The CONSTANT QUEEN

JOANNA COURTNEY

PAN BOOKS

First published 2016 by Macmillan

This edition published in paperback 2016 by Pan Books
an imprint of Pan Macmillan
20 New Wharf Road, London N1 9RR
Associated companies throughout the world
www.panmacmillan.com

ISBN 978-1-4472-8107-8

1 3 5 7 9 8 6 4 2

A CIP catalogue record for this book is available from the British Library.

Typeset by Palimpsest Book Production Ltd, Falkirk, Stirlingshire
Printed and bound by CPI Group (UK) Ltd, Croydon, CR0 4YY

For Emily, Rory, Hannah and Alec,
the best kids in the world.

ENGLAND
1066

SCOTLAND

GODFRED

NORTHUMBRIA

Stamford
Bridge
York
Fulford
Riccal

Rhuddlan
Caernarvon
Gwynedd
Chester
MERCIA
Powys
Billingsley
Coventry
EAST ANGLIA
WALES
Hereford
St.
Davids
Deheubarth
Glamorgan
Gloucester
Nazeing
London
WESSEX
Wilton
Abbey
Winchester
Senlac Field
Britford
Bosham
Hastings

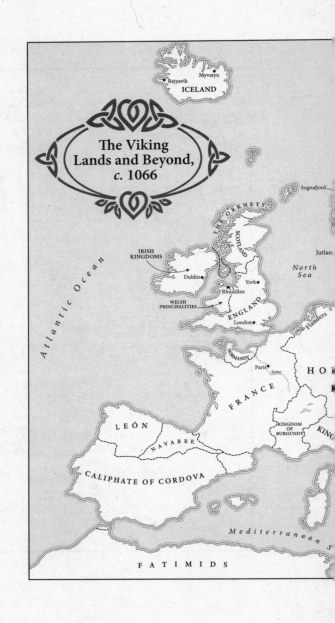

The Viking
Lands and Beyond,
c. 1066

ICELAND
Rejyavik   Myvatyn

Sognafjord

THE ORKNEYS

SCOTLAND

Jutlan

North
Sea

IRISH
KINGDOMS

Dublin

York

Rhuddlan

WELSH
PRINCIPALITIES

ENGLAND
London

Flanders

Atlantic Ocean

NORMANDY

Paris   Seine

HO

FRANCE

KINGDOM
OF
BURGUNDY

KING

LEÓN

NAVARRE

CALIPHATE OF CORDOVA

Mediterranean S

FATIMIDS

orwegian Sea

FINNIC PEOPLES

ratt
•Stikelstad
•Bymarka
Nidaros

•Oslo

SWEDEN

Sigtuna•

•Ladoga
•Novgorod

Baltic Sea

BALTIC PEOPLES

KIEVAN RUS

MARK

SLAVS

POLAND

Kiev

Vitichev•

Dnieper

PECHENEGS

OMAN
RE

Buda•

HUNGARY

CROATIA

Black Sea

•Constantinople

BYZANTINE EMPIRE

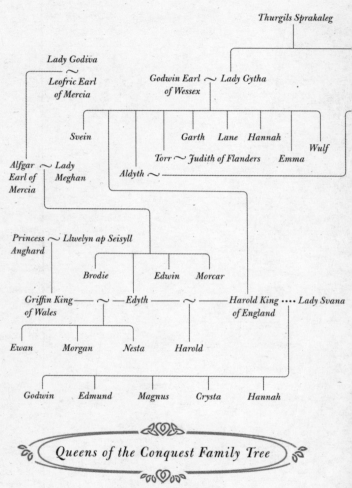

Thurgils Sprakaleg

Lady Godiva
~
Leofric Earl
of Mercia

Godwin Earl ~ Lady Gytha
of Wessex

Svein   Garth   Lane   Hannah

Torr ~ Judith of Flanders   Emma   Wulf

Aldyth ~

Alfgar ~ Lady
Earl of Meghan
Mercia

Princess ~ Llwelyn ap Seisyll
Anghard

Brodie   Edwin   Morcar

Griffin King —— ~ —— Edyth —— ~ —— Harold King •••• Lady Svana
of Wales   of England

Ewan   Morgan   Nesta   Harold

Godwin   Edmund   Magnus   Crysta   Hannah

Queens of the Conquest Family Tree

Note: A dotted line indicates a handfast marriage

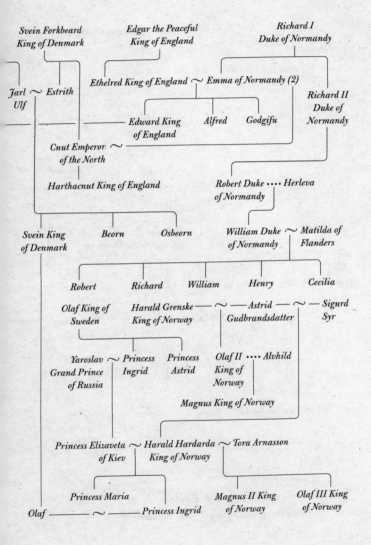

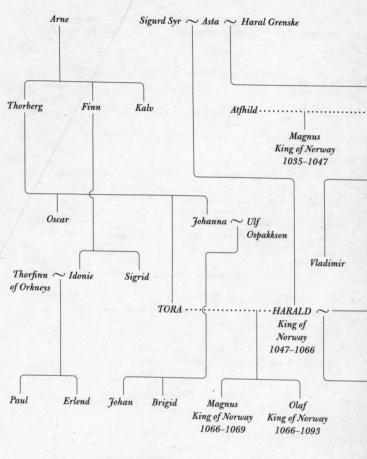

Arne   Sigurd Syr ∼ Asta ∼ Haral Grenske

Thorberg   Finn   Kalv   Atfhild ....

Magnus
King of Norway
1035–1047

Oscar   Johanna ∼ Ulf
Ospakkson

Vladimir

Thorfinn ∼ Idonie   Sigrid
of Orkneys

TORA ····················· HARALD ∼
King of
Norway
1047–1066

Paul   Erlend   Johan   Brigid   Magnus   Olaf
King of Norway King of Norway
1066–1069   1066–1093

Constant Queen Family Tree

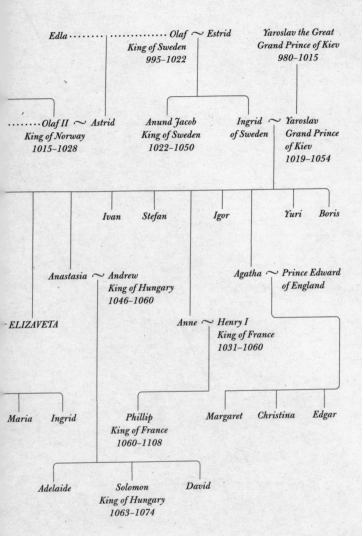

Edla · · · · · · · · · · · · · Olaf ∼ Estrid
King of Sweden
995–1022

Yaroslav the Great
Grand Prince of Kiev
980–1015

· · · · · · · Olaf II ∼ Astrid
King of Norway
1015–1028

Anund Jacob
King of Sweden
1022–1050

Ingrid ∼ Yaroslav
of Sweden   Grand Prince
of Kiev
1019–1054

Ivan   Stefan   Igor   Yuri   Boris

Anastasia ∼ Andrew
King of Hungary
1046–1060

Agatha ∼ Prince Edward
of England

ELIZAVETA

Anne ∼ Henry I
King of France
1031–1060

Maria   Ingrid

Phillip
King of France
1060–1108

Margaret   Christina   Edgar

Adelaide   Solomon   David
King of Hungary
1063–1074

THE CONSTANT QUEEN

Sometimes, when she closes her eyes, Elizaveta can feel it still — the headlong, giddy challenge of pitting herself against the world — and she yearns to recapture it. Even through the river-mist of too many years past, she can still feel the surge of water through the thin skin of the tiny canoe, the glitter of spray in her eyes, the rush of warm air against her face. And, above all else, she can feel the roar of her young heart as, at last, she crested the tumbling Dnieper.

It was a beautiful day for the Great Kievan Rapids Race. The walls of the city, high on the cliff, sparkled in the sharp light as they leaned in, willing her on or, perhaps, waiting for her to up-end. The sun-blurred faces of the crowds hung over the bank, all wide eyes and open mouths, their calls of encouragement scattered on the light breeze. And then there was the blue of the water; the endless, treacherous, glorious blue of the water — hers to master.

Girls weren't allowed. Too dangerous, they said, but she'd known that was foolish; she was brave enough to race and skilled enough too. She'd often sneaked out of the palace at first light with her brother, Vladimir, when the rest of the royal household were snoring in their feather beds and the guards on the walls were too blurry-eyed to spot their slim figures slipping down the steps in the dawn mist. She'd known how to spot the vicious downward suck of a whirlpool, the dark shadow of a rock too close to the surface, and the eerie light of a sandbank. She'd known how to find the current that would carry her, swift and true, to the great rope strung between the grandstands on the lower plains to mark the finish line. She'd known it all and she'd been determined to rise to it.

Elizaveta shudders, even now that years and sense have taught her how little such a petty triumph should matter, as she recalls the jolt. She ducks the pain as she remembers the dark cloud of the preying net, its sticky, grasping fingers yanking her up and back, ripping her from her craft which, unpiloted, twisted, lurched and smashed onto the rocks, whirling into the air in a splintering of timbers, drawing a collective gasp of delighted horror from the massed onlookers.

'How dare you?' she shrieked at her captors, fighting the clawing hold of the net and the sharp, bitter grip of humiliation. 'How dare you stop me?'

But the poor guards glanced downriver to the Grand Prince, her father, standing a livid, ugly red at the centre of the finest grandstand, and simply said: 'How dare we let you continue?'

Later, though, when one of them – the younger one – sneaked some food to the bedchamber in which she was incarcerated in disgrace, he turned the question back on her: 'How dare you, Princess? How dare you ride the rapids?'

Elizaveta just shrugged. It had been no dare, no whim, no cry for attention or accolades, but rather a deep need, like an itch in her soul.

'I wanted the adventure,' she told him and he shook his head ruefully and thrust the stolen soup and ale towards her and said, 'Next time, Princess, please adventure on someone else's watch.' At that she smiled. She smiled all the long, hungry night and the lonely days of her imprisonment that followed. She smiled because he'd said 'next time' and it was enough.

PART ONE

CHAPTER ONE

Kiev, April 1031

'Tell us a story, Mama – *please*.'

Elizaveta smiled at Anne's request. Sometimes little sisters were useful. At twelve years of age she considered herself way too old to be begging for bedtime tales but she loved to listen all the same, especially to her mother. For Ingrid told of the north, of the lands over the Varangian Sea where ice covered the hills all year round, and the sun never set at midsummer, and trolls still roamed the great forests. Ingrid knew about it because she had been born there, a princess of Sweden, and had been betrothed to King Olaf of Norway before her father had decided Grand Prince Yaroslav of Kiev would be a more lucrative match and shipped her south.

'Do you wish you'd gone to Norway, Mama?' Elizaveta had asked her once.

'Of course not, Lily,' Ingrid had laughed. 'I am happy here in Kiev – who would not be? It is a glorious city with a glorious future and there is nowhere in Norway that's as grand or as forward-thinking as Kiev.'

She'd sounded so certain and yet Elizaveta had been convinced that she'd heard a tiny, wistful hesitation in her mother's voice and she remained intrigued by the northern land that had so nearly been Ingrid's destiny. Now, Elizaveta sank onto the window seat on the courtyard side of the great stone hall that housed the elaborate women's chamber and bowers and tried not to look too eager as her mother settled five-year-old Anne and two-year-old Agatha into their carved cot beds and composed herself for a tale.

'There was once a great king,' Ingrid started with a smile, 'called Harald Fairhair because he had the lightest, brightest hair anyone had ever seen and everyone said that it shone like Christ's very halo.'

'Except,' Elizaveta interrupted, 'that they were pagan then, so how would they know to say that?'

Ingrid eyed her sharply.

'You are right, Lily,' she conceded, 'but many have said it since.'

'Many who did not actually *see* him?'

'Maybe so.'

Ingrid looked briefly to Hedda, the plump nursemaid who was suckling her baby in the corner. Little Greta would be six months old when Ingrid birthed and Hedda would switch from feeding her own child to feeding the new prince or princess, as she had fed all of the others. Vladimir called her the 'royal cow', though only when she was out of hearing for her slap was as sharp as her milk was plentiful. Elizaveta saw Hedda smile at her mother as she drew in a patient breath.

'Very well,' she said slowly, 'everyone said it shone like Thor's hammer.'

'Was that not iron though?'

'Elizaveta!'

Elizaveta huffed and looked away; fair hair of any sort was a sore subject for her. Ingrid, even now she was past her thirtieth year, had hair as blonde as overripe corn. Her husband, Grand Prince Yaroslav, liked her to wear it loose at feasts and would wrap it around his fingers, stroking it as if it were spun gold. He called Ingrid his 'sunshine' and frequently invited foreign ambassadors to match his metaphor with others of their own making. All too often Elizaveta had watched them fighting each other with words until even Ingrid was embarrassed by the rain of praise.

Two of Elizaveta's sisters, Anastasia and Anne, had both inherited their mother's bright locks and nine-year-old Anastasia in particular spent hours brushing and styling hers until Elizaveta longed to hack it all off with her eating knife. Once, when she was younger, she'd dared to cut a few strands whilst Anastasia slept. She'd only wanted to try it against her own face in the copper looking-glass but there'd been such a fuss that she'd had to throw her precious treasure off the great city walls into the dark pines below. She'd mourned the loss for weeks and resented Anastasia even more.

Elizaveta had not so much as an ounce of gold in her own hair. It did not shine brightly around her face but lay black as a midnight shadow against her olive skin. Her father called her his 'beautiful little Slav' and said she was truly his own Rus baby, but Elizaveta yearned for Norse gold and wore her dark locks covered as often as she possibly could. And it wasn't just her hair that marked her out from her smug little sisters. She was short – Anastasia was already grown past her – and as slight as a peasant child but however many courses she devoured at the table, she never seemed to fill out into anything approaching her mother's soft voluptuousness. She was all angles, with elbows as sharp as spearheads and knees as bumpy as forest fungi and no sign whatsoever of breasts or hips.

'Maybe you're a boy, Lily,' her eldest brother, Vladimir, would sometimes tease her.

'I'm a better boy than you, Vlad,' she'd throw back and then strive to beat him at whatever game they were playing, but the words would scamper around her head when the oil lamps were all blown out and she was alone in her bed.

'I'm not a boy,' she'd mutter fiercely into her goose-down pillow but always her own voice would seem to creep back out of it: 'Maybe, but you're not much of a girl either.'

'So this King Harald, late in life, had a son,' Ingrid was continuing, 'a son called Hakon and, fearing his older brothers would keep him from power, Harald sent him into England to be fostered by his friend, King Athelstan. And there he became a good Christian.'

She looked pointedly at her eldest daughter but now two-year-old Agatha was bouncing up and down in her bed, calling: 'England, England.'

Elizaveta smiled at her littlest sister, cursed, like her, with dark hair and with a tangle of curls besides. Agatha had learned the name of the land of the Anglo-Saxons just last week and was fascinated by it. There was a lost English prince called Edward at Yaroslav's court – one of myriad exiles their father liked to harbour – and much to everyone's amusement Agatha had taken to following the poor young man around like a pet dog. Elizaveta didn't laugh though. England, along with Norway and Denmark, was ruled by the great King Cnut, Emperor of the North, and by all accounts it was a rich jewel of a country; Agatha was right to be fascinated.

'Why keep these exiles, Father?' Elizaveta had asked Yaroslav once. 'Why house all these lost princes?'

'Why?' Yaroslav had laughed fondly. 'Only a fool would not. These "lost princes" are only lost for now, Lily. If they find themselves again – if they find their thrones and their kingdoms – then think what they will be worth. How grateful will they be to the one man who did not abandon them in their need? And what does gratitude mean?'

She'd considered.

'Money, Father?'

Again the laugh – wide, indulgent.

'Eventually, yes, but first, daughter, alliances and alliances mean protection, trade, marriages. Your dear mother may have given me sons to rule after me, but she has also given me daughters and with daughters, Lily, I can weave my influence across the known world. As you know, though, if you have paid any attention to your needlework lessons at all, any fabric starts with small stitches.'

'Your exiles are stitches, Father?'

'Exactly! Small ones, yes, and ones that may be dropped without trace, but possibly ones that take hold and sew us into the very fabric of the vast kingdoms beyond the lands of the Rus.'

Elizaveta could almost hear her father's ambitious words now, echoing around the soft bedchamber, and she turned to look longingly out of the window to his grand courtyard below. The fountain at the centre of the princely kremlin splashed carelessly against its mosaic surround. Guarding the four paths outwards, the great bronze horses her grandfather had brought back from war reared proudly up, their gilded backs catching the last rays of the sun and shimmering rosy pink. To her right, the Church of the Holy Mother was glowing too as the light of a hundred candles flickered through the vast coloured windows, defying the coming dusk.

The sound of choral plainsong drifted out of the open church doors but Elizaveta knew that soon Vespers would be over and Yaroslav's *druzhina* – his courtly household – would flood out and across to the hall, opposite her own bower, to dine. Mother had said that if she was good she could join the courtiers and she had on her best gown in anticipation. She had persuaded the seamstress to pad the dress out a little to hide her spiky bones and a glance in the looking-glass earlier had almost pleased her.

The rich red wool suited her stupid olive skin and the pearls around the neck of her pleated linen undergown brought some light to her face. Not as much as blonde hair might have done but enough to make her smile just a tiny bit at herself. Now her feet itched to tread the stairs out of the stuffy bower and she reached down to run a finger inside her calfskin boots, dyed red to match her dress, as if she might physically scratch the urge away.

'Patience, Elizaveta,' Ingrid said softly, interrupting her tale to smile at her eldest daughter.

'Elizaveta has no patience,' Anastasia said primly. 'She cannot sit still for a minute.'

Elizaveta glared at her pious sister. Just because Anastasia liked endlessly stabbing ivory needles into scraps of fancy fabric, she thought she was so dignified. She only did it because she wanted prettier dresses than Elizaveta but if that was the cost, she was welcome to them. Anne was the same, ever working on her letters though she had not yet turned six, trying out fancy inks and scripts as if there was a whole world at her desk and not out of the window, waiting to be explored. Elizaveta couldn't understand it at all. She could only truly sit still when playing her treasured viol, for then, at least, her spirit was dancing free, riding the rise and fall of the notes like a bird in the sky, or an acrobat at a feast, or a boy on the rapids. Elizaveta bit back sudden angry tears.

'Tell us about the trolls, Mama,' she suggested sharply. 'The trolls who live in looking-glasses and leap out to bite the noses off little girls who stare at themselves for too long.'

Agatha giggled but Anastasia was up in an instant and flying across the bower, nails out ready to scratch her sister's words from her throat. Elizaveta, however, despite her slightness, was strong and held her easily at arm's length as she kicked and spat.

'Girls!' Ingrid pulled them furiously apart. 'There is no way you two are coming to dinner behaving like this.'

Elizaveta yanked away.

'She attacked me,' she protested.

'Only 'cos she was horrid about me,' Anastasia cried, flouncing back to her own corner by the mirror.

'What makes you think I was talking about *you*, Stasia?' Elizaveta threw after her.

'Girls!' Ingrid snapped again. 'Honestly, how will I ever make marriageable women of you like this?'

Elizaveta sniffed and turned back to the window. More talk of marriages – 'alliances'. Whatever her father's grand plans, she couldn't see herself as a bride; the poor groom wouldn't get much for his troubles. Anastasia, however, looked mortified.

'I'm sorry, Mama. She's just so mean.'

'A princess should be able to ride over taunts, Stasia.'

'You are right, Mama, and I will. Shall I have a great husband, do you think?'

Elizaveta rolled her eyes to the darkening skies beyond the bower; her future husband was far and away Anastasia's favourite topic of conversation.

'I'm sure your father will find you a worthy prince,' Ingrid assured her.

'Like yours did for you?'

'Yes, Stasia. I was very lucky.'

'But you should have married a king, should you not?'

'King Olaf of Norway,' Elizaveta agreed – she liked to hear her mother talk of this. 'But when her father sent her to Kiev, her sister married Olaf instead.'

'Astrid,' Ingrid agreed, 'yes, God bless her, for with Olaf dead she is back in Sweden with our brother.'

Elizaveta leaned in – this was better than talk of marriage. King Olaf of Norway had been in Kiev last year and his young son, Magnus – Astrid's stepson – was here still as another of her father's pet exiles. Many of Yaroslav's troops had returned to Norway with Olaf, only to be bitterly defeated at the Battle of Stikelstad. A few had limped home, muttering darkly of an evil enemy, but most were either dead on the field or had given themselves to Cnut's service. Elizaveta had tried to find out more but the men had been unusually reticent.

'Surely,' Anastasia said, pretty head on one side, 'Aunt Astrid will marry again?'

'Perhaps,' Ingrid agreed, waving away Elizaveta's groan of protest.

'She must. If she has been a queen once she must surely long to be a queen again? I know I would. Oh, I would so love to marry a king and have sons by him so they will be kings too.'

'That would be a fine thing,' Ingrid agreed.

Elizaveta groaned again, louder this time.

'What?' Anastasia demanded.

'Is that all you want for yourself – to produce kings?'

'It seems a worthy aim. Why, what do you want, Lily, that's so much better?'

Elizaveta stared at her sister, her father's talk of the 'fabric of vast kingdoms' jittering in her head; Anastasia had such a narrow view.

'I'd like to be a queen,' she asserted, 'a queen in my own right who can help my husband rule and shape a nation as Mother is helping to shape the Rus.'

Anastasia screwed up her face in disgust but Ingrid stepped across to Elizaveta and put an arm around her shoulders.

'Thank you for your high opinion of me, Lily, though I'm not sure I deserve it. I am ever in my childbed.'

She patted her belly, newly swelling with her tenth child.

'You are doing your duty,' Anastasia told her. 'Father is very proud of all his heirs.'

'Indeed,' Ingrid agreed lightly, 'though sometimes I wish he could sire a few of you on concubines as his father did.'

'Mother!' Anastasia's shock made Elizaveta long to laugh but down below she could see the Metropolitan Bishop of Kiev emerging from the church in his rich ceremonial robes, the choir in his wake, and she knew the dinner hour was nearly upon them. She couldn't afford any more antagonism.

'You are a good Christian, Mama,' she said, as meekly as she could.

Ingrid looked at her and, to Elizaveta's great surprise, gave her a quick wink before turning for the door with a mild, 'As are we all, daughter. Now, shall we to dinner?'

The smaller girls squeaked in protest as Hedda rose from the corner.

'You haven't told us about the trolls,' Anne begged. 'Do they really live in the looking-glass?'

Anastasia, who had rushed to check her reflection, flinched and Ingrid glared pointedly at Elizaveta.

'No, Anne,' Elizaveta forced herself to say, 'they live deep in forests.'

'*Our* forests?' Anne looked fearfully to the window. Kiev stood on a high, clear plateau but the slopes below its thick walls were crowded with pines.

'Not ours,' Elizaveta answered. 'Trolls dwell in Norway and every winter they dig deep below the trees to avoid the ice and suck sustenance from the roots until they grow so fat they divide into two and twice as many come out in the spring.'

'Truly?' little Agatha asked.

'I know not,' Elizaveta admitted, kissing her dark curls. 'But one day I will travel to Norway and find out for you.'

'To Norway? Nay, Lily, it's too far.'

'Not for me – nor for you either, little one. You could come with me and hop across to see your precious England.'

Agatha's eyes grew big as moons.

'Could I, Lily? Could I really?'

Ingrid swept in, nudging Elizaveta firmly aside as she tucked the covers around her youngest daughter with a crisp 'We'll see,' but her words were cut off by a great knocking at the south gates.

The sound was clearly made with a heavy staff or, more likely, a sword hilt, and it echoed around the princely courtyard like a thunder-clap. The girls, even the smaller ones, were up to the window in an instant, clambering out onto the rooved wooden walkway beyond. Ingrid and Hedda tried to stop them but all around others were doing the same – clerks and maids and nurses were emerging from the living quarters above the three great halls that, with the church on the fourth side, formed the central section of the kremlin. The women's quarters were on the furthest, west side and Elizaveta looked to the perpendicular south hall where her brothers were scrambling keenly along their own balcony towards the great kremlin gates at the end of it. They were all there, Vladimir, Ivan, Stefan, Viktor and Igor, every one of them blonde as the harvest and all pushing at each other for the best view.

'Can you see?' Elizaveta called to Vladimir who, as eldest, had grabbed the best view.

He leaned right out over the gates but shook his head. The visitors, whoever they were, must be close up against the far side, hidden by the high gate-towers. The guards were holding a furious discussion with them and now the Grand Prince,

Elizaveta's father, was striding out of the church and down the wood-paved pathway to take command.

'Who visits Kiev at this hour?' he demanded, his body as slight as Elizaveta's own beneath his long embroidered overcoat but his power still clear in his tone.

The answer from the guards was frustratingly quiet but, at a wave from Yaroslav, they turned to crank open the vast gates and the men were revealed. Three leaders rode through on high-stepping horses, followed by a troop of some fifty soldiers.

'Varangians,' Ingrid breathed at Elizaveta's side.

Elizaveta's heart quickened. Varangians – elite Viking soldiers from the northern lands. Her sharp eyes fixed on the three at the head of the procession as they swung themselves out of the saddle to bow low before the Grand Prince.

'Who is *he*?' Anastasia whispered, pointing a quivering finger at the man in the centre.

All three men were broad with the muscular shoulders and thick arms of trained warriors but the central one was so tall that, even kneeling, his head, topped with hair brighter and blonder than any Elizaveta's envious eyes had ever seen, came almost level with their father.

''Tis Harald Fairhair himself,' Anne gasped.

'Nonsense,' Elizaveta said, 'he died years ago,' but even so she pressed a little closer to her mother as the man spoke, his voice – despite a few unfamiliar words of a Norse tongue older than their own – so clear and fluid it carried easily around the courtyard and up to the parapets.

'Greetings, Grand Prince. We come in peace, seeking refuge. We are exiles from Norway where my brother, the sainted King Olaf, was viciously slain in battle. This is Ulf Ospakkson, this Halldor Snorrason and I am Harald Sigurdsson, Prince of Norway.'

'Prince Harald!' Anastasia said, delighted.

'Of Norway,' Elizaveta emphasised. This wasn't the Harald of her mother's stories but even so her heart beat faster as she turned to Ingrid. Perhaps now she would find out more about the evil battle and the fate of the Norse lands that so fascinated her. 'Please, Mother,' she begged. 'Please can we go down now?'

CHAPTER TWO

Elizaveta walked into the hall behind her mother, for once grateful to have Anastasia at her side, for the vast room – some fifty strides long – felt cramped and close with the whole of the Grand Prince's *druzhina* pushing for a sight of the visitors. This huge space was the heart of Yaroslav's palace. Normally it was flooded with light, reflecting off the mosaic flooring and the frescoes along the lime-washed walls, but today it was so packed that the window openings were obscured, as if the encroaching night had already fallen.

Servants were rushing to kindle the oil lamps along the side columns and on free stands, but the crowds were blocking both their way and the light of those flames they had managed to strike. Even as Elizaveta walked in, there was a scuffle in the corner as a minor count, climbing a stool to look over the myriad heads, collided with another on the same mission, sending both sprawling into a servant with a lit taper. One cloak caught and, in a cry of alarm and a crackle of smouldering wool, its owner darted for the doorway, a path clearing rapidly before him, and dived into the fountain.

'Try not to laugh, girls,' Ingrid murmured, though her own lips were pressed together to contain her mirth.

Now, though, they had been noticed by the courtiers who

fell deferentially back to let them through. Elizaveta forced her head up and, resisting the urge to tug her headdress over her escaping raven hair, followed her mother as calmly and elegantly as she could up the centre of the hall to Yaroslav's grand marble throne at the top.

'Ah my love, my Ingrid. You grace us with your golden presence.'

Yaroslav leaped down from the dais and held out his hand to his wife. Elizaveta watched, fascinated as ever by her parents' public face. Always Yaroslav treated Ingrid was if she were the most precious thing in the world and now he handed her carefully up to her seat at his side, though she was both taller and broader than him, especially in her advancing pregnancy.

Everything the Grand Prince did, from eating, to pronouncing laws, to departing for the privvie, was done with a flourish, a flamboyance designed to impress his confidence and grandeur upon his subjects, but he seemed to genuinely love Ingrid and she him. Anastasia was always sighing about how beautiful it was. Elizaveta wasn't so sure about that, but it certainly felt right, reassuring – as if a partnership so solid at the head of a nation would inevitably make the nation solid too.

Now she crept across to Vladimir – the only one of the princes permitted down to dinner – as Yaroslav introduced his wife to the visitors and they made their obeisance. They were a curious trio. The first, Ulf Ospakkson, was tall, though not as tall as his prince, and had a mass of curly hair tumbling down into a matching beard that he had tried – and failed – to tame into a plait below his chin. His mouth could hardly be seen through the bush of it, save when he laughed, as he seemed to do often, and it opened up like a pink cavern to reveal fine white teeth. His eyes, in contrast, were huge and dark, tilled-soil brown, and seemed to take everything in at once.

The second, Halldor Snorrason, was a squat, heavyset man,

nearly as broad as he was tall. His head was hunched into his massive shoulders so he looked less like a man and more like one of the Byzantine turtles Vladimir kept in a tank in his chamber. He was older than the other two, his hair sparse on top so that it seemed as if his forehead, sitting low on a heavy brow, had sought escape up onto his head. His remaining hair was caught up in a leather band at the back of his neck and his long beard was neatly combed and drawn into a forked shape with two similar bands. His tunic was almost black, an unusually dark shade for the colour-loving Vikings, with the edges picked out in assertive swirls of gold thread. Elizaveta thought him quite the strangest man she had ever seen and only pulled her eyes away when Prince Harald stepped in front of him.

She drew in a breath. Close up, Harald Sigurdsson was even more striking than he had been from afar. Although clearly no more than two or three years her senior, he stood almost a head taller than any other man in Kiev's great hall, his immacu-late hair so blonde as to be almost white. He wore no beard at all, though his moustache was long and neat, and up the side of his clean-shaven face, from lip to eyebrow, ran a raw scar that seemed to Elizaveta to enhance the pale clarity of the rest of his skin. She edged forward, intrigued, and her father spotted her.

'Ah ha – my eldest daughter. This, Harald, is the Princess Elizaveta. Come forward, my dear.'

Elizaveta tried to compose herself as she stepped up onto the dais but her dress caught in the embroidered tip of her boot. For an awful moment she thought she might fall but then Harald was reaching out his hand and her fingers found his as he drew her securely up at his side.

'Thank you, my lord.'

'A pleasure, Princess, and is this your sister?'

Elizaveta was forced to agree that it was, seething quietly as Harald's hand left hers to raise Anastasia up at her side.

'You're too kind,' Anastasia simpered, batting youthful eyelashes up at the Norwegian prince, but as soon as she was steady Harald dropped her hand and turned back to Elizaveta.

'Your father is very gracious to receive us.'

His language, although much the same as theirs, was tinged with a soft inflection that made Elizaveta think deliciously of the snowy northern pines and knife-edge fjords her mother had often described. She glanced towards Yaroslav, who was deep in conversation with Ulf.

'He loves visitors,' she told Harald, speaking with care, 'especially such honourable ones.'

'Ah, as for that, I fear I come without honour for I have fled a battle.'

Elizaveta caught something pass through Harald's pale grey eyes, like a glacier shifting beneath the surface, and longed to know more. He did not look like a coward so why had he fled? She looked at him carefully, recalling asking Yaroslav about his lost princes when she'd been younger and less careful with her questions.

'But Father,' she'd said, 'are they not "lost" for a reason?'

'How do you mean, daughter?'

'Are they not weak men to have got lost at all?'

Yaroslav's ready laughter had died in his throat and he had pulled Elizaveta closer to him.

'Perhaps, Lily. It is possible, yes, but the world is a harsh place. It throws many things at men, especially young men. Fortune's wheel, my sweet one, turns relentlessly. It can tip you down when you least expect it and the bravest are the ones who hold fast – who cleave to life and to hope – and who are still holding when she turns upwards again.'

'And if a man helps them to hold on . . . ?'

'They will owe him for the rest of their days. Yes.'

Elizaveta had swallowed, unsettled.

'Have you had to hold fast, Father?' she'd asked nervously and he'd smiled again.

'Many times, Lily, and so will you.'

'I will hold?'

'You will, I know it.'

She had thought over those words many times since, praying for the strength to prove her father right, but now she felt as if she were looking straight at a man who was holding on and it fascinated her. Before she could ask more, though, he had turned back to Yaroslav.

'We will not be a burden, Sire,' he told him earnestly. 'We are warriors and willing to do you whatever service you see fit.'

'I doubt it not,' Yaroslav agreed easily. 'My little empire has been all but built on Varangian service. Norse soldiers have never let me down yet and, besides, I believe I have your kin at court. Vladimir!'

He waved at his eldest son and Vladimir dutifully turned to look for young Magnus. Elizaveta sighed. The seven-year-old Prince of Norway was the youngest of her father's current exiles and, in her opinion, much the dullest. Quiet and studious, he was happier at his desk or his prayer-stool than outside, even when the sun was shining. Yaroslav had told Elizaveta that he was an 'admirable example of piety', which she supposed he was, but it wasn't an example she would choose to follow.

She preferred the English prince, Edward, for though he was also quiet, he at least liked to ride and was happy to talk about the bible rather than just burying himself in it. She'd had many lively discussions with him and his fellow exile, Andrew of Hungary, a suave, handsome young man, newly converted to Christianity and ringing with zeal. Edward hung on Andrew's every word and Elizaveta wished he'd recognise that his own ideas, though not as flamboyantly expressed as Andrew's, were far more thoughtful and meaningful. She'd tried on several occasions to talk to him about England but he had been spirited away as a baby, fleeing the conquering King Cnut, and knew less than she did of his native land.

Now she watched as Edward ushered little Magnus forward and Vladimir, grabbing his hand, dragged him unceremoniously across to greet his newly arrived uncle. Prince Harald leaned down to shake Magnus's hand, talking quietly to him, presumably of his lost father, and Elizaveta felt suddenly mean. The poor boy had been forced to flee his homeland, aged five. He had been separated from his stepmother, Queen Astrid – Ingrid's sister – who had been left in Sweden with her kin, and now he had also lost his father and with him any chance of returning home. Even as she thought about that, though, she heard Harald telling Magnus:

'We will take Norway back, I promise you. We will take it back for our dynasty, as is right and proper.'

'How?' Magnus asked, wide-eyed and almost shivering.

'How? Why, with might – might and right.'

'And with God's blessing?'

'That too but, Magnus, God smiles on those who seek their own fortune, especially in battle.'

'He does? Does Christ not say we must be peacemakers?'

'He does but how do you think we can bring peace to Norway until we ensure it is ruled by a just king? We must make war in order to bring peace – do you see? We must bring light into the darkness but we must do it ourselves for do you not think, Magnus, that God has enough to do without fixing battles for us? No, we must strive for our own fate and if we do so he will reward us with his favour.'

'Oh.'

Magnus's brow furrowed and Elizaveta could already picture him poring over his books tomorrow. She smiled and edged over.

'You will need soldiers then, Prince Harald.'

He looked up.

'I will, Princess. Many soldiers. Cnut rules Norway, Denmark and England so he has a fearsome force at his disposal. I will certainly need soldiers and for that I will need gold. Men may defend without any reward save the protection of their homes and loved ones, but they rarely attack unpaid. I must find riches if I am to reclaim my kingdom.'

'*Our* kingdom,' Magnus said behind him but neither of them paid him any heed.

'So where will you find such riches?' Elizaveta asked.

Harald looked straight at her, his grey eyes bright and clear and flecked with gold in the flickering candlelight.

'As all good Varangians must – I will win it by the sword. I have seawater in my veins, Princess, and I will travel wherever the sail takes me. I will fight for your father, if he'll have me, and for any count or king besides. I will take my wages and I will seek treasure.'

Elizaveta looked up at him, intrigued. This man was not just holding fast to fortune's wheel, but seeking to drive her round. Most of her father's exiles seemed content to sit around his court dreaming of their return to power over a glass of their host's finest wine, but this man was alive with restless energy and purpose and it set her curiosity aflame.

'And what will you do with this "treasure" then?' she asked.

'*Do* with it?'

'Where will you keep it, my lord prince, so it is safe until you need it?'

He tipped his head on one side, considering.

'I have not thought that far,' he admitted. 'I will need some-where secure.'

'My father has great vaults in the north, in Novgorod. They are guarded day and night by the finest men.'

'You think I need such a vault?'

'I do. He has several spare. I could speak with him on your behalf.'

'You could?'

'Of course, I am his eldest daughter.'

Elizaveta drew herself up tall, though she scarce knew what she was saying and why, save that this man seemed so passionate about his lost country and she yearned to help him if she could.

'That would be very kind. I swear to fill it as fast as I can. I will fight every day God grants to me.'

Elizaveta smiled.

'Not *every* day, surely? You must rest. And, besides, you need not justify yourself to me.'

'Oh but I should, if you are to be my treasure-keeper.'

'I? Oh Prince, I did not mean . . .'

'Call me Harald, please. I do not deserve the title Prince, not yet.'

At that, though, Elizaveta shook her head.

'It does not work that way. A man need not deserve a title, for it is his birthright and it is more in honour of his forebears that he carries it than of himself.'

Harald blinked.

'You speak well, Princess. But he should surely live up to it?'

'As I am sure you will, Harald.'

'You will have the gold to prove it, Princess.'

'Elizaveta.'

She blushed as he bowed low but thankfully at that moment the burnished gong behind them was rung for the *druzhina* to be seated to dine and she was able to escape – though not for long.

'Harald, you will sit at my wife's right.' Yaroslav ushered his guest into the favoured spot. 'My daughters shall sit with you and your good men. No, no, do not protest. You are my honoured guest, whatever hand fate has dealt you, and you will share our table.'

The three men bowed low and moved to their seats. Elizaveta slid in between Harald and Halldor with Anastasia and Ulf beyond. She glanced at her sister and for once the pair were joined in delighted disbelief. Usually they were fortunate to find seats halfway down the hall but tonight they had somehow stepped up to their father's side and Elizaveta was determined to make the most of it.

As the meal advanced, a first course of spiced river-fish giving way to a rich game pie layered with forest mushrooms, Elizaveta began to feel almost dizzy with the effect of concentrating on the jumble of conversations around her. She barely touched her pie but was still not hungry when the servants cleared it away and lifted a spit-roasted boar from the central hearth, parading it around the assembled company before setting it on a golden oak table to carve.

To her left, her mother and Harald were deep in talk of people Elizaveta had only ever heard mentioned in Ingrid's stories. She longed to learn more but feared demonstrating her own ignorance so she turned to Halldor on her right who had, until now, been buried in his food.

'Are you also from Norway, my lord?' she asked politely.

Halldor shook his funny balding head.

'Nay, Princess. I am neither a lord nor a Norwegian. I am from Iceland.'

'Iceland?' So that explained his language – more guttural

than Prince Harald's, though curiously melodious. 'Is that not very far away?'

'Not so far under a strong sail. My good friend Ulf hails from there also.'

His 'good friend' leaned over, his dark curls bobbing wildly.

'What is he saying of me?' he demanded, his tone similar to Halldor's, though lighter and more full of laughter. 'What scurrilous tales is Halldor telling you, Princess?'

'None, truly,' Elizaveta replied. 'He says simply that you are both Icelanders.'

'Ah, well, that much is true – though the similarities end there, do they not, Hal?'

'You are both soldiers,' Elizaveta objected.

'We are,' Halldor agreed. 'Both Varangians, both sworn to the service of young Harald, both fleeing for our lives from Cnut, Emperor of the North – we have much in common, Ulf, friend.'

Ulf smiled wryly.

'True, true, yet *I* am not half troll.'

Elizaveta gasped.

'You're half troll?' she asked Halldor.

The hunched man's brow furrowed.

'You could believe that?'

Elizaveta's heart lurched at her foolishness as Ulf laughed his big, pink laugh.

'I would like it to be true,' she said quickly, 'for my mother has told me all manner of wonderful things of trolls.'

'Like that they eat children?' Ulf suggested merrily. 'And that they hide in caves and cleave to the night and are very, very ugly?'

Ulf laughed again and clapped Halldor on the back. Elizaveta felt even worse but Halldor did not seem ruffled.

'Or mayhap that they have hair so wild you'd swear their brains had all fallen out,' he shot back at his comrade.

Anastasia's blonde head bobbed from one man to the other, uncertain whether to be horrified or amused.

'Are trolls real?' she asked.

Ulf, catching her fearful eyes, shook his head kindly.

'Nay, lass, I think they are only real in stories.'

'And therefore very real indeed,' Halldor countered instantly. 'Shall I tell you of them?'

Elizaveta heard Ulf groan but Anastasia was nodding keenly and Halldor was sitting back on their bench, his neck unfurling from his tight shoulders and his brow lifting as his hazel eyes lit up like autumn sunshine.

'I met a troll once, when I was but a boy about your age, Princess Anastasia.'

'You did? Where? Where, sir?'

'In the forests, of course. I was hunting birds with my new sling and strayed too far in, beyond the sunlit copses at the edges and deep along the paths until they were paths no more but just faint imprints of brave footmarks. The trees leaned their branches over my head to pick at my hair and stuck out their roots to catch my feet and the vines reached out from the bark like snakes, keen to plunge their fangs into my flesh.'

His hands were moving now, casting shapes in the smoky air, drawing them into the pictures his throaty voice was creating and, despite herself, Elizaveta was lost – far away from the clatter of Kiev and down a dark, hidden path with Halldor.

'The troll?' she whispered.

'Ah, the troll! He was in a tangle of roots at the base of a great oak. I saw his eyes first – big as harvest moons and every bit as yellow – and they were following me, tracing my stumbling progress, getting ready . . .'

'Ready to pounce?' Anastasia asked, her voice squeaking.

'So I thought, child, but no – ready to *run*. He feared me, you see. They are quiet creatures, trolls, happiest left to their own funny little ways. It is only when cornered that they lash out.'

'But you did not corner him, Halldor?'

'Nay, lass. I ran screaming and he ran screaming and I went sprawling over a root and he, more fleet-footed on his tiny toes, leaped over me and straight up a giant pine, his long nails leaving scratch-trails all the way up the thin bark. And then he was gone.'

'Gone,' Anastasia breathed, delighted.

Elizaveta, pulled out of the trance of his storytelling, looked sceptically at Halldor.

'You made that up,' she accused.

He smiled.

'Maybe I did, maybe I did not, but whilst it lasted it was real, was it not?'

Harald turned their way.

'Halldor spinning yarns again?' he asked Ulf.

''Fraid so,' Ulf agreed but Anastasia was having no criticism.

'It was a fascinating tale,' she said stoutly and Elizaveta was glad of it.

'He speaks well,' she agreed.

'He does that,' Harald said. 'A good tale brings old Hal here to life in a way that it takes most men ten horns of ale to achieve.'

'Then he is lucky,' Elizaveta said.

Harald considered.

'I warrant he is, Princess. In Ringerike where I was raised . . .'

'In Norway?'

'Yes, in Norway, in the south, just above the great fjord. There people value stories very highly, art too. My mother always told me that poetry is real tales with stronger detail, just as art is real pictures in brighter colours.'

'Lies, you mean,' Ulf fired at him.

'Half-truths,' Harald allowed, 'but the better half. Oh come, Ulf, our stories are all we will leave behind in the world when we are gone to dust; surely we must make them as good as we can?'

'By our deeds,' Ulf agreed gruffly, 'but not with fancy words.'

'But "fancy" words exalt our deeds.' Harald turned to Elizaveta. 'Ulf likes things plain,' he told her.

'And you?'

'I do not seek to *create* my life with words but I see no fault in honouring it with them. Poetry is a great skill.'

'A great skill that will not keep you alive in battle,' Ulf grumbled.

'No,' Harald agreed, 'but one that will keep your memory alive long after the battle is done.'

Ulf grunted again but smiled and Elizaveta had the feeling that this was a debate they had held many times before and would hold many times again.

'Well I like a good story, well told,' she dared to assert.

'Then you shall have one, Princess. Hal – tell the hall of Stikelstad.'

'No!' Ulf protested. 'No, Harald, we lost.'

'We fought the odds,' Harald allowed, 'and for once the odds defeated us but we live to fight again – though my brother, God bless his soul, does not, nor his banner either. The enemy tore it down but we will, one day, raise a new one and until then the tale deserves to be told, to remind us of our duty and to honour his memory. Would you like to hear of our battle, Grand Prince?'

'Gladly,' Yaroslav agreed. 'It will give our stomachs a chance to find a little space for the pastries. Please, my lord . . .'

Halldor rose.

'I am no lord, Sire,' he said quietly.

'Maybe not,' Yaroslav countered, 'but if you tell a good tale, I shall make you a count.'

Halldor glanced disbelievingly at him but, as the great hall fell silent and turned his way, he drew himself up and Elizaveta saw him again fill out from a squat, twisted-featured solider into a sweet-faced poet. She pushed her half-eaten boar aside and focused on this strange Icelander as he began his tale.

'We topped the Kjolen Mountains at dawn,' Halldor started, 'King Olaf at our head, his landwaster banner flying high above him bearing his own golden dragon, roaring defiance. He rode to the ridge and looked down across the great valley and he threw his arms wide. "See that," he called back to us, his men, "see those pines, stood proud to the skies and those rivers crashing towards the sea and that lake, catching the clouds in its stillness – that is all of Norway before us now. It is glorious and it is ours to reclaim." And we came forward then and joined him on the ridge and before us was, indeed, Norway, and behind us four thousand troops, primed and ready to fight for their rightful king.

'"We shall reclaim it," we called into the sharp morning air and our voices seemed to echo all the way down the valley as if already making the first charge against the usurper. Oh, we were strong in heart and we were strong in arm and we were strong in right – for Olaf was the true king of ancient Yngling blood – but we were not, alas, strong in numbers. For the enemy, the usurper, when we joined with him in the great plain at Stikelstad some hours later had summoned some ten thousand of the devil's own soldiers to his back and we knew when we saw them that it would be a hard fight – yet we would not back down.

'The sun had tipped over noon by the time the horns

sounded and we made the first charge and, though we were few, we splintered them apart time and again. We drove spears deep into the hearts of the men in the front line, forcing them into those behind so that they quailed back and it seemed the victory would be ours and Norway would be returned to King Olaf. But then . . .'

Halldor paused and Elizaveta felt the whole hall draw in its breath.

'Witchcraft,' he whispered into the silence.

There were gasps, a couple of small shrieks, swiftly muffled. Some of Halldor's Old Norse words were lost on the crowd but there was no missing the tone and Elizaveta could not take her eyes off him as he raised his hands.

'Cnut sent a devil with a black cloak across the sun. We saw the shadow cross the blessed disc, drawing false night across the battlefield finger-space by finger-space until it consumed us and we, who did not know the ground so well as they, were lost.' Halldor's voice dipped. 'It was a rout, my lords and ladies – a treacherous, devious rout, for they sent their extra numbers round the back of us under cover of their hellish shade and we, poor innocents, had no place to go, save to carve our way out – and that we did, but in the darkness it was every man for himself and battles cannot be won that way. We tried to save our dear king but they followed the gold of his dragon banner to his last stand, slashed it to shreds and then cut him out of our arms.'

Halldor pushed back a wide sleeve to show a livid wound almost from wrist to elbow. The hall gasped again.

'Three of them there were,' he went on, his voice more forceful now, 'great lords all by the richness of their armour, though I knew them not in the evil mist. One struck him in the thigh.' Halldor thrust forward suddenly, right to the edge of the dais and those nearest flinched back. He prowled along the edge then suddenly jabbed his arm upwards. 'One thrust a spear beneath his mail coat and the last . . .' Now he grabbed young Vladimir, sat at the end of the high table, and made a dramatic gesture across his throat ' . . . cut his sainted neck.'

Vladimir obligingly sank onto his bench as if slain. There was a faint titter but all eyes were still on Halldor as he strode back to the centre of the dais.

'He was gone,' Halldor told the hall, his voice now echoing round the high, painted walls and into the over-reaching arches of the wooden parapets and roof above. 'King Olaf was gone and our cause with it and we had no choice but to flee to preserve our bodies and souls for vengeance.'

His voice rose on the final word, a thunder-clap of sound, and the released Kievan crowd roared their approval. Yaroslav rose, clapping, and everyone joined him until it seemed the very heroes in the frescoes were applauding too.

'You shall be a count, Halldor,' Yaroslav announced. 'I shall confirm it in court tomorrow.'

Elizaveta saw Halldor flush, the colour creeping visibly into his pock-marked cheeks and shooting up his squashed nose and out across his pate, and as it did so he hunched in on himself again and, with a modest wave, collapsed back onto his bench.

'And all that is true, Princess,' he said to Elizaveta, 'as God is my witness.'

Elizaveta could see now why no man had wished to talk of the evil day.

'Cnut called down the night?' she whispered.

'I saw it with my own eyes, though I know not how.'

'And that is why,' Harald put in, his own fair face sober at the memory of the dark battle, 'we will need a very great force to take Norway back out of his thieving hands.'

Elizaveta nodded slowly.

'You will do it, I know. You will take Norway back.'

'I will, and rob him of Denmark and England too.'

'England?'

'Why not? 'Tis but a day or two's sail from our western shores.'

Elizaveta looked at him, stunned by the glorious ambition shining from his fierce eyes.

''Tis a high aim, Harald.'

'Then I will need the very best arrows. You will keep my gold, Elizaveta?'

His voice had stilled, grown solemn. She looked into his grey eyes and saw swirls of dark blue and gold within their steady colour, as if sunlit rivers were flowing through them, keen to reach their destination.

'With all my heart,' she agreed.

CHAPTER THREE

Kiev, October 1031

'News of the Varangians!'

Vladimir came running into the boathouse where Elizaveta was sitting watching Jakob, the master boatbuilder, lovingly fit the first side strakes to the curved keel of Yaroslav's new trading vessel. It was a wide ship made for transporting furs, wax and weapons south down the Dnieper to Byzantium and not as sleek as a wave-slicing warship, but it was beautiful all the same. Elizaveta had been happily absorbed in Jakob's work for some time but now she leaped up and ran to her brother.

'What news?'

'I don't know.'

'You said there was news, Vlad.'

Elizaveta grabbed his arm impatiently. Yaroslav had given Prince Harald and his men a commission in his guard and despatched them to the north to help quell a rebellion on the coast. They had been gone all summer and Elizaveta was desperate for news of them.

'There is,' her brother agreed, maddeningly calm. 'I just don't know what. Three riders came in the gates an hour or so back.'

'An hour? Why did you not find me sooner?'

'Because, sister, you are very hard to find. I've been all over the bowers.'

Elizaveta grimaced.

'It is too sunny for the bowers, especially with winter on its way, but no matter – how do you know the men have come from the Varangians?'

'Because one of them is him . . .'

'Prince Harald?'

'No, not him. The other one – Ulf, is it?'

'Ulf Ospakkson, yes. Are you sure?'

'Course I'm sure. I've never seen a wilder mop of hair on a man. Will you come up to the palace, Lily?'

'I certainly will.' She ran over to the old boatbuilder and planted a kiss on his weathered cheek. 'Thank you, Jakob.'

'Pleasure, Princess, as always. Perhaps I will craft *you* a ship one day?'

'Oh I do hope so – a sleek, curved one with fine carvings and an eagle's head at the prow.'

'An eagle?' Jakob raised a shaggy eyebrow. 'Very well then, I shall start practising my birds.'

'Do.'

Elizaveta beamed at him then took Vladimir's arm and headed outside. The boathouse was at the water's edge in the trading district of Kiev known as the Podol, or Valley, as it stood far below the royal kremlin up on the great plateau. The wooden walkways here were raised to escape the spring flooding and the houses, workshops and stores were similarly lifted on strengthened cross-beam foundations.

It was a rough, crowded, busy part of Kiev with the fenced plots tight up against each other, but Elizaveta loved the vibrancy of the mish-mash of inhabitants, some Slav, some Norse, many a mix of the two or immigrants from the various tribal nations around the still-growing state of the Rus. It was with reluctance, therefore, that she took the great wooden steps up out of its streets and through the curved ravine to the north gates of her father's kremlin. The promise of news from Harald, however, spurred her on and picking up pace, she gained the top quite out of breath. Vladimir regarded her uncertainly as the guards admitted them.

'Perhaps you should change, sister?'

'Change, why?'

'You are a little . . . damp. And your hair is all over the place and your dress is coated in . . .' He shook it and pale flecks fell to the ground. 'Sawdust,' he finished.

Elizaveta groaned.

'You're right. Will you wait, Vlad?'

'Of course, but be quick, Lily. They have been fighting the wild men in the north-west and I wish to hear all about it. Father says that in a few years I can travel to Novgorod to rule as its sub-prince so I should learn all I can about the area.'

Elizaveta nodded.

'I'll be quick,' she promised him and darted into the bower.

The lower half of the long building was split into several rooms for the women's daytime pursuits and, as Elizaveta made for the central staircase, she could see servants rushing all over, tidying threads from around the looms in the weaving shed, mopping the floor of the dairy, strewing fresh herbs and rushes on the floor of the receiving hall and brushing down the wall-hangings.

She tore up the stairs and into the chambers above to find Ingrid, Anastasia and Anne all being helped into fine gowns whilst the new baby, Yuri, wailed in Hedda's arms and little Agatha ran around tugging on skirts and getting in the way.

'Elizaveta!' Ingrid exclaimed. 'Thank heavens. Quick – you

must dress. Your father is coming with a guest and we must be ready to receive him.'

'Coming here? To the bower?'

'To my receiving hall, yes. I have just had word. Make haste.'

So that explained all the activity downstairs; Elizaveta's mother often entertained in her rich receiving rooms, but rarely at such short notice.

'Surely it's only Ulf?' Elizaveta said as two maids tugged her out of her filthy day-dress and pushed her into a clean one of a beautiful sapphire blue. She looked down at it, puzzled. 'Why do I need my best gown?'

'I know not, Elizaveta, only that your father gave orders for us to be ready – you in particular.'

'Me?! Why me?'

Elizaveta edged to the window, dragging the two maids with her as they clung to the side-laces of her dress. Her second brother, Ivan, was with Vladimir below, clearly apprising him of the situation as the two of them were smoothing their own tunics and looking nervously towards Yaroslav's hall opposite.

'Her hair!' she heard Ingrid call and suddenly there seemed to be a mass of combs in her dark locks, tugging viciously at the knots.

'Ouch!'

'Hush, Lily. You must look your best.'

'Whatever *for*?'

Frustrated, Elizaveta stamped her foot and her mother was at her side in a trice. She put her hands on Elizaveta's shoulders and forced her to be still.

'I do not know what for, Elizaveta. I have not questioned your father and neither should you. He wishes you to look beautiful so you will.' Elizaveta huffed and Ingrid's face softened. 'You *will*, Lily – you are growing very pretty.'

Elizaveta shivered.

'I am too dark, Mama.'

'Nonsense, child. There are many ways to shine. Is a wooden carving not as lovely as a mosaic, or a rune stone as a fresco? Truly, you need not be blonde to be fair. You look lovely. Now quickly, I hear your father in the courtyard and we must make haste down the stairs.'

Ingrid led the way, Anastasia and Anne jumping after her, and Elizaveta bringing up the rear, with a squirming Agatha wailing at being left upstairs with Hedda and the baby. Elizaveta's heart was thudding strangely against her over-tightened gown and she glanced self-consciously down at her finally budding chest, to see it visibly pounding through the rich wool. Vladimir's knowing grin when he saw her did nothing to quell her nerves and she was grateful to take a seat at her mother's side on the little receiving dais at the top of the room as her seven brothers and sisters settled around them. Prince Magnus scuttled in and took a seat to one side, sneaking glances at the little leather book clipped to his belt, and Elizaveta glared at him.

'Why is he here?' she hissed to her mother.

'The messenger comes from his uncle – it is right he should hear him.'

Elizaveta groaned but now, in a fanfare of horns, Yaroslav was shown in with Ulf and his two riders and she turned nervously towards them.

'Ah, my lovely wife!' Yaroslav came up and kissed Ingrid firmly on the lips. 'And my beautiful daughters. How fine you all look on this lovely day, especially you, my sweet Elizaveta.'

It was all Elizaveta could do to stop her eyes narrowing; suddenly she was part of Yaroslav's ostentatious public display, but why? Oh, Lord, *why*?

'Thank you, Father,' she managed, glancing to Ulf, 'and I see you bring a visitor.'

'I do. You remember Ulf Ospakkson, Elizaveta?'

Elizaveta inclined her head, aware of Anastasia's eyes jealously upon her; that was one good thing in this strange situation.

'Greetings, my lord,' Elizaveta said, rising as Ulf came forward and dropped to one knee before her.

Dust from the road clung to his clothes and in the curls of his brown hair. He had clearly made an attempt to slick it down for several strands clung to his sun-browned forehead but the rest was already escaping and Elizaveta watched, fascinated, as one by one the curls sprung free. She heard Ingrid clearing her throat and glanced over to see her pointing urgently to her hand. Just in time she held it out for Ulf, flushing as he kissed it.

'You have fared well in the north?' she forced herself to ask, as no one else seemed inclined to speak.

'Very well. We fought the wild men back into their own kingdom and indeed beyond.'

'You have been inside the Iron Gates?' Vladimir burst forward, desperate to know more of the legendary pagans who reputedly lived in a vast forest cage of their own fashioning, and Ulf turned to him.

'We have, Prince, and it is a dark, dark land of caves and treetop dwellings, but rich in fur and iron. We have brought your father great booty.'

'And taken your share too,' Yaroslav said, though easily; he was never one to deny a man his reward if it was well-earned and he was clearly pleased with the haul his new recruits had brought him.

'That we have,' Ulf agreed, 'and that is why, Elizaveta, I am before you now. May I rise?'

Elizaveta flushed again.

'Oh yes, yes of course.'

Ulf stood and rummaged in the big leather pocket attached to his plaited leather belt. Carefully he drew out a small package wrapped in costly cream silk.

'A gift, Princess, from Prince Harald. He personally entrusted its delivery to me and promises there will be more – many more. Please . . .'

He held it out and, with a glance to her father, Elizaveta rose and took it. The fabric was soft and so smooth it almost slipped through her fingers. She hastily sat down again, nestling it in her lap to undo the binding-ribbon as her sisters leaned eagerly in to see. Her fingers were shaking ridiculously but she finally freed the knot and the silk opened out like a miniature flag to reveal, shining out of its folds, a thick neck chain of the softest rose gold.

'Oh,' she cried, 'it's beautiful.'

She lifted it up and the sunlight criss-crossing the room from the opposing windows caught in it, sending a thousand stars around the whitewashed walls.

'I am glad you like it, Princess,' Ulf said. 'Harald asked me to tell you that it is but the beginning. He sends these too.'

Now he produced another parcel. Elizaveta could feel Anastasia's eyes boring into her and rose to take this second gift more slowly, relishing the moment.

'Thank you, Count Ulf.'

'Just Ulf, Princess.'

'Nay,' Yaroslav put in, 'you shall be a count for this honour you do my daughter, as your friend Halldor is for his tales.'

'How does Count Halldor?' Elizaveta asked.

'Well, thank you. Very well. He has fought valiantly and won himself great riches.'

Ulf's brown eyes were sparkling and Elizaveta looked at him quizzically.

'Something special?' she asked.

'To him, Princess, yes. A slave girl called Elsa whom he prizes greatly and who seems very fond of him in return.'

'Of Halldor?' Anastasia asked incredulously.

'Anastasia!' Ingrid snapped. 'Why should she not love the Count Halldor?'

'He's just so . . . unusual-looking.'

'Maybe,' Ulf said smoothly, 'he has hidden talents.'

Ingrid spluttered and quickly turned it into a cough.

'He brings a story to life like no other,' she said quickly. 'I am sure a woman could fall for a man with such a tongue.'

'Indeed, my lady,' Ulf agreed, dipping his head and again Ingrid coughed.

Elizaveta looked from one to the other, puzzled, but her parcel was burning a hole in her fingers and she turned thankfully from the adults' strange jests to open it.

Inside was a small charm – a beautiful clear ruby in a woven gold setting with a clasp to fit it to the neck chain – and alongside it a golden key, also with a clasp. Elizaveta held it up, intrigued, and Ulf waved to his two companions who had lingered at the door. They shuffled forward, backs bent over a large casket which they brought to Elizaveta's feet. It was clasped shut with a fine gold buckle and Elizaveta looked down at it and then back to her key.

'Try it,' Ulf urged.

She glanced to her mother who looked a little bemused but nodded her forward all the same. Elizaveta handed the ruby to Anastasia who turned it over and over in her hands, looking wonderfully tearful at the sight of such a jewel that didn't belong to her. Elizaveta knelt before the casket. The little key fitted neatly into the lock and turned with a satisfying click.

Slowly she raised the lid and there, before them all, lay a mass of treasure – silver dirhams from Arabia, gilded cups and platters, jewel-studded knives and little ivory-carved boxes and game pieces. For a long time no one spoke and then Anastasia said: 'Is that all for her?'

Elizaveta was first to respond.

'Of course not, Stasia. It is Prince Harald's wealth. He sends it to me for safekeeping until he is ready to spend it on troops to reclaim Norway.'

'He is too good,' Magnus exclaimed from behind Yaroslav.

Elizaveta resisted the urge to contradict him. She wasn't sure what part Harald intended his nephew to play in the fight for their Norwegian inheritance but doubted it was a large one – and why should it be? Did Harald not have every bit as good a claim to the throne as Magnus? The boy might be Olaf's son, but only by a concubine. Harald was Olaf's half-brother and a descendant of the ancient Norwegian dynasty of the Ynglings in his own right and she knew which of them would make the better king.

'He has clearly worked hard,' she said, shutting the treasures away and locking the casket. 'Thank you, Anastasia.'

Elizaveta held out a hand for the ruby which her sister, with all eyes upon her, furiously returned. Then she carefully clipped both the charm and the key to the neck chain before fastening either end to her shoulder brooches. It dipped elegantly across her chest and gleamed against the blue of her gown.

'It becomes you well,' Ingrid said, then looked to Ulf, 'but what does it purport?'

'Nothing,' Elizaveta said crossly. 'It "purports" nothing, Mother, save that I promised Prince Harald I would see his treasure securely stored whilst he is out in my father's service.' She turned to Yaroslav. 'Can we use one of your vaults in Novgorod, Father, please?'

'We?' Yaroslav asked, raising an eyebrow and smiling across at Ingrid.

'I, then. Please, Father, I ask it of you as a matter of state.'

'Of state?'

He was smiling still; it infuriated Elizaveta.

'Just because I am but thirteen, Father, does not mean I cannot understand matters of state.'

He bowed.

'I apologise, daughter. So tell me, is marriage a matter of state?'

'Father!'

Anastasia leaped up.

'Is Elizaveta to be married, Father? Already? To Prince Harald?'

'Stasia!' Elizaveta all but shouted. 'Be silent.' Everyone stared. 'This is not about marriage,' she snapped, biting back tears.

She felt as if all the lovely treasure was suddenly raining down on her, crushing her. If Harald heard of this he would be mortified. He would take back his treasure and entrust it to someone who did not wish to make stupid claims on him.

'It's not like that,' she insisted. 'This is not about marriage or any such foolishness.' Her parents were looking at each other in that supercilious way again, laughing at her supposed foolish innocence, but maybe they were the fools here. 'Prince Harald trusts me as his treasure-keeper, no more, no less, and I value that trust and would appreciate it if you did too.'

She glowered at them all and now her mother rose.

'Elizaveta is right,' she said softly, looking to Ulf. 'No proposal comes with these gifts?'

The Varangian bowed low.

'No, my lady. I am sure, were the prince to seek such a weighty alliance, he would come direct to the Grand Prince himself, and on his knees. He appreciates all that you have done for us poor exiles, Sire, and seeks only the favour of your treasury. It is as your daughter says – their arrangement is between states people, not lovers.'

'See,' Elizaveta blurted, though this truth, put so baldly by Harald's right-hand man, sounded less reassuring than it should have done. She looked again to her father. 'May I have your leave, please, Father, to go and see this treasure safely stored until it can be escorted to Novgorod?'

Yaroslav hesitated a moment but then, at a look from his wife, moved over and dropped a kiss on Elizaveta's forehead.

'Of course, daughter. I am pleased to see you taking this trust responsibly, though I am sure Count Ulf will see the casket safe to my treasury here in Kiev until you can make your arrangements.' He leaned over, lifting the neck chain and running it softly through his fingers. 'You will need to look after this gift, daughter. There are many links on this beautiful chain and I suspect our Varangian prince intends to fill them all with keys.'

Elizaveta pressed her hand over her father's.

'I shall take the greatest care,' she assured him, drawing back.

Her heart was pounding beneath the ruby charm and she had to escape. Bowing low, she crossed the receiving room, moving as slowly as she dared, then grabbed at the door. Springing free, she picked up her skirts and, new chain jangling excitedly with her frantic steps, darted for the north gate, seeking out the fresh, uncomplicated air beyond the kremlin and drawing it into her lungs as if they might burst for the want of it.

CHAPTER FOUR

The banks of the Ros, June 1032

'Dignity,' Elizaveta reminded herself.

It was a lesson her mother had drummed into her in the preparations for this royal progress south but not, truthfully, something that came naturally to Elizaveta. Anastasia, riding to her left, was dripping with it, sitting erect in the saddle, her riding gown immaculately spread out around her and her wretched blonde hair flowing loose, so long now that she could almost trap it between her prim bottom and her saddle. Prince Andrew, riding at the rear of the procession with Prince Edward, had taken to paying her ridiculous compliments and Anastasia, sadly, had taken to believing them, making her even more insufferable than before. Elizaveta forced herself to sit up a little straighter and felt for her own hair.

Hedda and little Greta had insisted on winding the front sections into two plaits this morning to keep it back from her face, for which she was grateful, but the nursemaid had also threaded them with meadow flowers and although Ingrid had pronounced the results to be 'perfect' Elizaveta wasn't so sure. She felt awkward with the fragile stems clipped in with little wires and worried that she looked silly, but it was too late to pull them out now. They were approaching their destination

– Yaroslav's new southern settlements – and she must prepare to ride though the crowds that had gathered to see the royal family pass through.

The whole family was out today. Vladimir and Ivan rode behind Yaroslav with Elizaveta and Anastasia in their wake and then Stefan, Anne, Viktor and Igor all following on their own mounts. Ingrid was bringing up the rear in a richly dressed wagon with Hedda and Greta, a fidgeting Agatha, and baby Yuri. Although Yuri was nearly a year old and growing big and fit on Hedda's ready milk, Ingrid had struggled to regain her usual good health and Elizaveta was worried. Today, though, with a hot sun shining across the fertile plains south of Kiev, her mother was smiling brightly and waving to the crowd. Elizaveta swallowed and did the same.

The procession wound its way slowly along the hammered dirt track and up through the rough gates onto the wooden streets of the first of Yaroslav's new villages. Concerned at the lack of an agricultural population around the ever-growing city, the Grand Prince had been steadily 'encouraging' his poorer subjects to move into the lands between Kiev and the great run of protective Snake Ramparts. These triple earthworks, topped with viciously sharpened palisades, were designed to halt the vicious Pecheneg horsemen of the Steppe tribes who threatened Rus trade down the Dnieper and sometimes sought to advance on the city itself. Elizaveta had heard much about the Snake Ramparts and was eager to see for herself but first they must visit the new settlements.

These ran mainly along the banks of the Ros, an east-to-west tributary of the Dnieper and a natural extension of the ramparts. They provided both a border post for guards and a rich farming community to grow grain and raise livestock for Kievan tables and Yaroslav was fiercely proud of them. They were populated with forest people from the north and, more recently, prisoners from a war with Poland that had broken out earlier in the year and had been won, thanks in great part to Prince Harald and his fearsome Varangians.

Word had it that the prince's personal troops had grown to over two hundred men as ambitious soldiers flocked to his leadership and, with the war over, Yaroslav had put Harald in personal charge of establishing the mass of civilian prisoners in his new villages. He was waiting, they'd been told, to welcome them to the area and Elizaveta was keen to see him and assure him his treasure was secure.

Harald had scarcely been back to Kiev in his first year of service for Yaroslav, moving from the northern wars into the harsh round of winter tribute-collecting along the frozen rivers of Yaroslav's kingdom, not even joining the *druzhina* for Christ's mass. He had returned with the first thaw, though, and Elizaveta had hoped to see him ride the rapids but news of the Polish attacks had come days before the event and he had been gone almost immediately, his Varangians with him. It had been a poor race in their absence, though Vladimir had won and been so delighted that Elizaveta had almost forgotten her chagrin at being stuck on the bank.

Now, though, she would see Harald again and she prayed he would notice that, at fourteen, she was a woman at last. She had grown so fast that her mother had twice had to set the seamstresses to sew extra trim to the bottom of her skirts and, praise the Lord, she was taller than Anastasia again. Her breasts had also grown full, though her hips remained as slim as Vlad's – slim enough, were she only allowed, to fit in a canoe.

Elizaveta smiled at the thought and waved to the crowds of villagers who were pressing forward against the row of guards keeping the wood-paved streets clear. She could not, however, prevent her eyes drifting past her father to the little square at the heart of the settlement where a small dais had been raised, on which stood a man tall and blonde enough to look into her confused dreams.

Children were throwing petals into their path and one caught on the light summer breeze and whirled up into her eye, jabbing it in the corner so that she yelped. Elizaveta put up a hand to wipe furiously at the sharp tears it had drawn, blinking against the pain and praying her damned eye did not redden. Yaroslav had pulled up at the front of their parade and Harald had stepped forward to personally hold his bridle as he dismounted. Yaroslav clasped his captain warmly by both shoulders as Vlad and Ivan swung their legs free of their stirrups to jump down and still Elizaveta's tears came. Closing her stinging eyes desperately she let the warmth of the sun on her eyelids soothe her and the happy calls of the crowd wash over her.

'Dignity,' she reminded herself, then she felt a check on her horse and a warm hand on her ankle and a thrill, like the crackle from iron on a stormy day, rushed up the very centre of her body. She opened her eyes and there was Harald, his face level with her new curves, so close that she could – had she dared – have leaned down and run a finger along the scar on his cheek, less raw now but still a clear mark of his harsh warrior life.

'Princess Elizaveta, welcome.'

'Prince Harald, I thank you.'

'May I assist you to dismount?'

She nodded and his hand tightened around her ankle to steady her, though the tips of his fingers seemed to ripple across the stockingless skin above her boots, making it feel somehow overripe. She swung her second leg hastily over the back of her horse and now his other hand was resting on her waist, lightly and just for the moment it took her to drop to the street, but more than enough time to let her body know it liked it. Long enough, too, for her mind to recognise that, whatever her protestations to her nosy family, she wanted to be so much more than a treasure-keeper to this Varangian prince.

'Thank you.'

'My pleasure. I must speak with you, Elizaveta. I have fresh keys for your chain, if you will accept them?'

'Of course.'

'But I must wait, I fear, for first there is much ceremony to endure . . . enjoy.'

He was already turning to help her sisters down but not so fast that she missed the quick wink he sent her way. It tugged at his scar, sending his face slightly askew, and somehow drawing his other, unmarked eye closer so that she felt pulled right into the swirls of gold in their grey depths. Then he was gone and she was being whisked up onto the dais and someone was pushing little Agatha's hot, sticky hand into her own and the moment was lost. But it would come again. Surely, she prayed, casting her eyes down the tumbling Ros to the rolling plains and God's shimmering horizon far beyond, it would come again?

Elizaveta had to wait for what felt like an eternity, through speeches and a tour of the houses – built on firm foundations with neatly fenced plots that the displaced prisoners seemed content to own – and a service in the little stone church. Then there was a simple but, to Elizaveta, ridiculously long feast in the village square before, at last, the tables were pushed back and a bonfire lit. Musicians struck up a jig that pulled all the villagers out to dance and finally Harald was stepping her way.

'You are free, Princess?'

'To dance?'

Elizaveta looked warily at the rough-and-tumble peasants' reel. Agatha had dragged the long-suffering Edward into the steps and it did look fun but she feared her precious 'dignity' might suffer if she attempted to join in.

'If you wish,' Harald said, 'though in truth I have not learned many dances.'

'You have not, I imagine, had time to do so.'

'No,' he agreed, drawing her aside into the shadows just beyond the firelight. 'I'm afraid all my dancing has been with swords, but this is no time for such talk, Elizaveta. I have a new key for you – two new keys.'

'Two? Your wars in Poland, then, went well?'

'They did. I won safe borders for your father and much gold for myself – for Norway. You will keep it safe?'

'You may trust me with that.'

'Oh, I do. Here . . .'

He produced a parcel wrapped not this time in silk but in hemp. He grimaced as he handed it into her pale hands.

'It is not as pretty as the last, is it? I apologise. Ulf found me the silk – he is a smoother courtier than I.'

'It matters not,' Elizaveta assured him. 'The keys are the important thing.'

She hastily opened the parcel to reveal, as promised, two golden keys and between them a new charcoal-black charm.

'Your fee.' She flinched at the mercenary word and Harald must have seen it, even in the edges of the flickering firelight, for he leaned in and said, 'And to show my appreciation, Elizaveta. I chose it especially for you. See.' He lifted it up. 'The stone is jet, all the way from Whitby in England. I bought it from a Saxon trader for it is as dark and shining as your hair.' Elizaveta frowned and Harald's brow furrowed in reflection. 'What is it? What's wrong?'

She looked down at the scuffed ground.

'I hate my hair.'

'You hate it? Elizaveta, why? I think it quite the most beautiful thing I have ever seen.' Elizaveta laughed bitterly but he persisted. 'I jest not. It shines like a river of night.'

'Like a witch then?'

'A witch? Ah, Elizaveta, there is more to the night than witchcraft, I promise you.' His voice had grown husky and she felt it like a touch across her skin, a kiss even. 'Truly,' he said, stepping closer yet, 'I think your hair is beautiful. Look . . .'

He gently reached out and separated one of her dark locks from the flower-encrusted plaits, then did the same with his own ice-blonde hair. He twisted the two strands together so they lay in a twirl of contrast, pulling their heads close.

'It is a pretty pattern,' Elizaveta allowed, staring at it. 'Yet if I were blonde like my mother, you would not see the difference at all.'

He ran his fingers down the interlinked strands.

'And where, Elizaveta,' he asked, 'would be the joy in that?'

She lifted her eyes to his. They were so close now that she could feel his breath on her cheek.

'You may be right,' she conceded, her voice low.

They had both somehow stepped further from the light and she could see very little beyond his face. The scar seemed to stand out and she could not resist putting up a finger to touch it. He jolted back and their joined hair tugged.

'I'm sorry.'

'Don't be. It is a part of me, I suppose, albeit an ugly part.'

'It's not ugly. It's . . . art.'

'Art! Warrior art?'

'Exactly. It tells a story.'

'A bitter one.'

'Did you get it at Stikelstad?' He nodded in response. 'Can you tell me?'

'I have not Halldor's skill.'

'I need it not.'

He let their hair drop and glanced towards the villagers, rioting shadows against the leaping flames, then back to her.

'I will tell you, Elizaveta, if you promise not to hate your hair any more.'

'My ugly hair?'

'As ugly as my scar?'

She smiled.

'I promise.'

'Then I will tell, though there is not much to it. I had fought before Stikelstad, of course. I'd trained with my brother's great friend Finn Arnasson and he had led me out many times, but just in scuffles and sieges. Stikelstad was my first pitched battle and I was so proud of myself. I led seven hundred of my father's men to meet Olaf and I felt like a king at their head – fool that I was.'

'You were young.'

'Fifteen.'

Elizaveta calculated; that made him seventeen now, hardly old, and yet he was a seasoned warrior already.

'What happened?'

Harald shrugged.

'It was as Halldor said. We seemed to be winning. Our troops were hammering theirs and then the darkness came. It was evil, Elizaveta, truly. I was cut from my horse and from then on I was just fighting in the blackness, lashing out at any who assaulted me, friend or foe. I did not even see my brother cut down, nor his banner torn.'

'You can make a new banner, raise a new dragon.'

He shook his head and she looked at him in surprise.

'Not a dragon, Princess. I will have a raven – ravager of the battlefield. I will never be weak in a fight again. I know not when I took this wound, nor the others that mark me beneath my clothes, but at some point my legs would carry me no more and I had to crawl through the fighting and curl under a bush like a woodland animal. It was pathetic, truly.'

'It was not pathetic,' Elizaveta countered, 'for if you had not escaped you would not be here today and there would be no one to reclaim Norway.'

'That is true but that, too, is down to Ulf and Halldor more than myself. A day and a night I lay under that bush, till the enemy had done feasting and taken hostages and departed the field and the wounded had drawn their last pained breaths and gone to God all around me. I was barely sensible but Halldor found me, somehow, and he and Ulf carried me to a peasant's farm up the valley from the battlefield. They saved me.'

'They are true friends.'

'That they are. The others had fled over the Kjolen Mountains into Sweden and Harald and Ulf could have gone too but they chose to remain. All winter they worked that peasant's land. They ploughed up new fields and dug drainage and built a byre in exchange for my nursing until, in the spring, they had created the finest farm around and I, I had my life. I owe them everything.'

'You are a good lord to them.'

'I try, for a lord is nothing without his men, a king even less. I value them as highly as the treasure you hold for me and I will need them every bit as much as I need it to take Norway back.'

'Then you must keep them as safe as I keep your gold.'

'I must. Elizaveta . . .'

But whatever he intended to say was lost as a heavy clap on the back sent him sprawling forward and Elizaveta's father stepped up at her side.

'Plotting in the shadows, Harald?'

'Nay, Sire,' he said, recovering, 'just taking the chance to offer your daughter two more keys to my treasure troves.'

Elizaveta proffered the parcel but Yaroslav barely glanced at it.

'My daughter is a treasure richer than any gold or jewels, Varangian.' His voice was low and Harald bowed to it.

'That I know, Grand Prince.'

'Do not presume to what you are not entitled.'

'Father!' Elizaveta protested but Harald held up a hand as the Grand Prince nudged them back towards the light of the fire.

'I presume to nothing, truly, bar her kindness as my treasurer.'

'Good, though were you to offer her not just caskets but a crown . . .'

Elizaveta's protests stuck in her throat and Harald simply bowed again.

'I swear I will rule Norway one day, Sire.'

'*You* will?' It was a new voice, a thinner, higher one, and Elizaveta groaned as Magnus joined them. He, like her, had grown in the last year and his gangly frame intruded awkwardly on their group. '*I* am King Olaf's heir, Harald Sigurdsson,' the boy said, squaring up to his uncle, though Harald cast twice his shadow against the flames.

Harald looked down at him.

'How do you know?' he asked mildly. 'Were you at his side when he died?'

'You know I was not. Had I been, I might have protected him better.'

Harald bristled and Yaroslav stepped quickly between them.

'Come now – you are kin, joined by blood and a shared aim. You must fight your enemies, not each other. You can rule together, as I ruled with my own brother for several years.'

Elizaveta shifted. Her uncle had been the last of Yaroslav's eleven brothers to meet an early death and the thought of it made her uncomfortably aware of the harsh secrets of a man's world.

'If you wish to rule,' Harald said, 'you need men and for

men you need gold. I am gaining gold, nephew, but where is yours?'

'God will see me safely to my rightful place,' Magnus returned easily.

Harald growled.

'I told you, Magnus, God helps those . . .'

'Who strive for themselves? You did, but maybe, Harald, God helps those who devote themselves to his service? How can we know?'

'I am sure,' Yaroslav said hastily, 'that God loves all men who serve in whatever way they can and I pray that he sees you both safe in your homeland.'

'As kings?'

'If it is your destiny, yes.'

'With queens at our side?' Magnus looked slyly up at Harald. 'You are betrothed, are you not, Uncle?'

'No.'

Harald's answer was quick; too quick. Elizaveta looked at him but he had let his blonde hair fall forward and his eyes were shaded by it.

'No?' Magnus echoed in his stiff little voice. 'But weren't you promised to Finn Arnasson's daughter?' He turned to Elizaveta. 'The Arnassons are very great jarls in the north of Norway, Princess. They hold much land and much power.' He smiled thinly and Elizaveta shivered.

'Then it will be a useful alliance for you, Prince,' she said stiffly to Harald.

'There is no alliance,' he replied, pushing back his hair and looking straight at her. 'There is no promise. Magnus knows not what he is saying. It was talk, nothing more – you know how it is?'

Elizaveta drew in a long breath as she considered this. Her

father was always dangling betrothals before the young men of the *druzhina*, as he had indeed just done with Harald.

'I know,' she agreed quietly and her fingers clasped tight around her keys and the little black charm. 'And now, you must excuse me, gentlemen. It seems you have much to discuss and I think my mother looks for me to see to Agatha.'

It wasn't true. She'd seen her littlest sister being carried furiously away by Hedda some time back, but her joy in the evening was gone. She felt confused, lost even, and for once she longed for the peace of the ladies' bower. She curtseyed, then turned and strode away, past the bonfire and towards the comfort of the church that was to stand as their accommodation that night.

'Elizaveta!'

Reluctantly she turned back to see Yaroslav pursuing her.

'Father?'

'Do not let this boyish posturing upset you, my sweet.'

'It has not.'

'Indeed? Good.' He tucked a finger under her chin and lifted her face. 'Men will seek you, Elizaveta.'

'Because I am a Princess of Kiev?'

'Yes, but more than that – they will seek you for your spirit. A man needs a wife with spirit if he is to succeed in life.'

'As you have, Father?'

'I am blessed, Elizaveta. I married your mother for my nation but I have grown to love her for herself. I hope you find such fortune too and will do my best to make it so.'

Elizaveta opened her mouth to try to thank him but he was gone, back to his dais to look over his people, and she was left to retreat to her bed, strangely comforted by his awkward words but no less confused.

CHAPTER FIVE

Banks of the Dnieper, April 1034

'❦lizaveta stepped up onto the grandstand beside her
sisters and felt the usual mix of elation and envy that
the Rapids Race always set swirling inside her. With
Yaroslav richer than ever on the trade and territory Harald and
his Varangians had brought him, he was planning a huge celebration and the competition area below Kiev looked magnificent. The race was always run at the height of the snowmelt
when the river shot down the tight path through the forest
cliffs, twisting between rocks, through pools and over little
waterfalls until it hit the open water at the bottom.

The two grandstands were stood down there on stilts either
side of the fastest run of the current, and this year they were
bigger than ever and decorated all along their wood-tiled roofs
with scarlet pennants edged in gold. There were raised walkways leading to both, the one on the far bank stretching a long
way round as the floods were high this year, forcing the lower
section of the river so far out across the plains that it sometimes
seemed, especially in the morning mists, as if the sea itself had
come to Kiev.

The watching platforms were some ten men deep and the
front railings were sturdy and strung across with several layers

of thick rope. A little higher up, where the river twisted between rocks and the best crashes were to be seen, there were more platforms, rougher ones built by the villagers. The most daring observers would also brave the natural ledges above the ravine towards the start of the race where the land was dry but the cliffs fell steeply down to the course below.

The racers, Vladimir and Ivan both amongst them this year, would be reaching the starting pool now, their boats carried over their heads as part of the ceremony. The craft were slim one-man canoes of animal hide stretched over a flexible birch frame and Elizaveta had had little trouble carrying her own on the glorious morning when she'd sneaked out in her brother's clothes and joined the line-up.

She sighed at the memory. Had it really been six years ago? She was sixteen now and no boy's clothes would hide her womanliness, but Ingrid – thankfully back to full, bossy health – had still set two maids to watch her from before she woke. Elizaveta hated it but could not blame her wary mother; she *would* ride again if she got half a chance.

She peered enviously up the river as Anastasia arranged them all along the railing, carefully making space for the lost princes to join them. Edward was twenty-three now so too old to qualify for the race, though he'd taken part several times before. He had not distinguished himself but he had made it to the end and Elizaveta had admired him for trying. Prince Andrew, however, although still young enough to race, had simply said with his usual easy flair that he was not a boatman. It was fair, she supposed – a man, as Anne had primly said, should know his own strengths – but she struggled to admire him for it.

Andrew seemed to her to float around the kremlin looking very elegant but doing little of any use, though he had been receiving visitors recently – dark-eyed Slavs from his homeland who looked to restore him to his crown. Anastasia was very excited about it and forever hanging on his long, thin arms, flicking her blonde hair and gazing up at him, asking to know more of Hungary. She was after a husband, that much was clear, and, feeling mischievous, Elizaveta slid herself between her sister and the prince.

'Who do you think will win, Andrew?' she asked.

'Oh, your royal brother, I am sure,' he replied in his smoothly perfect Rus.

'Which one?'

'There is more than one in the race?'

Five-year-old Agatha, standing next to them with her hand in Edward's, laughed out loud but Anne stepped hastily forward, shushing her little sister.

'Both Vladimir and Ivan are riding,' she told Andrew. 'Vlad won last year and wishes to keep the cup and Ivan is desperate to take it off him.'

'I see,' Andrew said calmly, 'and who will succeed?'

'Vlad,' Agatha said promptly, pushing past Anne, 'because he's biggest. That's right, isn't it, Edward?'

Edward smiled down at her.

'Perhaps, Agatha, but I fear both your royal brothers will be challenged by Gregor, the young Count of Smolensk.'

Elizaveta looked admiringly at Edward; as usual he had quietly noticed exactly what was going on.

'I agree,' she said. 'I have seen Gregor practise and he is so fast down the rapids it takes your breath away.'

Andrew squinted down at her.

'You have watched the practices, Princess?'

'Oh yes,' she confirmed, 'otherwise how else would I know who to place a wager on?'

Andrew's eyes widened further.

'You have wagered?'

'Why yes. Not myself, of course, but Hedda has secured my stake.' Elizaveta drew a small birch sliver from her pocket, carved with Gregor's rune-mark, and Andrew looked fearfully around, as if she were holding a still-bleeding pagan sacrifice.

'Princess,' he begged, 'put that away or you will be in terrible trouble.'

'Oh no,' Elizaveta assured him, 'we all do it – well, except Magnus. He just mutters stuff about Christ throwing the moneylenders out of the temple, but this is no temple. Even Anne pulls herself away from her books long enough to wager. It adds to the excitement, do you not think?'

Prince Andrew clearly did not. Anne looked uncomfortably at her feet and Anastasia seized her chance.

'I did not wager,' she said primly.

Elizaveta spluttered and was about to point out that Anastasia had been the first to go to Hedda that morning when she caught sight of an ice-blonde head moving through the crowd towards them and her thoughts were instantly scrambled.

In the last two years since she had visited the Ros settlements she had seen Harald rarely. He and his men had barely been allowed to stay in Kiev for more than a few weeks between successful ventures on her father's behalf. The two of them had stolen what time they could, but it had been all too short, save for a precious month last summer when they had both accompanied her father on a visit to Novgorod, the northern capital of the Rus, to inspect the vaults.

Yaroslav had allowed Elizaveta to conduct the visit and, feeling very royal, she had led the way down the low stone corridor that ran deep beneath the chill city. Harald had followed dutifully behind, and she had been achingly aware of the warmth of his big body at her back. The guards at the vast oak doors had bowed so low to her that their noses had almost scraped the cold rock floor and had stood deferentially back as they had stepped inside. Fifteen big caskets, locked to the floor with great chains, had stood before them – a wall of wealth – and she'd heard Harald's breath catch.

'You have worked hard,' she'd murmured and the look he'd given her had fired her skin, despite the ice of the stone chamber.

'So have you.'

He'd stepped behind her to look upon the wealth he had gathered to secure Norway and for a moment Elizaveta had been frozen by the thought of how he had done so. It had not, she'd known, been by smiling or asking nicely. When he was abroad on her father's service Harald worked in blood and she'd been painfully aware that these spoils she kept like some little dragon were a sparkling veneer over the necessary violence of his life as a soldier. She'd taken a step back, suddenly afraid, but his hands had closed gently on her shoulders, steadying her.

'I want you with me, you know,' he'd said, his voice low. 'I want you with me in Norway.'

She hadn't dared look at him.

'Do you not have a woman waiting?'

'Not one like you.' He'd dropped his hold and strode forward, running his big warrior's hand across the caskets. 'Look what we've done already, Elizaveta.'

'I have done little.'

'Not true. You have understood me. You have understood my ambitions and you have started us on the path to achieving them.'

It had been the 'us' that had reached into her, sending prickles through her whole body. Gathering herself, she had moved forward to join him, carefully unclasping her neck chain so that they could check every casket. He had spoken no further of a union but as they had knelt side by side on the Rus stones, their faces aglow with the light from the gold that would win

Norway, she had been sure that this had become their shared destiny.

That, though, had been last summer. Recently she'd begun to wonder if she had imagined the cave, as Halldor might imagine the trolls that could live in it, and she shifted awkwardly as Harald drew close.

'Welcome to our great Rapids Race,' she offered shyly.

'I am very glad to be here,' he responded, though his eyes were upon her, not the river.

Thrown, Elizaveta looked down at the water bubbling close to the platform. It had been a hard winter and the river still carried lumps of ice. If a rider caught on one it could cut the skin of his canoe and send him down in moments.

'The waters run hard,' she managed.

'They will carry us fast south then.'

Elizaveta looked up at that.

'You are taking the trade boats to the golden city?'

'To Miklegard, yes.'

'Miklegard!' She smiled at the ancient Viking term for Constantinople, the capital of the Byzantine Empire. 'The seawater in your veins is itching?'

'A little, perhaps. This is duty – the traders were sorely attacked by the Pechenegs last year so your father has assigned us as guards – but I confess that I am eager to see the place. They say it takes a man a full day to walk around the walls.'

Elizaveta felt envy stir inside her again. She had heard many tales of the beauty of Miklegard – the Great City – and longed to see it for herself.

'I am told the Hagia Sophia is the largest church in all God's world,' she said.

'And the richest. The central cupola rises to the heavens themselves, wide enough to hold a very choir of angels and lined with gold so thick you could make ten armrings from one panel.'

'Even you would do well to claim that treasure, Harald.'

He looked hurt.

'I am not *such* a heathen, Elizaveta. I would like to see the cathedral for its beauty, not its worth.'

'I'm sorry. I would like that too.'

'Though the treasure would not hurt.' He winked, then leaned a little closer. 'Our caskets are safe, Princess?'

Her body sung; he had not forgotten their visit. The troll cave had been real – but had the words spoken been real too?

'Your caskets are safe, yes.'

'*Our* caskets, Elizaveta. I would like . . .'

But now Agatha bounced up between them.

'Harald! You made it. Are you not racing?'

Harald gathered himself and smiled down at the five-year-old.

'I am too old to qualify, Agatha.'

'You're more than eighteen?' she asked, her wonderment at his great seniority making them both laugh.

'He *is* eighteen,' Elizaveta told her. 'He has been at war too long and missed his chance.'

'At what, Princess?'

Harald seemed very close, his grey eyes sharp as new-mined crystals.

'At racing, of course.' Elizaveta licked at her lips, suddenly dry, and added as Agatha bounced away again, 'I rode the rapids once.'

'*You* did?'

He looked down at her, his grey eyes swirling with something that was either admiration or disgust.

'Yes, *I*,' she said defiantly. 'Or rather, I rode them halfway.'

'You crashed?'

'No!' She glared at him. 'I rode very well.'

'I don't doubt it. So what happened?'

'I was netted.'

He blinked.

'Netted? By whom?'

His tone was playful but the memory was still painful for Elizaveta and she had to put up a hasty finger to catch a rogue tear before it could smudge the kohl her mother had finally let her use on her lashes.

'There are men stationed in groups along the banks with great nets on wooden poles to catch any riders who are tossed from their canoes and may be in danger from the rocks,' she explained. 'The boys are young and no one wishes to see them die.'

'Of course not, but you, Elizaveta – you were not in any trouble?'

Despite herself, she smiled.

'I was in *much* trouble, Harald, but not from the water.'

'Your father did not approve of you racing?'

She shook her head.

'Girls are too delicate for such sports, or so he says, though I do not see why. We are lighter and more agile than boys and I had practised harder than any. I was hurt more by that stupid net scooping me out of my boat than I would ever have been if they'd let me finish.' Harald looked at her again, seeming to scrutinise every part of her face until she shifted awkwardly. 'What is wrong? Am I smudged?'

He smiled.

'No, Elizaveta, you are not "smudged". I was merely wondering . . . why?'

'Why did I ride? Why should I not?' She could hear her own voice rising in a way her mother would undoubtedly condemn as undignified, but she could not stop it. 'Has anyone ever asked Vlad why he rides, or Ivan? No! It is a fine thing for them to wish to test themselves, to rise to the challenges that nature has set, to pit their skills against those of their peers, so why, then, is it so strange for me? Are we so different, men and women?'

'In some ways,' Harald said, his voice so low now it stopped her own in her throat and made her heart push at her breasts. His eyes followed the motion and she swallowed. 'But you are right. I think women every bit as brave and fiery and determined as men.'

'Oh?' she retorted, confused. 'And you have known many women, have you?'

'A few.' He raised a slow eyebrow and her stomach flipped inside her. 'Though none that mattered – yet.'

Elizaveta's throat felt very dry. Who had he known? Concubines? Pretty, wild little street women who'd crawled over his scars with their lithe, practised bodies? His chest was tight up against hers and for a treacherous moment she longed to put her hands against it and feel his strength. He was staring at her still, his glacier eyes fixed on her lips as if he might kiss her right there, in the royal grandstand, as if she might let him, and she pulled back, flustered. She was not one of his street women, won with honeyed words and a muscled chest.

'The race will begin any moment,' she said stiffly, turning back to the river.

'Elizaveta, I did not mean . . .'

A shout went up from the riverbank and she turned gratefully to look up at the great scarlet flag waving in the trees at the top of the ravine. It indicated that the racers were in the starting pool and an expectant silence fell on the hundreds of watchers lining the river. Guards stood to attention, netters braced themselves against rocks and, at the centre of the grandstand, Grand Prince Yaroslav rose, picked up a golden hammer and swung it cleanly into the centre of a richly patterned gong. The sound shivered, sweet and low, across the water and was joined by another up the bank and then another in the trees and a fourth hidden in the ravine. The mingled sounds filled the spring air and then suddenly the forest flag went down and the race was begun.

The nobles in the grandstand, forgetting themselves in the excitement of the moment, pushed forward as hard as the commoners on the banks and Elizaveta suddenly found herself forced against the railings. To her left Prince Edward lifted Agatha onto his shoulders as Anne, never one for fuss, stepped back a little. Prince Andrew flapped ineffectually at the crowd, Anastasia attempting to soothe him as she let herself be crushed against his chest and Elizaveta felt a little crushed herself. For a moment she fought for breath until suddenly the ebb and flow of people was stopped as Harald reached his long arms out around her, forming a shield. She was grateful for his solid presence, though not sure she felt any safer, but now, on the ridge, a flag went up and her attention was caught.

'Green,' she said excitedly, daring to glance back at Harald. 'The flag is green.'

'Is that your man?'

She nodded. Gregor was wearing green. Vladimir was in purple, Ivan in scarlet and blue and the five other young men in various other colour combinations.

'Who do you have?' she asked him, unable to take her eyes off his arms, the muscles rippling against the push of the crowd.

'Green too,' Harald admitted. 'I saw the lad ride yesterday; he was fearless.' They watched in silence for a few moments then he added: 'I would have liked to see you ride the rapids, Elizaveta.'

'I would have liked the chance.'

The boats were not visible yet but on the platforms at the top of the rapids the people were going wild. Agatha was screaming excitedly, bouncing up and down on poor Edward's brave shoulders and pointing upstream. Elizaveta leaned over the parapet to see, but suddenly Harald's face was beside her own and his chest tight against her back.

'Elizaveta.' His voice was low, urgent.

She turned and found herself in his arms.

'Harald, please. People are looking.'

'They are not.' That much was true. 'I must speak. Your father will send me to muster the trade fleet down in Vitichev within a few days and I seek your leave to talk to him.'

Elizaveta's ears were filled with the excited calls of the crowd but she seemed to hear only him.

'You can talk to him any time, Harald,' she stuttered, fearing she was reading his intentions wrong. 'You are his man.'

'But I wish, this time, Elizaveta, to talk to him of *you*.'

'Oh.'

'To ask his permission to take you as my wife – my wife and future queen.'

She strained to catch the words. All around people were pressing to the waters' edge and their roar was grabbing at Harald's words, tangling them so they would not enter her brain.

'There,' someone called, 'there they are!'

'Elizaveta,' Harald urged, 'may I talk to him – may I talk to him of us?'

Us? The word lit a memory of them both knelt before the caskets in Novgorod, their future shining before them.

'Yes,' she gasped out. 'Yes, Harald – you may. And now,' she giggled, embarrassed, 'may *I* watch the race?'

He smiled too then took her face in both his hands, so big they wrapped all the way up to her ears.

'In just one moment.'

His lips pressed against hers, so fast and sure that she had no chance to protest, even had she wanted to. For a moment she was drowning deliciously in the kiss, but then he was spinning her round and pointing up the river as if nothing had happened at all. His hand, though, was still on her waist and the musky scent of him was all around and his words were rippling through her mind as if she were truly riding the rapids this time.

''Tis Gregor!' Edward cried and Elizaveta forced herself to pull away from Harald a little as the green tunic whirled into view upriver, Vladimir's purple close behind.

They took the first turn around the rocks almost together, Vlad pressing hard and then suddenly the top of the Prince's canoe clipped the other boat and Gregor slewed wildly sideways and disappeared. The crowd gasped.

'Where is he?' Elizaveta asked, grabbing Harald's hand without even thinking.

Vladimir's boat wobbled on the edge of a tricky whirlpool. The stern tipped and shivered and then, thankfully, he righted it but still Gregor was nowhere. Elizaveta scanned the river desperately and then suddenly Harald pointed to the far side where, miraculously, the young count's canoe had popped up below the rocks, barely a hand's breadth behind Vladimir. The boy was soaked to the skin and shaking his head wildly to throw the water from his eyes but he pushed on, his paddle flashing in the spray, and now he was gaining on Vladimir. Vladimir sensed the danger and picked up his own pace but he was too late. Gregor shot between the grandstands to a hero's roar and beneath the rope to victory.

'How did he do that?' Elizaveta gasped.

'Nerve,' Edward said admiringly, swinging Agatha down to the floor. 'Nerve and not a little luck. He must have caught an undercurrent through the channel. And look, here comes Ivan in third. A good day for your family.'

'Indeed,' Elizaveta agreed softly. Agatha was bouncing excitedly, Anastasia had seized the chance to fling her arms around Andrew, and even solemn Anne was clapping, but it all felt dreamlike. Had Harald really spoken of marriage? Had he truly asked for her hand or had she just been mixed up in the race?

'Will you excuse me?' Harald said, strangely formal. She *had* imagined it. 'I must seek out your father.'

'Now?'

'Whilst he is in a good mood and likely to look favourably upon an exiled prince. You are sure, Elizaveta?'

He *had* spoken.

'Sure,' she squeaked.

'Then I shall go.'

Harald bowed low and began to fight his way towards the Grand Prince. Elizaveta watched his fair head weave through the crowd and hugged her arms around her chest. The canoes were gathering at the finish and she was glad to be distracted by them and pleased to see Vlad slapping Gregor on the back and towing him to the bank, for the lad was shivering violently. Men helped them onshore and threw great fur cloaks around them as slaves pulled the canoes to land and then they were brought to the grandstand to receive their prizes from Yaroslav.

'A great race,' the Grand Prince proclaimed. 'Perhaps the greatest ever and a worthy victory by Gregor the Seal.'

The crowd roared in delight at this byname and Gregor beamed. He was trembling too much to take the cup but he beckoned up Lady Beatrix, his voluptuous young fiancée, to accept it on his behalf. She did so and then, to even more uproarious approval, kissed the victor full on the lips before them all.

'Must be catching,' Elizaveta said quietly, feeling the recent imprint of Harold's lips on her own.

Anastasia squinted at her.

'What must be?'

'Oh, nothing.'

'What, Elizaveta? What's catching? What's happening?'

'The feast, I think,' Elizaveta said wickedly. 'Shall we go?'

She turned down the walkway, falling into step with Halldor Snorrason.

'True love?' Halldor grunted, nodding to the victor and his clinging woman.

'I don't know, Hal,' Elizaveta threw back with a smile. 'I hear *you* are the expert on such matters these days.'

Halldor grimaced.

'It makes fools of us all.'

'Happy fools,' Elizaveta said, watching Gregor depart with both Beatrix and his trophy beneath his cloak. Behind them Harald was escorting Yaroslav along the walkway and Elizaveta's heart lurched. What if her father said no?

'Mayhap,' Halldor was agreeing and she turned gratefully back to him.

'Elsa is here?'

'She is. She has been watching from the far bank. I asked her to accompany me into the grandstand, but she insisted she knew her place.'

'Her place is at your side, Hal. You should marry her.'

'Marry? Nay, I'm not one for ceremonies, Princess. I have pledged her my troth and it is enough. Besides, she carries my child.'

Elizaveta spun round to face him.

'That's wonderful news, Halldor – you will be a father.'

'I will, poor mite. 'Tis a good job he will have such a fine mother.'

'Oh, Hal,' Elizaveta chided, 'do not underestimate yourself.

He or she will have the finest bedtime stories of any child on God's earth. Elsa will go to Miklegard with you?'

'She will.'

'She is lucky then.'

'You think serving women freer than princesses, Elizaveta?'

'No, I am not so foolish nor so arrogant as that. I know myself to be very lucky but Elsa is, I think, blessed too.'

'I hope so,' Halldor said, his eyes fixing on the girl, who was now in sight, standing at the end of the walkway, her slim hands over her swelling belly as she waited quietly for him. 'Happy fools,' he echoed, trying it out. ''Tis true, Princess, yet love is a fearful business.'

'Fearful?'

'A terrible admission for a Varangian, is it not? But it is true. Loving Elsa has made everything seem more worthwhile but it also means there is more to lose. My own life is more precious now and that is both a blessing and a curse, especially in battle.'

He looked so earnest, so troubled, that Elizaveta longed to kiss his funny, wrinkled brow but she feared embarrassing him so instead took his arm and led him towards his mistress.

'Best then,' she suggested, 'if you make the most of every moment of it – especially in peacetime.'

Halldor laughed at that, a big, open belly-laugh, and patted Elizaveta's arm.

'You are wise, Princess. And I hope,' he added, 'that you can heed your own advice. You will come to Norway with us, I think?'

There was little point dissembling.

'I hope so, Hal,' she admitted, glancing forward to where Harald and Yaroslav were taking the steps up to the kremlin together. 'I truly hope so.'

CHAPTER SIX

Giske, Norway, Midsummer 1034

Tora Arnasson dug her toes into the rough sand and looked out across the rolling sea to the muted mainland beyond. Behind her, up on the cliff, the elders were lighting the beacon and she could hear the crackle of the tinder and the low shout of approval from the men as she caught the first sparks reflected in the frothing sea's edge. Within minutes the fire would be ablaze, sending out its burnished path across the water like a miniature sun to call the Arnassons' people to feast.

Glancing nervously up the cliffs, Tora saw three heavy figures silhouetted against the nascent flames. In the centre was her uncle, Jarl Finn, the man who had taken command of the Arnasson family when her own father, Thorberg, had been lost to an enemy sword. Already widowed, Finn had raised Tora and her siblings, Otto and Johanna, with his own daughters, Idonie and Sigrid. He was a tough man but Tora had always found him fair and certainly far more so than his hot-headed younger brother, Jarl Kalv, stood brooding dangerously to his right.

She shivered and looked the other way, but there was no comfort to be found there either, for to Finn's left was the equally dangerous Einar Tambarskelve, the only great land-holder in the north who was not of her father's kin. Einar's family were less deeply rooted in the land than the Arnassons and he was ever on the alert for opportunity, political or military, to advance himself. When Cnut, already king of Denmark and England, had first driven King Olaf out of Norway six years ago, Einar had cleaved to him and gained himself much power as a result. Recently, though, Einar had been mithering about Cnut's regent in Norway, his son Steven by his English concubine, and Tora feared he would draw the Arnasson men into his plotting.

She cast her eyes back out to sea, searching for the bobbing mast-lanterns of the first fishing craft that would bring the locals from their lonely farms along the coast to see out the midsummer night on their jarl's beach. Long trestle tables had been set up on the high sand where the sneaky sea could not lick at legs, and in a cluster of pavilions in the lee of the cliff servants were preparing the feast. A huge fire had been set in a circle of stones and Tora could hear grunts as porters lifted a vast iron sheet across it on which the fish – fresh-caught this morning – could be fried and served straight onto the bread trenchers sat beneath linen on a table behind.

Over another fire, a lamb was turning on a spit and on a third bubbled a large pot of honeyed apples, flavoured with spices traded in from the orient and spiked with firewater from Kalv's own brew house. The same had provided the barrels of ale which were sat in the shade of a cavern for it had been a hot day and promised to be a warm evening. The sun would not sleep tonight, nor the people of Norway either, and the air bristled with anticipation.

'There!'

Tora's younger sister Johanna ran to the water's edge, pointing eagerly outwards.

Following her finger, Tora saw three lights bobbing with the swell of the rising tide coming from the western end of the mainland.

'They are on their way,' she agreed with the calm befitting her nineteen years, though she could not prevent herself leaning into the half-night to try and catch the voices of the revellers as memories battled inside her.

Harald had come like this back in 1027. His had been the first boat into the bay and he had sailed it himself, though he was – like her – but newly turned twelve and recently fostered into Finn's household from his own home in the south. Wearing a wolf's mask fashioned from a real skull, he'd put back his white-blonde head and howled to the moon-sun as he splashed through the shallows.

'I am come to hunt you, Tora Arnasson,' he'd called, catching sight of her, and she'd run, sand spraying up behind her scrabbling feet as he'd given chase. 'I will catch you, Tora – you know I will.'

'And what will you do with me then?' she'd called back over her shoulder, ducking round the fires and making for the cliff path.

'I will eat you,' Harald had said and her heart had scudded and her steps faltered and within moments he'd caught her ankle and tumbled her onto the sand.

'I will not taste good,' she'd protested, squirming to escape.
'I will risk it.'

He'd flipped her onto her back, the sand catching in her loose blonde hair, and crawled up over her, his big body shadowing her slimmer one, though he'd held himself up on his muscular arms like the haunches of the very wolf he was pretending to be.

'Don't eat me,' she'd whimpered, feeling his breath hot on

her neck and his hair tickling her cheek and his maleness like a fever across her pale skin.

'Why should I not?' he'd growled, dipping lower.

'Because, pup, she is my niece!'

And with that, Harald had been lifted by the scruff of his neck high up into the air and flung aside.

'Sorry, Jarl Kalv, sir. I'm sorry. 'Twas just a game – just midsummer foolery.'

'You're too young for such games,' Kalv had snapped back, 'or maybe too old. Get up, Tora, and wipe yourself down and try, for once, to behave like a jarl's daughter and not a peasant girl.'

That had stung, the scornful 'for once' pricking at her summer-hot skin like a barb, as if she'd been some sort of disgrace to her dead father's memory and not the ridiculously well-behaved girl she'd half-despised herself for. It had lit something inside her, or maybe simply fanned the flames Harald's wild chase had sparked.

Simple sense had dictated a need for caution, at least until the sun was low enough to make the beach more shadows than light. But as the ale had flowed and the fish had been picked to the bones and the men had taken their wives on their knees around the fire leaving the youngsters with the darker reaches of the sands, Tora had looked again for her wolf.

'You have feasted well, Harald?'

'That I have.'

He'd thrown off his wolf cloak and had stood before her in just a linen shirt, his torso, despite his youth, already muscular and clearly defined through the thin fabric.

'You are, then, full up?' she'd asked cheekily.

'I may have a little space, if something especially tasty were to tempt me.'

'A honeyed apple perhaps?'

'No. No, not that – too sweet.'

'Some crisped skin from the lamb then?'

He'd stepped closer.

'Too dry.'

'Some ale from my uncle's barrels?'

'I have had plenty of that.'

She'd tipped her face up to his.

'What then, wolf?'

He'd smiled in the half-light.

'The lips of a jarl's daughter,' he'd whispered, then his hands had been on her waist and his lips against hers, and she'd felt as drunk as if she'd drained the apples of their pungent juice.

'Oi! Harald Sigurdsson!'

'Not again,' Harald had groaned against her lips and, though fear had spiked inside her at the sound of the call, she'd giggled.

'Is that my sister you're chewing on?'

They'd both relaxed and Harald had spun round, hands still on Tora's waist, to face their accuser.

'I was not "chewing", Otto,' Harald had objected. 'I was far more delicate.'

'Were you indeed?' More of the local youngsters had been gathering and Otto had drawn himself up tall. Although barely eight, he'd been a tall, confident lad and had enjoyed the audience. 'Well, with our father gone, I am the guardian of her honour and I say that if you wish to chew on her – delicately or nay – you must first be betrothed.'

'Oh yes,' Johanna had clapped, 'a betrothal. Come, Tora, you must have flowers in your hair.'

'No, Johanna, I . . .'

But already Johanna, Idonie and Sigrid had been pulling her away and plucking clover from the cliff side to thread into her wind-tangled hair.

'And you, Harald,' Otto had gone on, 'you must, must . . .'

'Dance!' someone had supplied. 'Dance like the wolf you claim to be.'

'Wolves don't dance,' Harald had objected.

'And they don't kiss either, southern boy,' Otto had retorted, 'but this is midsummer so normal rules don't apply – now dance!'

Tora smiled at the memory. That night, as Harald whipped the crowd into joy, she'd been able to cast off the grief of losing her father at last and it had felt so good. Now, she put a hand to her fair hair as if the clover might still be clinging to its fine strands and sighed.

The boats were landing. The westerly three were first but already others were sailing in from across the sea and around the coves of the jagged coastline. Men were leaping out, pulling their craft up onto the shore and lifting their womenfolk to the dry sands, calling greetings to their neighbours and blessings on their jarls who had made it down to the beach and stood, feet planted wide in the sand, with Einar still just a step away.

Everyone was half-merry already, though the barrels had not yet been broached. It was a lonely existence farming out on these wild coasts and families could go weeks without seeing anyone beyond their own farmsteads, so they were all disposed to enjoy every last sociable minute of the feast. Tora was glad to see it but as the final boats pulled up she knew, with a sinking heart, that once again he – Harald – would not be arriving.

'Lady Tora, good evening.'

The man before her, bone-thin with age and his clouded eyes unusually bright as they drilled into hers, could not be a greater contrast to her previous suitor on this beach.

'Lord Pieter,' she said guardedly, crossing her hands involuntarily over her chest as he drew close – too close.

'Such a pleasure to see you.'

'And you,' she forced out, unpeeling her hands as she caught her uncle nodding her to take the proffered arm.

Lord Pieter owned extensive fertile lands on the isle of Giske and Finn had recently opened marriage negotiations with him. The thought of being shackled to this skeleton of a man tore at Tora's heart as, more sharply still, did the knowledge that such a match would cut her tenuous ties to Harald. But, then, Harald was not here.

She had not expected it, not really. He was in the land of the Rus, fled from King Cnut's oppression, and was as likely to sail a boat into this bay for midsummer as a real wolf, but a tiny part of her always looked for the miracle anyway on this strange night where the old magic – if there was any left – was most likely to cast its spell across Norway.

Reluctantly, Tora allowed Lord Pieter to escort her towards the tables where, all around, people were being ushered to their seats. Servers were bringing round jugs of ale and men and women alike were eagerly unclipping their cups from their belts. The first fish were on the great cooking platter and their smell caught the air and roused a cheer as the jarls looked benevolently on.

'Must just, er, relieve myself,' Pieter said, dropping her arm and scuttling into the shadows of the great cliffs at the back of the beach.

Tora hung gratefully back, relishing the space he left at her side, before suddenly becoming aware of her uncle standing close by.

'We are too good to them, Finn,' Kalv was saying to him.

She glanced over and saw the younger jarl watching grumpily as his precious barrels were broached.

''Tis once a year, Kalv,' Finn replied. 'If a few barrels of ale secure their allegiance until the next one it's a price well worth paying. And besides, 'tis a hell of a party. Have you seen the farm girls, brother? I swear they grow prettier every year.'

'Or you older, Finn.'

'And blinder!'

The brothers laughed but now Einar stepped forward.

'Blinder for sure, for you cannot see what is going on under your own nose in Nidaros.'

Instinctively Tora shrunk back but she did not move away.

'Easy, Einar,' Finn warned.

'Well, 'tis true. Cnut's damned regent is bleeding the country dry and not one of you will do a thing about it.'

'How can we, Einar? We have seen Cnut's might, seen it carved black across the field at Stikelstad. You were not there – too busy creeping to Cnut over the sea in bloody England – but I was and I will never forget it. Kalv was the only one of us wise enough to fight for Cnut and 'twas only his mercy that saved me from certain death that day. I will not be fighting against the Emperor of the North again.'

'Not Cnut,' Einar growled, 'just Steven, his concubine's bastard, set over us all in his stead. The king should have put one of *us* into the regency.'

'Meaning you, Einar?'

'I was his most senior general, yes, but Kalv led troops at Stikelstad so he would have been a good choice too. We understand Norway, we know her people far better than that English bastard who doesn't even know how to scratch his own scrawny backside. It's ruining us.'

'Must we discuss this now, Einar?' Finn protested, taking a few steps towards the feasting tables but Einar grabbed his arm, pulling him back.

'If not now, then when? Life can't be all feasting, Finn Arnasson.'

'I know that,' Finn snapped and Tora looked away, scared

that he might see her listening in. Pieter was returning, shifting his tunic into place as he came, and she took a wary step towards him but Einar's next words drew her inexorably back towards the men: 'We need the true heirs back from the Rus.'

'Harald Sigurdsson?' Kalv asked.

'Perhaps,' Einar's voice was smooth, too smooth, 'or perhaps young Prince Magnus. He is Olaf's son, after all – his first in line.'

'He is just a boy, Einar.'

'So ours to tutor.'

'To control, you mean,' Finn snapped. 'I say Harald is the better bet.'

'You would.'

'What does that mean?'

'You think he's yours just because of some whelp's ceremony too far back to remember.'

Tora's heart leaped – so Finn had not yet fully given up on Harald.

'You seem to remember it well enough, Einar, and 'twas no whelping. They were twelve – adults in the eyes of the law.'

'The law was not there.'

'Of course it was – every man and woman there witnessed the ceremony.'

'Ceremony?' Einar spat. 'Pagan ritual, no more.'

'We shall see,' Finn said softly, 'we shall see, Einar. Now come – we can talk more of this on the morrow. For now let us drink and forget our troubles for midsummer.'

They moved away, an uneasy grouping, leaving Tora to slide into a place at Pieter's side with a smile that surprised and delighted her ageing suitor, though it was not, in truth, for him. Clearly Finn had more than one set of negotiations going and she couldn't help wondering if at last the old midsummer magic was finding its strength. The past called to her again and she looked out to the blush-pink sea, trying to capture it more clearly.

'Dance, Harald!' they'd cried all those years ago and dance he had, flinging up his limbs before the moon-sun, howling and stamping in the rapidly formed circle. He'd twisted round girls and boys alike and by the time Tora's self-appointed maidens had drawn her forward, bedecked in so many flowers her very hair seemed imperial purple, the adults had been upon them, keen to find out what was taking place.

'What's this . . . ?' Kalv had started but this time Finn had put out a hand and stopped his protests.

''Tis just a game, brother. Let it be.'

And Kalv, for once, had listened and let the revelry continue. But it had been no game to Tora when Otto, his cloak draped around him like a bishop's robes, had clasped her hand into Harald's and wound seaweed, fresh from the water's edge, around their intertwined fingers and pronounced them joined; no game when they'd been carried, shoulder-high, around the smouldering fire; and no game when they'd been set upon a rock so small they had to cling to each other not to fall off and urged to 'Kiss, kiss, kiss.'

One touch, that's all she had, one lingering touch of his lips, one whisper of a tongue, tentative but so sweet she had met it with her own, before her uncles had pulled them apart.

'Happy midsummer,' Finn had said kindly before quietly taking her to sit with him out of harm's way.

She'd been furious back then, Tora remembered, but Finn seemed to be glad of her 'games' now, whatever he had said to Lord Pieter. She dragged her eyes from the sea to watch him sit down at the head of the table, Einar tight at his side, and wondered if next year, or maybe the year after that, Harald's boat would finally sail into her bay. So long she had waited for him and with good reason – though not one Finn could know.

'Happy midsummer,' she whispered, turning from the fawning Pieter back to the shimmering sea to send the greeting up into the night air and south – a long, long way south to wherever Harald was, in the hope her words would somehow, some way, pull him home.

CHAPTER SEVEN

Kiev, Christ's Mass 1035

'I hear Norway calling me, Elizaveta.'

Elizaveta looked at Harald. They were sat side by side at Yaroslav's Yule feast, for tonight the Grand Prince would announced their betrothal. Last spring he had told Harald he must earn Elizaveta's hand by distinguishing himself in the service of the Byzantine Empress Zoe who was seeking his aid. Harald had risen to the challenge, becoming commander of two hundred men within weeks and securing three Saracen dhows of treasure in his first campaign against the infidel pirates in the Greek seas. Yaroslav's vaults were full and the Grand Prince was finally satisfied. He had told them earlier this evening that their marriage was assured and since then her Varangian suitor had been all jokes and flirtation. This sudden solemnity threw her.

'Southern seawater is not enough for your veins, Harold?'

He smiled.

'The seawater suits me fine, Elizaveta, but the gold of Miklegard pales after a time. It is a beautiful place, truly, but almost too rich for a simple northern Viking. It's a little like eating a banquet at every meal – dizzyingly wonderful at first but then suddenly you yearn for a simple stew around the fire or a hunk of coarse bread and cheese in the fields.'

'Coarse bread, Harald? Surely not. I don't believe anywhere can be *too* beautiful.'

'Maybe not for you, my sweet, for you are more refined than I. I hope Norway will not be too wild for you.'

Again the sombre shadow crossed his handsome face and Elizaveta put her hand over his.

'I long to see Norway, Harald. I always have. Why these dark thoughts? 'Tis Christ's mass – a time of celebration.'

She gestured around the vast hall, ringing with chatter and laughter. As it was a celebration, Ingrid had allowed all ten of her children to stay up for the feast, and the top table was crammed with chattering royals. Even four-year-old Yuri was there, though Hedda was keeping a careful watch from the sidelines, her little daughter Greta playing quietly at her side.

The family were flanked by the lost princes, Agatha sat happily up against Edward at one end and Anastasia, to Elizaveta's great amusement, by Andrew's side at the other, even though it had pushed her out to the edge, not somewhere she liked to be. Anne had taken her place beside Vladimir and, now ten years old, sat rigid and proud. She had, though she realised it not, grown very pretty, and Elizaveta knew it must have cost Anastasia much to cede her place to her. She grinned and turned back to Harald.

'All is well, truly.'

He shook himself then, his blonde hair catching in the light of the huge fires set all the way up the bright hall to stave off the winter ice.

'You are right, my princess. I've just been remembering the Yule five years back that I spent behind a hide curtain in the rear of a peasant's farmhouse. They sheltered me there for four months at great danger to themselves and do you know why?'

'Because Ulf and Halldor built them a byre?'

'No – though that helped – it was because they believed I should be king. *I*, Elizaveta. They thought their own lives and those of their dear children were worth less than my own kingship and I have to honour that.'

Elizaveta looked into his eyes and saw amber fire burning in the grey.

'You look to the horizon?' she suggested gently and he nodded. 'You will sail to Norway soon then – this year?'

'Not this year.' He turned his eyes to the rafters, wreathed in smoke. 'I need more gold.'

'Are you sure?' Elizaveta fingered the chain across her chest. 'We have seen your caskets, Hari, and it seems to me that you have treasure enough to buy an army that could take on the whole world.'

Harald reached out and placed his fingers over her own, tracing the shape of the little keys.

'It is not just money, Elizaveta, but reputation. If I am to lead an army into the frozen north of Norway against the great King Cnut I will need men who follow me not just for pay but because they believe in my leadership, as that peasant family believed in it. The emperor wants me to lead men into Italy and it could be a good chance to rally fighters to my cause. The Lombards in the area are challenging his rule and they have invited Normans in to bolster their cause.'

'Normans?'

'Indeed, and they could be the ones I need. They are a race that love fighting more than most and have many young swords for hire. Their duke has just died leaving a bastard boy, William, as his heir but he is only seven and the nobles are scrapping for control. Italy is a good place to send them to work off their ire and a strong sword arm is always welcome there to challenge the imperial overlord. The Normans are fierce, so I'm told, but it is no surprise, for they are Vikings at heart – and who better to defeat Vikings than a Viking?'

'Is that not cannibalism?'

He laughed.

'That is war, Princess.'

'And it makes you a hero?'

'Maybe. Is that wrong?'

'Poetry is real tales with stronger detail,' she suggested. 'Is that not what you told me?'

He nodded.

'I draw my inspiration from the Vikings of old.'

'Pagans?'

'Just so. I fear sometimes, Elizaveta, that I have a pagan's heart.'

'And is that so bad, as long as you have a Christian soul to match?'

Harald stared at her, then suddenly seized her hand and lifted it to his lips, catching the neck chain and sending it jangling wildly.

'Ah, Elizaveta – we are cut from the same cloth, you and I, and I adore you for it. You shall be my necklace goddess.' He pulled her closer and the chain caught against her arm, making her wince as one of the keys pinched her skin. 'It hurts you?'

'No, of course not. It is, I admit, a little heavy now so I wear it only on special occasions like this one.'

Alarm flitted across his face.

'Where do you keep it the rest of the time?'

'In my father's treasury in a casket all of its own that I had made specially.'

'And the key for that casket?'

Elizaveta touched her fingers to her chest.

'I keep it on another chain around my neck.'

He looked down, his eyes burning into her.

'I see it not.'

She licked her lips.

"Tis against my skin, safe.'

She saw his chest rise and fall and for a moment he struggled to speak then he said, 'I should like to see it.'

'And you will, my lord, when we are wed.'

Harald groaned and his desire tugged deliciously on her deeper reaches, making her glance awkwardly around in case her siblings had seen her wanton response.

'No one is looking,' he whispered.

'But they are here.'

'You would rather we were alone?' Elizaveta flushed and could not bring herself to answer; he knew anyway. 'I would rather it too, my sweet. Perhaps later, when the *druzhina* is busy dancing . . .'

'Harald!'

'Oh, I would not dishonour you, Elizaveta, truly. Well . . .' He screwed up his nose looking suddenly so sweet that she almost leaned over and kissed him right there, at her father's table. 'In truth, I would love to dishonour you – though I would not see it as such – but I know my place and we will marry soon.'

'When, Harald?'

He linked his fingers through hers one by one.

'I need another year,' he said. 'Another year in the emperor's service, two at the most, and I will be ready. I am sure of it. I will come back to Kiev with the best mercenaries treasure can buy and I will marry you, Lily. I will make you my own and then I will make you my queen. Can you wait another year?'

Elizaveta nodded, though in truth, were her father to suggest it, she would wed him now, tonight and bed him besides. She closed her eyes against the delicious, wicked thought. Perhaps she had a pagan heart too?

'I hear things are unsettled in Norway,' she managed eventually.

'You do? From whom?'

'There are traders at court – many traders. Edward and I talk to them for we are both eager for news of the north, though sadly Cnut seems very secure in England where he spends most of his time. He is safe, too, in his homeland of Denmark where his son Harthacnut is widely accepted as regent, but Norway is not so stable. They say the northern jarls are kicking against the rule of Cnut's bastard regent, Steven. They say there is talk of rebellion. A man called Einar?'

'Einar Tambarskelve? Lord, yes! If ever there were to be trouble he would be at the heart of it. The Arnassons too?'

'Your betrothed's family?'

Harald tapped a finger on her nose.

'*You* are my betrothed, Elizaveta, and your father is about to announce it to all.'

She grimaced.

'My father speaks loudly,' she allowed, 'but I do not believe that even he can reach across the Varangian Sea to Norway.'

'Of course he can – the traders will take the news.'

He was right and Elizaveta felt comforted at the thought. Besides, by the time they sailed for Norway they would be married, joined in church before witnesses, and no childhood alliance could override God's law.

'Then,' she said stoutly, 'we must see that they also take news of your great fame. Where is your storyteller, Harald, to sing your praises to the hall?'

'Halldor?' They both cast around the hall but it was Harald who spotted his old friend first. 'He is there, in the corner, looking as if he might try and climb into his ale cup.'

Elizaveta's gaze followed Harald's direction and saw his dear friend huddled over his tankard.

'Poor Halldor.'

Elizaveta's heart ached for the funny warrior, for he had ridden into Kiev behind his leader two weeks back with his young boy tight against his chest and sorrowful news. Elsa had died in her childbed last year, in a rough army camp on the shores of the Greek sea where she had accompanied Halldor as part of Harald's supply train. The boy had been safely born but Elsa had caught a fever from which she had never recovered.

For three days and nights, Harald had told Elizaveta, Halldor had sat at her side as she fought the infection but on the third night, in the very darkest hour, it had overcome her. Harald said Halldor had wailed so loud that the whole camp had heard him and they had risen and gathered outside his pavilion and when he had carried her dead body outside they had sung the Lord's Prayer to the skies.

Halldor had carried Elsa to the shore and laid her in a boat and rowed her out beyond the breakers and still they had all sung. When he'd tipped her into the ocean's dark embrace they had feared he would throw himself in after her. Instead, though, he had sat alone in that boat until the sun had risen, violent pink, behind him. Then he had turned and rowed back and, taking up the boy, had strapped him to his broad chest and vowed before God and all Harald's men to be both mother and father to him from that point.

'And so he has been,' Harald had assured Elizaveta. 'The boy, Aksel, had a wet-nurse at first, another slave girl who had lost her own baby, and we all hoped that maybe Halldor would take her into his heart, as he had with Elsa. But Halldor said there was no space inside him for love of any but Elsa's memory and the boy and once Aksel was weaned he dismissed her. He has cared for Aksel ever since.'

Elizaveta strained to pick Halldor out of the smoky air and

saw one-year-old Aksel asleep, curled up on the bench against his father's broad back.

'Is Aksel always with him?' she asked Harald.

'Always, save in battle – then he leaves him with the camp followers.'

'Concubines?'

Harald flushed.

'Cooks and, er, water-fetchers and whatnot.'

Elizaveta felt a flash of strange, uncomfortable fury but she shook it away; this was about Halldor.

''Tis no life for a child,' she said. 'Perhaps I could help release your poor storyteller a little.'

'How?'

'Wait and see.'

She rose and, squeezing out from behind the high table, crossed the hall to Halldor, giving the central fires a wide berth, for they spat sparks from the snow-damp wood. It was another bitter winter and everyone was wrapped up in as many layers as they could afford. Most wore a tunic between their usual under- and overgowns to keep out the worst of the chill. This year Elizaveta had the finest of them all as Harald had brought her a bolt of Byzantine silk, a more precious gift even than the amber charm that had come with it.

The simple tunic her seamstresses had sewn from it, exclaiming at the supple fabric with every tiny stitch, was like a miracle. So thin it barely padded her now-womanly shape at all and yet warmer than the richest combed wool, it was like a fairy skin. The other women of the *druzhina*, Anastasia in particular, were fiercely envious and Elizaveta had taken to storing the precious garment in the treasury with her neck chain. Now she tugged its silken sleeves down to show beneath her woollen overgown as she moved up the hall to Halldor.

'Cost him a month's wages, I heard,' Elizaveta caught a

woman telling her neighbour as she moved down the packed hall.

'Ah, but I heard that his wages are only the half of it. He has more treasure than the Arabian Caliph himself.'

'And more balls besides,' the others returned, 'lucky girl,' and with that they melted into giggles.

Elizaveta forced herself to keep her head up but inside questions were flying around it. 'I should like to see that key,' Harald had told her and suddenly she was picturing him unfastening her gown and easing it off her shoulders and parting her silken tunic. Her whole body tingled with spiky longing and it was all she could do to keep walking.

Halldor looked up at her, confused, as she approached. He started to rise but the little boy shifted in his sleep and he hesitated.

'Please,' Elizaveta said quickly, 'stay seated.'

He sank gratefully back down and Elizaveta slipped into a space at his side, hastily vacated by a lowly count.

'Why are you down here, Princess?' Halldor asked, gesturing towards the high table.

'To see you, Halldor. I am so truly sorry that you lost Elsa.'

He turned his soft hazel eyes on her.

'Not as sorry as I.'

'I know that and my heart aches for you. She meant much to you.'

'More than a slave girl should?'

'Nonsense. Who has said that?'

'Camp gossip, I'm sure. They think I am weak. They think I am mad not to have taken another into my bed; nearly as mad as I am to keep the boy with me.'

'Aksel is lucky to have you.'

Halldor grunted. 'I don't know about that. I am a rough and ready sort of a father.'

'You have no choice.'

He laughed bitterly.

'Of course I do. If I was a truly decent man I would give up running around the Greek sea like a wild thing, take my share of Harald's booty, and buy a farm back in Iceland. That's what a child needs – a secure home, land of his father's to run about on, and milk from his father's beasts on which to grow strong, not a ship that turns on the tide and the remnants of a whore's cooking pot.'

'I agree.'

Halldor looked startled.

'You think I am a poor father?'

'No! No, not that, Halldor, definitely not that.' Elizaveta looked at the boy sleeping trustingly in the crook of his father's big arm. 'But I think you are right that he needs a home.'

'I should buy a farm? I knew it really, I . . .'

'No farm, Halldor – not yet. Harald needs you and you would be wasted behind a plough. Leave the boy with me.'

'With you, Princess?'

'Yes. Well, with Hedda in the royal nursery. Aksel will be safe with her and well cared for until such time as we sail for Norway.'

'*We*?' he teased, his voice lightening slightly. 'Harald is a lucky man, Princess.'

'I only hope he can love me half as much as you loved Elsa, Halldor. Will you let me take care of her boy?'

Halldor smiled at last.

'If you do, you will be a treasure-keeper indeed, for he is dearer to me than any gold.'

'I will care for him as I will my own sons.'

'May God bless you with many. I accept – if you are certain, Princess?'

'Elizaveta, please, and yes, I am certain, on one condition

– that you tell us of Miklegard and of your adventures on the Greek seas. Harald has spoken of it but he is a poor poet besides you.'

'You want a tale?' Halldor tried to keep reluctance in his voice but Elizaveta could hear his ready imagination bubbling up through it.

'Please, Halldor – consider it my Yule gift and Harald's too for there are men here from Norway and we must send them home with news of the great man who will one day be their king.'

Halldor smiled wider.

'I see that in you, Elizaveta, Harald has won himself brains as well as beauty.'

'Please, Hal,' Elizaveta protested, embarrassed, 'save your honeyed words for the tale.'

She grabbed his hand to tug him up and, pausing only to unfasten his bear-fur cloak to wrap around his sleeping child, he allowed her to lead him up to Yaroslav.

'I bring a tale, Father,' she said, 'an adventure tale for the Yule court.'

All heads were turning their way now and Yaroslav, spotting his moment, stood.

'Our Varangians are returned from the Byzantine Empire,' Yaroslav pronounced as a hush fell over the great hall. 'They have brought gold – enough gold to win back their leader's crown in Norway, home of our forefathers. Enough, indeed, to also win their leader a wife – though I wish him luck with her, for she is an unruly one indeed.'

Yaroslav nodded Elizaveta furiously back to her place and she retreated as Harald rose to take her hand, to the applause of the gathered *druzhina*.

'My lords and ladies,' Yaroslav proclaimed, his voice ringing sonorously out of his slim chest and around his great hall, 'I give you my daughter Elizaveta and her betrothed husband-to-be, Harald of Norway.'

The crowd, already merry on Yule ale, roared their approval and Elizaveta felt it like the warm rush of sauna-steam across her skin. Hotter yet, though, was the touch of the man at her side.

'Now that it is official,' Harald whispered over the clapping, 'may I kiss you?'

'Later,' Elizaveta told him and saw his eyes darken wickedly. 'Later?'

'Yes, if you are lucky – but for now you must hush for we have a story.'

'Unruly indeed,' Harald muttered, though he did not sound cross and as Elizaveta sat down, she was very aware of her hand still clasped in his.

She watched, as calmly as she was able, as Halldor stepped up onto the dais and lifted his arms wide, casting his sorrow from him – for this moment at least – as he had cast off his cloak to make a bed for his motherless child. The *druzhina* took some time to settle but he waited patiently until all eyes were turned his way.

''Twas the middle of the Greek sea,' Halldor began, his voice lilting across the expectant crowd, 'a sea as blue as Our Lady's gown and as clear as any maiden's conscience.' Someone tittered and Halldor raised a hand in acknowledgment. 'The sun lay ahead, heaving in the hot skies, the seabirds rested on our mast and even the flies buzzed only about the smelliest sailors.' More titters but then Halldor broke across them: 'Then suddenly, over the edge of the world, like a spear piercing the heart of the hazy peace, rose a ship – a ship flying the black sail of piracy like the wings of a raven over a battlefield.'

The crowd gasped obligingly and Elizaveta saw Halldor's head lift a little further as if their appreciation was blowing life back into him. Her own heart soared at his words for she had managed to save a large rectangle of the silk from her tunic and, with a little help from ladies more skilled and more patient than herself, was stitching a huge raven into the centre. It would be Harald's new banner – his battlefield ravager under which he could recover Norway – and it was all she could do to contain herself from telling him about it. She smiled delightedly and forced herself to focus on the tale.

'Were we afeared?' Halldor was asking, his voice rising.

'No,' came a call from the back.

Halldor smiled.

'Oh, but we were. Pirates have hearts as black as their sails. They fight to no rules and they acknowledge no laws, neither of God nor of man. We were afeared and we will be afeared again but our leader, our Prince, would not let that stop us for we were there on those aquamarine waters to keep them safe for the emperor's own boats to sail and he knew his duty.'

Halldor paused, letting his eyes drift to Harald who inclined his head graciously and, beneath the table, squeezed Elizaveta's hand.

'We were to arms immediately,' Halldor said, drawing the crowd back into his spell. 'We clipped the sail tight and rode the side winds towards the foe, turning hard on the steer-board to come round flank-on to her evil crew. We could hear them laughing – twisted mirth from their twisted pirate mouths – for they'd seen our boat, gifted us by the emperor, and they thought they had the measure of us.'

Halldor paused again, pacing the dais, leaning forward as if sharing the secrets of the beginning of time.

'They are small, the boats in which they ask us Varangians to ride the waves. They are long, yes, but narrow – so narrow that only those sailors as skilled as Prince Harald can handle them without tipping into a watery grave and yet so narrow too that, handled right, they can outpace any other craft – nay, outpace dolphins, God's own water horses, at full leap. And they have magic in their bows . . .' Halldor looked around the hall, his eyes gleaming, 'they have Greek fire.'

More gasps. Everyone had heard tell of the hellish weapon but no one in Kiev had seen it for themselves – until now.

'We sailed close, my friends, so close that we could smell their rotten breath and see the whites of their scarred eyes and the black tar-stumps of their hacked limbs as they leaned forward, grapple-hooks in what hands they had left to them, ready to mount our boat and kill us. Fools.'

His voice dropped.

'Greek fire lives in a barrel, specially soaked and girded thrice round with iron. Whilst it is sealed it lies as quiet as olive oil but unleashed . . . ah, it can set the clouds themselves aflame above your heads! Prince Harald swung himself up into the mast.

'"Say your prayers, pirates," he called, "for we have God's own fury in our hold!"

'"There is no God," the pirate leader called back, his voice a rasp through lips as dry as snakeskin, "save perhaps myself."

'Then he threw back his dark, salt-encrusted locks and gave a screech of a laugh and his men bobbed and roared and waved their cutlasses as we crept closer still and then, as they lifted booted feet onto the gunwales ready to make the leap to our boat, the Prince cried, "Unleash the fury," and, with the roar of a dragon, the flame shot from the bowels of our boat and fried them before our very eyes.'

Halldor paced the front of the dais, all eyes following him. Elizaveta noticed Anne with her hands to her delicate mouth, and Agatha leaning so far forward she was almost atop the table. Even her brothers, the older ones almost men now, looked nursery-young again, caught in the tale.

'I will never,' Halldor cried, 'forget the sight of pirate eyeballs sizzling at the edges and then popping from their unworthy sockets to burst on the tips of the spewing flames. I will never . . .'

'Thank you, thank you, thank you!' Grand Prince Yaroslav leaped to his feet and clasped Halldor's hand, pumping it up and down. Several of the ladies of Kiev – not used to Viking tales – were pressing linen squares to their brows or hiding their faces in their husband's cloaks. 'Thank you indeed, Halldor Snorrason. Here – an arm ring for your eloquence.'

'But . . .' Halldor started and then, with a glance at a giggling Elizaveta, subsided. 'You are too kind, gracious prince.'

'And you too vivid, my lord. You must be thirsty.'

Halldor bowed low and allowed himself to be drawn round to Yaroslav's side for a drink. Elizaveta turned to Harald.

''Twas a good tale,' she said, 'though for myself I would have liked to hear the end. Is it true?'

'As true as it ever is.'

'But the Greek fire . . . ?'

'Oh that is true. 'Tis a fearsome substance.'

'And you hanging from the mast?'

'Less true,' Harald allowed with a grin. 'It would upset the balance of the ship dreadfully, though it does wonders for the balance of the tale. But now that Halldor has made a hero of me, may I claim my kiss?'

Elizaveta looked around. The *druzhina*, enlivened by Halldor's story, were rising, stepping away from the tables, recharging their coloured Yuletide glasses and moving towards the minstrels, Anastasia and Andrew at their head. Hedda, ignoring their loud protests, had whisked the younger ones away with her own Greta. Yaroslav was talking earnestly to an energised Halldor, Anne and Vladimir with him, and the rest of her siblings were gratefully escaping the confines of the table.

Even Ingrid had disappeared, as she so often did, poor woman, to the latrines. No one would miss them.

'You may,' she agreed, her face all Greek fire of its own as Harald led her to the small door behind the dais that Yaroslav used to make a grand entrance but which also served well as an unseen exit.

'Where are we going?' she asked.

'To look at Norway.'

'She is calling you still?'

'A little – come.'

Harald led her behind the hall and up the staircase in the west tower to the top of the city walls. A guard strode towards them as they topped the wooden walkway but, recognising their faces, he bowed low and scurried into the corner tower, leaving them alone with the night.

Harald drew his cloak – a huge wolf-pelt lined with marten and padded with wool – around them both, pulling her close against him, and led her along above the city walls towards the northerly side. To her left Elizaveta could look down into the neat fenced plots of the artisans and merchants rich enough to afford land within the kremlin and to her right the snowy pine forests dropped away to the iron ribbon of the frozen Dnieper below. Her breath cut the air like the dawn mist and her face tingled with it, though not as much as her body against her bethrothed's. Suddenly Harald stopped.

'See there,' he said, 'the North Star.'

He pointed to the brightest of the thousands of stars, shining as fiercely tonight as if announcing the Christ child all over again.

'I see it,' Elizaveta agreed, looking up at him.

'Beneath it lies Norway, Elizaveta – Norway and our thrones.'

'Our . . . ?' she breathed.

'Our,' he confirmed softly, turning her in towards him so

their bodies were pressed together. 'You hold the key, my Princess.'

His hand ran up from her waist and brushed lightly across the chain at her breasts. She gasped and suddenly his lips were upon hers and he was pulling her up against him so that her feet almost left the ground and she had to clasp her hands around his neck to hold on or, perhaps, to draw him closer yet, her breathing quickening as his hands tightened.

'Elizaveta.' Her name bruised against her own lips as it was forced from him. 'Oh Elizaveta, it will be a long year. You will wait, my love?'

'Of course,' she agreed huskily. 'Of course I will wait. Now hush and kiss me more.'

CHAPTER EIGHT

Kiev, February 1036

Winter lay over Kiev like a kitchen dog over a rat. It had clamped the city between its icy jaws and the city was helpless beneath it. The royal log store was getting lower and the trunks of the great pines beyond the walls were so gripped by the endless frosts that even the hardiest axeman could not break them. Every day servants cleared the snow from the paths across the courtyard and every night more fell. The fountain at the centre had frozen unexpectedly one harsh night before Yule and sat in a perpetual cascade, never moving but never ceasing to move. Even Yaroslav's bronze horses seemed to paw at the throat-ripping air more in desperation than triumph.

The kremlin was still and empty. The lords and ladies of the Yule court had retreated to hunker down on their farms and see their servants kept their stock alive until the blessed thaws released the shoots from the ground. The artisans were holed up around their braziers, trying to keep their fingers warm enough to work goods for the great spring trading run, and the merchants and soldiers were out on their sleds and their skates and their skis, traversing the frozen rivers that formed the winter pathways across Yaroslav's lands. Over the hardest months of the year they would go between the outlying tribes and villages, collecting tribute and buying goods to bring back to the eager denizens of the ever-expanding city, and it was very quiet without their bustling presence.

The royal family were left with their sparse personal *druzhina* of less than a hundred guards, servants and officials and life was unbearably calm. They rarely ate in the great hall now, preferring Ingrid's cosier receiving rooms and leaving the servants to enjoy the warmth of the big kitchens for their own meals. Ingrid, after five health-restoring years without bearing a child, was weighed down with the last stages of an unexpected pregnancy and liked it quiet. Yaroslav, too, was content to see out this iron month in relative privacy, but Elizaveta was bored. Harald had ridden back to the emperor's service, and was even now fighting Norman predators in Southern Italy, leaving her with little to do save twitch at the loom or at tedious needlework and she longed for spring to bring the men back to the hall.

Even the lost princes had gone. Andrew had announced his intention of joining the Grand Prince's troops in the punishing winter tribute gathering and Edward had hastily – if not altogether eagerly – followed. Elizaveta had pitied his painful need to prove he was as brave as the Hungarian and missed his earnest company. As for little Agatha, she had seemed lost for weeks until Anastasia, now fourteen and pining dramatically for the glamorous Andrew, had begged Elizaveta for music.

Playing the viol was tough in winter. If she played too far from the fire, her fingers would not work the strings as they should, and if she moved too close, the wood of the precious instrument warped and wrecked the sound. Having Anastasia at her mercy, however, had been too hard to resist and so she had lifted it carefully from its case and let her lightest notes loose.

Her reward had been the sudden spark of fun in little

Agatha's trusting eyes; the sight of fierce little Anne putting down her pen, her feet twitching beneath her desk; and the thanks – genuine thanks – from proud Anastasia. Even Hedda's little daughter, Greta, usually kept quietly in the shadows, had joined in.

The sisters had danced loudly and laughed louder and before long their brothers had run across the courtyard to join in. For a brief time they had been merry but it had not been long before the quarrels had broken out. They all needed new company and it was with delight, therefore, that Elizaveta greeted the messenger slipping and sliding across the courtyard to their rooms one dark afternoon. Such haste could only mean one thing – visitors.

'What is it, Alexei?' she asked the young guard as he slipped around the door, trying to keep the winter winds outside. 'Who is come?'

'Nobles, Princess. Nobles in fine furs riding down the Dnieper on horses bigger than any I have ever seen.'

'Down the Dnieper? From the north?'

'Yes, Princess. From *far* north. They carry a flag nigh on as big as a sail in reds and whites. Captain Gustaf says it is the colour of the Norwegians.'

Elizaveta's eyes widened.

'He does? You must come in then and quickly.'

'I was trying to, Princess.'

Elizaveta glanced guiltily over her shoulder to where the rest of her family were pressing forward and stepped hastily out of the doorway to let Alexei through. He bowed low before Yaroslav but the Grand Prince had clearly heard Elizaveta's exchange and was already waving servants to bring his overcoat. Hunching himself into the wide sleeves, he made for the door, brushing aside the poor lad trying to fasten the ties in his haste to reach the gates. Elizaveta moved to follow but Ingrid yanked her back.

'The visitors will come, Elizaveta, when your father is content for them to do so and we must be ready to receive them.' Ingrid turned to the servants hovering excitedly. 'Stoke up the fires, please, and fetch logs and pour more wine into the mulling cauldron. Run and tell the cooks we will need more food and find herbs for the rushes. We stink like peasants.' She looked around at her children – all ten in workday gowns and tunics, chosen for warmth, not show – and sighed. 'There will be no time to change for they will not linger at the gate in this cold, but straighten yourselves at least.'

Ingrid set about brushing down little Yuri with her fingers. Anastasia produced a fine ivory comb from her pocket and pulled it through her already immaculate blonde locks before reluctantly helping Anne to do the same. Agatha shrunk away, for her dark brown curls were beyond any comb yet invented, and Vladimir, Ivan, Stefan and Viktor were content to cover their unruly mops beneath the furred hats they normally only wore outside. Only Magnus amongst the boys, sitting over a book at one end of the table, produced a comb of his own which he had soon drawn through his thin blonde hair. Elizaveta half-heartedly pulled on her own ruffled locks and edged over to Vladimir.

'Who can it be at this time of year?' she whispered. 'They must be mad to travel so far.'

'Or brave,' Vladimir said, looking eagerly to the door. 'Maybe they are Varangians, Lily? Maybe they have come from Novgorod and maybe I can go back with them?' Yaroslav had finally promised his eldest son he would install him as Count of Novgorod once the thaws came and he was every bit as fed up of the winter as Elizaveta. 'Maybe there has been a battle in Norway and they are fled, as Harald fled?'

Elizaveta bristled instantly.

'Harald did not flee,' she said, 'he retreated.'

Vladimir raised an eyebrow.

'Hell of a retreat, Lily.'

'But one worth making,' she shot back. 'His reputation grows with his treasure.'

'As you well know, *necklace goddess*.'

Elizaveta flushed.

'Why do you call me that?'

Vladimir grinned wickedly.

'I heard Harald do so – and other things besides. He is very sweet on you, Lily.'

'As he should be if we are to be married and you, Vladimir, should not listen in to private conversations.'

'Then you, Elizaveta, should canoodle somewhere further afield.'

'Canoodle?! We do not . . .'

But her protests were silenced by the clatter of iron-soled boots across the courtyard and the ten princes and princesses of Kiev spun to face the door. It was opened wide, wider than any had attempted since the cruel frosts had slathered the step, and Yaroslav entered on a frozen blast, two dark figures behind him. For a moment Elizaveta feared her father had brought beasts from the forest to their hall, so grizzled were his visitors, but as they moved forward she saw they were men, though fearsome ones.

Ingrid, one hand cradling her swollen belly, stepped up and reluctantly offered the other to the first icy creature.

'Jarl Kalv Arnasson,' he introduced himself in husky Norse. 'An honour to meet you, Grand Princess.'

Arnasson! The name rippled through Elizaveta, colder than the winds the servants were now fighting to bolt the door against. She looked Kalv up and down as Ingrid raised him, withdrawing her fingers from his cold-bruised ones as soon as she dared. He was not especially tall and, as he threw back his huge cloak in a shimmer of melting snow, she saw he was slimmer than many of his kind, though sinewy with taut muscle. His face, too, was thin and his narrow eyes darted about the room as if totting up its worth. Elizaveta shivered again and looked to the other man, now kneeling in his turn, but found little comfort there.

'Jarl Einar Tambarskelve at your service, Sire.'

The words came from his lips but not, Elizaveta was sure, from his heart, if he even had one. He did not look like a man who would willingly serve any lord. Though his head was bowed, his hooded eyes were looking up, and though he was on his knees, his shoulders were rigid and his hand tight upon his rich scabbard. Elizaveta glanced to the door and was grateful to see the guards had the visitors' swords – long, heavy weapons with jewelled hilts. This man, this Einar, twitching even as he kissed Ingrid's hand, looked unpredictable, dangerous. What had Harald said of him? *If ever there were to be trouble Einar would be at the heart of it.* Well, it seemed there might be trouble now and with Harald not here to meet it.

As if reading her mind Einar looked around the room, counting them all off as Kalv had done.

'You are an intimate group, Grand Prince,' he said slyly.

'We are,' Yaroslav agreed. 'Few venture to Kiev at this time of God's year. Your mission must be urgent to bring you so far south?'

Einar did not take the bait. Instead, he fixed on the slender figure of Magnus, standing behind Vladimir and Ivan, and suddenly, in a move that sent the two princes skittering aside, he flung himself to his huge knees before the boy. Magnus looked stunned, Yaroslav no less so, especially at the big jarl's next words: 'May God bless you, King Magnus.'

'K . . . k . . . king?' Magnus stuttered.

'King?' Yaroslav echoed.

Elizaveta looked to Vladimir who shrugged as Kalv, after a strange sidelong glance at his compatriot, also fell to his knees before their exiled cousin.

'Cnut is dead,' Einar intoned, clearly relishing the effect, which was considerable.

'Cnut, Emperor of the North, dead? How?' Yaroslav demanded.

Kalv glanced at him.

'A fever, Sire, or so we are told. It was last November.'

'*November?*'

Elizaveta watched Yaroslav grasping for words and knew how he felt. It seemed impossible that the great Cnut, whose vast Norse kingdom had straddled the cold northern seas for so long, could have died four months ago without them knowing. She and Harald had spoken of him at Christ's mass and already, it seemed, he had been dead in his grave.

'He was in England at the time,' Einar said hastily, 'and the seas have been rough. We came as soon as we heard; came to fetch the rightful heir to Norway home to his people.'

'Me?' Magnus asked, swelling visibly. 'You have come for me?'

Again Kalv glanced at Einar but the other man did not even flinch.

'Yes, Sire.'

Yaroslav put up a hand.

'On whose authority? Was not Cnut's son, Steven, ruling Norway? Why has the throne not been left to him?'

Einar looked shifty.

'It was, Grand Prince, but Steven did not understand the ways of the Norwegians. The people made their displeasure known and, wisely, he fled.' Yaroslav moved to protest but Einar rushed on: 'Harthacnut is proclaimed king in Denmark and Harold of the Harefoot in England. Cnut has sons enough on the thrones of his kingdom; there is room for Olaf's ancient line in Norway.'

'Do all the jarls support this move?'

'They do. We bear writs to prove it and with your noble permission we will escort King Magnus to his stepmother, Queen Astrid, in Sweden and from there into Norway to be crowned.'

Yaroslav still looked uncertain, but twelve-year-old Magnus puffed out his scrawny chest and flung back his slender shoulders. He looked imperiously around his foster family.

'It seems God does help those who devote themselves to his service,' he said, touching his fingertips piously together.

It was too much for Elizaveta.

'No!' The word burst from her mouth before she could stop it and, as the two Norwegians turned their calculating eyes upon her, she felt Vladimir tug on her gown.

'Lily, hush.'

But she could not.

'Harald is the rightful king.'

Kalv flinched but Einar was already up and advancing on her and the other jarl was quick to follow.

Elizaveta felt them loom above her, dark and menacing, but stood her ground. Let them try and threaten her – she was a princess and this was her hall. She would be heard.

'Prince Harald is King Olaf's brother,' Elizaveta asserted boldly.

'Half-brother.'

'Yes and legitimately born of the ancient line of Yngling, unlike Magnus, the son of a concubine.'

'Elizaveta,' Yaroslav warned but Einar just gave a curled smile.

'A son is a son, Princess. But you know much of our country?'
Yaroslav coughed.

'My daughter is betrothed to Prince Harald.'

'She's what?' Kalv demanded, clearly startled, but Einar
seized his arm.

'My comrade here begs your pardon, Princess. He is just
surprised, that is all, as we in Norway know the Prince to be
betrothed to another – Jarl Kalv's niece, Lady Tora, a Norwegian
noblewoman of some standing.'

Anger ripped through Elizaveta's chest like a pain. Harald
had lied to her. Or, she reminded herself hastily, this prowl-
ing man before her was lying now. She must not be too quick
to judge and she definitely must not give them the satisfaction
of hurting her.

'Oh, I know of her,' she said, letting her own lip curl a little.
'A childhood game, no more.'

Kalv's eye twitched and, with relief, Elizaveta knew she had
hit her mark. Einar leaned forward. His cloak dripped snow
onto her soft indoor boots but she refused to step back.

'And where, pray, Princess, is your betrothed?'

Elizaveta swallowed and looked to her father.

'Harald has ridden south,' Yaroslav supplied. 'He serves the
Byzantine emperor and has won much praise in his army.'

'And much gold too, I hear,' Einar agreed easily. 'He always
was a ruthless fighter.' He rolled the word 'ruthless' round his
tongue as if relishing it.

'Effective,' Elizaveta substituted defiantly.

'If you wish, Princess,' Einar said, 'though sadly not effective
enough to claim Norway now.'

'No,' Elizaveta protested again, 'you are wrong. That is
exactly what he fights for. He is a bold and committed warrior
and he will make you a valiant king if you can only wait a little.'

Einar looked at Kalv.

'Sweet,' he said. Elizaveta's eyes narrowed and Vladimir tugged harder on her gown. 'But the trouble you see, Princess, is that we need a king *now*. Norway's throne is empty and an empty throne is a dangerous thing. If Harald were here . . .'

Einar spread his hands wide as if they were discussing a pleasure ride or a trip to market.

'Harald *will* be here,' Elizaveta said desperately. 'I will send for him.'

Again Kalv seemed to hesitate and she took a step towards him but Einar cut in front.

'All the way to Miklegard? In these snows? 'Tis a long trip, Princess, and a longer one back. Harthacnut of Denmark could have seized Norway by then and we cannot allow that. Besides, I am sure Prince Harald will be delighted to see his own dear nephew on the throne.'

'He will,' Magnus agreed eagerly in his silly, reedy voice.

It grated across Elizaveta's fury like a whetstone across a blade and she could contain herself no longer.

'You,' she said, stabbing Jarl Einar in his broad chest, 'want Magnus for your king because he is small and young and ineffectual. You want him to play kings for yourself. You want . . .'

'Elizaveta – enough!' Yaroslav's voice thundered around the chamber and killed her protests dead in her throat. 'These men are our honoured guests, come to offer our dear foster son a route home, something we have all prayed for on his behalf, have we not?'

Elizaveta dropped her head. She would not answer; could not answer. It was so wrong, so very wrong. Could her father not see these men for what they so clearly were – power-hungry opportunists braving the Rus ice in pursuit of their own personal glory?

'Have we not, Elizaveta?' Yaroslav's voice was low with warning but Elizaveta could take it no more.

'I have prayed, indeed, Father, for the rightful king of Norway to be restored to his throne but this – this is not right and God will know that. Good day.'

She swept a curtsey, yanking Vladimir's hand from her gown as she did so, and then departed the room, ignoring her father's furious calls and the gratingly obsequious reassurances of the men who had come, she knew, to steal Harald's dream.

CHAPTER NINE

The walls of Kiev, November 1036

'How can you say that, Harald? *You.* How can you be so . . . so pathetic?'

'Pathetic?'

Harald looked surprised, amused almost, and it fanned the anger that had been smouldering inside Elizaveta all summer long. Magnus had ridden out of Kiev barely days after the Norwegian jarls had come for him, escorted by a royal guard which had included Prince Vladimir, bound, to his huge delight, for Novgorod. Elizaveta, confined to the bower and glad of it, had watched Magnus go from her window, his stupid slim frame all rigid and proud on a magnificent black stallion that had dwarfed him and that she had prayed would throw him to the ice.

She could not blame young Magnus. Edward had patiently explained to her, on his return from tribute collecting, that the boy would be a fool to turn down this thunderbolt of an opportunity and she knew it to be true but Magnus had not so much held onto fortune's wheel as let it roll right over him.

'He is young,' Edward had said. 'What did you expect of him? He cannot ride out as Harald can.'

'Nor rule as he can.'

'That may be true, Lily, but Harald's time will come. Some men are made for greatness.'

He'd looked sad then.

'Your time will come too,' Elizaveta had assured him, thinking of the rich little island of England that had cast him out so long ago.

'I fear not.'

His eyes had swum and Elizaveta had been grateful when she'd heard Agatha's cheery voice calling his name outside.

'Agatha looks for you.'

'She is very sweet. Everyone here is so very kind but I fear I will never be able to pay your father back.'

'You do not know that, Edward. Men came for Magnus; perhaps one day they will come for you.'

He'd bitten back a harsh laugh and she'd quashed her anger about Norway for his sake but she was furious at her parents for taking Einar's substantial bribes – 'payments for your care of our royal lord' – and letting him go so easily. And she was even more furious at the hood-eyed men who must have been laughing all the way up the Dnieper at their seizure of such easy prey. She was sure that Norway would not thank the Grand Prince for letting those two loose on their government and had yearned for Harald to return so they could ride north to make good his own claim. Now, though, he was telling her, as if she were some simpleton peasant girl, that it wasn't 'as easy as that'.

'What are you afraid of?' Elizaveta challenged. 'Einar Tambarskelve and his bully soldiers? Or is it the Arnassons? Is that the issue, Harald? Jarl Kalv told me of your betrothal. He seemed very sure of it.'

'Did he?' Harald's hand shot out and grabbed her wrist, trapping the neck chain she had drawn from its casket for this, his first night back in Kiev, and pressing the sharp edges of the keys into her flesh. 'Why then, Elizaveta, if I was his sworn kin, would he take Magnus instead?'

'I think he might indeed have taken you, Harald, but you were not here and Einar was swift to pounce on Magnus instead.'

'I could not help that.' His face was so close to hers that she could see the groove of his scar where the sword had cut deepest. 'I was out fighting to further my cause.'

'Or maybe just to fill your pockets. Do you truly want Norway, Harald? Is it truly seawater in your precious Varangian veins or something softer – like honey? Do you secretly like it down there in the south with its warm air and its exotic food and its pliable concubines?'

'Stop it!'

Harald grabbed at her other wrist and pulled her tight against him, sucking the breath from her. Elizaveta glanced over her shoulder but they were alone on Kiev's walls. She had brought him here to plot their journey to Norway but it had not worked out that way.

'Why are you not angry, Harald?' she asked desperately, fighting his grasp.

'Oh Lily.' Harald leaned down and dropped a kiss on her forehead, so soft and so sweet she was surprised into stillness. 'I am furious,' he whispered. 'My belly feels as if it has Greek fire inside it and my heart as if it might crawl out of my chest and take up a sword itself, but what good does that do?'

'What good? *Every* good, Harald. A man must have passion to reclaim his throne – that's what you told me. A man must believe and must make others believe. He cannot just give up because some beardless youth got there first.' Harald laughed softly and suddenly he was kissing her again, on her forehead, her nose, her lips. Elizaveta pushed him furiously away. 'I know not what you are used to from your Byzantine women, Harald, but I am a Princess of Kiev and am not to be won with kisses.'

He sighed.

'How can I make you see that I am in the empire fighting, Elizaveta, not whoring?'

'You have never been with a whore?'

Harald hesitated and her anger bubbled crazily inside her so she could almost feel it prickling her skin from within. She yanked away and strode off down the wall, clutching her cloak around her, though more for protection from his touch than the Rus cold. Why could no one else see how terrible this was? Why was she alone in her fury?

Her father had persuaded himself that her outburst had been one of love and chosen to overlook it as a girlish fancy. Her mother, close to giving birth to her eleventh child, had been grateful at this chance of familial peace after a few tense days and only Anastasia had looked to keep Elizaveta at bay longer than a week. With the spring, though, had come a vicious Pecheneg attack, right on the very plateau beyond the Grand Prince's kremlin, and with Yaroslav visiting Vladimir in Novgorod, it had been Andrew who had led the defence, turning all her sister's thoughts to her heroic general.

The Kievan forces had defeated the tribal attackers in a huge battle, played out before the eyes of the city, and Elizaveta had watched with the rest, momentarily distracted from her own bitter concerns by the violent cut and thrust of the waves of death lapping at the walls of her dear home. Prince Andrew, she'd had to admit – though no way near so loudly or effusively as Anastasia – had shown strong leadership and within days the war had been won and all had been triumph and feasting.

As the autumn leaves had covered the rotting corpses, however, and the first snows had fallen over their remains, Elizaveta had taken to pacing the walls looking for Harald's return. The landwaster banner she'd been working on so long with her ladies had finally been finished and looked magnificent with the swooping raven dark and challenging against the regal gold of the silk. It had cost her many hard, dull hours and endless pricked fingers but it had been worth it. She'd longed to present it to him and her frustration had mounted with every day he did not come.

She had written to Vladimir in Novgorod, telling him she would soon be there to visit on her way to the Varangian Sea, and even to her Aunt Astrid in Sweden, saying how much she longed to see her. She'd persuaded a young traveller to teach her the Norwegian forms of their language and badgered him endlessly for information on towns and customs. She had ordered her seamstresses to make new gowns in the warmest, richest fabrics she could squeeze out of her newly benevolent father and, like a little girl again, had begged her mother for tales of the north.

'Harald will not ride, Lily,' Ingrid had told her, 'not yet,' but she had newly given birth to yet another son, Boris, and Eliza-veta had put her negativity down to the weakness of the childbed.

When Harald was back, she'd been sure, things would be different but now Harald *was* back and it was all infuriatingly similar.

'You are grown soft, Harald,' she flung at him now. 'Soft and self-indulgent.'

His reply skidded along the cold walls.

'No one else talks to me as you do, Elizaveta.'

'Which is precisely why you are grown weak,' she flung over her shoulder. 'You are too used to being the hero, Harald.'

'Rubbish. I am a soldier, no more. I do my duty and I do it well. I have been promoted to the elite guard.'

She spun round to face him.

'How nice for you. I'm sure the uniform is very pretty.'

'It is actually, it . . .' Harald cut himself off. 'Lily, please . . .'

'Do not call me that.'

'You are disappointed.'

'Disappointed? Hah! I am furious, Harald.'

'And I understand that.' He came cautiously towards her. 'I am furious too but fury is not enough to carry a man into battle. Battles require logic, timing, calculation.'

'Courage.'

He winced.

'I am sorry you think so poorly of me.'

'I am sorry too.'

'Lily . . . Elizaveta, please. This is a setback, no more. It does not change my plans to reclaim the throne, just delays them a little.'

'Really? I have something for you.'

He stopped before her, surprised.

'You do?'

She cursed her own impatience. The raven banner was beneath her cloak but now was not the time for it. She turned away.

'It doesn't matter.'

'Lily!'

He caught at her arm and she lost her grip on the parcel. It fell to the ground between them and they both stared at it. Elizaveta started forward to gather it up but she was too slow.

'A present?' Harald asked. 'For me?'

'That was the idea,' she agreed crossly, 'but I don't suppose you'll need it now.'

He turned the parcel over and over in his hands, then suddenly pulled on the ribbons that bound it. The flag fluttered open and caught in the sharp breeze cutting across the top of

Kiev. For a moment the raven seemed to soar above them and Elizaveta heard Harald gasp.

''Tis magnificent.'

She flushed despite herself.

'You like it?'

''Tis the finest thing I have ever owned, truly. You stitched it yourself?'

'Of course.' Pleasure flooded through her as he ran his fingers reverentially over the fine stitching, picking out the edges of the legendary bird. 'It was meant to lead you into Norway.'

He grabbed her hand so that the silk tangled between them.

'And it will, Lily. Truly it will. How can I fail with such a gift – with such a wife? We must just bide our time, that is all. Magnus is proclaimed as Norway's new king. He is Olaf's son and I hear tell that they are hailing Olaf as a saint now for his work in taking Christ to our nation. Can you not see that if I ride against Magnus, even under such a beautiful banner, I will be the usurper, the tyrant, not the saviour?'

'You will be the rightful king.'

'Bless you for thinking so, my sweet, but in truth I have no more right than my nephew.'

Elizaveta laughed bitterly.

'Your nephew has few rights, Harald. He is in the hands of the northern jarls and they will play him to their own ends.'

'And keep him safe too. It would be a futile challenge, Elizaveta.'

'But a glorious one.'

Harald nodded slowly and leaned over the parapet to look out across the plateau. The snows were covering the blood-stained battlefield and Kiev looked peaceful and proud. Yaroslav had declared after the battle against the Pechenegs that he would extend the walls, make them as long as those of Miklegard itself, to keep all his people safe and Kiev buzzed with the promise of the New Year. Up here, though, outside the chatter, nothing felt right.

'Perhaps you speak true, my Princess,' Harald said softly, running the flag tenderly through his calloused warrior's hands.

'True about what?'

'That I should ride home and die in glory, not hide down here in shame. 'Tis the Viking way after all – Valhalla welcomes valiant fools.'

'Harald! Valhalla is a pagan myth.'

'As the raven is a pagan symbol – and a good one. What, then, does our Christian God seek from us, Elizaveta? Surely he would rather I turned the other cheek and gave my blessing on Magnus's reign?'

Elizaveta shifted uncomfortably.

'You could rule jointly,' she suggested. 'You spoke of it before.'

'You would like to be half a queen, my sweet?'

She glared at him.

'I would like to be your wife.'

'I would like that too, truly, more than anything.'

He tried to take her hand but she shook her head, cross again.

'That's just not true, Harald.'

He sighed.

'No,' he agreed heavily, 'it is not exactly true, no more than it is for you. Neither of us could retire to a farm and live just for each other.'

'I did not mean . . .'

'Could we? Truly? We are royal born, you and I, Elizaveta. It is a privilege and a responsibility. I *will* marry you, my love, and I *will* make you a queen but the time must be right. We must be patient.'

'Patient?'

'Tis not your strength, my love?'

'I am not patient, Hari, no – but I am constant.'

He smiled and pulled her close.

'My constant queen?'

He leaned in to kiss her but she pulled back at his words.

'I would be, Harald, given a chance, but it seems I will never be a queen, constant or otherwise.'

Anger flared inside her once more, the same bitter rage that she had nursed across a long, hard summer and all for nought. She took the landwaster from him, folding it small.

'I still do not see it,' she protested. 'If you wait, Magnus will only grow stronger.'

'And Einar weaker as a result. Norway can no longer be won just by war, Lily, but by diplomacy and it is a more devious game. Our time will come.'

'You swear it?'

'I swear it.' He leaned in, his lips grazing her neck, and softly took back the banner, tucking it carefully into his belt. 'I swear, Elizaveta, that I will make you a queen; Queen of Norway, Denmark and England – Empress of the North. Can you trust me, my necklace goddess? Can you trust our future to me?'

Her fingers gripped the wooden parapet as his face pressed closer to hers. Her head was spinning with the ambitious list of titles but they were not reality yet.

'I have little choice, Harald,' she said tartly. 'I can hardly ride north alone.'

He groaned.

'You are very sexy when you are angry, do you know that?'

'And you are very pathetic when you are grovelling.'

'Tis true but I want you so badly, Lily.'

He yanked her suddenly in against him and she felt his desire ripple up her body and her own pulse raced treacherously in response.

'I want you too,' she admitted, her voice cracking.

'We are, you know, to be wed . . .'

Her eyes narrowed.

'Do you, then, take all your betrotheds to bed?'

'Lily . . .'

'I told you not to call me that.'

The anger was back and she pulled away and stalked down the walkway, longing to run but fearing she might slip on the icy boards. Harald skittered after her and she stopped dead so that he all but tumbled at her feet.

'No, Harald,' she flung at him. 'We are royal, remember? It's a privilege and a responsibility and I am not birthing your bastard whilst you play soldiers in the Greek sea.'

He looked so sad, staring down at her, looking for apologies she might believe, but she was done with apologies. He was right – she was disappointed, torn apart by disappointment, and much as she ached for him, he had to understand that.

'If I must wait,' she told him firmly, the words misting in the Kievan night, 'then so, too, must you.'

CHAPTER TEN

Austratt, Northern Norway, September 1038

ora kicked her horse into a canter and rode the autumn winds, tossing back her hair and welcoming the thin tears they drew from her eyes. She should have cried before. She should have cried when they laid Pieter, her husband, in the ground and said prayers over his wasted body. Her mother had cried, her sister Johanna too – though she cried at anything – but Tora had just felt numb.

She had been forced to the church door with Lord Pieter when Einar had brought not Harald but the boy-king Magnus back to Norway, a defiantly shamefaced Kalv in his wake, but it had been a poor marriage. Pieter had been a kind enough husband, but feeble, and she had been more nurse than wife. Already, just days after his passing, her brief marriage felt like a rogue part of her life – more story than memory.

'God bless his soul,' she called into the newly sharp air as her horse stretched out across the great plain above the jagged cliffs of the northern coastline.

She meant it truly but to her shame she was glad to be riding away. She should miss Pieter, she knew, but she did not. Maybe, she tortured herself when waking from an easy sleep every morning, she was just weak-hearted?

It would do her good to be back in Austratt where she had grown up. It was so much livelier in her Uncle Finn's town-edge farm than out on Pieter's remote island of Giske. Travellers called all the time on their way down the fjord to Nidaros to trade and Finn kept his doors wide open. There were often entertainers in his hall – skalds and poets, acrobats and musicians. Rarely were there less than a hundred men sleeping in the alcoves of his huge farmhouse and often there were pavilions erected on the flat land in front of it to house more.

They brought gifts for their lodgings, these men – sometimes game or fish for the table, sometimes ale or mead or strange firewaters that made the men splutter and kindled their ever-ready laughter as high as the hearth flames. Sometimes, though, she recalled them gifting Finn stranger things – birds in cages with feathers as colourful as their tails, bright-eyed little dogs, not hounds to run in the hunt but curiosities to keep in the bower. They brought exotic foodstuffs and spices – Tora would never forget the one they called chilli that had felt like a brazier had been lit in her mouth. They delivered wonderful glassware and jewellery and unusual tools that kept the artisans wondering for weeks. And news – news even from Constantinople where she heard tell Harald was fighting the Saracens in some island called Sicily.

Tora kicked her horse into a gallop as their little group turned inland towards Austratt, pushing against the raw truth that she could not grieve for Pieter as she should because of the giddy joy that she was free again – free for when Harald returned. The thought that he might have wed elsewhere had often tormented her but surely such news would have travelled back to Norway? Besides, how could it happen? Harald was Tora's; and she his. She knew that and she just prayed that he remembered it too.

It had been the night before he rode to battle in 1030.

They'd both been fifteen and had seen plenty of each other since their midsummer 'betrothal' three years before, though usually it had been amongst others. The northern lords often gathered for celebrations – Yule, All Hallows, Easter, midsummer, weddings, christenings, funerals; the usual turns of life – as well as travelling across Norway for the great assemblies that formed the backbone of the country's government. Harald and Tora had usually been with the other youngsters and, though they had danced together often, they had kissed but rarely – until that night.

Tora had not seen fifteen-year-old Harald for some months as he'd been off a-viking with her Uncle Kalv and she had been fascinated by his sudden transformation from boy to man. He had always been tall but he seemed to have shot up so he was already on a level with Finn, no small man. His shoulders had squared off and his moustache grown thick and full and as shiningly blonde as his long hair. He had seemed, too, to move with new confidence and purpose, for he was mustering men to lead into the hills to meet the returning King Olaf, his half-brother, and to help restore him to his throne.

He'd had a new mail coat and a gilded helmet, paid for from his own pelt-trading at Nidaros, and he'd looked every inch the warrior. It had seemed to Tora that girls followed him everywhere, pointing and giggling and trying to engage him in conversation – or more. Their betrothal was still talked of but increasingly as a fairy story, an example of Harald's reputation as a lover rather than a confirmation of his commitment to Tora Arnasson. She'd had to act.

It had taken all her courage and a healthy dose of some strange, clear Rus spirit she'd sneaked from her father's table, to get her to Harald's door. He had been sleeping in a rich pavilion amongst the seven hundred or so men who'd answered his call to arms, eschewing his usual rich bed in Finn's hall to be amongst his soldiers, so she'd waited until the farmstead and camp were silent at last and escaped the bower. She could remember now how her heart had pounded so loudly she'd feared the men would think it a drum calling them to arms and come from their tents. She could remember how her hands had shaken as she'd hidden in the trees at the edge of the camp to remove her linen nightdress and wrap her nakedness in her cloak and how it had been such a warm night that she had been sweating beneath its heavy layers by the time she had approached his pavilion.

She'd felt so wanton, so daring, dressed thus. It had been a trick she had overheard one of her aunt's ladies telling her friends in the bower. Newly wed, she had apparently surprised her lord out on the hunt by riding forth clad only in her cloak and the resultant passion, so she'd assured her goggle-eyed listeners, had been more than worth it.

'Besides,' she'd giggled, 'it felt so good riding naked I almost climaxed before I even reached my lord.'

There'd been lots of 'oohs' and 'oh you are wicked's but 'wicked' had seemed, in this context, an admirable quality so Tora had considered it worth a try. Besides, she'd feared that if Harald had to untie her laces there would be too much time for thought and this needed to happen fast. She'd wanted to make him hers. She'd wanted to seal the pact they'd made, official or nay, on that midsummer beach. She'd wanted him to go to battle with her scent upon his skin and, above all else, she'd wanted him to follow that scent home again. She had still, though, been terrified.

When she'd crept into his pavilion and seen him sprawled out across the rough bed with just a light blanket over his golden body, she'd almost run away there and then. It had only been his squire awakening and scuttling swiftly out when he saw her in the doorway that had kept her rooted.

'Harald?'

He'd started awake, reaching for his sword, but when he'd seen her he'd relaxed.

'Tora. Is all well? Is there a problem at the farm?'

'No problem, Harald. I just wanted to . . . to see you. To wish you luck in battle.'

'Thank you.'

He'd rubbed sleep from his eyes and sat up further so that the blanket had fallen from his bare chest and she'd seen the dusting of fine hair across it. He'd looked so beautiful and she'd swallowed, urging herself on.

'And to give you something.'

'Really? What?'

'This.'

She'd thrown back the cloak and, to her gratification and immense relief, he'd gasped in something like awe.

'Truly?' he'd whispered.

'If you want it – want *me*.'

'How could I not?' he'd said huskily. 'You are beautiful.'

She'd glanced down at herself and instantly wished she hadn't. Her hips had looked so wide, her breasts so bulbous, her stomach so slack. She'd sucked it in but he'd already been up and moving towards her, reaching out tentative hands to cup first one breast and then the other, and he'd groaned, his whole body twitching in a way that had made her instantly forget her own.

'You are sure, Tora?' he'd breathed.

'We are betrothed.'

'We are,' he'd agreed, though his eyes had not been on her face and his hands had already been moving down her body, pulling her against him so their skin rubbed together. 'Yes,' he'd murmured. 'God, yes.'

Then he'd been unfastening her cloak and lifting her into

his arms. He'd laid her on the bed and crawled up over her as he had done on that beach three years ago when they were still young, still innocent.

'Have you done it before?' she'd asked him, though the words had seemed to scrape her throat.

'Never,' he'd said and she'd sighed happily and let him part her legs. 'Can I touch you?'

She hadn't expected that but he'd looked so eager that she'd nodded. He'd run a hand down over her stomach and between her legs and a sensation had shot through her, half pleasure, half fear. She'd longed to clasp her legs shut or, at least, to draw the blanket over her private parts, but he had been exploring them so delightedly that she'd dared not.

'Oh, Tora!'

Her name had sounded so sweet on his lips and then, at last, he'd been kissing her and pressing himself against her and – ow! She'd had to bite hard on her lip to keep the cry inside. It had felt as if someone were ripping her apart.

'Oh, Tora,' he'd said again, 'that's good. That's so good.'

And though she hadn't felt good – though her body had been screaming and her head tangling with the sin of it – it had been enough. She'd put her hands around his back and traced the lines of his muscles with her nails and then clutched at him as he'd picked up pace and, thank the Lord, within seconds she'd felt his whole body shudder and he'd cried out so loud the whole camp must surely have heard, and it had been over.

Afterwards it had all felt worth it. He'd stroked her and kissed her and fussed over the blood and told her again and again how beautiful she was and how he would come home to her victorious and King Olaf's most trusted jarl and he would make her his for always.

'What if I have a child?' she'd asked him.

'Oh, I will be back long before that matters,' he'd assured her but in the end there had been no child and he had not come back.

Her stomach churned at the thought of the lost chance, for a child would, surely, have called him home? Harald had wanted to do it again that night but she'd used the coming dawn and his imminent march as an excuse. Instead he'd walked her back to where she'd hidden her nightdress and kissed her farewell and by the time she'd woken from an exhausted sleep he'd gone and all his soldiers with him. She hadn't seen him since. Had she sinned? Was this God's punishment? If so, it seemed very unjust. She heard hooves thundering up behind her and turned to see Finn catching her up.

'You ride hard, Tora.'

She blinked away the past and looked at her uncle.

'It is a fine day for it.'

'It is and, look, we are nearly there.' Finn pointed over the wide fjord to the long roof of his great farmhouse, just visible on the far bank. Tora felt her heart lift a little at the sight of it but Finn was still talking. 'I am glad you have come back to Austratt with me, Niece, for you are a sharp girl and I need your help.'

'You do?'

'We must keep an eye on Einar. He is ever at King Magnus's side and the boy has come to rely on him so much that he swells with power. I swear it was he who told the king of Kalv's sad part in Stikelstad.'

His eyes clouded and Tora reached out and patted his wrinkled hand, a useless gesture really but what more could she do? It had been a bitter time when someone – almost certainly Einar – had dripped into young Magnus's ear the names of the men who had killed his father, King Olaf, in the blackness at Stikelstad, one of them Kalv.

Despite his valiant part in Magnus's restoration to the Norwegian throne, the young king had condemned Tora's second uncle to death and he had been forced to flee across the western seas to exile. Finn had received word that he was safe with the legendary Jarl Thorfinn on the Orkneys which had been some comfort, especially as Finn's eldest daughter, Idonie, had recently become Thorfinn's wife, but the resultant rise in Einar's power weighed heavily upon him. Now he swung out of his saddle before the jetty and, stretching his old back, beckoned Tora down at his side.

'Perhaps,' he said as she dismounted, 'you could become friendly with the king? He might like a woman's touch.'

'Uncle!'

'Oh, not like that, Tora. You have done your duty by me with Pieter and I am not sorry that you are free of it.' He winked, surprising her. 'More . . . maternal. Unless, of course, things develop. In truth, it would be another good match for you, and a great support for the family.'

'Magnus?' All Tora's joy in the bright journey to Austratt faded away. She had taken one meek husband; surely she did not deserve another? 'What of Harald, Uncle?'

'Harald Sigurdsson?' Finn drew in a sharp breath. 'I think you know that I still harbour hopes in that direction, Tora, but there is little even I can do with a childhood contract that was never ratified.'

'It was,' she flung back and then, scarlet, pulled away and walked a few paces, glancing nervously at the ferryman waiting eagerly in his boat.

Finn looked at her curiously.

'Was it indeed? Ah, Tora, you surprise me.'

She turned back.

'I'm sorry, Uncle.'

'Nay, do not be sorry.' His eyes were flickering across the

horizon, as if thoughts too great to be kept inside were battering at them. 'Lord Pieter never complained and much good could come of this. As I said, you are a sharp girl. You have done well.'

'You are pleased with me?'

She could scarce believe it, but now Finn came up and chucked her under her chin.

'Very pleased. I like a woman who knows when to act.' He looked out down the vast fjord, cutting its determined way from the northern seas towards Nidaros and beyond that over the keel – the mountains that formed a ridge across Norway – to the Varangian Sea and the southern lands beyond. 'You have decided me, Niece – it is time to act before Einar crushes us all. We must send messages to Harald. We must remind him of his responsibilities here.'

'You want him . . .' Tora lowered her voice though the ferryman was busy readying his oarsmen and Johanna and the servants were still far back. 'You want Harald as king?'

He put up a hand.

'Let's not rush forward too fast, Tora. I want Harald in Norway as his nephew's supporter and as a great jarl and as your husband. Let the rest unfold as God wishes it.'

Tora's eyes glowed. *As your husband!* She had not sinned after all and now, it seemed, she might finally have her reward. Except that . . .

'I hear things of a Princess of Kiev,' she said nervously.

'Oh, I do too, but they are not wed, Tora. He can . . . side-step such an arrangement.'

'Or he could "sidestep" me, Uncle.'

'And all our family with you? All of Norway indeed. I think not, Tora. Now, come, let us take the boat across to my farm and hope there are acrobats awaiting us and messengers ready to ride south, for there is work to be done, much work, and you, my dear girl, are at the heart of it.'

CHAPTER ELEVEN

Hagia Sophia, Kiev, August 1039

'May God bless this couple and grant them happiness in His sight. May His light shine upon them and may the world be gracious to them.'

Elizaveta huffed quietly. She had no doubt the world would be 'gracious' to the shining couple; the bride would allow no less. As they turned from the glittering altar, Anastasia beamed on the assembled dignitaries radiating . . . what was that? Smugness, Elizaveta decided meanly. Yes, definitely smugness. Her sister did look beautiful though. Her dress, in blues and greens as luminous as the newly painted frescoes on the walls, was a work of art. Her blonde hair shone like an angel's and it was topped with a tiara that glittered as if the North Star itself had landed on her head. Prince Andrew, at her side in a regal tunic of forest green trimmed with gold, seemed a little dazed by his new wife. It was a feeling Elizaveta was sure he would have to get used to.

'Stop it,' she berated herself. 'Stop being bitter and mean and . . .' She stopped short of the word 'jealous' even in her own head though she knew it to be true. It had been her choice not to marry Prince Andrew. It could have been her there now, standing at the altar of her father's magnificent new Hagia Sophia cathedral. He had ordered it built on the site of his victory over the Pechenegs two years ago and had shipped in craftsmen and stonemasons and architects from Miklegard to create it in grand Byzantine style. Harald had brought most of them with him last winter and then returned to the emperor who had apparently tired of fighting Normans in Italy and instead employed them to liberate some island called Sicily from the infidel. Harald was one of the men set to command these fearsome mercenaries and Elizaveta worried for him, clashing swords with Arabs in the diseased heat of the south, and longed to hear news of his progress.

Harald had spent half of his brief Yule visit in conference with Yaroslav, telling him all he knew of Byzantine art, culture and politics. Yaroslav was plotting something, Elizaveta was sure of it, something more than Greek cupolas and frescoes, and Harald was caught up in it. She had quizzed him several times but he'd just said it was 'architectural trifles' and insisted they did not waste their short time together in such boring talk. Then he had distracted her in ways that made her body burn in memory.

'No dishonour,' he had assured her, unbuttoning the pearl fastening at the neck of her undergown and kissing the hollow at the base of her throat. 'Just pleasure.' And oh, it had been pleasure. He'd gone no lower and she had not given him licence to do so, though her body had fought her will with the force of a spring flood. But they had kissed. They had kissed time and again until they'd kissed 1038 into the past, but in the New Year he had gone to Sicily and all she'd had of him since were letters brought by Yaroslav's dusty craftsmen and keys to more and more damned treasure.

'It's not right,' she thought now as the newly cast bells rang out in triumph and Andrew took his bride on his arm and led her down the aisle towards the great doors, thrown wide to let the vast crowd beyond see the riches within. In truth the cathedral was not fully finished. Several of the thirteen circular towers had not yet been fitted with their golden cupolas and a number of the side chapels were bare but no one was looking into those dim corners now. No, all eyes were on Anastasia as she waved and smiled and soaked up the glory of the day like riverbank moss in the spring thaw.

Yes, Elizaveta was definitely jealous. She was the eldest daughter and she had been betrothed for nearly two years but her groom was off fighting Saracens and Anastasia had delightedly stolen her moment from under her. As Vladimir and Yaroslav followed the bridal couple down the aisle, Elizaveta took her place with her mother whilst Ivan, Stefan, Anne, Viktor, Igor, Agatha, Yuri and three-year-old Boris slid smoothly into the princely procession behind them. They all began to move slowly through the church and Elizaveta smiled at the assembled guests, then froze as, at the back near the great doors towards which Anastasia was now tugging Andrew, she spotted a familiar armoured figure. Ulf! Her eyes cast eagerly past him but she could see no blonde hair topping the Sunday crowd; no groom come to claim her whilst the guests and the choir and the Metropolitan were all in place to wed them.

'Smile, Elizaveta.' Elizaveta glanced at her mother and plastered a false grin across her face. 'It will be your turn soon, my sweet, I am sure.'

'Are you? I am not, Mother. I am not sure at all. I swear with every year he spends in the south Harald thinks less and less of Norway. It has become a land of trolls to him, no more.'

'That's not true, Lily.' Ingrid was smiling and nodding to important figures in the crowd, but still kept up her quiet conversation with Elizaveta. 'I have spoken to him myself and he is passionate about his homeland.'

'You have? When?'

Ingrid smiled.

'He does not spend all his time in Kiev kissing you, Lily.'

'Mother! He does not kiss me – well, barely.'

'I am not blind, daughter. I know it is hard for you, especially today. Your sister is not the most tactful of brides.'

Elizaveta groaned in assent; Anastasia had been unbearable for weeks. Even patient Anne had snapped at her when she'd turned the conversation yet again to the richness of her bridal gown and Agatha had learned to make herself scarce whenever seamstresses were near. Now nine years old, Agatha was a striking child, with curls to match Ulf's all the way down her long back, but she was far happier on a horse than in the bower. Elizaveta didn't blame her.

'I just don't see,' she said now, 'why Harald and I cannot be wed whether we travel to Norway or no?'

Ingrid patted her hand.

'Your father is just protecting you. He does not want you shackled to an adventurer.'

'Why not? It sounds like fun.'

'Elizaveta – try and be sensible. You are a Princess of Kiev. You have your dignity to maintain, and that of your family.'

'Always dignity,' Elizaveta muttered and her mother leaned in to kiss her cheek.

'Besides,' she whispered, 'your father may have other plans for Harald.'

'What?'

Elizaveta stopped, stunned, but her mother nudged her forward.

'I am just saying, try and be patient.'

'I hate being patient. What do you mean, Mother? What plans?' Ingrid glanced nervously around. 'Mother,' Elizaveta begged. 'I will be twenty-one next year. I am not a child and this affects me – surely I have a right to know.'

Ingrid nodded tautly.

'Miklegard is weak, Lily. The emperor is wasting away and

the empress is old and has no children. They are much pre-occupied by securing Italy and Sicily. There may be a chance . . .'

'Father as . . . ?'

'Hush, Lily. Your father seeks to further the prosperity of the Rus peoples in whatever way he can. His borders are ever extending and he sees no reason to limit that process. If we can aid Andrew to take back Hungary that will extend our influence west. Magnus already owes us a debt of gratitude in the north and, who knows, maybe one day we will see gentle Edward in England, but for now we look south.'

Elizaveta could hardly believe what she was hearing. Truly she had underestimated Yaroslav but now it all made sense.

'And that is why Harald lingers in the service of the Byzantine Empire?'

'He is working with your father to . . . investigate matters.'

'But Norway?'

Ingrid shook her head.

'I have filled your head with tales of the north, Lily. Too much perhaps. Norway is a wonderful country but Byzantium is an *empire*. And your father would not, of course, wish to leave Kiev . . .'

'Harald? And, and . . . me?'

Ingrid kissed her.

'It is in the hands of God, daughter, of God and of men. But hush – this is not the time and nothing is settled. Please just try and enjoy life. Whatever his other plans, your father is working wonders here in Kiev. The city grows daily. Is that not exciting?'

They were nearly at the door now and the roar of the crowd was intense. Yaroslav's plans for his extended city included a network of paved streets, elegantly fenced plots and any number of public buildings, not just churches but oven-houses, a library and a monastic school. The people would benefit greatly and as their Grand Prince stood at the top of the marble steps and held his arms wide to them, they hailed him as, if Elizaveta was hearing right, the 'Emperor of the Rus'.

'Emperor?' she muttered, testing the word nervously but now Yaroslav was looking round for his wife and instantly Ingrid slipped from Elizaveta's side.

Elizaveta stood and watched her parents' joined figures alongside the bridal couple acknowledging the accolades of the crowd and felt suddenly very, very lonely. If Harald was plotting all sorts of wonders with her father why was he not here? Why was he not at her side?

'Princess?'

Elizaveta swung round to see Ulf, his hair as wild as ever and his big brown eyes trained upon her. She stepped aside to join him in the shadows of a column, gratefully letting the other guests surge past.

'Count Ulf, greetings. You travel alone?'

'Alas, Princess, yes. Prince Harald has led great victories in Sicily. We have taken Messina and are even now marching on Syracuse. He cannot be spared, for the infidel is strong in opposition and the Normans on our own side need fierce control, but he sent me in his stead to honour your sister and to bring you this gift.'

The package was silken again, a rich blue this time, but Elizaveta did not take it.

'I do not need your silk, Ulf, thank you.' Ulf blinked and shifted the parcel awkwardly from one calloused hand to the other. 'Is Halldor not with you either?'

'He is with Harald.'

'Aksel will be disappointed.'

Elizaveta looked around for the child, now five years old and ever in scrapes, and was grateful to see him playing tag around the columns with Yuri and Boris. Aksel was always asking about his colourful father and would be sad not to see him. She did her best to tell him tales of Halldor's grand warrior life but she had not his skill and although the boy was devoted to her and had touchingly proclaimed himself her squire on his fifth birthday, she often caught him looking longingly over the city's south wall. But then, she was often doing the same herself.

'I am sorry,' Ulf said. 'Halldor longed to come too but we did not wish to leave Harald unprotected.'

Elizaveta raised an eyebrow.

'You two are the only men in Harald's troop of renowned soldiers who can keep him safe?'

Ulf did not even hesitate.

'Yes, we are. Please accept the gift, Princess. I have travelled many days to bring it here.'

'I did not ask that of you.'

'You did not,' Ulf acknowledged, 'but all the same I ask *this* of you.'

He held the package out again and reluctantly she took it. The myriad guests were flocking out of the Hagia Sophia and only sharp-eyed Agatha, her arm on Edward's like a true princess, noticed them behind the half-built pillars. Slowly Elizaveta undid the ribbon and looked at the now familiar keys, two this time. Between them, though, was an object tied up in an exotically embroidered bag. Her curiosity piqued, Elizaveta handed the keys carefully to Ulf and opened the tiny bag. Turning it over she let its contents tip into the palm of her hand and looked down, stunned.

It was a finger ring, melded of gold and inlaid with a tiny, intricate mosaic of ruby, sapphire and emerald. Written around it in runes was the conceit: 'Mine is Yours is . . .' Round and round forever, eternally binding.

'It's beautiful,' she breathed.

'Harald had it made especially in Miklegard.'

Miklegard! The word, once so magical, grated against Elizaveta's heart. Always it was about Miklegard. Miklegard was even, thanks to her father's building work, come to Kiev – but Harald was not. No plans, however grand, seemed worth his absence.

'It's beautiful,' she repeated, 'but empty.'

Elizaveta held it up and regarded Ulf through the hole at the centre.

'But Princess, that is for . . .'

'I know what it is for, Ulf, but tell your precious master this – I will never wear this ring upon my finger until he is come to place it there himself. Take it.'

She shoved it at him but he put up a hand in protest and it caught her own, sending the priceless ring pinging across the darker reaches of Yaroslav's freshly cut marble flooring. Elizaveta bit her lip but stood her ground as Ulf scrabbled for – and thankfully found – the ring up against a pillar.

'Princess,' he protested, his eyes as hurt as if she had spurned him and not his far-off master, 'Harald does you great honour with this ring.'

'Harald,' she corrected him, her heart aching, 'will do me honour when he stands at the altar with me, as Prince Andrew has stood with my sister today. I will keep his treasure safe, as I have sworn to do, but until he leaves his southern seas and comes north himself he has no claim on me.' Ulf's eyes hardened. She hated to see it but she could do nothing else. 'I love him, Ulf,' she said simply and then spun away and buried herself in the crowd, fumbling for her linen square as hot tears fell.

She had started this journey as Harald's treasure-keeper and it seemed she was that again – no more, no less. It had been a long, hard way to come for so little.

CHAPTER TWELVE

Miklegard, April 1042

*H*arald kicked at the wall. A tiny scrap of mortar flaked off but these walls, he knew, were almost as thick as a man lying on his side. He could kick all century without getting through and he might have to.

'We stayed too long,' he growled, pacing the tiny cell for the hundredth time that morning.

It was hot and the stench of his own piss assailed his nostrils from the rough bucket in the corner. It was foul. He'd not had a bath since he'd been thrown in here and the crust of sweat and dirt was itching at his skin. The guards had even taken his comb. He'd been momentarily pleased that they considered him so dangerous they could not even leave him with those tiny ivory teeth but three weeks in, with his hair birds-nesting, he was no longer amused. It wasn't that he was vain but his hair was his mark; his men looked for it in battle. How could he expect them to follow this mop?

'We should not have returned here from Sicily,' he raged. 'We should have taken passage north with those Normans.'

'The ones heading back to try and assassinate their own duke?' Ulf said scornfully.

Harald laughed bitterly.

'It does seem to be their favourite sport. Young William must be enchanted to have avoided so many swords – but 'tis not his fate that need concern us now. We should have fled to Kiev whilst we had the chance.'

'The emperor had just died,' Ulf grunted and Harald looked round. His friend was sat in a corner whittling at a stick with a nail he'd found on the floor just beyond the bars. Surely guards who took combs from their prisoners should watch for such things? 'We needed to be here, remember, to . . . what was it, Halldor?'

'Hammer whilst the blade is hot,' Halldor supplied gloomily.

The older man was sat in the opposite corner, staring into space. He'd done a lot of that recently and Harald sometimes wondered what he saw. Whatever it was, it had to be better than this.

It had all been going so well. With the poor young Emperor Michael fading into a cripple before everyone's eyes, Miklegard – or Constantinople as they were learning to call it – had become a viper's nest of factions and plots. Empress Zoe, the direct ruler in the imperial line, would remain in place but there must be an emperor too. The dead Michael's nephew had been named as Michael V but he was weak and unpopular and there were plenty keen to challenge his frail rule.

The empire was, as Harald had reported hopefully to Yaroslav last year, ready to crack wide open and Yaroslav had been preparing a fleet to do just that. Harald had seen the ships safe in Vitichev, away from the prying eyes of the Kievan gossips. He had inspected them with the Grand Prince last Yule, discussing where Miklegard was weakest and what it would take to steal her but now things had gone wrong. Young Michael, perhaps sensing trouble, had sent his generals to throw Harald and his men into this rat-hole where they could aid no one against him, least of all themselves.

Harald rattled at the great bars of his cell in frustration. It was he who should be holding the power, he and Yaroslav together, but the imperial faction had moved too fast for them. If he were not stuck celebrating Christ's resurrection in a five paces square hole in the depths of the old palace they would have been there, in Vitichev, preparing to attack. Yaroslav would be emperor, they had agreed as much, but Harald would have first right of succession and would rule as the sub-Imperatrix in the golden city itself, Elizaveta with him. They would ride under her beautiful raven banner, currently tied uselessly around his waist like a Greek fashion trifle. She would like that, he'd been sure. She would agree, once she came here, that Constantinople was a worthy place to rule and she would forget Norway as he had forgotten Norway. Or nearly forgotten.

Letting go of the bars, Harald turned back into the cell, his long legs physically itching at their confines. His hand went to his pocket in which he kept the missives that had arrived all too often from Finn Arnasson. He'd half-hoped the guards would take them with his comb but they had just laughed at the strange lettering and stuffed them back in the leather pouch at his belt, cracking the birch but not the messages it held. They'd been wiser than they knew, for those letters more than anything else, save perhaps this damned imprisonment, were shaking his resolve to bid for the Byzantine Empire.

Harald leaned against the wall, grateful for the cool of the stones through his sticky tunic, and pictured him – Finn Arnasson, the man who had brought him up from the age of twelve; the man who had taught him the art of war and of court-ship; the man who had taught him how to be a man. His own father, Sigurd, God bless him, had been a gentle soul, happiest, despite his royal lineage, with his sheep and Harald had been nearly as restless on their Ringerike farm as he was now in this hell-hole of a cell. His mother, Asta, had luckily been made of more ambitious metal and had secured him his place with the Arnassons. With Finn.

Harald stared into the empty air, much as Halldor did, and for once saw images of his own. Finn had brought him to life. His raucous, wild household had been heaven after years of sheep-shearing and Harald had thrown himself into his martial training with fervour. From Finn and his top warriors he had learned skill, poise and cunning, and from Finn also he had learned the joy of the battlefield. Sigurd had liked to talk of peace and Finn, too, embraced it as an ideal but it was when he spoke of war that Harald's foster father's eyes lit up. For Harald that had been the greatest release of all. He'd been born to battle, he knew it, but it was Finn who'd shown him how to embrace that desire and how to *use* it. He owed him much.

His fingers rasped across the letters, written not on birch twigs but on the bark – a flatter, wider surface where words could be not just commands but expressions of feeling. Finn had told him of Einar's increasing power and of Kalv's banish-ment. Harald had felt a momentary flicker of pleasure that the slyest Arnasson was gone, for Kalv had ever worked to get him into trouble as a youth, but he had soon seen past that. Magnus was a fool. If Kalv had dealt Olaf his death-blow it was a hurt, certainly, but one that he could have used to bind the man to him, not to cast him out where he could plot and scheme. Besides, much as Harald disliked Kalv he could see that he had only been obeying orders and if you started punishing that you had nowhere left to go. Magnus was not a soldier, that was the problem. He ruled with his pampered exile's heart; no wonder Einar was in charge.

If you have any ambition for Norway, Finn had written to him, *you should come now. Einar grows dangerous and, unchecked, will have Norway on her knees. We look eagerly for you, son. We*

would welcome you. Tora, especially, would welcome you as I know
she has welcomed you before.

Harald pulled his fingers from the pocket as if it might
suddenly bite him. Tora! He owed her much too. He had heard
tell she was married and had felt the news as a release, but
now it seemed she was widowed and her tenacious uncle was
harking back to their supposed childhood alliance. He thought
of his erstwhile sweetheart. If he strained, he could still see
her standing in the doorway of his pavilion; could still see her
voluptuous body unveiled from the thick cloak; could still feel
himself harden at his first sight of female beauty.

He could see too now, too many years later, how she had
held herself – guarded, fragile. He had not noticed it then,
had seen only her ripe breasts and the inviting tuck in her
pubic hair. He did not blame himself – he'd been fifteen and
about to ride to his first battle so he had not so much questioned why she was there as revelled in the joy of it. Now,
though, the questions ran round and round in his head.

'We are betrothed,' she'd said to him. That, too, he had
barely regarded, his mind focused on more immediate needs,
but it haunted him now, in this cell full of memories and too
much time to think. He'd hoped that with her marriage she
had forgotten him, moved on, as he had moved on. He would
not be a good husband to Tora Arnasson. If his wanderings
drove Elizaveta wild, they would kill the quiet Norwegian
woman.

His fingers went instinctively to the ring Elizaveta had sent
back. He'd been furious when Ulf had returned it with her
message. He had railed against her arrogance and denounced
her pride and vowed he would forget her and her damned
father besides and sail for Norway on the morrow. He'd
stormed through the war camp outside Syracuse, tearing strips
off his men and setting extra training for all and working himself

into a lather with swordplay until Halldor had calmly taken him aside and suggested he 'look at it from her point of view'.

Harald had thought him mad. He had little truck with other people's points of view. They were rarely as clear or as focused as his own and would only weaken him as a leader. This time, though, with Halldor fixing him in his funny, wizened stare and his men panting behind, he'd tried. Or, at least, he'd listened as Halldor elaborated it for him in his usual fancy way.

He'd seen how frustrating it must be for Elizaveta, shut up in Kiev never knowing when he would come for her and now, imprisoned in this damned cell, he understood it better than ever. It was not, though, Halldor's persuasive stories that had made him string the ring on a leather cord around his neck but just the very thought of her. He did not need to understand Elizaveta to want her. She nagged at his soul. She would make a terrible wife – Yaroslav had said as much at their betrothal – for she would be all rebellion and demands, but so was life.

'You're right,' he said out loud. 'It was my fault. I chose to stay and I was wrong.'

Ulf rose.

'It's good to hear you say so for once, Hari, but truly you were not to know that one of the plots was against *us*.'

'But I should have done, Ulf. I have a soldier's daring, not a politician's cunning, and now look where we are. We have to get out.'

'So you keep saying, but how?'

Harald kicked the wall again. This time it did not even yield a flake of stone, just sat there solid and uncaring. And now his toe hurt.

'Bribe the guards?' he tried.

'With what?' Ulf asked. 'Sexual favours?'

Harald shuddered.

'Promises,' he suggested. 'Halldor can do it; he's the word-smith. You could spin them a tale, Hal, surely – tell them what riches and honour will be bestowed upon them if they aid us to overcome the evil emperor?'

He looked to Halldor but his friend was up and pressed against the bars, straining forward.

'Looks like he's going to try biting his way out,' Ulf laughed but Halldor put up a hand.

'Hush a minute, you two – listen.'

'What is it, Hal?'

'Listen!'

Harald and Ulf moved up to stand at his side. Harald closed his eyes on the murky cell and the murkier corridor beyond and did as he was asked. Halldor was right – there were noises and not just the usual heckles of market, but shouting, cursing. And now he heard bells ringing out, clattering a wanton tune as if their ropes were pulled in haste – or desperation.

'Riot?'

'I think so,' Halldor agreed. 'It's been coming.'

Harald and Ulf turned on him.

'How do you know?'

'Because, unlike you two, I only speak when there's some-thing worth saying. The rest of the time I listen. The guards talk.'

'In Greek.'

'Which I have learned.'

'Really?' Harald looked at his old friend, impressed. Most of the nations they met with – Swedish, Danish, Rus, Norman, even English – spoke a form of Norse, developed differently but still recognisable as the same tongue. The Greeks, though, were different and their words sounded to Harald like the cackle of hens. 'When did you learn Greek, Hal?'

'Just picked it up. I like words.'

'As do I,' Harald objected.

'And I like meanings. They say that the new emperor has overreached himself. They say he plots against the great Empress Zoe herself.'

'Against the empress?' Harald asked, impressed again at Halldor's understanding. 'The people will not like that.'

'No indeed.'

Halldor's gaze flicked out of the bars again and now they could all hear the unmistakable chant of 'Zoe, Zoe, Zoe!' growing louder every minute. Whatever force was on the march out there, it was coming their way.

'Shout!' Halldor urged. 'Make those useless lungs of yours count for once.'

Ulf and Harald needed no second asking and the three men clung to their prison bars and yelled. No guards came and, encouraged, they yelled louder. Harald felt as if his chest might burst but there was no way he was being left to rot in this locked casket of a room. He would ten times rather crawl from a battlefield with a sword in his chest and his own blood pumping a path for him than waste ignominiously away unnoticed, especially if there was a riot to be had.

'Here!' Harald called. 'In here. Help!'

It probably sounded foolish but so what? He could hear the guards down the corridor now, panicking, begging for mercy in sharp, high-pitched cries that were cut off with a gurgle as someone's knife slit blood across their dying vocal cords.

'Pray whoever it is likes us,' Ulf muttered and then suddenly the corridor was filled with the rebels and, to the three men's huge astonishment, the foremost amongst them were women.

'Your harem, Harald?' Ulf asked drily.

'If only,' Harald threw back but now Halldor was talking to the women as one of them fumbled a big key into the lock.

'Sweet nothings, Halldor?' Ulf teased.

Halldor glared at him.

'I asked them why they're fighting,' he said.

'And?'

'They say everyone is fighting. The emperor has had Empress Zoe shorn and sent to a nunnery. It is too much, they say. Zoe has ruled Constantinople as consort for fourteen years; she cannot be cast aside. They say it is the duty of every woman in the Byzantine Empire to rise for her.'

Harald blinked but now the doors were wide and he cared not who had opened them. This was no time for debate but for action. He dived out into the golden city to find the mob ruling the streets. They surged between the houses, pushing down fences, cracking pavements and setting upon any official foolish enough to get in their way as they drove towards the vast imperial palace at the heart of the city like a wrecking tide. There was nothing golden about Miklegard tonight.

As Harald joined the throng he pictured the city as he had first seen it, rising up from the aquamarine of the Bosporus in a wondrous jumble of towers, spires and cupolas like a vast playground for the old gods. He remembered his awe at the open harbour, row upon row of jetties and every one clean and ordered and policed by officials in dazzling white tunics emblazoned with the imperial crest. He remembered the streets, wide enough for two wagons to pass and paved in stone ground smooth so no wheel caught.

He remembered being shown into the palace complex, a succession of buildings, each one larger than the last, that seemed to have been carved from giant blocks of marble and dipped in gold. He remembered the mechanical tree at the heart of the complex that moved by hidden pulleys and cogs and in which metal birds of all colours somehow sang songs sweeter than their real fellows outside. And he remembered the imperial rooms, decorated in the rich purple that gave the great dynasty their title – Porphyrogenita.

Harald saw now, though, cut dark across the faces of the furious mob, how foolish he and his men had been to think they could challenge such a rule. Empress Zoe might be in her sixty-second year, she might have worked her way through more husbands than was natural in her desperate quest for an heir. She might keep poisoners in her retinue and sorcerers to keep her young. She might be mad as a monkey in season, but she was born in the purple and nothing could replace that. Not some Rus prince, self-styled as 'grand' and certainly not some jumped-up Varangian from way above the snowline with only a few ounces of royal blood.

'The empress!' Harald roared. 'We must protect the empress.'

Grabbing Ulf and Halldor he turned east, off the main avenue to the imperial gates and round the back to the Bucoleon Palace – the headquarters of the emperor's Varangian guard.

The three of them were greeted with delight. The men were in chaos, uncertain which side to take and needed a leader.

'No sides,' Harald ordered, blood surging round his body at the chance to act at last. 'We take no sides. We keep order and we keep Zoe safe. She is the lynchpin; let the rest play out as it will.'

It was a mantra they kept to through a long, dark night and it was Harald who was stood on the shore at dawn to see the Empress Zoe, rescued from her momentary exile, safely back to her people.

'Thank you, Varangian,' she said as he handed her personally into a chariot, as dignified in sack-cloth and with head shorn as she was in full imperial garb. 'I shall see you rewarded.'

But Harald did not want reward. Not now. Harald did not want this world of hot-headed factions; he had been insane to ever think he did.

'We must go home,' he told Ulf and Halldor as they followed close alongside the chariot, keeping the eager crowds back from their returning mistress.

'Home?' Halldor queried and Harald's heart ached as he was not used to it doing save when Elizaveta yanked at it.

'Home to Norway,' he elucidated. 'Though first to Kiev.'

'To claim your bride?'

Harald thought guiltily of Tora but dismissed the idea. She had married once; she could do so again. He would find her a good husband once he was king. Ulf should settle down. Yes, uncomplicated Ulf would do nicely for Tora and she would get more joy of him than of a man enslaved to a dark-haired Rus Princess.

'To claim Elizaveta, yes, and to warn Yaroslav.' Harald glanced warily around but no one could hear their words above the roars of the triumphant crowd. 'He cannot attack now. It would be like setting fire to dry hay. I shall ask the empress permission to leave as soon as I can.'

It was several days before he could secure an audience. Empress Zoe had been busy hanging traitors and the walls were strung with them as he was shown into the great purple chamber. The empress was reclining on a couch. Either her sorcerers had been at work or, more likely, her wigmakers for she had a full head of hair and wore a gown so sheer he could see every part of her aging body through it. He fell to his knees and made his request but Zoe eyed him coldly.

'You would leave me, Varangian? Leave *me*?'

'I would rather not but my duty is in Norway, Empress.'

'Your "duty" is wherever I say it is.'

She sat up, fangs bared, and fixed him in her viper's stare. He had to think fast.

'I have considered serving you not a duty, Empress, but a pleasure.'

She smiled then, a lazy smile.

'You are quick, Varangian. I like that. And strong. I hear men follow you – even the brigand Normans – and I like that too. I could raise you up, you know, if I chose.'

'You have already done me much honour, Empress.'

She rose and walked idly around him as he shifted helplessly on his knees before her. Then suddenly she leaned over his shoulder, her fake hair scraping across his face.

'I could marry you.'

'Empress?' Harald had never been more scared in his life.

'If I wanted,' she went on, her voice honey-sweet. '*You* would make babies on me, I am sure.'

Had Harald at that moment been asked to fight the whole Sicilian army single-handed he would have taken it as the easier option.

'Truly, Empress,' he managed, trying to keep his voice from shaking, 'I would consider myself dead and gone to God's very heavens to have such a chance but I am too lowly.'

For a moment he thought she would challenge him. He saw himself dragged into her bed with her sorcerers casting spells over her womb as he pounded useless seed into it and her poisoners waiting in the wings for him to fail. Is this what it had come to? Was this his punishment for keeping two women waiting? Was this the mystical female vengeance he'd seen in the eyes of the citizens who'd broken him from his prison?

Harald chided himself, head bowed, for ever thinking this imperial woman would embrace him as a son and begged God as he had never begged Him before, not even at Stikelstad, that she would not embrace him as a husband. But then, as if bored by it all, Zoe spun away.

'You are right. Your muscles are thick, Varangian, but your blood is thin and, besides, I have a husband planned.'

Harald dared to look up.

'I may go then, Empress?'

She laughed, a high-pitched rattle that shook her frame beneath the transparent gown.

'You may go from the palace, yes, but dare to leave Constantinople and I will have you caught and tied up and fed to my ladies piece by piece – heart last.'

'Ah.'

'I may be old, Harald Sigurdsson – yes, I know your name – but I am not stupid. Yaroslav is plotting and you and your friends are forever running back and forth to his little upstart of a city. You are a captain of my guard and you will stay a captain of my guard and be glad of it – will you not?'

There was only one thing to say – 'I will, Empress' – but he knew, despite her command, that his days here were numbered. Somehow he had to get out. That night he and Ulf and Halldor sat up until the North Star faded in the dawn and a week later, they were ready.

CHAPTER THIRTEEN

Kiev, June 1042

'It was the darkest hour of the night when we made our move.'

The nobles of Kiev were fixed on Halldor as he took up his favourite place at the front of Yaroslav's dais, arms stretched wide to draw the assembled company into the world of his tale. 'And yet!' Halldor raised his hand with his voice, these days polished in the Rus form of Norse. 'It is *never* dark in Miklegard. Oil lamps burn in the main streets to keep the thieves at bay and they cast beams like prison bars across the water. And that's exactly what they would have been for us had our ship been caught in them – prison bars. Nay, worse. The Empress Zoe is a hard woman; she does not like to be crossed.'

'Show me a woman who does,' someone called and Halldor smiled.

'You have it right, my friend, but few – luckily – have the power to order our deaths. Just days before our escape, the empress told Harald she would feed him to her ladies piece by piece. Heart last, she told him, so he would be alive to feel the pain of it for as long as possible, and I bet we all know which piece first . . .'

The company roared delight and at Elizaveta's side Harald shifted.

'Is that true?' she whispered to him.

'It's what she said,' Harald confirmed. 'Truly, Elizaveta, Empress Zoe makes *you* look meek.'

'Indeed? I shall have to improve then.'

He groaned.

'Please do not. You are quite frightening enough.'

'I'm delighted to hear it,' she said and was rewarded with a snatched kiss but now Halldor was off again.

'Jesting apart, good people, we would have been dead men if her guards had caught us. Harald and Ulf and myself would even now be hanging from Miklegard's great walls with seagulls feasting on our eyeballs and all our fifty-strong company with us. We *had* to succeed.

'We stole to the harbour via the back streets, our cloaks over our heads and our swords drawn against the vagabonds who lurk in the shadows. There are row upon row of jetties in Miklegard like you've never seen and ours, praise God, was in darkness. We took off our boots so as not to clatter on the wood and felt for the jetty's edge with our toes and the boat's blessed side with our fingers, like blind men seeking a woman. And, oh, my friends, she felt so good; better than any woman I've ever known . . . save one.'

Halldor paused and looked down to where Aksel was sat at his feet and ruffled the boy's head fondly. Now eight, Aksel was growing tall and strong and was already joining the older lads in martial training whenever he was allowed. He longed to impress his warrior father and several times Elizaveta had secretly watched him as he checked his new muscles in the looking-glass or strained to measure his height against the notches on the bower wall. He had not left Halldor's side since the men had ridden in at noon and Elizaveta felt her own feet strangely cold where he was usually wont to sit. She was pleased, though, to see her 'squire' so happy and Halldor was clearly revelling in his strong son's attention.

The *druzhina* held its breath as, for a moment, Halldor seemed lost, his eyes fixed on a ghost in the mid-distance, but then he snapped back into motion, the story with him.

'We could not raise the sail. It would signal our departure like a beacon, so we had to row, and we had to row quietly. We fifty hulking Varangians had to row as if we were nothing more than a fish rising for a fly – one fish. We had to row together – we're good at that – and we had to row delicately – we're not so good at that.' Halldor barely allowed the laugh before adding, 'But it's amazing what a man in fear of his life can master.

'It was a thankfully rough night and, with God's help, we crossed that harbour like a mere sigh of wind amongst the rest, with Harald on the steer-board guiding us between the probing lights. It was slow and I swear no man dared even breathe for fear of the bells ringing out and the harbour filling with the empress's men and the sleek warships being set on us, breathing Greek fire that would char us like hogs on a spit. That would . . .'

Halldor checked himself.

'No one came. We got past the reach of the lamps and skirted the harbour wall towards the exit. Ten boat lengths and we would be safe. Nine, eight . . . We could taste freedom on the salty air. And yet . . .'

He dropped suddenly off the dais, making Aksel visibly jump, and paced along the lines of diners either side of the hall.

'And yet, we had one more obstacle to cross – and our greatest. We were not safe. Indeed, we were in the most fearful danger yet. For the good harbour guards at Miklegard like to protect their precious trading vessels from the pirates who creep across the seas beyond. And they like, also, to keep their precious trading vessels in harbour until their dues are paid and that is why, my lords and ladies, there is a chain stretched across the entrance, right on the sea's surface.

'It is a chain thicker than a man's arm and it will snare the bows of any vessel that attempts to cross it and, like as not, snap her bow-strakes and let the greedy sea inside. There is little choice, then, but to leap from the deck and submit to the mercy of the guards and, believe me, Empress Zoe's men have *no* mercy.' He mounted the dais once more, an actor in his own Greek theatre. 'They consider it sport to shoot men in the water. They enjoy the artistic effect of red blood across the blue.'

'How though,' Ivan asked, 'would they see you in the darkness?'

Halldor leaned over and tweaked the Prince's cheek.

"'Tis the golden city, man, home of Greek fire. They have lamps so bright a single one could light up this whole hall. They do not normally kindle them at night so the pirates are kept in the dark but they *can*. Within moments they can be ablaze and then . . .'

He mimicked drawing back an arrow, and then staggered, as if he were his own victim. The crowd shifted uncomfortably.

'So how then,' Anne squeaked, stung into speaking out by the horror of the tale, 'did you escape?'

Halldor put a finger to the side of his squint nose.

'Cunning, Princess,' he said. 'Cunning and daring. As soon as we were close we put up the sail. The wind was brisk and it caught immediately, propelling us forward. We yanked in the oars and stood ready, every man focused. We could see the creaking chain in the moonlight, like a thousand silver teeth waiting to devour us. We had to time it exactly right. Ulf was up on the prow, arms wrapped around the dragon's neck to better judge the distance and, as we drew within a leg's space of the chain, he gave the command and we ran. We ran, all the rest of us, to Harald in the stern and as we did so, for we are not small men, the boat rose up, her bows lifting way above the water and the evil chain.

'And then, as fast as we had run to Harald, we turned and ran back to Ulf. For a moment, a terrible moment, the keel teetered on the great iron barrier and then the boat see-sawed down and the stern lifted and we were free, free of the empress, free of the mob and the bitter factions tearing Miklegard apart; free to live. We raised Prince Harald's glorious landwaster up the mast and flew home beneath his raven, like birds of the air ourselves – and here we are.'

He bowed suddenly as the courtiers rose to their feet cheering and clapping and Yaroslav came out to clasp his hand. Aksel leaped up and threw his arms around his father's thick waist and Halldor pulled him close, smiling in delight.

'You really did that?' Elizaveta asked Harald.

'We did. Halldor's stories are mainly truths, Elizaveta, I promise you, just with embellishments – like a golden trim on a plain gown.'

'Real tales with stronger detail?' she suggested, borrowing his own words. 'But how did you know it would work?'

'Ah!' Harald grimaced. 'We did not.'

'You had not tried it before?'

'Never.'

'But you have heard of others who have done so?'

'Not as such.'

'No one had done it before? Ever? Harald, are you mad?'

He leaned in and grabbed the hands she hadn't even realised she'd been waving.

'I wanted to get back to you.'

'That badly?'

'Yes, that badly. I have been away too long, Elizaveta. I was a fool and I bless you for waiting for me. I will make it worth your while, I promise.'

He kissed her, harder this time, and she felt herself melt like sealing wax in a candle. It had been hard, it was true. Anastasia had moved into her own quarters with Andrew and took precedence over Elizaveta at all meals. She had given birth to a daughter, Adelaide, and Ingrid fussed over her first grandchild in a way that sometimes made Elizaveta feel physically sick. She longed to make a home of her own, as Vladimir had done in Novgorod, but she was a woman and she needed Harald to make that possible. Nay, she just needed Harald.

'And how,' she found breath to tease, 'will you do that, my lord?'

'Marry me and you will find out.'

'I will.'

'Soon?'

'Very soon.'

'Tomorrow?'

'Done!' She glanced along the table. 'Well, maybe the next day. You know how Father likes his ceremony and it might kill Mother to arrange all that in one night.'

Harald smiled.

'The next day I can just about wait for.' He rose. 'I will put it to him.'

'Now?' Elizaveta gasped.

'Now. I am the hero of the hour, Lily!' He winked. 'The Grand Prince will surely not refuse me?'

Elizaveta shook her head, a strange thrill suffusing her body as Harald leaped the table and went on one knee before a very surprised Yaroslav.

'Grand Prince,' he said, his voice ringing around the hall.

'I have suffered much to return to you and I ask one boon – your daughter. I cannot live a moment longer without her as my wife.'

There was an ooh of delight from the women in the hall and, though Elizaveta looked modestly down, her body sang. She sneaked a look at Anastasia and was pleased to see her usual smug expression wiped from her fair face. Beyond her, Agatha was grinning wildly. Elizaveta's youngest sister was nearly thirteen now and had had her own share of proposals but she stuck steadfastly at Edward's side and, in her usual forthright way, had made it clear that she intended them to be wed. Elizaveta might be making it to the altar just in time not to be beaten by another of her sisters.

'In that case,' Yaroslav said, playing the crowd, 'we must have a wedding.' Cheers greeted this. 'We will have it one week hence.'

Harald looked back to Elizaveta and grimaced. She giggled.

''Tis only a week,' she mouthed.

''Tis a week too much,' he mouthed back and her body tingled.

'Yes,' Yaroslav said, putting out a hand for Ingrid who, as always, rushed to his side. 'A wedding, then a few days for you to . . . get to know each other.' Whoops of delight. 'And then we will sail.'

The crowd were still calling their approval but Elizaveta saw Harald stiffen and felt the noise fuzz around her.

'Sail?' he asked Yaroslav.

'Yes, for Miklegard. We cannot, I'm sure you will agree, afford to wait.'

Harald rose, one foot at a time. He looked stiff suddenly, almost old.

'Your Highness, we must talk about this.'

'Talk?'

157

Yaroslav's eyes narrowed and the delicious thrills around Elizaveta's body were instantly chased out by a shiver of cold dread. The mood had changed. Everyone knew it. Even the youngsters at the back of the hall had stilled and the sudden silence was suffocating.

'The situation in Miklegard is not as we thought,' Harald said. 'Not as it was.'

Yaroslav advanced on him and though he was two heads shorter than the Varangian he seemed to tower over him.

'Not as *we* thought?'

'Not as we *hoped*.'

'*We* hoped, Harald? *You* said Miklegard was cracking. *You* said she was weak. *You* said we could take her.'

'And it seemed true,' Harald protested. 'Nay, I thought it was true. We all did.'

He looked desperately to Halldor and Ulf who rose now and came to their leader's side, his supporters, his protectors. They were no use, though, against Yaroslav's rising anger.

'And what then, pray, *is* the situation in Miklegard?'

'Unsettled,' Harald managed. 'The emperor is dead and there is not yet a new one.'

'Then,' Yaroslav snapped, his voice a whip-crack, 'we must move now. Your wedding can wait.'

'No!' Elizaveta cried and then smothered it in a napkin.

This mission was so important to Yaroslav. More than that, it was driving him and had been for months. He had taken Elizaveta to see the fleet, a magnificent group of ships that must have cost half his silver to build. He had called Vladimir back from Novgorod and spent hours with the boy – now a man and as eager for the glory of this bold plan as his father – plotting their every move. He had even employed the greatest minds in all Rus and beyond to find a coating for the ships that would repel the legendary Greek fire. The project had consumed him and he would not let it go. *Should* not let it go. She looked angrily at Harald. Why was he so scared? He had escaped Miklegard a fugitive, so surely he must seize the chance to return a victor?

'It is not just the emperor, though, Sire,' Harald was protesting. 'There is the empress too.'

'The empress!' Yaroslav scoffed. 'You are afeared for your manhood, Harald?'

The *druzhina* laughed but it was a terse, nervous sound.

'Your Highness,' Elizaveta heard Harald urge, his voice low, 'please can we discuss this in private. It is complicated. I would not wish you to send your beautiful ships into destruction.'

Yaroslav's eyes narrowed further, like slits in a full-face helmet.

'You doubt my fleet?'

'No, Grand Prince. No, I . . .'

'You doubt my son, perhaps?'

He gestured to Vladimir who came forward, flanking his father as Ulf and Halldor flanked Harald.

'I doubt him not,' Harald insisted.

The Rus nobility were edging forward, eager to hear, and Elizaveta saw Ulf and Halldor square their shoulders and glance to their company, as if readying to fight. No swords were allowed in the great hall but these men of Harald's, these strange, wild, fiercely loyal men, had hands as deadly as blades wielded by others. Were they threatening her father? How dare they?

Elizaveta rose too. Her mother waved her frantically down but she was a part of this and she would not stand back and let her future husband, her oh-so-glorious hero of a future husband, destroy all of Yaroslav's plans.

'Harald,' she said and all eyes swung her way. 'Explain yourself. You say Miklegard is weak, leaderless, so why . . .'

159

'Not leaderless,' Harald broke in. She bristled and he made a visible effort to check his tone. 'They have the empress.'

'But she is a woman and an old one besides – and mad, too, or so they say.'

'Perhaps, but she was born in the purple.'

'This all turns on the colour of the empress's bedhangings?'

'Yes!' Harald's voice broke across the listeners, sharp as a slap, and Elizaveta flinched back. 'Yes,' he repeated, more quietly but her anger was rising now.

'You do not wish to attack?' she asked icily.

'I don't consider it wise to attack, no. The people of Miklegard . . .'

'The people?' Elizaveta spluttered. 'So now we are to cut our plans to account for the common will?'

'Miklegard is a vast, cosmopolitan city, Lily.'

'And Kiev is not?'

'Miklegard is different. You would not understand, you . . .'

But Elizaveta had heard enough. Years she had waited for this man. Years she had dreamed of him and planned for him and yearned for him. Years she had believed in him but it turned out that he was not the man she'd thought.

'Oh I understand, Harald,' she said. 'I understand very well. You are but a storyteller's hero, all transitory adventure and tiny, petty, personal triumphs. You sail alone. You and your precious pair of bodyguards and your ship full of bachelor soldiers. This country, my father's country, has sheltered you and nurtured you and kept your precious treasure – *I* have kept your precious treasure – but when we ask you for just a little in return, you refuse us.'

'Elizaveta, that's not true. I seek only to protect Kiev.'

'No, Harald – you seek only to protect yourself. Here.'

She unclipped the great neck chain that she had taken from its casket before dinner with such pride. It was thick with keys and charms now, worth more than most men, nay, than most lords, would see in their lifetime and she had felt honoured to wear it. Now, though, she despised it.

'Take it!' She thrust it into his hand. 'Take it and take your precious men and go. Go north to Novgorod and release your damned treasure and return to Norway where you belong – where you have always belonged.'

She felt the weight of the *druzhina*'s eager stares and knew the bowers would be a-buzz with this tomorrow. She caught sight of Anne, frozen in horror at the argument, and Agatha's kind eyes swimming with sympathy, but looked away before she could catch Anastasia's inevitable triumph. Even that, though, felt right; she had been seduced by Harald as surely as Yaroslav had and she must pay.

'We will attack Miklegard without you,' she told him.

'No! No, please.' Harald looked to Yaroslav. 'The golden city is as closed off in its mind as it is by its walls. No one will welcome you, not the fleet, not the empress and not a single man, woman or child. You would have to kill them all.'

'Then,' Yaroslav said, stepping over to Elizaveta and putting an arm around her shoulders, the solid weight of it making her realise how she was quivering, 'maybe that is what we will do. It is no concern of yours now, Harald. As my daughter says, you should leave.'

Harald looked from one to the other. He turned and let his eyes roam the vast room. Ulf and Halldor pressed close to his side and suddenly Elizaveta hated them. They would take him away from her. Already her anger was cooling, leaving her clammy and nauseous.

'I love him,' she'd told Ulf. Had they laughed at that? Had they gloried in another of his conquests?

Slowly Harald nodded.

'If that is your wish, Grand Prince, though I sorrow in it.

I shall go to Norway and if I am such an empty hero to you, Elizaveta, I shall find a wife elsewhere. Good night and good luck.'

And with that he swept a clipped bow to Yaroslav and leaped from the dais, Ulf and Halldor swift at his heels and Aksel only a heartbeat behind them. Briefly the boy glanced back at Elizaveta, sorrow in his young eyes, but at the clack of the soldiers' boots across the marble floor, he turned and was gone.

The hall sat, frozen, as outside the Varangians called for their horses. They all listened as the gates cranked open, their chains creaking as Halldor's had done in his story barely a candle's mark past and then, in a riot of hooves and shouts, they were gone. Harald was gone and Elizaveta was alone.

CHAPTER FOURTEEN

Novgorod, January 1043

'More ale!'

'More? Any more, Harald, and you'll drown.'

'More ale! Aksel!'

Harald waved his tankard at the boy who rushed forward with an apologetic look at his father.

'Let him,' Halldor sighed. 'Perhaps a sore head will bring him to his senses.'

'Who needs senses?' Harald drawled. 'Who needs feelings?'

'Ah!' Ulf clapped his leader on the back. 'Now we get to the heart of it.'

'Don't talk of hearts.' Harald sensed as much as saw his old friends rolling their eyes over his head. 'And don't laugh at me.'

'We're not laughing, my lord. We are simply wondering how much more of your hard-won treasure you intend to pour into a tankard and out of your own foul bowels before we can set sail. We have a fleet. We have men.'

'It's winter.'

'Not the best time to sail, I grant you, but the Varangian Sea never freezes and at least this way we might surprise them. If we sail now we can be in Norway within a week and paying good King Magnus a nice surprise visit in his winter residence. If the messengers are to be believed, King Harthacnut is dead. England has passed to Edward, Ethelred's son, but Denmark has gone to Magnus. That's another kingdom handed to him on a plate and it's not right. Let him cede Norway to you and go and relax in the fertile Danish lowlands. You said yourself that Finn Arnasson has paved the way for a peaceful entry and the men are ready just in case he is proved wrong. There is no farming to be done, and no trading either. 'Tis the perfect time to sail.'

'It's not right.'

'What?'

Harald looked up.

'I said it's not right.'

'Sailing to Norway?'

'No! I mean, yes – *that's* right. What's not right is sailing alone.'

'You are not alone, Harald. We have five hundred men. We have . . .'

Halldor clamped a hand over Ulf's mouth.

'Go and check on them, Ulf.'

Ulf looked startled.

'Check on the men? Why?'

'Because if they are as ready as you say – and I believe they are – they will be restless, troublesome. See they are not bothering the good citizens of Novgorod, will you? And take Aksel – it's time he had his first street brawl.'

Ulf sighed but rose.

'Fine, fine. We'll leave you two to cosy up. Come on Aksel, lad, let's go and crash some skulls together.'

Aksel leaped up eagerly and followed Ulf from the tavern. Halldor settled himself on the bench at Harald's side.

'It's her, isn't it – Elizaveta?'

Harald drank. He didn't talk about women; no man did – or should. All autumn he had busied himself with trading treasure, commissioning boats, mustering men. All autumn he'd turned his blonde head determinedly north but the first snows had crept under his skin and suddenly it all felt wrong.

He'd read Finn's letters again and again and even written to say he was sailing in the New Year. Finn had assured him that Magnus was ready to 'welcome his dear uncle' and though he doubted that was true, he had also sent letters to Ingrid's brother, King Anund of Sweden, to be sure of safe housing there until the way was clear into his homelands. Ulf was right – Magnus had Denmark now and he was sure the boy would eventually make at least a pretence at settlement and he could move forward from there.

He'd lain awake trying desperately to picture Tora naked beneath her cloak but every single time an image of Elizaveta spitting fury at him in front of all Kiev had intruded and proved many times more erotic. Elizaveta wouldn't be just a wife but a partner and he'd wondered time and again how he'd let some stupid, ill-thought-out public argument rob him of all that. He drank again.

Halldor drank too but then he said: 'When Elsa died I wanted to take my dagger and plunge it into my own heart.'

Harald looked at him, shocked.

'But that's . . .'

'A sin?'

'Not that so much as . . .'

'Cowardly? Inglorious? I know. I hated myself for it but I hated the world without her in it more. And I might have done it too if it hadn't been for Aksel.'

Harald rubbed at his eyes as if he might be dreaming.

'Truly, Hal?'

'Pathetic?'

'Pathetic.'

Both men drank again. Neither spoke until eventually Halldor added: 'I still think of her, Harald. Every single day I think of her and it may be pathetic but I can't help it and in a funny way it keeps me going. I think, maybe, some women are just special. Elsa was one and it seems to me that Elizaveta is another.'

Harald rounded on him.

'I have a betrothed in Norway.'

'I know. You are a greedy man, Harald Sigurdsson, but I do not see you setting the sails to get to *her*. Instead we're all kicking our frozen heels in Novgorod waiting for you to get up the balls to go back to Kiev and apologise.'

'You think that's why we wait?'

'Do you not?'

'No! There's the ice and the troops and the . . .' Even drunk Harald heard how useless his excuses sounded – how pathetic. 'She won't have me,' he bit out instead.

'Maybe not.'

'She hates me.'

'It's a good sign.'

'This isn't a story, Hal.'

'Of course it is. It's *your* story, Harald, so you should write it the way you want it. Her father's fleet sailed for Miklegard and it was a disaster. They limped home just as you said they would and the young Prince Vladimir barely escaped with his life. Elizaveta will know now that you are not a coward, but a wise general.'

'Wise? Come now, Halldor.'

'You're right. I get carried away with words. Moderately sensible – is that an improvement?'

Harald clapped his friend on the back.

'I think maybe, Hal, *you* are the wise one. You think she might have me still?'

'I think it's worth a chance and, besides, if she does not, you have your spare in Norway.'

Harald pulled a face at his crinkled friend and drank again, trying desperately to disguise the smile creeping across his face. Could he ride?

'You crossed the chain at Miklegard,' Halldor's voice whispered into his ear. 'You fried pirates on the Greek sea. You braved the empress in her lair and came out alive. Surely you can ask a girl to forgive you?'

Surely he could, Harald thought, but it seemed far harder than anything he'd done before.

CHAPTER FIFTEEN

Podol, Kiev, January 1043

*E*lizaveta felt the rush of heat across her face as, with an animal roar, the men of Kiev flung their torches into the great galley ship set on the thick ice of the Dnieper and it flared proudly. The flames balled briefly in the very centre of the old vessel before licking out along the rowing benches and dancing along the gunwales towards the great dragon head high up on the prow. The crowd in the crazy streets of the Podol cheered madly and Elizaveta, stood in the royal grandstand with Anne and Agatha, felt as warmed by their joy as by the heat.

'This bit makes me sad,' a voice said behind her.

She turned to Jakob, the master boatbuilder who was honoured as part of the royal party at this special fire festival, and smiled.

'The ship was old, Jakob.'

'But beautiful.'

'They all are, and you will build more.'

Jakob sighed a harsh, rasping sigh.

'I built many last year, Princess, just to send them to the bottom of the Greek sea with your brother, God bless him.'

'Vladimir did not sink, Jakob,' Elizaveta said sternly, looking for her father who, thankfully, was absorbed in the fire as the ice cracked beneath the ship and it shifted, keen to be off on its final journey.

Her pagan ancestors, not so many years back, had believed they were sending it to Valhalla to win favour for the year's trading and raiding ahead and she was sure many of the wide-eyed watchers in the Podol still clung to that belief. Many young men were making dangerous runs across the melting ice to fling gifts – rings, horseshoes, gowns, drinking cups, all the symbols of their individual trades – into the flames. They did it more to impress the young women of Kiev than any lingering gods, but the superstitions were still strong beneath the whole ceremony. It was the sort of night, were they in the northern lands of their forefathers, when the trolls would be roaming free.

Elizaveta shivered, despite the heat of the blaze. Would Harald be celebrating the winter fire festival in Norway? Would he be watching his own galley burn, no longer needed now he was secure at home, with King Magnus on one side and his blonde Norwegian wife on the other?

'Don't think of it,' she told herself, as she had done all winter.

Her family had been very kind in the wake of Harald's dramatic departure. Agatha and Edward had taken her out riding, driving the horses hard to force her mind off her troubles. Anne had brought her a book of prayers, beautifully inscribed 'for my courageous sister' in her own golden lettering, and even Anastasia had seemed genuinely concerned, though perhaps it was just jealousy at her dramatically tragic status.

Ingrid had secured the services of a talented viol player from Bavaria to help her develop her music and it had been a blessed distraction. Yaroslav had bought her jewels and taken her on a tour of the ever-growing Snake Ramparts and then, at Christ's mass, invited a dozen eligible young counts and princes from neighbouring tribute-lands to pay her court. It had not gone well. Elizaveta had tried her best to be polite but, truly, they had all been simpering idiots compared to . . .

'Don't think of it,' she told herself again.

Vladimir, home from the terrible expedition to Miklegard, had returned to Novgorod where he had married the daughter of the previous count. Ivan was betrothed to a princess of Miklegard, as part of the prolonged peace negotiations following their defeat, and Yaroslav had finally given in to Agatha's determined entreaties and offered her to Edward. The earnest prince, now into his thirties, had been delighted but embarrassed, repeating what he had oft told Elizaveta – that he had little chance of ever paying his exuberant benefactor back. Agatha, however, had pronounced firmly that her happiness was all the thanks Yaroslav needed and the wedding was set for next year when she turned fifteen.

In the meantime, an ambassador from no less a court than France had been dancing attendance on Anne, looking for a wife for the widowed Henry I, and it felt to Elizaveta as if all of Yaroslav's older children were doing their part in extending his web of influence, save her. It hurt, though not enough to encourage the pale-livered princes on offer.

'In the spring, Elizaveta,' Yaroslav had told her on Twelfth Night, barely curbing his rising impatience, 'we will choose a husband. If *you* cannot then *I* will – and you will accept my choice graciously. You are twenty-four, daughter, and we must marry you before your womb shrivels and no one wants you at all.'

He was right of course, but as Elizaveta watched the flames grasp the neck of the great dragon-prow she felt sudden sympathy for the poor ship. She had loved Harald. Recklessly and foolishly she had loved him, and that love had burned her as the dragon-ship was burning now.

She watched sadly as with a strange, sucking sound the last of the ice around the ship melted away and it bobbed on its self-created pond. Soon its charring strakes would split apart and it would sink beneath the surface where, before morning, a thin crust would already have formed over any floating remains, trapping them until the spring thaws sent them spinning south.

To the left of the grandstand an impromptu band had struck up. Elizaveta spotted her viol teacher at the heart of them and looked for the tug of the music inside her but it did not come and she stood sombrely at Jakob's side, the two of them fixed on the sinking vessel as the rest of Kiev began to dance. Then, suddenly, a call ripped through the crowd from the people furthest upriver.

'A spirit!'

'A spirit from Valhalla, come to claim his ship!'

'Nonsense,' Yaroslav said quickly but he, like the rest, moved forward to look up the Dnieper where many fingers were now pointing and from where, over the crackle of the flames, the night air was filled with the sound of spiked hooves pounding the ice. Into view came a horseman, riding up in the stirrups of a huge stallion, wearing a scarlet cloak and a helmet fixed with ceremonial wings on either side. He did, indeed, look like some warrior spirit as he took the bend in the solid river and bore down on the ship.

'Who is he?' the crowd asked each other, delighted.

'He's a dead man if he rides any closer to the ship.'

'Spirits cannot die!'

All eyes watched as the figure galloped alongside the galley, a huge, dark shape against the orange glare, his mount's hooves seeming to skim the dangerously thin ice. Then, just as it looked as if he would pass on down the dark Dnieper, he flung himself from the horse and landed square on the dragon's head so that the insistent flames reached eagerly up to devour his boots. The crowd gasped and pressed forward as the man – if man it was – held up an arm.

'I am here to die with this ship,' he proclaimed. 'To die for my sins against this glorious nation of the Rus, as I justly deserve.'

'No!' the crowd protested.

He silenced them with a hand.

'Only one thing can save me . . . the love of a woman.'

The crowd ooh-ed, delighted at this living story.

'What woman?' they called, volunteers already squirming keenly to the front.

'The Princess Elizaveta,' came the reply, then the heroic figure swept the helmet from his head and a curtain of ice-blonde hair fell over his scarlet cloak.

'Harald!'

Elizaveta could hardly believe it and didn't know whether to berate him as a fool or embrace him as her hero. The crowd, however, were in no doubt and all looked keenly to Yaroslav to release their 'spirit' from his hellish flames.

'You abandoned us, Harald,' Yaroslav called across the river.

'I know it, though I did so with all honest intentions. You have seen, I hope, that I advised you out of my small warrior's wisdom and not pride or cowardice?'

The flames were eating into the dragon's neck now and Harald climbed a little higher, clutching at the beast's carved ears as the crowd clutched at each other.

'I will make reparation, Grand Prince,' Harald went on. 'I will make your beautiful daughter Queen of Norway and then of Denmark and of England too. Together, Yaroslav, we will rule the north, I swear it, but I must have Elizaveta as my queen. I beg this of you.'

The ship creaked. The fire at the centre had burned through the base and now one side splintered, sending the whole vessel rocking. Within minutes it would fold in on itself, dragging the prince into the inferno and down to death in the Dnieper.

'Grant it!' the crowd begged their own prince.

Elizaveta saw Yaroslav's eyes flicker across the dying ship and knew that, as much a showman as Harald, he was judging the time he had left.

'You will treat her with all honour?' he demanded as, with a shriek of tearing wood, the mast fell, slamming into the ice and sending the ship tipping wildly.

'I will,' Harald called and now Elizaveta caught real panic in his voice.

'Serve him right,' she muttered, 'for his damned hero tricks,' but her heart was in her mouth and she stepped up to take Yaroslav's arm.

'You consent, daughter?' her father asked her, one eye on the ship.

'I consent,' she agreed, as loudly as she could.

'Then, Prince Harald,' Yaroslav called, 'come and claim your bride.'

Harald stilled, bowed his head a moment, and then leaped from the dragon. He landed on the ice with a thud and skidded towards the bank where eager hands waited to lift him clear just as the ship burst. The dragon's head seemed for a moment to rear up before collapsing backwards into the flames as the water frothed around them. Elizaveta put a hand to her chest to keep her heart within, for it was beating like a blacksmith's hammer against the anvil of her bones. Now, though, Harald was being brought before her, lifted onto the grandstand on the shoulders of the people of Kiev and her sisters were pushing her keenly forward. She must compose herself.

'A grand entrance, Harald,' she said drily as he knelt before her.

He looked up through his curtain of hair, the golden flecks sparkling in his soft grey eyes.

'I wanted to impress you.'

'By singeing your boots?'

'And I wanted to make it hard for you to say no.'

She shook her head.

'You certainly did that, but Harald . . .' She put out a hand and raised him so his great body was against hers. 'Even had you crept in on a donkey I would not have said no.'

He kissed her hand and the crowd whooped.

'I am unendingly glad to hear it – but your father might have.'

Elizaveta saw the sense of it; this crazy charade had offered Yaroslav a chance to climb down with honour, even with a flourish. And yet . . .

'Why did you come back, Harald?' she whispered.

He wrapped her hand in his and pressed it to his chest.

'Because, Elizaveta, fool that I am, it seems . . . it seems I love you.' He blushed and stumbled on quickly. 'And I heard tell that maybe you loved me too?'

'Maybe. Though you hurt me, Hari.'

'I know it and I regret it more than the loss of a thousand ships. I won't do it again. Let me show you . . .'

Harald pulled his eating knife from his belt and held it to his throat. The crowd, drunk on the continuing action before them, gasped but Harald simply slit the leather cord around his neck and released the rich ring Elizaveta had returned to him.

'May I?'

He took her hand again and, before everyone, slipped the glorious ring onto her finger. The crowd cheered and cheered.

'Tomorrow,' Yaroslav said sternly. 'Tomorrow in the Hagia Sophia, you will be wed.'

'Before my womb dries up?' Elizaveta dared to ask him and his eyes narrowed.

'See it stays safe until then, daughter,' he instructed and turned to lead Ingrid into the first dance as the fire festival reluctantly let go of its impromptu interruption and resumed its usual festivities.

'Yes, Father,' Elizaveta murmured to his back but there was no way she was waiting any longer.

'Come,' she said, taking Harald's hand to lead him from the grandstand.

'Now?' he asked, eyes darkening to the colour of the bubbling Dnieper.

'Now.'

Elizaveta led him to Jakob's workshop, unlocking the huge doors with the key the boatbuilder had ordered cut so she could enter whenever she wished to look at the eagle-prow he was working on for her. Holding Harald's hand tight she drew him round a half-built trading ship, through the rack of sweet-smelling wood waiting to fulfil its destiny beneath the axe, and up the ladder to the loft above. Here Jakob kept his tools, his carvings and his experiments; here, Elizaveta's eagle was taking shape beneath the rafters; and here Jakob had a soft feather bed for the nights he worked too late with his beloved boats to go home to his wife.

'You're sure?' Harald asked but in answer she just pulled him down beside her and kissed him and then they were tearing at each other's clothes as if the boat were still burning beneath them.

Elizaveta felt his hands all over her body and in her turn explored his, seeking out the scars with her fingertips, her mouth locked onto his and her every sense singing. She could smell a glorious mingling of fresh wood, sweat, and smoke, and the softness of Jakob's bed beneath her contrasted deliciously with the hard body of the man she had not dared to believe would return.

'I want you,' she murmured, pulling him up and over her. 'I want you now.'

He held himself there for a moment, looking down on her, teasing her.

'Now?'

'Right now, or you ride north alone.'

'Never.'

He dipped and ran soft kisses down her neck and between her breasts until she arched up to meet them and then, slowly and deliberately, he entered her. There was a sharp pain and then a wonderful, overwhelming rush of sensation.

'Yes,' Elizaveta muttered, clutching him deeper inside. 'Yes, Harald. Please.'

'It does not hurt you?' he asked, pausing.

'Only when you stop.'

Harald smiled at that and began moving again, filling her with the sort of rush of feeling she'd been craving for so long. He paused again, kissed her, then suddenly rolled over, pulling her with him so that, still locked together, she was straddling him.

'Harald!'

'Your turn, my sweet.'

'Really?'

'Try it.'

So she did, moving slowly at first but then picking up pace as the sensations swelled inside. She was riding the rapids again, her body surging with adrenaline, feeling the rush of the wind and the power of the water beneath her except that this was no cold river but Harald, her Harald, and she rode him high until, with a cry of pleasure, the water took her and she knew herself to be exactly, completely, and gloriously where she ought to be.

CHAPTER SIXTEEN

Austratt, February 1043

'Harald will sail for Norway.'

'I know,' Tora agreed, trying to sound composed. 'You told me. In the New Year you said and now it is New Year. Indeed, it's been a new year for so long now I'd say it is barely new at all.'

'True,' Finn conceded.

He sounded odd and when Tora looked up from her embroidery she saw he was twisting his hands together like an old woman considering a knot in her loom.

'Is something wrong, Uncle?'

'Something is . . . different.'

Finn did not make 'different' sound enticing. Indeed, in Tora's experience, different was rarely enticing; it was so unreliable.

'But Harald is still coming?' she probed.

'So his letters say, yes. He plans to land in Sweden and cross the Kjolen mountains down to Nidaros.'

'Good. We can be there, then, to welcome him.'

'We can. Him and . . .'

'And what, Uncle?' Tora demanded impatiently, shoving her needle into the linen pattern and rising.

Finn took a visible breath.

'Him – and his wife.'

Tora's world spun. The half-woven pattern on the loom danced before her eyes. The needlework dropped from her fingers and the fire in the brazier seemed to rise up before her. She'd thought news of this magnitude would have reached her. Nay, she'd thought such news was impossible; thought he was hers.

'The Rus princess?' she forced out. Finn's bowed head was all the answer she needed. 'How could he?'

'He writes it was a political imperative,' Finn said, babbling now. 'He writes he was bound to the Grand Prince. He writes that he still honours our family above all others in Norway.'

'Damn our family.'

'Tora!'

'He promised himself to me, Uncle.'

'Then you married another.'

She flinched. It seemed so cruel that her marriage to Pieter, such a paltry aside to her life, might rob her of the one man she'd ever truly wanted.

'That was not my choice,' she snapped.

'I made that match for you in good faith and you know it. Besides, this can still work, sweetheart, I promise you. He says he will see you wed with great dignity to . . .'

'He will see me wed to no man,' Tora snarled, 'save himself.'

'Tora . . .'

'And you, Uncle, will support me in that, I am sure.'

She could hear herself, low and menacing. Anyone listening outside the doors would think there was a stranger within and maybe there was. Everything Tora had thought she stood for, had thought she lived for, seemed to have been pulled away from her. Did Harald think she was so meek as to just accept this? To marry his substitute groom with smiles of gratitude and support him in his bid to put another woman on the throne?

Well, he was wrong. For many, many years Tora's only real purpose in life had been to marry Harald Sigurdsson and she would not be denied it now. Let him come and his Slav bride with him; the wretched woman would soon see who held the strings in Norway.

PART TWO

CHAPTER SEVENTEEN

The Bay of Malaren, September 1045

The wind grabbed viciously at Elizaveta's hair and threw salt into her eyes, heedless of the hot tears already blinding them. She huddled lower into her sleeping sack, more like a slug than a queen, and prayed for this merciless journey to be over. For so many years she had dreamed of sailing over the Varangian Sea, imagining herself stood at the prow facing the glorious waves, but the reality had turned dark and wet and bitter and now she cursed her naivety. This was not some Rus river trip but a tough, cold battle against the open ocean. She clutched at her belly, swollen with Harald's precious child, and prayed for land.

Two seasons in a row they had been ready to sail and two seasons in a row the wild men of the North Rus had attacked Novgorod and Harald's troops had been forced to assist Prince Vladimir in seeing them back into the forests. Elizaveta's grateful brother had paid well and there had been much booty besides but it had seemed to Elizaveta that they were in danger of sinking under the weight of these war profits if they did not sail soon.

There had been only one benefit of the delays – the chance to attend Agatha's wedding to Edward, a day that had touched her heart. She had grown so used to her littlest sister following the quiet English prince around Kiev that it had been strange to see them stood side by side as man and wife, but right too. Now the bridal pair had departed for Hungary with Andrew, Anastasia and baby Adelaide for rebellion was rising in Andrew's homeland and emissaries had ridden into Kiev asking for him to return to lead them. Edward had offered Andrew his sword, saying he was sick of waiting for a summons from England that he knew would never come, and the two couples had ridden west together.

Ivan had also left Kiev to serve the emperor, his new father-in-law, in the Greek seas and Stefan had been sent to the growing city of Chernigov to control their father's eastern borders. Yaroslav's children were spreading out across the known world, just as he had always intended, and as Elizaveta had prepared to sail for Norway the thought had both terrified and excited her. She had made her sisters, even Anastasia, promise to write and had stocked up on vellum of her own but there had been no chance to send a message whilst in the grip of the relentless sea.

At first they had sailed west, tracking the southern shore of the barren lands of the Fins and all had seemed well, but earlier today they had struck out into the open sea towards Sweden and a sudden storm had crashed in on them, roaring menace. Now, although the sun should be reaching its highest point, it was darker than night, a strange green gloom that crept into Elizaveta's heart like a weed. She pushed back against the side of the ship and watched, mesmerised, as wave after wave rose over them. Every one looked as if it must surely suck them all under, before the brave little vessel crested each foaming top, the crew hanging onto their oars as if the thin wood might grow feathers and fly them to safety.

At Elizaveta's side, Greta was on her knees, praying to the

louring skies, her near-blue lips muttering supplications over and over, her dress dark from the relentless spray and her hair whipping around her face like a pirate's lash. Elizaveta felt for her. Hedda had offered the services of her daughter, Greta, now fourteen, as a wedding gift and Elizaveta, touched, had gratefully accepted the girl as her maid. In Novgorod she had proved herself a quick learner and had been a great comfort in Elizaveta's two previous pregnancies, both of which had come to nought.

Elizaveta's heart twisted at the remembrance of those losses and she pushed her hands even further around her belly, as if she could keep this baby inside by force of will. She could feel cramps and a dull ache in her back and knew, from too many times with her mother, what that might mean.

'It cannot,' she shouted, her words being sucked up into another giant wave as all around the men fought to turn the spinning craft head-on to avoid destruction. 'I *cannot* lose another.'

She looked for Harald but he was at the steer-board with Ulf, his muscles tense through his soaked tunic as he battled the ocean. She sucked in her breath as another pain came; there was no doubting it now. Both times before she had bled so early as to have barely even dared to hope the seed had taken in her womb. This time, though, the babe had quickened and her belly had gently swollen and she had set sail so confident of taking Norway not just a new king but an heir besides. It seemed that the Varangian Sea, however, had other plans and if it were not base superstition, Elizaveta would almost dare to think the old gods of the north were playing with her.

'My lady?' Greta put a hand on her shoulder, leaned close. 'My lady, do not be afeared. God will see us safe to shore.'

Elizaveta tried to smile to bolster her poor maid's simple faith, but at that moment, just as they were cresting a wave, another came from sideways on, curving across the first and catching the boat in a vicious surge. It slewed sideways, like a cart on ice, and shot to the ocean valley, landing with a crash that sent its helpless sailors tumbling. Elizaveta, trapped in her sleeping bag, could not grasp a hold in time and was flung against the mast. Pain knifed through her and she jerked in on herself.

'My lady!'

Greta's scream was loud enough to pierce even the roar of the next wave and suddenly men were crowding around them. Elizaveta sought amongst the faces for Harald and saw him fighting to her side, white hair shining even amid this blonde Viking crew.

'I am losing him, Hari.'

For a moment his face clenched with pain, as if a sword had run through his guts, but he forced it aside, muttering love as he pulled her up and out of the treacherous bag in one easy movement. She saw the blood as he did, as they all did. It ran down her skirts and across the deck, mixing with the frothing churn of the ocean.

'Hold the mast.'

She did as he asked, clutching at the straining wood as Greta, her young eyes set hard, stood the other side and pressed her forehead against Elizaveta's.

'You must push, my lady.'

Elizaveta nodded and gritted her teeth to try, but her body knew it already. She could feel the muscles digging in as tight as she dug into the mast. The boat rocked and tipped, the men at the oars roared with effort, the clouds swirled so close they could almost touch them, and the simple expulsion of a womb seemed ridiculously small at the heart of all that action. Elizaveta felt a strange pulse within and then the sickening slap of flesh against her bare ankle. Somewhere she heard Harald let out a single, shattering cry and then all went black.

'Broth, Lily?'

Elizaveta blinked awake to see Harald crouched at her side holding out a leather cup of rough soup. It smelled salty – everything smelled salty – but meaty too, and it was warm. Tentatively she released her hands from the sleeping sack and cupped them around it. The heat seeped into her wizened fingers and she drew in a ragged breath.

'How . . . ?' she asked.

''Tis calm enough now to set a fire.'

Harald indicated the far end of the ship and, squinting through the squall, Elizaveta saw low flames glowing in a metal pit which squatted on the deck like a hot-bellied beast. Over it, dangling from a tripod, hung a big cooking pot, the steam escaping defiantly into the cold sea air.

'Drink it, Lily,' Harald urged. 'Halldor made it specially. It will do you good.'

Elizaveta resisted the instinctive response that nothing would do her good. She risked a look around. The boat was battered but intact. The waves no longer topped its sides and the clouds had cleared. She saw Halldor at the fire, eleven-year-old Aksel at his side. She saw Ulf still at the steer-board and Greta crouched at her feet. They were all here, all alive, and somehow she was alive too. She had to be strong for Harald. She had asked to come on this great journey – asked and asked – and she must not complain. But, oh, her belly ached and her heart ached even more.

'Good news,' Harald was saying, watching eagerly as she took sips of the broth. 'We have sighted land.'

'Truly?' She sat up a little. 'Where?'

'To the west, praise God, or the navigators would have done

a very poor job. The land birds are circling and the water is
paler – we are close, Lily.'

'Close to Norway?'

'Sweden first, remember – your mother's land.'

A thrill ran through Elizaveta at the thought and she handed
the broth back to Harald so she could ease herself out of the
sleeping sack. Her legs felt shaky and her body ached all over
but there was no pain and, praise God, no blood, save that
dried onto her dress. It was a mess; the green wool as creased
as an ancient's neck and stained with salt and dried blood. She
shivered with distaste.

'I must change,' she said, pressing her feet more firmly into
the sturdy wooden boards. If the ocean had not drowned her
she would not let grief do so either.

'Change, Lily? Here?'

'Where else? I do not see a bower floating past, do you?'

Harald smiled wryly.

'I am glad you are feeling better, my sweet.'

Elizaveta leaned in against his chest and his arms went
instantly around her.

'I confess, Hari,' she whispered up into the curve of his
throat, 'that I am sad.'

'I too, my sweet. It was a terrible loss.'

'Where . . . where is the baby?'

'I gave him to the waves.'

'Him?' Her breath caught and for a moment it was a struggle
to stay alive.

'But you are well,' Harald pushed on and her heart remembered to beat again. 'You are well and that is what truly matters.
God will see fit to grant us a child once we are safe on Norwegian shores.'

'You think so?'

'I know it. Now, look!'

He pointed and, following his finger, Elizaveta saw the rise of land breaking the flat horizon. The sun was sinking over it as if guiding their way and she felt a surge of hope as golden as this new land in the evening light. Halldor and Aksel came to stand at their side and she sensed the solidity of their care like a wall against her back.

'Will we find shore before nightfall?' she asked.

'No. Sigtuna, where the royal palace lies, is far up the Bay of Malaren, but we will be there to dine with your aunt and uncle on the morrow.'

Elizaveta tried to take in his words. Her mother's brother, Anund, was King of Sweden and their sister Astrid had not remarried after Olaf's death and resided here still. Elizaveta carried great gifts for them both from Ingrid and the thought of meeting her northern kin bolstered her will.

'I must change,' she said again. 'Now.'

She did not wish to be seen by even a peasant fisherman of this, her mother's homeland, in anything less than her best and, bedsides, this dress was creased with sorrow. Let the waves have it; she would start afresh.

'Elizaveta, welcome, welcome! How is my dear sister? How are all your siblings? How many now? Eleven of you, is it? The messengers can scarcely travel north quickly enough to tell me of one birth before another is on its way. Oh, but look at you – so beautiful. How did you get so dark, my dear? Your father I suppose.'

Elizaveta flushed. Astrid was every bit as fair as Ingrid, with the same soft blonde hair and kind blue eyes, and the sight of her was a balm to Elizaveta's aching heart. She blinked hard, grateful for her lessons in Old Norse and trying to decide which of her aunt's tumbling questions to answer first. Thankfully, though, Astrid seemed not to need any response.

'And you, my dear – how are you? The messengers told us you had lost a babe on board ship? How awful. You poor thing. The sea is a fearsome place at the best of times, never mind in such terrible travail. Let us get you to the bower immediately. I ordered the sauna heated the moment we were told of your ships in the mouth of the bay so it should be ready for us very soon. Oh, Elizaveta, I am truly glad to see you.'

Elizaveta grinned over her shoulder at Harald as Astrid drew her away from the menfolk in the great hall, but she was grateful for her aunt's kindness. Astrid was far more voluble than Ingrid but exuded the same soft care and after her tortuous journey Elizaveta was happy to fall into such tender administrations.

She let herself be bathed, luxuriating in the soft rose-scented water that cleansed away the last of the blood still clinging to the insides of her thighs, and stepped into the blissful warmth of the sauna. The dry heat from the stone kiln at the centre of the wooden room was new to her, for in Kiev they boiled water on the top to fill it with steam, but as it crept into her frozen bones she felt life return to them at last and with it, hope. She looked to her belly, already shrunken back in on itself, and pressed it gently. There was no pain.

'So, my dear,' Astrid said, sliding her ample body in at her side, 'you will be Queen of Norway?'

'Maybe,' Elizaveta agreed cautiously, 'if Magnus welcomes us.'

'Oh, he will. My stepson is not one for strife, God bless him.'

'His supporters may be, though.'

'Einar Tambarskelve? That's true. I do not like that man. You can never tell what he is thinking, save that it will be something bad. But he is devoted to Magnus.'

'He is devoted to his own cause.'

'Which comes to much the same thing.'

Elizaveta looked sharply at her aunt, sitting naked on the

wooden benches, fanning herself with peacock feathers. Astrid winked.

'I am not as silly as I look,' she said, 'though I find people – men in particular – rarely work that out. Magnus is fond of me, Niece. I will write to him personally, pressing your cause.'

'You would do that for us?'

'Of course. Would you not do it for your own sisters' children?'

Elizaveta considered.

'I would,' she agreed. 'Well, maybe not Stasia's but she wouldn't need me to. She gets everything her own way.'

Astrid laughed.

'I used to think the same of Ingrid.'

'Mother?'

'Yes. She was Father's legal daughter, you see, and I just the child of a concubine. That's why he sent her to Kiev to be a Grand Princess and I got despatched to Olaf as his consolation prize.'

'You were Queen of Norway,' Elizaveta protested. 'That, surely, is more than just a princess?'

Astrid laughed again.

'Perhaps, though do not say so to your mother. Besides, my reign only lasted a few years before Cnut robbed me of my title – may he rot in hellfire.'

Her voice caught, suddenly harsh, and Elizaveta looked more closely at her in the comforting gloom of the sauna.

'That, then, is truly why you would help me?'

Astrid inclined her head.

'You see much, Elizaveta. You will be a good queen, I think, and I will consider the circle of my fate complete if I can help one of my own blood to my throne again.'

CHAPTER EIGHTEEN

Bymarka, Norway, Easter 1046

The horses broke through the trees and Elizaveta drew in a stunned breath at the long curve of green valley before her. Norway! She had been riding through it for four days now and still every turn in the path, or rise of a hill, or edge of a forest unrolled new vistas, each one seeming vaster than those that had gone before. Would she ever grow used to this country? Would she ever grow accustomed to the green spaces and the soft lakes and the rolling mountains? Would she ever cease to find it strange that she could turn all the way around and, despite the horizon being a day's walk away, still see less than a handful of roofs? And would she ever truly feel like the queen of it all? Elizaveta thought of the court awaiting them just a short ride further on and nerves shook her insides like a falcon his jesses.

Astrid had been true to her word and less than a month into the new year Harald had received a terse invitation to 'talks' with Magnus. They had followed the snowmelt over the Kjolen mountains to meet Norway's young king who had ridden out to a hunting lodge on the border to greet them. Though he was now twenty-two, Magnus had not seemed to Elizaveta much changed from the bookish boy she remembered. He'd worn a magnificent crown and sat on a magnificent throne, carried up into the hills by poor cart ponies, but it had been Einar Tambarskelve who'd controlled the negotiations. For three long days they had huddled in a dark lodge in the forest and, as far as Elizaveta could see, no one had said a word they truly meant, smoothing over the hatred with much flowery discussion of 'mutual interests' and 'the good of the country'.

Still working hard to understand Old Norse, Elizaveta had grasped less of the words and more of the true meaning and it had all been very clear. The northern jarls, especially Einar and Kalv, were bitterly unhappy at losing their easily controlled young king but were afraid of Harald's fierce Varangian troops. Magnus (or, rather, Einar) had declared that he would tolerate Harald as a joint ruler of Norway but he was clearly distrustful. Both sides were proceeding in a show of support and togetherness but it merely masked the bitter rivalry beneath as thinly as the ice crust over a firefestival galleon.

Today that charade would truly begin for Magnus had ridden ahead to prepare the Easter court and now Harald and Elizaveta were to take their place at his side. It was to be a 'celebration of unity', but even so Harald's men were in full armour and their eyes darted continuously around the beautiful landscape, looking for treachery. Elizaveta's stomach fluttered again and she put a hand to it.

'He kicks?' Harald asked eagerly, riding up at her side.

Elizaveta shook her head but smiled.

'He will kick soon.'

'Now that he is home,' Harald agreed and Elizaveta prayed it would be so.

This new child had, she believed, been conceived in Sweden at Christ's mass – a true gift from God – and she prayed for it every day. She had rested as much as possible, even when journeying, letting Greta tend to her like a child and keeping so quiet that she had barely recognised herself but this time, she was certain, it would be worth it.

'There, Lily – over there. Look!' Harald's voice suddenly rose like a child's and he leaped up in his stirrups, pointing eagerly. 'There is the royal residence. Is it not beautiful?'

Elizaveta scanned the rolling green plain but could see no turrets or cupolas, no walls or gateways, nothing but an over-sized peasant's dwelling on the far slope of the valley.

'Where, Hari?'

'There!' he said impatiently, pointing straight at the barn-like building. 'Come on – race you!'

He sounded so excited that Elizaveta spurred her horse on behind him, revelling in his happiness. Glancing over her shoulder, she saw Ulf, Halldor and Aksel excitedly urging their own mounts forward and even young Greta kicking her pretty pony into a gallop. There must be more to this place than met the eye. Perhaps the palace was hidden down in the trees, behind the byre? But no, Harald was cantering straight up to the long wooden structure and as Elizaveta drew close she saw that it was the only building around.

It stood nearly a hundred paces long, the low walls padded with moss and turf so it seemed to magically rise out of the very earth itself. The huge roof of thatched straw seemed similarly homegrown on the giant hillside and it was only as you moved closer that you could see the stamp of human endeavour on the massive farmhouse.

The thatch stuck out over the walls, supported by a long run of pillars to create a sheltered walkway for shade in the summer and some protection from the harsh snows in winter. In the centre of the main wall a wooden porch jutted, richly carved and painted in glowing reds and blues to draw out the patterns and pictures. The doors were similarly decorated with vibrant vines and leaves and they were secured with an iron lock, though that small device

seemed to be the only protection for this supposedly royal residence. There were no earthworks, no walls, not even a palisade
fence, and Elizaveta doubtfully drew rein at Harald's side.

'This is it, Hari?'

'It is.' He caught the look on her face. 'You do not like it?'

'No, no, it's lovely. Beautiful. Just . . . very different to what
I'm used to.'

'I suppose it is,' he agreed, handing her down from her horse,
'but you will love it. Wait until you see inside. Everything in
one place – so cosy.'

Elizaveta blinked and rubbed at her eyes. Was this really
Harald, her Harald – the man who'd fought pirates and
defended empires and won battles, the man who, over the last
three years, had bedded her anywhere and everywhere until
her body often sang with longing just at the sight of him – her
Harald admiring something for being 'cosy'?

'It has no defences?' she hazarded.

'No defences? Oh, no *walls*!' He laughed. 'Look around you,
Elizaveta. You could see an enemy coming from miles away.'

'And then?'

'And then you'd ride out and defeat them, of course.'

'Oh.'

'In Norway, my love,' Harald told her, chucking her under
the chin as her father might, 'we say that you do not need stout
walls for defence, just stout hearts.' He looked up at the farm
and suddenly seemed to shrink a little. 'You think it a poor
palace for a king, Elizaveta?'

'No indeed, Harald.' She rushed to reassure him. 'It is beautiful, truly. I cannot wait to see inside.'

'Good. It is very . . .' He looked for a word to impress her.
'Very grand. It was built by my brother, King Olaf.'

'Then it must be special to you.'

'Nearly as special as you are,' he said, kissing her long and hard before whispering, 'and one day it will *all* be ours.'

'Sssh!'

The huge door was creaking open before them and she kissed him back to silence him, though the words thrilled through her all the same. It seemed that Harald had become joint king of Norway without a drop of blood shed and for that they must be thankful, but as Magnus stepped out, feet planted proprietorially in the doorway, she knew their fight had only just begun. She shuddered and placed a hand to her belly as a small movement, more tickle than kick, jumped beneath her skin.

'Oh!'

'What is it?' Harald asked.

'I think maybe the babe truly is kicking – here.' Elizaveta grabbed Harald's hand and slid it round across her swelling belly. 'Do you feel it?'

'I do!' He beamed. 'I do feel it. Little Olaf is saying hello. He knows he is truly home.'

'It seems so,' Elizaveta agreed, awed, but now Magnus had stepped forward and the dark shadow of Einar Tambarskelve filled the doorway behind him.

Elizaveta instinctively tried to move back but Harald held her tight.

'My son is practising his war dance,' he told their grim-faced greeters, hand still placed across her. 'He is happy to be here in his ancestral home.'

Magnus, however, just looked blankly at them and Einar shot forward, face as dark as a midnight squall.

'Mayhap it will be a girl.'

Harald beamed more broadly than ever.

'A princess would be welcome too, Einar, especially if she is as gorgeous as her mother.'

Magnus rolled his eyes.

'All this devotion, Harald, is it seemly, do you think, for a king?' Harald stepped forward to shake his hand.

'God gave us women, nephew,' he said. 'I am simply enjoying his gift.'

Magnus tutted.

'You will find, Uncle, that you have not as much time for such frivolities as women now you are a king.' And with that Magnus turned, slim shoulders tight, to lead the way into the hall.

'Frivolities?' Harald mouthed to Elizaveta, amused, but they could hear the Norwegian court waiting excitedly inside the farm, and he moved purposefully to Magnus's side as the younger king stepped through the door.

Elizaveta fell obediently in behind them, though her heart was thudding as if a hundred babes were kicking it. She felt Einar's louring presence over her shoulder and was grateful to note Ulf and Halldor slide in behind him with Aksel between them. Apart from Harald and Greta, these faithful warriors were her only true friends in Norway. She thought longingly of Sweden and Astrid's soft, homely welcome and missed her aunt both for her hospitable self and as a shadow of her faraway mother.

What would her family be doing in Kiev now, she wondered as she followed the two kings into the enormous farmhouse and up the central aisle? The Rus' Easter service would be in Yaroslav's magnificent new Hagia Sophia, with its glowing marble floors and rich mosaics and soaring cupolas. His *druzhina* would kneel before the gilded altar and take communion from a jewelled cup and the richly robed monks would sing to the resonant notes of the silver pipe organ.

Then they would all process through the newly paved streets of Yaroslav's growing city whilst a mass of Kievans threw flowers before them, and on up into the great kremlin with its fountain and its bronze horses and its three stone halls. There would be a hundred musicians and acrobats and clowns with new tricks to amaze them and they would feast on a range of fragrant dishes from all over the vast tangle of the Rus lands and beyond.

The contrast to her current situation could not be more pronounced, but the great and good of Norway were leering at her from either side, and she had no more time for musings. Already the tiny procession had made it to the top table and Magnus was taking his place on the great throne, leaving Harald to move into the lesser chair on his right. The men were joint kings in everything but Einar had insisted that when they were together Magnus would have precedence and he clearly intended to enforce that rigidly. Elizaveta moved past him towards her own place, feeling all eyes upon her, though not, as in Kiev, to admire her, but more as if waiting for her to fall. She sighed and Harald leaned solicitously in.

'You are well, my sweet?' he asked, as he handed her into her seat.

'Quite well. Just thinking of home.'

He frowned slightly.

'This *is* your home, Lily.'

'Of course. I know that, Harald, truly and I am so glad to be here with you – a solid partnership at the head of a nation makes the nation solid too.' He squinted at her and she blushed. ''Tis something my father used to say.'

'And he was right.' Harald kissed her firmly. 'We will build our own farm, my sweet. We will build it however you want it.'

'Really?'

'Of course.'

'Of stone?'

Harald frowned again.

'I'm not sure that would be possible, Elizaveta – you've seen enough of Norway to know that trees are more plentiful here. Besides, it is prettier. Wood lives.'

'It does, Hari,' she agreed, looking around at the decorated pillars and panels and roof-beams, 'and there are some truly talented carvers here. It's just so . . . brown.'

'Of course it is brown, Lily. What other colour would it be? Is the baby rotting your brain?'

He laughed but there was an edge to his mirth and she knew that over the riotous, nervous feasting ahead she would need him close. Now was not the time to tell him that the dark, heavy colours of this strange Norwegian farm depressed her spirit.

'It must be,' Elizaveta said lightly and squeezed his arm as Einar took a seat alongside a large, sour-faced woman.

'My wife,' he said shortly, 'Lady Brigid.'

Brigid leaned forward and glared at Elizaveta.

'The Arnassons should be here at any moment,' she announced without a word of courtesy. 'I am so excited. I haven't seen dear Tora since she was newly widowed and it's been far too long.'

Elizaveta's throat contracted. Brigid spoke fast, and her Norse was thick with a northern inflection, but Elizaveta did not mistake her meaning. This was another reason she needed Harald close – the infamous Arnasson family were due here at any moment to 'welcome' the new arrivals and she was dreading meeting Harald's one-time betrothed. Harald had told her a little of Finn, the man who had raised him and who he so clearly admired. He was looking forward to seeing him again and that worried Elizaveta, but not nearly as much as the fact that he had told her nothing at all of Tora.

'You are queen,' she reminded herself sternly, 'and you are carrying Norway's heir.'

She placed quiet hands over her swelling belly. This child was as much her weapon in this strange new country as Harald's sword was his and she cradled it tight as the keen neigh of a horse cut into the hall from outside.

'Here they are now,' the dour Einar said, sounding disorientatingly jolly at the prospect of trouble.

All heads turned to the door, then back to Elizaveta, as the court waited eagerly to see their new queen meet the woman they believed she had supplanted. Elizaveta rose slowly. She reached for Harald's hand but he had stepped away, joining Magnus at the front of the dais as the doors swung open. Elizaveta shivered and Aksel leaped forward, offering his strong young arm. She clutched at it, tears of gratitude springing to her eyes, as a man strode into the hall and bowed low.

'Finn!' Harald called and jumped down to clasp the man's shoulders.

'King Harald,' Finn said carefully, 'welcome home. We have missed you, have we not, Niece?'

He turned and drew forward a woman dressed in a gown of purest blue, topped with a snow-white cloak of ermine fur. Elizaveta watched, frozen, as Harald took her hand and, bowing lower than she'd ever seen him do before, kissed it. Her eyes, though, were stuck on the woman who was everything she suddenly realised she had known she would be.

Tora Arnasson was tall and voluptuous, with soft, feminine features and a curtain of honey-blonde hair. Her eyes were wide and as blue as her dress and her skin was pale and clear. She was the perfect Norse woman, beautiful in a way Elizaveta had always craved. Indeed, as she stood there, teetering on the dais of an unknown hall full of unknown customs, the dark walls seemed to crowd in and the great wooden rafters threatened to fall on her head and the smoke from the huge central hearth pricked at her eyes. For this woman, this rival, was the incarnation of Ingrid, her mother, and Elizaveta was torn between an ice-cold desire to see her dead and a sharp, intense longing to throw herself into her arms.

CHAPTER NINETEEN

*T*ora, painfully aware of the woman stood just above her on the royal dais, forced herself to keep her head high and her eyes up as she greeted Harald. Even after sixteen years, it was unmistakably him, but he looked so different. He was even taller than he'd been at fifteen and much broader. His arms alone looked twice their previous width and she hated to imagine the number of sword-swings it had taken to build so much muscle. His face, once so smooth, was lined and weather-worn and down one side, as if the devil had drawn across him, was a long trace of a wound, faint, but to Tora's eyes as livid as if it were new-won.

'Stikelstad?' she whispered, stepping forward and putting up a hand but not daring to touch.

Harald's own fingers went to his cheek and he nodded. For a moment the word seemed to shimmer between them, laden with memories, and then, as if snatching it away, he said: 'Much has changed since then.'

Instinctively Tora looked over his shoulder to his new wife.

'And many promises have been broken,' she said sharply.

Goodness, the Rus girl was beautiful – so slim and fragile, like a sprite, and with such fine features. Her eyes were as dark as her night-time hair, her skin an alluringly dusky shade and her lips full and inviting. She was the opposite to big, blonde

Harald in every possible detail and for a second Tora could almost see them entwined between the sheets. She blinked the rogue image away. This girl was the total opposite to herself too and if this was the sort of beauty that had captivated Harald down in the south she stood no chance. Never had.

'I am truly sorry, Tora,' Harald was saying, his voice low, 'if you had . . . expectations of me.'

Tora had so much to say to that, so much she wanted to remind him of, to demand answers for but not now, not here with all of Norway watching on.

'You must introduce me, Harald, to your wife,' she said loudly, cutting through his attempt at intimacy.

Harald looked stunned and Tora was glad; she was not here to make him content – not now.

'Of course,' he agreed, recovering. 'Er, Lady Tora Arnasson, this is Queen Elizaveta.'

'Of Kiev?' Tora asked, taking a single step forward.

'Of Norway,' the dark girl said stonily, taking a mirrored step.

Elizaveta did not hold out her hand and for that, at least, Tora was grateful for she could no more have kissed it than she could a weed-strung toad. Instead, they both bowed their heads in a curt greeting, more for the eagerly watching Norwegians than each other.

'And how,' Tora asked, 'do you find your new country?'

'Very agreeable,' came the swift reply, laced with an exotic southerly inflection, but Tora saw the edge of Elizaveta's full lips twitch and knew she'd hit a nerve. Good.

'It must be very quiet after the bustle of home,' she suggested.

Elizaveta's eyes narrowed.

'This *is* home,' she shot back, 'and I welcome the quiet – it is good for the babe.'

One of her slim hands rested pointedly on what Tora now saw was a swelling belly. Damn. She'd heard tell of a

'Twenty-one? In one place?'

'Yes, my lady.'

'Why so many?'

'Well, I suppose because there are ten thousand people living there and they all need somewhere to worship.'

Ten thousand! Tora felt faint. Were there even that many in the whole of Norway?

'You will be bored here, then?' she stuttered.

'Me? No. No, I am ready to build a farm and find a wife.'

Ulf looked intently at her and anger fired inside her again. So this was the man to whom Harald would see her 'wed with great dignity'. No way. No way was she being forced into marriage with one of Harald's warrior friends as some sort of consolation prize.

'I am bound by a long-established contract,' she said stiffly.

Ulf nodded slowly, his crazy curls bobbing.

'I heard,' he said, 'but I do not think that contract stopped you marrying before?'

'That was not my choice.'

'I see. But your "choice", Tora . . .'

'Lady Tora.'

'Your choice, *Lady* Tora, is surely no longer available to you.'

'And you consider yourself an adequate replacement?'

Ulf laughed.

'Clearly you do not.'

Tora shook herself. She was acting the stranger again and she did not like it.

'I'm sorry. I do not mean to be rude.'

Ulf shrugged then pointed at Halldor, deep in conversation with the Rus impostor.

'Halldor there had a woman once, a slave girl. He loved her very dearly but she died giving him a son.'

Tora's eyes opened wide. She looked to Elizaveta's belly and back to Ulf.

'What on earth are you saying?'

He followed her gaze and flushed.

'Not that! Lord, no. May God keep Queen Elizaveta safe. I was simply saying that Halldor has never found anyone to replace her.'

'Oh.' Tora felt ridiculous. Was this big, bluff soldier pitying her? She looked awkwardly past him and was grateful to see her sister being shown into a seat on his other side.

'Ah, Count Ulf,' she said hastily, 'meet Johanna, my little sister.'

He looked around.

'Not so very little,' he said admiringly as Johanna turned her big eyes up at him and suddenly Tora found herself free of her awkward conversation. Indeed, of *any* conversation.

She looked across at Harald. Finn was standing, leaning easily on the back of the new king's seat, the two men chatting as if nothing had happened between them, as if Harald had not betrayed their family by bringing home this darkly beautiful Slav bride. And now they looked over at Ulf and Johanna and it was clear from their nudges and nods where that was going. Tora was being smudged out already, painted over, left to rot as the court wound its fickle way onwards.

'No!' she said into her meal, making the troll-man jump.

Tora hastily stabbed a piece of elk and stuffed it into her stupid mouth but the word rang round and round in her head all the same – no, no, no, no, no! She wasn't going to disappear; why should she? She cleared her throat.

'You must come and visit us at Austratt, Harald,' she said clearly. The top table looked her way. 'Must he not, Uncle?'

'Of course,' Finn agreed, though he was regarding her warily.

'I hope you might like it there, my lady,' she said directly to

Elizaveta. 'It is not Kiev but as a key trading post it is a little livelier than here.'

Elizaveta glanced at Harald.

'That's very kind, Tora,' he said. 'We would enjoy that, would we not, Elizaveta?'

Elizaveta looked back to Tora who held her in her gaze, willing her to crumble, but the damned woman just took Harald's hand and, toying openly with his big fingers, said: 'We would, Hari.'

Hari! Since when had he become 'Hari'? Was that a Rus affectation? It made him sound more like a dog than a man.

'Lovely,' Tora managed through clenched teeth. 'Perhaps for Whitsun? That would give me time to source some special dishes to give you a true taste of Norway.' She looked to Finn. 'We could dig up the shark perhaps, Uncle?'

'Dig up?' Elizaveta asked faintly.

Tora smiled at her.

'Shark meat is poisonous so it has to be left under large stones to crush the toxins from it.'

'For . . . for how long?' The Rus girl's wretched olive skin had gone pleasingly green.

'About three months.'

'But how does it stay fresh?'

'Fresh? Oh, it doesn't stay fresh but a little fermentation adds to the flavour. It used to be Harald's favourite dish, did it not, Harald?'

'Maybe,' Elizaveta said, leaning across him, 'his tastes have changed.'

'Or maybe,' Tora shot back icily, 'he's just forgotten how good his old favourites were.'

'If his tastes ran to rotten fish,' Elizaveta flashed, 'I somehow doubt it.'

'It's a very mature flavour. One he may have lost in the sickly dishes of the south. It lingers.'

'So I see – or should that be *smell*?'

Tora glared at Elizaveta who glared back but now the eyes of the court were turning their way and Finn slid himself between them.

'I hear Count Halldor tells a wondrous tale,' he said loudly. 'Perhaps he would entertain us with something from the golden city?'

'I'm sure he would,' Harald agreed. 'Halldor?'

The troll-man grunted but rose and, to Tora's astonishment, a sudden smile transformed his wizened face and his hunched body unfolded as he moved out before the crowd.

'Twas a night of a thousand stars . . .' he began and everyone turned contentedly his way, but all Tora could see now, with an empty space between them, was her rival.

'You think you've won, don't you?' she hissed at her.

Elizaveta just smiled a slow, infuriatingly beautiful smile.

'I know I have. Harald loves me.'

Tora nodded slowly. She'd be a fool to deny his infatuation with this girl, but they were in the north now and the new queen stood out like a reed amongst pines.

'Perhaps,' she agreed, with a smile of her own, 'but he needs *me*.'

CHAPTER TWENTY

Bymarka, May 1046

'You will be polite to the Arnassons, Lily?'

Elizaveta looked up from her viol practice as Harald came so close as to obstruct the movement of her bow. She stared at him, surprised. Usually he loved to watch her play, especially when, as on this deliciously warm evening, she was doing so naked.

'I will be every bit as polite to them as they have been to me,' she said curtly.

'That's what I'm afraid of.'

Harald turned away and reluctantly she put down her instrument and went after him as he paced up the side of their 'bedchamber', a dark, windowless room dominated by a magnificent bed. It had carved wooden sides and a pile of feather mattresses and furs so soft she'd slept surprisingly well every night. Harald told her it was all the 'fresh' air of Norway and if by fresh he meant crisp and salted and endless then he might be right.

She had to admit the beauty of the place was growing on her. Up until yesterday she'd been out riding every day, marvelling at the freedom afforded by not meeting a soul. Greta usually came with her, Aksel providing an escort if Harald was busy

– as increasingly he was – and together the three of them had explored much of the Bymarka forests, lakes and plains.

'It looks,' Aksel had suggested one morning, when they'd ridden far out to the edge of the Nid river, 'as if a giant cleaved it from the earth with his sword.'

It had been such an accurate image Elizaveta had almost seen the mythical creature before her.

'You have your father's gift with words, Aksel,' she'd told her self-proclaimed squire but he'd just blushed, glanced self-consciously at Greta, and then ridden off up the next slope. Elizaveta, however, had paused for a moment, looking up the long scar of a waterway towards Finn's town of Austratt and wondering what would meet her there – as still she wondered now.

'Hari?'

He spun round and looked down on her. She thrust out her breasts a little, hoping to distract him from the strange conversation, but for once it did not work.

'Tora is not a nasty person,' he said earnestly. 'I know she has been a little prickly with you . . .'

'Prickly?' Elizaveta stuttered. 'Indeed she has. Speaking with her is like being battered with a mace. She and her cronies call me the "witch queen".'

'Witch queen?' He rolled the words across his tongue. 'I like that.'

'Harald – you can't. It's mean.'

'It's exciting. You told me yourself once, on the banks of the Ros, that your dark hair made you a witch, remember?'

'I do, Hari, and I also remember you telling me that there is more to the night than witchcraft.'

He grinned.

'A truth I hope I have more than proved. But you *have* bewitched me, Lily.'

'Not like that, not with black magic.'

'No, no not like that but with your beauty and your spirit and your damned fiery stubbornness. Let them talk, my sweet; it keeps their idle minds occupied and surely it is *my* opinion that counts, not theirs?'

Elizaveta dipped her head. He was right, she supposed, and at least Tora had ridden back to Austratt to prepare for their visit. Elizaveta was not looking forward to it. She had no desire to see her blonde rival again, nor her precious town either. She was used to sparring with women – she and her sisters had done it all their lives – but this was different. There was no undercurrent of togetherness here and there'd been times since she'd ridden into Norway that she'd missed even Anastasia.

She'd sent letters to the Hungarian court but there had been no time yet for a reply and she yearned to know that they were safe and, pray God, that Andrew had taken his throne. As for her mother – sometimes she longed to talk to her so much it physically hurt. A letter from Ingrid, bless her, had been waiting at Magnus's court and she had devoured its simple, domestic content. She and Greta sometimes talked of Kiev, but Elizaveta knew Harald was right that Norway was her home now and she tried to restrict such stolen conversations.

'Tora is defensive, that is all,' Harald was saying now.

'Offensive more like,' Elizaveta retorted.

'Because you are queen, Lily, and because you are beautiful and because I cannot get enough of you.' Suddenly he dipped his head, burying it between her breasts and kissing them one after the other. 'Especially like this,' he added. 'When did they grow so large?'

She giggled, relieved at his change of tone – and subject. ''Tis the babe.'

'Clever Olaf – a gift for his papa before he is even born.'

'I think,' she admonished, 'that they are more for him than you.'

'Then I'd best make the most of them before he arrives.'

He began kissing her again and drew her towards the bed but as she landed on the soft covers Elizaveta squirmed uneasily beneath him. Yesterday she'd bled. Just a little, a few spots like the drops from a needle-prick on a tapestry frame, but she'd called the midwife immediately. The woman had reassured her that it was not uncommon but had suggested that her husband should 'keep to his side of the bed a while'.

'Hari,' she started but he was already on his way down her body, rubbing his hands lovingly round her bump as his tongue headed south. 'Hari!'

Harald looked up, peeping over her belly like a hare behind a hillock, so gorgeous that for a moment she was tempted to ignore the midwife but she dared not risk the child.

'The midwife says not to.'

'No to . . . ? Oh! Why not?'

He was up at her side in a moment, all concern.

'I bled a little – a very little. It's not a concern but we cannot . . .' she tried to remember the words ' . . . rupture the seal.'

Harald screwed up his nose.

'Well,' he said drily, 'that picture has put me off at least. You must rest, Lily.'

'Yes. No riding, she said.'

'No riding me?'

'No and no other stallions besides.'

He kissed her.

'You will soon be bored then, my sweet.'

'Are you suggesting, my lord, that "riding" is all I do?'

'I wish it were.' He kissed her again. 'I suppose you will have to take it easy in Austratt then. I shall have a litter made to carry you around in.'

'No!'

'Yes. You must be kept safe. It will be a magnificent one, I promise, draped in scarlet.'

'The colour of blood, Hari?'

'Purple then – the colour of empresses! Finn is gathering forces for me, my sweet. After our visit we will sail on Denmark. Magnus, fool that he is, set Svein Estrithson as his regent on Cnut's death and the whoreson has taken the throne as his own.'

'Svein Estrithson?' Elizaveta queried.

'Cnut's nephew through his sister. He was born and brought up in England but he came to Norway when Magnus took the throne. Seems Magnus, the fool boy, took a shine to him and look how Svein has rewarded that! He claims he has the backing of the Danish people but we will see how supportive they are with our swords in their faces.'

'Magnus will sail with you?' Elizaveta asked.

'He certainly will; 'tis his fault we must fight. Besides, I'm not leaving him behind, nor Einar either. They're plotting against me, I know it, and I can't let them out of my sight. If I'm lucky they'll take a lethal wound.'

'Hari – ssh!'

Elizaveta looked pointedly at the light around the door that just about separated them from the great hall. Einar's bed was the other side. He'd had it set there amid much grumbling when he'd been forced to vacate this room for the new joint king. There were only two chambers in the farmhouse, the rest of the court sleeping either in their own pavilions outside or in the alcoves on the wooden platforms along the hall, and he had not been impressed at joining the masses.

'He could sleep with Magnus,' Elizaveta had suggested wickedly to Harald.

'He could,' he'd agreed, 'he and his fat wife both. Then they'd truly be on top of him.'

It had seemed funny then but now Elizaveta had seen more of the workings of the court it was less so. Einar prowled mercilessly, cornering lords and ladies wherever he went, binding them into his complex political webs like a preying spider. He was as good with words as Halldor but he used them not to entertain but to coerce.

'Must you attack Denmark?' she asked now.

Harald looked strangely at her.

'Of course. We cannot let Svein rob us of our birthright. And besides, my sweet, if we defeat him, Magnus can go and be king there. It's a softer life in Denmark, he'll like it and we will be free of him.'

That *was* tempting but Elizaveta was still worried.

'Will you take Halldor and Ulf?'

'Of course.'

'With Ulf newly married to Johanna? The poor man.'

'Not that new, Lily – it's been two weeks.'

'Oh and you'd had enough of *me* within two weeks, had you?'

He smiled.

'I will *never* have enough of you, my sweet.'

His hand slid to her thigh.

'Hari, the babe!'

He groaned.

'When is it due?'

'Autumn.'

'Autumn! I will shrivel up by autumn.'

'Mayhap, then, it is a good thing that you are going a-viking?'

He nodded ruefully.

'Mayhap it is – though a man usually likes to be sent on his way with a smile . . .'

Elizaveta rolled her eyes but reached down to stroke his manhood. It leaped into life in her fingers.

'Don't worry – I will make you smile, Harald Sigurdsson.' He groaned with pleasure and she increased her pace. 'You will leave me Aksel though?'

'Hmmm?'

'Aksel. I want him here with me.'

'Why? You will have Greta to care for you.'

'But not to protect me.'

'Protect you? You will hardly be here alone, Lily. I will leave a good guard.'

'A Norwegian guard. It's not enough.'

'What?'

His eyes twisted with the effort of concentrating and he squirmed. She tightened her hold.

'Einar's wife is always talking of how "sad" it would be if I lost the babe. I fear her intentions, Hari. Hers and the Arnasson girl's besides.'

'Tora's?' Harald yanked away, leaving Elizaveta reeling. 'You're accusing Tora of plotting against you? That's not fair, Lily. You may not like her but there's no need to cast a slur on her character.'

She looked at him, confused, as his lust for her visibly shrank.

'You accused Einar of plotting against *you*.'

'That's because Einar is a vicious, hard-headed political vulture.'

'And Tora is not?'

'No!'

Elizaveta pulled the bedclothes around herself, suddenly cold.

'You like her still?'

'Of course I like her. Why would I not?'

'Because she takes every opportunity to put me down.'

His eyes narrowed.

'This is mean of you, Lily. Mean and petty. Ever since you've been here you've been critical. Maybe Norway isn't as advanced as Kiev but it's a fine country, with fine people.'

Guilt spiked through her. She *had* been critical. She *had*, perhaps, scorned some of the Norwegian customs, but she *had not* imagined Tora's hatred of her. Somehow she must make Harald see the other side of his pretty little childhood sweetheart. She grabbed his arms.

'She told me plainly, Harald, that she would have you off me.'

He strained away from her.

'She wouldn't do that, Lily.'

'Oh but she would, Hari – she *did*. And how do you think she'll do that? How do you think she possibly can? She can hardly marry you until I'm dead, can she?'

Harald leaped up, pulling away from her and snarling around the bed like a bear.

'You're blind, Lily. Tora would never plot to kill you; it's not in her nature. Just because I chose to marry you does not give you the right to treat her like dirt. Apologise.'

'No.'

'Elizaveta!'

He pounded his fist into his palm but Elizaveta wasn't going to be intimidated. She stuck up her chin.

'No, Hari. I was simply voicing my concerns and if you cannot listen to them then you are a very poor husband.'

'I am *your* husband and you will obey me.'

'When you command me correctly I will willingly do so.'

Harald sprung forward, gripping the bedrail so tight she could see the veins bulging on his hands and the knuckles turning white but she would not give in. She was a Princess of Kiev and he should respect that and besides, she was right, she was sure of it. She'd heard Tora and Brigid discussing their damned shark poisons too often to feel secure once the men were gone.

'Perhaps,' she said icily, 'you should go to Austratt and see your precious Tora without me.'

He stared at her for a long moment and for the first time ever she struggled to read the swirls in his eyes. She pouted up at him, willing him to pull her into his arms, to lose this quarrel in love-making, whatever the risk, but he did not.

'Perhaps I should,' he said instead. 'It might give you a chance to rethink your attitude to your country, to your queenship.'

She'd offended his homeland; that had been wrong.

'Hari, I'm . . .' But the word 'sorry' stuck in her throat and before she could reach for him, he was gone.

The next morning he rode to Austratt without her, a scowl not a smile on his face, and somehow Elizaveta was alone again.

CHAPTER TWENTY-ONE

Austratt, Whitsun 1046

'Poison her?' Tora looked up at Harald through carefully incredulous eyes. 'I would never poison her, Harald; I would never poison anyone.'

'I know that,' he agreed. 'I told her as much but she's a wildcat when she's angry.'

'I hope, then, that you did not get scratched.'

Tora prayed no one was listening. She sounded so shallow, but Harald was drawing closer so she could not stop now. She'd been delighted when he had arrived in Austratt without his queen. The official story was that Elizaveta was unable to travel because of her health but Tora had seen the shadows behind Harald's eyes and had been assiduously attentive to him. Now, as the ale barrel emptied and courtiers retired sleepily to Finn's next-door guest-hall, the true story was coming out. She filled his cup.

It was true that Tora would not poison Harald's wife, however haughtily beautiful she was. She had not the stomach for it. But it was true, too, that she had wanted to plant the idea in her rival's mind. She felt a little ashamed that it had worked but she could not let that get in her way now. She knew

Finn was watching her and she redoubled her attentions to Norway's joint king.

'If you are so set on Harald,' her uncle had told her during their preparations for the royal visit, 'we can use that.'

'How?' she'd asked uneasily.

'You do not need to be a man's wife to bear him a child, Tora.'

'But . . .'

'And you are, after all, morally his wife in God's eyes.'

'I . . .'

'And it's not as if you haven't done it before . . .' He'd taken her hand. 'A king needs a mistress, Niece. It befits his status and helps ensure heirs for the country – Arnasson heirs.'

'But the queen . . .'

'The queen is slight. Birthing will not go easily for her.'

'Uncle!'

'It is a simple truth, Tora, nothing more. She has lost three already. You, though, you are a proper woman. Pieter was not man enough to make the most of that, but there is little doubting Harald's seed. You would like children, would you not, Niece?'

He'd cut her where she was already wounded; the lack of children from her first marriage was its only sadness.

'I am not a concubine, Uncle,' she'd insisted, struggling to resist the lure of the suggestion.

'Of course not,' he'd soothed. 'You would be a royal consort and you would have such status. You will bear him fine boys, I know it. Fine *kings*. And if the Rus girl were not, God forbid, to rise from her childbed it would be good for Harald to find consolation, would it not? Especially if that consolation were already carrying his babe.'

'But the Roman church, Uncle . . .'

'Is safe in Rome. Come, girl, most of our people still marry beneath a tree at midsummer without a priest in sight unless he be in the bushes taking his own pleasure. And we have only Harald's word for it that he is truly wed to the Slav. Here in Norway, it is more as if *she* is his mistress and *you* his true wife.'

It had been nonsense of course, she'd known that really, but such seductive nonsense. Finn himself had been delighted with the notion. Einar was plotting still and he needed to bind Harald to the Arnasson cause. Johanna marrying Ulf, promoted to the rank of Harald's marshal and second-in-command, had helped them but not as much as blending the two families' blood would do. She steeled herself.

'You look tired, Harald.'

'I *am* tired. I barely slept last night.'

'It must have been very upsetting for you. Shall I help you to your bed?'

He looked up and seemed to see the emptying hall for the first time.

'No need,' he said. 'I might as well kip down with the men.'

He waved to the hard core of his Varangians, still drinking around the fire. Tora looked too and saw Finn stood in the shadow of a pillar nodding her on. She thought fast.

'You cannot do that, Harald,' she said, 'you are the king now.'

'One of the kings.'

'Even so – you do not see Magnus sleeping with the common lords, do you?'

That seemed to work. Harald rose and she was swiftly up at his side but so too was his troll-friend, Halldor, who had been lurking at the end of the table. Luckily he was not the only one; Tora had never seen her uncle move so fast.

'Count Halldor!' Finn called. 'Just the man. I have this delicious golden spirit sent to me from the Orkneys. You must try it.'

Halldor was helpless in his persuasive clutches and Tora

was free to follow a staggering Harald to his chamber. The door led directly off the hall and she knew plenty of eyes were still open enough to watch her move in behind him. Her cheeks flamed but her steps did not falter. This was Harald, she reminded herself – *her* Harald, her wolf-boy. She was entitled to him.

'Very tired,' he was mumbling, throwing himself onto the bed, and now it was Tora who had to move fast.

'A last drink,' she suggested, sloshing wine into a goblet from the jug on the side table and offering it to him, taking the chance to slide onto the pillows at his side as she did so.

Harald looked at the goblet in askance but then shrugged.

'Why not.' He drank deep. 'Elizaveta is not like you, Tora. You are all . . . soft.'

Tora moved a little closer so he could feel exactly how soft.

'She has too much spirit?' she suggested.

'Ha! Yes.'

'That must be very challenging for you. I would not be so. I am too meek.'

'Meek is not a bad thing in a woman, Tora.'

'I don't know. I think I would always just want to please you, to do your bidding.'

'That's not a bad thing either.'

'No?'

Tora knelt up, fumbling for her courage with her dress-brooches.

'I still,' she said, keeping her voice low, 'want to please you, Harald.'

The brooches snapped free and her overdress fell to her waist. Harald sat up a little, thrusting his goblet aside, and, encouraged, she undid the lace of her undergown so that it, too, fell loose.

'*Do* I please you, Harald?'

He ripped the shift from her shoulders so fast she almost cried out in alarm. It seemed she did please him, but then he just sat there, looking her nakedness up and down, but making no further move to touch her. It needed more. Drawing in a deep breath, Tora pushed herself up to stand on the bed above him and let both gowns fall to her feet. She was naked before him again, as she had been sixteen years ago, though she was older now, less lithe – would she tempt him still?

Harald moaned and she saw his trousers bulge. Emboldened, she knelt again and released him. She could almost feel her uncle's eyes on the door and hated herself as a whore but she was here now and suddenly she was desperate for Harald to want her – not for Finn, not for the Arnassons, not even to annoy Elizaveta, but for herself.

'You belong with me,' she murmured.

'I am wed.'

'I know that. I challenge it not. You can have me too.' She knelt over him. 'A king should have a mistress, Harald – it befits his status – and I am yours.' She leaned in, letting her full breasts touch his face as Pieter had liked her to do. 'So take me.'

'Yes.'

He was up and over her instantly, pinning her wrists to the bed and pushing between her legs, driving into her. She longed to grasp him, hold him close, but she could not move, could only lie there at his mercy, fighting to enjoy her triumph. He closed his grey eyes as he thrust, lost in a world of his own and Tora knew, with sick certainty, that it wasn't her he wanted. Indeed, it wasn't her he was bedding at all as, with a cry, he spilled his precious royal seed inside her and collapsed, spent.

In the morning he was tender. Tora woke to find him looking down at her and had the uneasy feeling he'd been doing so for some time. He took her again, slower this time, watching her as if expecting something, though she knew not what.

'We sail for Denmark soon,' he said when it was over. Tora struggled to make the connection. 'We can be together until then,' he explained, like this was a gift; no, like a promotion, as if he had moved her up the ranks of his soldiery. Then he added, 'Your uncle will expect it now.'

'My *uncle*?!'

'And I,' he added hastily, 'would like it.'

'A king should have a mistress,' Tora repeated numbly.

Harald smiled.

'It befits his status?' She nodded and he kissed her. 'I will make sure you enjoy it, Tora.'

And he did, or least she assumed that was his intent when he flipped her and touched her and watched her, and the unease grew that he was looking for something more from her. His body was strong and powerful and, unlike frail Pieter, he made her feel small and pleasingly womanly beneath him. She liked the feel of his skin on hers and she loved lying in his arms after he was spent, but there was none of the thrill she'd yearned for and that confused her. How could she have waited so long to feel so little?

'You are very quiet,' he said a few nights later.

'Quiet?' She glanced to the door. 'I have to be, surely – everyone is outside.'

He'd laughed at that.

'They know what we're doing, Tora.'

She knew that; oh God, she knew that. The endless winks and nudges and knowing smiles told her that every minute of the day, as did the glares from Count Halldor's dark brow and the reports back from Johanna that 'Elizaveta will be furious'. She tried to be pleased about that but more than anything else she felt ashamed. She had expected glory in their coming together. She had been uncertain what form it would take, but had been sure that the rightness of their union would manifest itself in the sort of ecstasy she had not found with Pieter.

Instead, as the days went on, she came to almost fear nighttime, not because of Harald's lack of feelings but because of her own. As the triumph of winning him melted away, she was left wondering, yet again, if she had a weak heart and her overwhelming emotion when the men finally sailed out the mouth of the fjord to reclaim Denmark from the usurper Svein Estrithson was relief.

'Well done, Niece,' Finn said, holding her close as he bade her goodbye on the jetties. He clutched a big hand to her stomach. 'Let's pray you bear fruit.'

'I am not a tree, Uncle,' Tora said stiffly.

'No indeed, but please don't be prim. Not now. The family has advanced and you have had fun – all is well!'

Then he winked and hugged her again and was gone, leaving her holding her belly and feeling certain she was missing something and even more certain it was something that Elizaveta, with her dark eyes and sensuous lips, knew all about. Harald would not, she was sure, be back in her bed and she wished with all her confused heart that it bothered her more.

CHAPTER TWENTY-TWO

Bymarka, September 1046

'Lily! I came as soon as I could.'

Harald ran into the chamber to find his wife looking even more beautiful than he'd remembered and at least twice as large. She was standing holding onto a bedpost with one hand and her back with the other and panting like a dog out at hunt. She looked at him and something in her eyes made him wave the two well-padded midwives away. Greta hurried them to the door and then, with only the slightest hesitation, slipped out too.

'As soon as you could?' Elizaveta said drily once they were alone. 'You've been gone four months, Harald.'

'Four very profitable months, my sweet.'

'You defeated Svein Estrithson then?'

Harald grimaced. They had not defeated Svein, quite the opposite. The bastard had played cat and mouse amongst the islands, refusing to engage them until finally, somehow, he had trapped their ships and they had been lucky to escape intact. Then, after days in a dank fog, Magnus had been taken by a terrible fever and gone to God leaving, to everyone's surprise, a will giving Denmark over to Svein.

Harald had denounced this as a fevered insanity and moved

to take the fleet back to Jutland to seize the throne as the rightful heir. Einar, however, had blocked the move, insisting that their duty was to escort their royal lord home to Norway in all honour and, with so many men in the jarl's direct charge, Harald had been powerless to override him. His only consolation was that it had brought him home in time to be with Elizaveta. Not that she needed to know all that now.

'We took Samso,' he told her cautiously.

'Samso?' She wrinkled her nose. 'Where's that?'

'It's an island off Jutland.'

'A big island?'

'Very,' he said firmly – she wasn't to know.

'Funny,' came back the swift reply, 'because I heard it was less than an hour's walk across and home to little more than a half-wit shepherd and his flock.'

'You did? Who from?'

'Aksel. He told me too that Magnus is dead – which is a blessing, yes, though I know we must not say so – and that Svein is King of Denmark now.'

'He told you that?'

'Oh yes. He talks to everyone who comes through.'

'Ah. I see. I'm so glad I left him with you then.'

Elizaveta almost smiled, then suddenly her face contorted and she gripped the bedpost and, closing her eyes, began panting again. Harald darted forward but she put out her other hand to ward him off and, ridiculously frightened, he stopped.

''Tis passing,' she said eventually, recovering herself.

'Does it hurt?'

'Of course it hurts!'

'I'm sorry. I don't like you hurting.'

'Really?'

Elizaveta pushed off the bedpost and moved away from him, both hands in the small of her back, stretching out so he couldn't help but notice the swell of her breasts pushing against her light shift. He truly had forgotten how beautiful she was; and how much he desired her. Not that she would thank him for such thoughts now.

'Really,' he said earnestly.

She spun back.

'Why then,' she demanded, 'did you bed the Arnasson girl?'

Harald flinched.

'You heard that too?'

'Aksel . . .'

'Talks to everyone. I know.'

'And there were plenty of ladies keen to discuss it with me too, Harald. *Very* sympathetic they were, as I'm sure you can imagine.'

Harald flinched again. He'd seen the ladies of courts all over the world attacking a good piece of gossip and they were as vicious with it as hounds with a hare.

'I'm sorry.'

Elizaveta moved towards him. He put out a hand but she did not take it.

'Why, Harald?' she asked. 'Why did you bother bringing me to your precious homeland if you were just going to run off to her when you got here?'

That stung.

'I did not "run off" to her. You sent me to her, Elizaveta. You told me yourself to go to her.'

'But not to *bed* her. How long did it take, Hari? The first night, was it?' He tried to stare her down but her dark eyes were too sharp. 'I'm so glad our wedding vows – vows made before Christ's own altar and my father, your liege lord for so many years – meant so much to you.'

She was panting again now, though whether from pain or fury it was hard to tell. Harald drew himself up.

'A king needs a mistress; it befits his status.'

Elizaveta snorted.

'Says who?'

'Says . . . says the world.'

'And since when did you care what the world says?'

She spoke true. He edged forward.

'Please don't be angry, Lily. You are my wife. You are having my child.'

'Don't I know it?'

A hiss of pain escaped from between her teeth and Harald seized the chance to reach out for her. For a moment she rested against his chest, burrowing her head into him, her little feet stamping beneath her shift as she fought the birth-spasm, but then it must have passed for she sprung away.

'I thought you loved me, Hari?'

'I *do*.'

'So?'

'So, I was angry with you and you weren't there and she, she was.'

'That's it?'

He spread his hands wide.

'Need it be more?' She looked confused and he pressed his advantage. 'I don't love her, Lily. She was just . . .'

'Convenient?'

'No! Well, maybe a little, but it runs far deeper than mere physical cravings, Lily. It's about power. Not over her,' he added hastily. 'You are the only woman I crave power over, Lily, and you are the one I fear I will never master.' Nearly she smiled. 'Einar is plotting.'

'And bedding an Arnasson helps, does it? Why not go the whole hog and leap between the sheets with the man himself?'

Harald shuddered.

'He looks very hairy.' A giggle escaped his wife's throat, a light, happy sound and he snatched at it. 'Things are tense, Lily. Magnus's faction is hardly pleased to have me here in Norway and I need as many friends as I can get, even with him gone.'

'Are you going to bed them all?'

'Only if you want me to – you can come along if you wish.'

Elizaveta cried out in sudden pain and he ran to her.

'I never,' she said between gasps, 'want to have . . . anything to do . . . with bedding . . . ever again.'

Harald stroked her back nervously. Her breathing was relaxing again but to his intense relief she did not pull away this time.

'How come,' she murmured into his chest, 'this babe of yours was so much fun to put inside me and yet it's so hellish to get out?'

He kissed the top of her head.

'It will be fun again,' he promised.

'Not just for you.'

'No. It's much more fun for me when it's fun for you too.'

It was truer than he'd realised. Tora had been attentive, almost embarrassingly so, but she had never seemed truly to enjoy herself and that had made him feel somehow useless.

'It's always fun for me,' Elizaveta said, 'or it was.'

This time he claimed her lips, briefly, tenderly.

'Just you,' he swore to her. 'From now on, Lily, it's just you.'

She tried to reach her hands up around his neck but her bump pushed her too far away and instead she grabbed at his hair, pulling his face down so their foreheads touched and he felt hers slick with sweat.

'I thought a king should have a mistress?'

'Says who?'

'She will not be happy.'

Harald thought about this.

'I think she might, Lily. She did not seem to find it anywhere near as enjoyable as you do.'

'Hari!' She batted at his chest. 'I don't want to know.'

'Just hear this then, Lily: she will be relieved to be rid of me. I will give her a farmhouse or something.'

Elizaveta rolled her eyes.

'You Norwegians and your farmhouses,' she said but the words stumbled and she grabbed at him, pulling his tunic so tight he thought it might strangle him.

Both of them fought for breath until the pain subsided and her hold loosened.

'You,' he told her when he could speak again, 'shall have your stone house, my sweet.'

'No.'

'No?'

'No. I've decided I don't want that and you don't either.'

'I don't?'

'No. A king should not live on a farm.'

'A big farm.'

'No, Hari. Come, you've lived in Kiev, you've even lived in Miklegard for heaven's sake so you must see – in this day and age a king needs a city.'

Harald stared at his tiny wife, her dark cheeks flushed with pain and her belly pulsing with his child.

'You want me to build you a city?'

'Build *us* a city, Hari, yes. Forget Denmark for now; let us make Norway great and let us start with a proper capital. I have had letters from my sisters in Hungary. Andrew is king, praise God, and Anastasia says they are working to develop a settlement on the Danube river called Buda into a worthy place from which to rule. She writes that she lives in a great new palace and that she has been given free rein to commission builders and artisans to make it greater yet. Agatha confirms it.'

She ground her teeth as another spasm rocked her.

'A city?' Harald said, testing the idea. 'A capital for Norway? But we have Nidaros, Lily.'

Elizaveta tossed her head.

'Nidaros is not a city, Harald. It is a market, no more; a rough little harbourside market. And what's more it's up here, in the north, where all those overblown lords rule the roost. You need a city in the sou . . . ow!'

He held her through the next pain. They seemed to be getting longer and closer together and he looked nervously to the door wondering if he could call back the midwives, though at the same time his mind was racing. A city in the south, deep within the safety of the great fjord in his Ringerike homelands? As Elizaveta returned to him he leaned back a little to look into her eyes.

'A city, Lily?'

'Yes. That will show Norway where its future lies and who it lies with. Who wants Magnus and his remote wooden farmhouse when they can have Harald in a palace for all to see, in a walled city full of churches and libraries, statues and courtyards and ooowww! Harald, it hurts. It hurts so much.'

'I'll call Greta.'

She nodded and he shouted towards the door for assistance. It flew back and Greta, no longer the timid girl he remembered, strode inside, the two midwives waddling in her wake.

'It hurts her,' Harald told them urgently.

'It will, Sire. It hurts all women, even queens.'

He crushed Elizaveta against him.

'She will be safe though?'

'We'll take very good care of her,' Greta assured him.

'You must. She is very precious.'

'As are all women,' one of the midwives intoned piously.

'No! She is far more precious than that.'

The poor woman cowered and Elizaveta, recovering again, let out a low laugh.

'All will be well, Hari.'

He looked at her. She seemed tired, frail. She had always had a fragile quality to her slim frame but never before had he feared she might actually break. She was tough, strong, wild. He held her against him again.

'I can't lose you, Lily. I love you – you know that.'

'I know, Hari.'

Her voice was wavering again.

'You and me,' he said urgently. 'It's just you and me now, my Lilyveta – you and me always.'

'You and me,' she echoed but the words were swallowed up in a roar of pain and the midwives rushed forward, somehow lifting her from him and moving her onto the bed.

'Let me stay,' he said desperately.

Greta put a gentle hand on his arm.

'No, Sire, please. This is woman's work and we will do it best alone.'

'I . . .'

'We will see her safe, Sire, I promise. Now please . . .'

'Lily!' he called out but she was lost in the spasm and could not reply and before he knew it, he was outside, staring at the door.

Behind him someone coughed and he turned to see Ulf.

'You look pale, Hari.'

'Pale? God, yes, it's horrible in there.' Ulf waved for a servant and pressed a goblet of wine into Harald's hand. He gulped at it gratefully. 'What do we do now?' he asked his friend.

Ulf shrugged.

'We wait.'

'That's all?'

'That's all.'

Harald looked slowly around him. The hall was packed. His soldiers were outside in their own camp but all the lords and many of their ladies, come to welcome them home from their raiding, were gathered around the hearth. A large pot of stew sat over it and many held steaming bowls.

'You should eat,' Halldor suggested now, coming up next to Ulf. 'Keep your strength up.'

'Eat? Don't be ridiculous, Hal. I'm not the one who needs strength right now.'

'Even so, it could be a long wait.'

'Nonsense. You heard her – the babe must be close.'

Halldor shook his head pityingly.

'If I remember Aksel's birth correctly,' he said, 'she's only just getting started.'

And so it proved. Hour after miserable hour rolled past. Night fell. The lamps were lit around the walls of the hall and more stew was brought. Harald even ate some. People talked quietly amongst themselves, trying not to stare whenever Elizaveta's screams drowned out their words. Harald paced up and down, up and down, with his men taking brave turns accompanying him as his temper grew with his fear.

'It's quite normal,' a low voice said suddenly in his ear.

'Finn!'

Harald turned to his foster father. Finn and Einar had marched away to see Magnus laid out with all pomp. They intended taking him to nearby Nidaros to be buried beside Olaf, his sainted father, and Harald was worried what that might do to the mood in the north. Magnus's death was his chance to unite Norway, not divide her. He looked cautiously into Finn's eyes but Finn threw an arm around his shoulder as if there was not a care between them.

'Honestly, Harald,' he said, nodding towards Elizaveta's door, 'it sounds as if they are being ripped apart but it's quite normal.'

'Really? It doesn't seem very fair.'

'No,' Finn allowed. 'I'd not be a woman, even for all the gold in *your* caskets.'

Harald grimaced.

'Nor I.'

'Planting the seed seems a deal easier than bearing the fruit. And you, Harald, seem especially good at planting seed.'

Something in Finn's voice caught at Harald and even Elizaveta's cries seemed to fade slightly. Was he saying . . . ? Surely not? Elizaveta would kill him – if she was not dying already.

'What are you telling me, Finn?'

Finn leaned in close.

'I have news from Austratt. Joyous news.' Harald felt the stew he had forced down fighting to return. He put out a hand and found Halldor's broad shoulder, but his old friend could do nothing to protect him from this one. 'Tora is pregnant.'

Harald closed his eyes. He longed to ask if it was his but knew that would be mean. Foolish too, as he had been foolish. He'd let himself be seduced by Tora's softness, by her connections, by memories that ran deep into his past but that might now wreck his future. A cry from Elizaveta, louder than any that had gone before, rang out around the hall and Harald felt it shudder all the way through him.

'A king must have heirs,' Finn said calmly.

'A king,' Harald snapped back, 'would rather have a queen.'

'Oh well,' Finn said, 'you have plenty of those too now.'

Harald stared at him.

'I cannot make Tora my queen, Finn. I am wed already.'

'And pray God your wife stays safe.' Finn looked pointedly at the chamber door. 'You could handfast, Harald,' he went on, his voice dangerously soft, 'as many have before you.'

'Tora would never agree to that.'

'Tora would do as she is told. As might a king who needed support against a possible rebellion in the north.'

'Are you threatening me, Finn?'

'Of course not. Guiding you, that's all. Magnus is dead, Harald; this is your opportunity – *our* opportunity. You are like a son to me, you know that. I just want to see what's best for you.'

'And you think that is two wives? Good God, man, I am suffering enough with one. When on earth will this be over?'

'I'm sure it will be easier with Tora. Her mother birthed very quickly.'

It was too much. Harald grabbed Finn's tunic, pulling him close.

'Now, Finn, is not the time for this. I am busy with my wife, my Christian wife, and . . .'

A new cry stopped him short – a tiny, plaintive but deter-mined little cry. He looked at the door as the whole court leaped to its feet.

'Not the time,' Finn agreed calmly. 'Go, Harald – see your child, your first-born but not, remember, your last. We will talk again.'

Harald heard the words. Some part of his brain stored them nervously away but for now all he wanted was to see Elizaveta. He ran for the chamber door but it was barred. He banged his fists against the wood.

'Let me in.'

'One moment, Sire.' The voice was wavery, faint.

'Now. Let me in now.'

'Please, you must . . .'

'No. No more waiting. Let me in or my axe will do so.' The bolt slid slowly back to reveal the older midwife, her ample frame blocking the gap. 'Where is she?'

'Your child is safe born, Sire, and . . .'

'Where is she? Where's my wife?'

'The queen just needs a little time. She just . . .'

But Harald had heard enough. He pushed her aside and stepped in.

'Lily?'

Elizaveta was on the bed, lying there so pale it looked as if every drop of her blood had been drained from her and maybe it had, for the sheets were soaked and her poor naked legs were caked red where they poked from her sodden shift. Greta was tending to her but seeing Harald she stepped back, bloody rags clutched to her chest. Harald's hands went to his mouth. He dared not move.

'This surely,' he whispered to Halldor at his shoulder, 'is not normal?'

Halldor's strained 'no' seemed to scratch at his very soul and he flung himself forward.

'Lily?' Her eyes flinched open. 'Oh, thank God. Lily, I thought you were . . .'

'Don't say it, Hari. I thought I was too but I am here.'

'You are here.'

'The babe?'

'The . . .' He looked around, confused. 'I almost forgot.'

'Hari! I go through all this and you almost forget?'

Her voice was faint but he heard the teasing within it and his spirits soared. Then, suddenly, she sighed and it seemed to shake her whole body.

'Lily – what's wrong?'

'It is a girl, Hari. I . . . I'm sorry.'

'Sorry? You're *sorry*? Oh my sweet – never be sorry. Where is she? Where is my princess?'

The second midwife brought forward a tiny bundle of white cloth and, taking it, Harald peeled back the warm folds and looked upon his daughter. Two big, dark eyes, so exactly like her mother's, blinked up at him and to his astonishment and horror he felt tears well in his eyes. Tears!

'She's beautiful,' he managed, blinking ferociously.

'Hari – are you crying?'

'No.'

Elizaveta laughed softly and he went back to her and sat gently on the side of the bed. Greta had pulled a fresh sheet over the mess and all looked pristine but he hadn't got so soft as to be fooled.

'Has the bleeding stopped?' he demanded of the midwives.

'We believe so, Sire, but she must rest.'

Harald looked at Elizaveta. She'd put out a hand to the baby but her eyes were closing and he felt the damned tears rising again. He stood up firmly.

'We shall call her Maria,' he said.

'Maria?'

The midwives exchanged glances at the strange Latinate name.

'Maria,' he repeated, 'to honour her Rus heritage and in praise of Maria, Mother of Christ, that she may keep Elizaveta safe.'

"Tis a noble Christian name,' one of them volunteered.

'For a noble Christian king,' Harald agreed, adding wretchedly to himself: 'who has – who *can* have – only one wife.'

He glanced back at Elizaveta but she looked little more than a shadow in the stained bed and he prayed, as he had never truly prayed before that, despite his many sins, God would look down on him today and bring her safely back.

CHAPTER TWENTY-THREE

Oslo, Christ's Mass 1046

'We were trapped!' Halldor's voice rang out around the packed hall. 'Trapped in a fog that wrapped itself around us as if our own dragon-prow were breathing fumes; trapped in a fjord as narrow as a maiden's passage and as steep as the granite walls of hell; trapped with Danish ships in an arc across our only escape route like a sickle of death.'

Elizaveta smiled. She had not heard one of Halldor's tales for some time and, despite the dark content, she welcomed it as a sign that all was well again. Harald had told her little of the men's bitter campaign against Svein this summer, dismissing it as 'a disaster', but listening to Halldor now it sounded a triumph. It seemed that even the worst events could be polished up by the funny warrior's rhetoric and she wondered what gloss he might find for her own travails.

If he ever told it, she did not want to hear. Living through the pain of Maria's birthing and the endless, terrifyingly slow days of recovery, had been bad enough without ever hearing it recounted, but live through it she had and for that she was unendingly grateful. She had held fast to fortune's wheel and fortune had lifted her out of the mire.

She and Harald had moved south once she had recovered, both to escape the prying eyes of the northern jarls and to look for the perfect site for their new city. They had found it on the banks of the river Lo and Harald had set his troops to building the great hall in which the courtiers were all now gathered.

The northern jarls were taking great pleasure in grumbling about its basic comforts but though it was true that it was rough at the moment, they had great plans for it. Some of the commanders had commissioned their own dwellings nearby and it gave Elizaveta great pleasure to see the city they were calling Oslo starting to take shape. She felt desperately proud of it and had personally supervised the plans for a great church. For now, they worshipped in an ancient wooden chapel, but new foundations had been laid and dedicated to Our Lady to give thanks for Elizaveta's survival and for their own little Maria.

She looked fondly across to her daughter, now a lively three-month-old and cradled in her father's big arm, her little hands waving and her dark eyes following Halldor's every exaggerated movement, though always her head flicked up if her father spoke. Maria was never happier than when she was with Harald and Elizaveta felt the accustomed whip of sadness that she was not a son, able to train with him as she grew. She forced it aside – why wish war on any child?

'It seemed,' Halldor intoned, arms high, 'that we were doomed. We had played the water-gods one too many times and they were sick of us.'

'Halldor,' Harald warned quietly.

He was still pursuing the devout Christian-king role that Elizaveta had long since realised was aimed at avoiding the handfast ceremony constantly demanded by the relentless Finn. She sighed. It had taken Harald weeks to admit to her that his wretched northern mistress was bearing him a second child and Elizaveta had seen no reason to make it easy for him, for it was as painful as hellfire for her.

'Just you and me' had been a blissful dream, remembered on a haze of birthing pain, but she'd soon seen that it would not now be possible and much as she hated that fact, she had learned to accept it. What other choice was there? She'd recalled her mother's laughing words about wishing Yaroslav would take a concubine and had tried to be glad that someone else would have to go through the horror of producing an heir for Norway. But it was hard and, despite her best efforts, her eyes narrowed as she glanced down the table to where Tora sat, her pale skin rosy, her blonde hair glossy and her belly as round as a full moon and every bit as pleased with itself.

Elizaveta rubbed at her beautiful finger ring, nervously tracing the pattern of Harold's love in the inset jewels. The Arnassons had come to Oslo two weeks ago and were housed in a sumptuous set of pavilions on the far side of the meadows – though not nearly far away enough for Elizaveta. All through the Yule period the damned woman had been wearing gowns specially cut to exaggerate the swell of her bastard babe and her damned uncle had paraded her on his arm everywhere they went as if she were some sort of jewel – which Elizaveta supposed for her family she was.

She had envied Tora for birthing in her own land with her mother close, until Harald – in one of their rare, awkward conversations about his mistress – had told her Tora's mother had died when she was still small. For a moment Elizaveta had almost felt sorry for her rival, and then she'd reminded herself that Tora had both a sister and a brother nearby and of course her devoted, pushy uncle to ever watch her back, and had returned to hating her, stoking her anger to avoid another uncomfortable truth – that, blooming in the seventh month of her pregnancy, Tora Arnasson looked more than ever like Ingrid and Elizaveta, cherishing her own hard-won child, yearned, with a sorrow that made her feel uncomfortably vulnerable, to be with her mother. Now, she tore her eyes away from Tora and, closing them, sent her thoughts across sea and downriver to Kiev.

Ingrid had sent gifts for Maria, Yaroslav too, and, more precious than the fancy toys and cups, ivory teethers and rich silks for tiny gown, a letter:

I wish so much I could be with you and your daughter, my own dearest girl, Ingrid had written, *and can only hope that she brings you as much joy as you have brought me – and perhaps a little less trouble.* Elizaveta had smiled through her tears at that and even more so at her mother's parting words: *say hello to the trolls for me.*

Her family seemed, these days, to be little more than a shadow on vellum. Anastasia had sent a brief note in a neat hand that Elizaveta knew was not her own, though the words had been sincere. She had praised the value of daughters, saying her own Adelaide was a delight to her but Elizaveta had heard the unspoken regret that Anastasia had not, as yet, produced a son either and had felt for her proud sister. Anastasia had always longed to produce kings; it must be hurting her to have so far failed to do so.

Agatha had written too, a long, rambling missive, full of praise of Edward and funny tales of Hungarian society and with word that she, too, was pregnant. It seemed Yaroslav's grandchildren were entering the world fast. Anne remained unwed, though the emissaries from France had returned to Yaroslav and he was negotiating her dowry. She'd written that Kiev was quiet these days and that she had heard much praise of Paris, the French first city, and Elizaveta had sensed how she yearned to move on. How far away was Paris, she wondered sometimes? Or Buda? Close enough to visit? She'd vowed to look into it, for in those long days recovering from her vicious childbed she'd felt very alone with just Greta and Aksel – and, of course, Harald.

For if Harald was seeing the woman bearing his next child, he was doing so very briefly and very secretively. Tora, so Elizaveta had learned from Greta, had a pavilion all to herself but she must be alone in it most of the time for Harald slept every night at Elizaveta's side and sat at every meal with her. In return, if occasionally he was gone from view for an hour or two Elizaveta let her passions loose on her viol and managed not to snipe or even comment on his return. She was secretly rather proud of herself – this, she hoped, was what her mother would finally recognise in her as 'dignity'. She blinked and forced herself to return to the present moment.

'What did you do?' someone called out to Halldor, though whether for dramatic effect or to hurry him out of the metaphors that seemed to grow longer and grander as he grew older, was hard to tell.

Halldor put up a hand.

'What *could* we do? We were . . .'

'Trapped,' his audience provided.

'Exactly! Trapped as a bug beneath a goblet, as a . . .'

'As an audience before a poet,' someone supplied and Halldor frowned.

'Very well. I shall cut to the chase. If we could not run and we could not dodge, we had to coerce. First we threw barrels full of the finest ale from Odense into the sea to tempt them. One boat went skittering after but it was not enough so we released caskets of treasure. We kept the treasure back, mind, all save a chain or two, artfully draped out of the clasp – Danes are easy to fool!' This won him a roar of approval which he acknowledged with a grin. 'They dived for those, losing formation and we edged forward, poised to duck through the gap, but Svein hollered them back and pressed on with the attack. We were, it seemed, doomed.'

Halldor paused dramatically and, hearing a gasp behind, Elizaveta glanced back to see her squire leaning eagerly forward as if physically pulled into his father's vivid story. She smiled. Aksel was twelve now and too old to sit at her feet but he had positioned himself, as ever, at her shoulder, poised to serve. The young man had sat at the door of her chamber as much as Harald after Maria's birth – nay, more, for no one had called him to kingly duties as they had her poor husband. Once she was sitting up, he had brought her fresh flowers to make her chamber smell sweet, and pestered the cooks for delicacies to tempt her pathetic appetite, and always been there to offer her his arm when she wished to try and coax her feeble legs back into action.

'My son is sweet on you,' Halldor was always teasing her.

'No, Hal,' she'd correct him, 'he is just sweet.'

In truth, she had a suspicion that it was Greta he was sweet on, for there had often been flowers and pastries for her maid too, but since they had come to Oslo, Halldor had drawn his son into training with the men. Looking at his eager face now, Elizaveta supposed it was time but she would miss him if he went raiding in Denmark next summer, and fear for him besides if Halldor's tales were even half true.

'There was only one thing for it,' the Icelander was crying gleefully, 'prisoners. No general can refuse to help his own men so over they went, screaming and yelling in their soft southern accents. Some we tossed high – you should have seen them cutting holes in the mist with their flailing arms and legs. Some we sent out on an oar balanced over the gunwale, teetering and tottering like infants learning to walk until their fat arses overbalanced them and they tumbled into the deep. Some we even drove up the mast at sword-point and made them jump from the very top like our landwaster raven flying high above, only without the wings!'

Halldor sighed happily.

'Fine sport! Soon the sea was awash with Danes weeping for their mamas and what could Svein do but sail in to scoop them up? And what could we do but slip away through the gaps, set our sails and make for the open seas, a hundred prisoners lighter and faster than he? And here we are!'

'Here we are indeed.' Harald rose, handing an indignant Maria over to Elizaveta, and clapped Halldor on the back. 'Though not quite all of us.' The court silenced instantly. 'Our Yuletide has been greatly saddened by the loss of my nephew, King Magnus.'

Elizaveta watched Harald intently. He had not, she knew, been in the slightest bit saddened by Magnus's death but she had been no better. At his memorial service she had tried to conjure up fond memories of the slim little boy she'd shared a schoolroom with back in Kiev but her thoughts had filled instead with pictures of her own vibrant siblings and all she had managed to remember of the young exile was irritation. She'd sent the news to her sisters but doubted they would feel any more sadness than she did. And, of course, Magnus's death meant Harald was now Norway's sole king. Rumours were flying, but even Einar did not seem to be able to make accusations of foul play stick and was contenting himself with obstructing his king in whatever ways he could.

'Our dear Magnus,' Harald went on, 'with many of our men, caught a fever aboard ship and though we sped him to land on my own personal craft – the fastest ship we have – we were too late to save him. His royal body is, as you know, interred where he would have wanted to be, with his saintly father and my brother, King Olaf, and I ask you all to pray, as I pray, for his soul and for the Lord's grace on those of us left behind without his light.'

Elizaveta kept her head low but over a squirming Maria she could see Einar glowering and feared that the repercussions of Magnus's sudden death had not yet even begun. The northern jarl had been fiercely devoted to Magnus, his protégé since he'd stolen him from Kiev, and at his funeral he had sworn vengeance on Harald. This icy show of friendship was as thin as the first frost, the waters beneath dark and tangled with dangerous currents.

The court shifted as Harald, their king, stood, blonde head devoutly bowed, but at last he raised his head, releasing them. Instantly the servants who were crowded at the back doors with the first dishes – curved blood puddings, crisp cheese and leek tartlets, and fat pink prawns – stepped forward. The goblets were filled and the chatter of feasting consumed the uneasy silence of grief. Not that anyone seemed very grieved bar Einar and that was more, no doubt, for loss of his power than loss of his king.

Harald sat down and Elizaveta, handing Maria to Greta with a kiss, poured him some wine from a small cask she had bought at great expense from a French trader. It was called a 'rioja' and was from a country far in the south called Spain. Anne had recommended it after the French emissaries had brought some to Kiev and Elizaveta had been delighted with its rich, fruity taste.

'Try this,' she urged.

He drank.

'Nice. Is it Greek?'

'Spanish.'

'Spanish?! You are making me sophisticated, wife.'

'Never!'

He kissed her and she felt desire stir deep within her healing loins.

'Remember, Harald,' she said softly, 'when I was birthing Maria . . .'

'How could I forget?'

He paled and she pushed hastily on.

'I told you then that I was never having anything to do with bedding ever again.'

He grimaced.

'That I do remember.'

She ran her lips lightly across his neck.

'Well, I've changed my mind.'

Harald turned, clasping her chin to look deep into her eyes.

'You have? Are you sure?'

His eagerness set her alight.

'Very sure, Hari, though you may have to be gentle with me at first.'

'I shall try, my lovely Lilyveta,' he said, 'though as I recall it is rarely me who sets the pace.' She giggled, and he pulled her closer, kissing her full on the lips. 'But how,' he demanded, 'with such a promise, am I meant to concentrate on eating?'

Elizaveta grinned.

'You have no appetite, my lord?'

'Oh I have appetite, Lily, just not for anything on these dishes. Perhaps I should take you prisoner now?'

'Like those poor Danes?'

'*Poor* Danes?'

'Did you really make them jump from the rigging?'

He flushed, looked away.

'Of course not.'

'Because it's hardly going to win Denmark, is it, playing silly games?'

'Silly games?! I'm not the one playing silly games. Einar is the one doing that.'

'But you . . .' Elizaveta caught herself. His eyes were flashing fury and now was not the time to discuss war tactics. 'You will sort Einar out,' she soothed hastily. 'I know you will. Svein Estrithson too, when the time is right.'

Harald drew in a deep breath and nodded.

'The only reason I cannot,' he said tightly, 'is because Svein ducks battle. If I could draw him into an open fight I would defeat him and he knows it so he hides amongst his islands and forces me into his "silly games". It is infuriating.'

'Patience, Harald.'

'I do not have much of that, Lily.'

'Nor I, Hari,' she agreed, drawing him close, 'nor I, but look, we are growing up enough, at least, to avoid a quarrel.'

He licked his lips.

'Oh I'm not avoiding it, wife, just saving it for the chamber when I can be more . . . creative in my arguments.'

Heat stole through her again and she longed for the evening to be over.

'You said you would be gentle,' she reminded him.

'If that is what you wish?'

Elizaveta smiled silkily but before she could answer there was a strange cry from down the table and she looked over to see Tora pushing back her chair, her blue eyes flickering strangely. Finn leaped up, calling loudly for assistance, and Elizaveta groaned. The wretched woman must have seen her close to Harald and was deliberately making a fuss.

'You are unwell, my lady?' she bit out, Old Norse smooth on her tongue these days.

Tora looked across and for a moment their eyes locked. Elizaveta saw something in the other woman's – not jealousy, not bitterness, not even any sort of challenge, just naked fear, one woman to another. Then Tora looked down and as Elizaveta's eyes followed she saw the Norwegian's fine skirts were soaked through.

'Her waters have broken,' she gasped. 'Get her to her pavilion.'

'It's too far.'

Finn looked scared and with reason; Tora could not cross the snowy meadow in that condition.

'Get her, then,' Elizaveta said without thinking, 'to *my* chamber. Now!' she added furiously as everyone looked nervously at each other.

Could they not see that Tora was before her time, maybe too far before it? She could be in danger and Elizaveta knew all too well how that felt. But as Tora moved up the rough temporary stairs to the royal chambers above, she realised what she had done. Now, instead of Harald making love to her in her beautiful bed, the one piece of luxury in their nascent city, his mistress would be birthing his child there. She felt a brief, evil wish that her rival might not make it through this but that died as the remembrance of Tora's face pulled at her heart. She could wish no ill on any poor woman in childbirth.

'I shall retire to the church,' she said.

'Lily.' Harald put out a hand to her. She placed her own in his but kept her distance and he lifted it to his lips. 'I love you.'

She smiled at him but could not bring herself to answer. Pulling gently away, she looked for Aksel who rushed forward, offering his slim arm. Clasping it tighter than anyone else needed to know, she left the hall. New snow was falling on the cleared log-paving and Elizaveta felt it fizz on her hot cheeks, cooling her as they headed towards the church.

'That was well done, my lady,' Aksel said softly in his newly deep voice.

'Dignified,' she told him, 'that's what I was looking for.'

'It was that indeed, but more besides, my lady; it was queenly.'

*

Elizaveta settled into the old chapel for a long night. Aksel fetched chairs and cushions and a brazier, and Greta came running with furs. None of them even pretended to pray. Aksel set wine to warm over the fire and Elizaveta sipped at it, hoping vaguely that this was not her costly Spanish grape he was mulling. But she had barely drunk a single goblet before a messenger scuttered through the big doors and they turned from their makeshift dinner to stare. He bowed low.

'Come forward,' Elizaveta urged. 'You have news?'

'Yes, my lady.'

Her heart beat madly as the man almost crawled towards her, head bowed low. He was here so quickly it could only be an ill report. She rose and looked up to the crumbling ceiling and it seemed as if even the angels in the faded fresco above her head leaned down to hear. The man traced a pattern in the earthen floor with his foot.

'The Lady Tora is safely delivered.'

'Already?' Elizaveta gasped.

'Yes, my lady.'

'Lucky her,' she muttered furiously, and then remembered herself. 'She is well?'

'She is.'

'Good.' She said it firmly, loudly, forcing it out to echo around God's church. 'And the babe?'

'Is small but breathing.'

'Good.' Again the word rang off crooked walls. 'It is . . . ?' The messenger sucked in his breath and with that she knew; had she not, indeed, known already? 'A boy,' she said heavily.

The lad nodded dumbly. Greta ran to Elizaveta's side and she heard Aksel pouring more wine but put up a hand to refuse such shallow comfort.

'A boy,' she said again.

She glanced out of the window opening to the stone

foundations of her cathedral – the little slice of Kiev she planned to raise to her daughter – and suddenly it seemed such a futile creation. What use to Harald were fancy stoneworks and glittering frescoes? All he truly needed to be secure in this farmhouse country of his was an heir and it was not she who had given them that. She drew her cloak close around her as once she had done out on the walls of her childhood city when she had urged Harald not to be an empty hero. She had seen such a future for them then, a storyteller's future, but the story was proving harder to craft than she'd ever dreamed possible.

'What have they named him?'

They! She did not want there to be a 'they' – only a 'we'.

'Magnus.'

It was not the messenger who spoke but a deeper, lower, far more familiar voice.

'Harald?'

He was standing in the doorway, lit up by the ghostly glow of the fast-falling snow beyond, and as she turned his way he came forward, covering the ground in long strides, his boots sending thunder-claps around the tiny church. The messenger ducked thankfully away and Greta drew Aksel tactfully into the shadows as Elizaveta went slowly to meet her husband.

'Magnus?' she dared to ask.

'In honour of our dead king.'

'That is . . . apt.'

His hand stole around her waist and though she longed to push it away she yearned for his touch.

'I thought so,' he said lightly.

'And yet you, you always said you wanted an Olaf as your heir.'

His other hand stole around her waist.

'I do, Lily, and I want him to be yours.'

She swallowed.

'You should not be here.'

'Yet I am.'

She dared to look up at him.

'You will have to handfast to her now.'

'Perhaps. Perhaps not. I have other plans for sorting Einar Tambarskelve.'

'Plans? Hari, don't do anything . . .'

'I will take care of it, Lily. *You* are my wife and the future King Olaf is yours to have – if you wish it?'

He was looking at her with such love, such concern. Across the snowy courtyard his son had been born yet he was here with her. Of course she wanted it, yet ringing in her ears were other words: 'You should not birth again,' the midwife had said to her. 'Truly, my lady, you should not; you are too slight. Another baby, especially a big one – especially a boy – could kill you.'

'I have to have a boy,' she'd told her, even then, with blood still drying on her thighs.

'It's too dangerous, my lady.'

Elizaveta had thought of the Rapids Race. Her mind, half-crazed, had seen the course as clearly as if she'd been riding that canoe into the head of the frothing water.

'I like danger,' she'd said. 'Tell no one this, do you hear – no one!'

The midwife had reluctantly agreed and now Elizaveta was glad. She reached up to run her finger slowly down the line of the scar that marked the day Harald had lost his royal brother Olaf back at Stikelstad, the battle that had sent him to her.

'I wish it,' she said and kissed him.

CHAPTER TWENTY-FOUR

Oslo, November 1049

'How dare she?'

Harald strode into the garden of Tora's city dwelling where she was helping Magnus to line up ants along the little wooden sword his father had ordered fashioned for him. It was a beautiful toy but two-year-old Magnus much preferred bug-play to war-play and Tora saw no need to change that.

'Something wrong, Harald?' she asked mildly.

'Ungrateful, that's what she is. Ungrateful and mean.'

'Elizaveta?' Tora hazarded, though of course it was Elizaveta; no one else ever roused the King of Norway to such rage.

'Yes, Elizaveta. Damn her.'

Tora shifted uneasily. She knew she should be pleased to hear him talk of his Slav queen this way – Finn certainly would be if he were here – but mainly she just found herself wondering if he would ever feel strongly enough about her to damn her. Or, indeed, she about him.

She loved him, of course she did – loving him was almost part of her blood – and she cherished him as the father of her child, but this crazed passion he had with Elizaveta, all smiles one minute and rage the next, looked exhausting. She had been delighted when their strange, brief affair had taken seed but the arrival of her son had cast further doubt onto her already confused feelings for his father.

The overwhelming, ecstatic love she'd felt towards little Magnus from the moment she'd held him in her arms far outweighed anything Harald had ever sparked in her, even back on the beach that first midsummer night. This heart-swelling maternal emotion had consoled her that she was not, after all, totally weak-hearted, but she still sometimes wondered at the furious love Elizaveta seemed to feel for Harald.

For her own part, Tora kept her relations with the king as businesslike as she could. Harald had ordered a beautiful house built for her just outside Austratt. She had a loyal household, a thriving farm, and her dear son. And even when, as now, she had to travel to Oslo to be with the official court, she had this beautiful house, several streets away from Elizaveta's fancy new palace. Tora longed to dislike Oslo but in truth it was very pretty and far more clement than Nidaros, plus she could spend precious time with Johanna and Johan, the son she had recently borne Ulf. Magnus was fascinated by his tiny cousin and Tora was fascinated by Magnus, and if Harald only visited her rarely, mainly to rage about Elizaveta, she did not much mind.

She usually roused herself to take him into her bed on the few occasions he requested it but mainly, she had to admit, more out of longing for another child than for him. Every so often Finn muttered about handfasting and some part of Tora would like the affirmation of a ceremony but, truly, the fierce love she felt for Magnus was all the alliance she needed, and his very existence bound her to Norway's bold king more than any ribbons could. Now she drew Harald forward, pushing him gently down into a seat. His hands were actually shaking with rage; what on earth had happened now?

'You'd think she'd be happy, wouldn't you?' he demanded.

'She is a very lucky woman,' Tora agreed tentatively.

'She is, isn't she? She should be on her knees thanking God for me, shouldn't she? Not screaming at me as if I am little Maria caught getting into mischief.'

Tora smiled at that, though she quickly raised a hand to hide it. Maria, newly turned three, was a headstrong child, always being caught where she should not be. Unlike Magnus who was happy, when allowed into a feast, to sit quietly playing with counters or just watching the adults, Maria was always up and down. Only the other day the All Hallows feasting had been violently interrupted by a hideous scream. Investigation had revealed that Maria had brought a toad into the hall 'because it looked hungry'. The creature, escaping his mistress the minute her attention had wandered – as it so often did – had taken a liking to one unfortunate lady's green skirts and sprung himself into her lap.

'She shouldn't dress like a lily leaf,' had been Maria's defence when she'd been unveiled as the culprit by her own cry of 'There you are, Filip!'

'Filip' had been returned to the fjord and Maria to her chamber but it had been clear that her doting father had only imposed the punishment for show and, as usual, it had not kept her down for long. Today's trouble, though, was clearly more than just child's play.

'What's happened, Harald?' Tora begged.

'Happened? She screamed at me, that's what's happened.'

'I see that, Harald,' Tora agreed. Sometimes she almost fell into calling him Hari but always she fought to resist the wretched shortening. 'But why?'

'Why? Oh. She thinks I was foolish to kill Einar.'

'Ah.'

Tora bit her lip. She should have guessed and for once she had to agree with Harald's wretched slip of a wife – not that she would say so. Norway had been a-buzz with the news ever since Harald had invited Einar to negotiations up at Bymarka and Einar had come out in a coffin. Einar, so the story went, vividly told by Harald's troll-man, had threatened the king – drawn a sword on him. There had been little choice, as sad as it was, but to strike in self-defence.

Even Halldor, though, had been unable to inject much true sorrow into the piece and another story was being whispered about the court – a story of ambushes, swords left outside, lights extinguished in an artificial Stikelstad. This other tale had a ring of truth but no one was yet challenging the official version for fear of Svein Estrithson getting his claws into Norway as he might surely do without the fearsome Harald securing her borders. Einar's family, however, were swearing a blood-feud and despite the fact that such ancient practices were banned by the church, news of it was being gleefully passed around.

'What was I meant to do?' Harald asked Tora now. 'Stand there and let him slaughter me?'

'No man could slaughter you, Harald.'

'He might,' he snapped, eyes narrowing, 'with surprise on his side and a force at his back.'

'He might,' she rushed to agree. 'Any man might kill another that way.'

He looked suspiciously at her but let it go.

'"Reckless", Elizaveta called me. Reckless – me! I am famed, Tora, for my calm decision-making. I am not reckless.'

'Of course not, Harald, or you would long be dead.'

'Exactly! You understand me.' He smiled at her but did not move closer, did not pull her into his arms to kiss her. '"Ruthless",' he raged on. 'That was another word she threw at me. She said Einar had called me that once, way back in Kiev, and now she knew he was right.'

'Ruthless?' Tora stepped closer, thinking fast. 'But is that not, Harald, a good thing in a leader? Strong, decisive, unwavering.'

He looked at her, surprised.

'I suppose it is, yes. *Hardrada.*' He rolled the older Norse word around his tongue. 'Harald Hardrada – it has a certain ring to it.' He pulled Tora in, kissing her at last, though when he pulled back he added, 'That'll show her!'

Tora sighed.

'Why does she think it was stupid, Hari . . . Harald?'

'Because of this wretched blood-feud. She says Einar was getting old and cantankerous and no one was paying him much attention anyway. She says that without Magnus he lacked power and if I'd just gone on ignoring him he'd have been no threat. She's so naïve.'

Tora wasn't convinced Elizaveta was the naïve one here, but she saw the chance and would be a fool to miss it.

'She does not, perhaps,' she suggested softly, 'understand Norway as well as you and I?'

'That's it exactly.'

'She does not, perhaps, see how easy it is to drive a wedge into a king's power in a country so divided by mountains and forests and fjords that men from different regions can go months without seeing each other?'

'She does not, Tora.'

'And she does not, perhaps, sitting in this fancy southern city, understand how strong the lords of the north are? Norway's defence lies less in stout walls . . .'

'And more in stout hearts!'

Harald grabbed Tora and swung her round. Little Magnus clapped delightedly and Harald glanced at him, as if seeing him for the first time, but then bent down and drew him, too, into his arms. Magnus squirmed. Tora sometimes thought his big, fiery-eyed father scared him a little and she prayed now that he would not cry.

'You listen to your mother, son, and you will make a great King of Norway. Stout hearts – that's it! I told Elizaveta that once, you know, but she does not listen to me, not ever.'

Magnus squirmed again and Harald, thankfully, put him down but the exchange had given Tora time to think.

'This blood-feud, Harald,' she said, 'it is more for show. You know how the northern lords cherish their independence and this is just a way to try and assert that. You need simply offer penance – some money, some land – and they will drop it. We are not pagans any more, even as far up as Tromso.' He laughed at the local joke and she moved closer. 'Send Finn.'

'What?'

'Send Finn to talk to them, to make peace.'

'Would he?'

'You know he would. Let's call for him.'

'Now?'

'Now. We can sort this out, Harald. We can sort this,' she dared to add, 'together.'

Harald nodded slowly.

'You are so calm, Tora.'

'Someone has to be,' she said lightly and went to the door to send for her uncle.

Finn arrived fast and was more than happy to help on two conditions.

'A handfast ceremony?' Harald suggested, too wearily for Tora's comfort, but Finn shook his head.

'I want Kalv back from the Orkneys, Sire. I want him out of exile with Thorfinn and Idonie and back in Norway. He will help me keep the balance of power in the north.'

'Balance – Kalv?'

Harald laughed bitterly. Tora thought of her hot-headed

uncle, who'd always been brewing trouble, and feared Harald was right not to believe her uncle's claims but Kalv was family and it was her duty to support her uncle in seeking his return.

'He's matured,' she suggested.

'You think so?'

'He must have,' Finn agreed hastily. 'And even if he hasn't, Einar's lot are scared of him.'

'That much is true. Fine, send for him. Second condition?'

Finn smiled.

'A handfast ceremony.'

They were bound together that afternoon in the forests above Oslo, in a clearing created by Elizaveta's many city builders. It was a brief ceremony, assembled quickly before Elizaveta could find out and attended by a ring of courtiers hastily scooped up to bear witness. Delighted with the unexpected excitement on an otherwise dull day at court, the clandestine party was surprisingly merry.

Johanna was there, Johan on her hip and Ulf at her side, magnificent in his marshal's uniform. Halldor was there too, glowering darkly and muttering about bigamy as if he was some sort of moral guardian and not a filthy-mouthed soldier with a son by a slave girl. Finn's choir of ill-rehearsed but sweet-voiced youngsters drowned him out and within what felt to Tora like moments she and Harald were being led round the back streets to her house.

'Bedding,' Finn announced, almost the moment they crossed the threshold.

'Bedding?' Tora gasped. 'Uncle, we have a son!'

'Only one,' Finn shot back. 'The court will see this done properly – as, Niece, will you.'

His meaning was shamefully clear and Tora found herself being bundled into bed by Johanna and her cousin Sigrid, though the winter sun was still high in the sky and she'd had no more to eat than a taste of broken honey-cake and a sip of bridal ale in the rough ceremony.

'Here.' Johanna reached forward and threaded flowers into her hair. 'Like your betrothal.'

They were hardy white winter roses, not soft clover flowers, but Tora appreciated the link all the same and kissed her sister fondly.

'This feels very strange.'

'It *is* a bit strange,' Johanna agreed frankly. She glanced at Sigrid, recently married with great ceremony to a worthy young earl, and hastily added, 'but it is better than nothing.'

Better than nothing! Tora touched her fingers to the flowers and wished she were back on a beach with twelve-year-old joy in her heart and simple seaweed to bind their hands. Those times were long gone though and now the men were delivering Harald to her, cheering raucously. She forced herself to look up at the door as they tumbled inside and, as she saw he was dressed in only a cloak, another shiver of memory broke the harsh cheer of the afternoon with something more tender.

'Your idea?' she asked, gesturing to the cloak. 'Sweet.'

'Oh Tora, if only I were.' Harald shut the door on the rest of the court and moved closer to the bed. 'I have used you ill.'

Tora reached up and touched his cheek.

'I am not complaining.'

'I know! That makes it harder.'

'You would rather I screamed at you?'

'No. I have enough of that from . . . No. Come here.'

He put out his arms and she moved into them.

'Are you doing this for my uncle, Harald?'

He shook his head.

'No, Tora, truly. The handfasting, yes. It is a nonsense cere-mony and I hope you and I know our ties to each other without

JOANNA COURTNEY

dancing them out in a wood. This bedding, though, this I do because you, Tora, are the sweet one – sweet and kind and soft and gorgeous.'

Then his mouth was on hers and he was pulling her beneath him and she clutched him close and wondered as he moved inside her how very glorious it would be to have him hate her as passionately as he hated – as he *loved* – Elizaveta.

CHAPTER TWENTY-FIVE

Oslo, April 1050

'It's all so perfect, Hari. Isn't it perfect?'

Elizaveta looked up at Harald, willing him to love her new venture as she did. The city of Oslo was growing swiftly under her careful guidance and today its myriad new citizens were all out to watch their young men dare to participate in the inaugural Rapids Race. The great seawater fjord did not freeze as the Dnieper had so there was not quite the same feeling of release but up in the forested mountains, the waters of the Lo were being set free and the current was more than strong enough to create an exciting race down into the open finish in the fjord.

Elizaveta had been delighted when she'd found the winding rocky tributary that rose up out of the north-west of the city into the hills and had been personally supervising the training of the men who would be Norway's first ever rapids riders. One of them in particular she had trained hard and as she, with the rest of the excited crowd, peered upriver, she prayed sixteen-year-old Aksel would fulfil his potential and take the prize – a jewelled cup she had persuaded Harald to part with from his still-bulging caskets of treasure.

'I hold the keys after all,' she'd told him, straddling him, naked of all bar her jewelled ring and her neck chain, wrapped like a scarf around her throat.

'You hold all the keys, Lily,' he'd agreed slightly ruefully, stirring, as always, beneath her.

'And don't you forget it!'

Now she squeezed his arm eagerly.

'Isn't it perfect?' she repeated.

'It looks quite good,' he agreed, his lip twitching.

'Quite good?! I think it's magnificent.'

'Then why do you care about my opinion?'

She pouted.

'I don't know, Hari. I sometimes wish I didn't – it would be much simpler if I could just let you come and go like Tora does.'

'Lily, hush.'

'Why?' she demanded, pulling three-year-old Maria back from the edge. 'It's true and it's not as if it matters. Finn is happy, there's peace in the north, Kalv is back – nasty creature that he is – and you have two new children on the way.'

'Lily . . .'

'I'm just stating facts, Hari. Not many kings can have such matching wives.'

Elizaveta ran a hand over the swell of her belly and looked across to a similarly bulging Tora, tying Magnus's tunic tighter against the crisp spring air. She had been furious when Harald had sheepishly admitted to his rushed handfasting but really, who wanted a husband you had to wed in the secrecy of the forest? Besides, Tora, strange woman that she was, did not seem to bother much with Harald any more.

'You know, Lily,' Harald said now, grabbing her hand and yanking her close to him, 'that save your bellies you and Tora are about as like as a deer to an eagle.'

Elizaveta laughed.

'You are calling me a deer, Hari?'

'You know I am not. Now hush – the race will start soon and you'll miss it with all this gabbling.'

Elizaveta smiled and turned to look upriver again, memories swirling around her. She felt a sharp jab of pain that none of her family could be here to share this moment. Greta had been a wonderful support but her maid could hardly join her on the royal grandstand and she missed her sisters.

Agatha was still in Hungary and had birthed two daughters. She seemed happy there, settled even, and Elizaveta almost envied her proximity to Anastasia. She had heard nothing much from her brothers, though her mother wrote that they were well. She thought of Vladimir, once the closest of her siblings, and suddenly saw him running into the boathouse to fetch her the fateful day that Ulf had visited with the first of Harald's treasure keys. The memory bloomed and she recalled the eagle-prow that Jakob had offered to carve for her – the eagle-prow that had watched benevolently as she and Harald had first lain together. No wonder that's how Harold saw her.

'Hari.' She tugged on his arm and he looked impatiently down. 'Hari, do you still have my prow?'

'Your what?'

'My prow. The one shaped like an eagle that Jakob carved for me in Kiev. We brought it to Norway, remember?'

Suddenly it seemed a matter of utmost urgency to see it again. Was Jakob still alive? Was he still lovingly fashioning wood down in the Podol? Did he ever think about the little princess who had wanted wings for her very own ship?

'I remember,' Harald said. 'It must be in the treasury.'

'Underground? It will be sad down there.'

'Sad? Elizaveta, it's made of wood. It cannot be sad.'

'You told me once that wood lives.'

Harald rolled his eyes.

'You are determined to be contrary today, my sweet. I will find your eagle, I promise, and release him to the winds if it will make you happy but today, please, can we just watch the race – *your* race? Look – the flag is up!'

Elizaveta looked into the dense trees and the sight of the great red and white flag stirred her heart.

'You must beat the gong,' she said to Harald. He shook his head and she frowned. 'You must, Hari. The boats will be ready and it is hard to keep them steady on the start.'

'As you know?'

'As I know, yes. Please sound it.'

'No.'

'But . . .'

'*You* sound it.' He pushed the hammer into her hand, taking hold of Maria, who was still tugging to be closer to the water, and nudging her forward. 'And quickly, Lily – the boats are hard to keep steady on the start.'

All eyes were upon her so she resisted the urge to stick her tongue out at her infuriating royal husband and instead lifted the hammer and brought it down with all her might into the big copper gong. The soft sound, rich with memories, rippled across the water and, further up the hillside, the others sang out like echoes until, to a whoop from the excited crowd, the starting flag went down and the race was begun. Elizaveta fixed her gaze on the trees, looking for the flag at the first turn and praying Aksel's red one would be raised. The crowd hummed curiously.

'What happens now?' someone asked behind Elizaveta.

'They are taking the first turn,' she explained, turning eagerly. 'They will . . . oh.' She stopped, for there was Tora, her big blue eyes as surprised as Elizaveta's own at who had chosen to answer her. 'They will drop into a pool halfway up,' Elizaveta forced herself to say, 'and the flag bearers will raise a colour in the trees to signal which rider enters the rapids first. There, oh there – look! It's red!' Unthinkingly she'd clutched Tora's arm at the sight and now she dropped it like a hot coal. 'That means Aksel is in the lead.'

'Your squire?'

'Yes.'

'That's good then.'

Elizaveta nodded, unsure what to do now. She rarely spoke to Harald's handfast woman and never kindly; it felt as strange as taking a sip of ale and finding it to be mead. Not unpleasant, just all wrong. Thankfully the canoes were soon tipping into view. The crowd upriver were leaping and cheering madly and the pulse of the competition rippled through the men and women at the wide finish, giving Elizaveta an excuse to turn away.

'Go on, Aksel!' she screamed. The young man was battling against a sharp Varangian, both boats tipping precariously as they dug their paddles into the churning water on the lower stretch of the race. 'Go on!'

'Dignity, Lily,' Harald's amused voice said in her ear.

'This is no time for dignity,' she retaliated, 'they're neck and neck.'

The crowd were roaring wildly, pushing up to the bank to see, and she tightened her hold on Maria who looked set to leap into the boat with their favourite. Then suddenly the other contender, trying to cut through along the near bank below them, caught his paddle on a root and slewed his boat. Aksel shot under the finish line, his rival coming through sideways just seconds behind and Elizaveta punched the air in delight.

'He won, Mama,' Maria called, every bit as pleased as her mother, and Harald bent down to sweep her into his arms. 'Can I give him the prize, Papa?' she demanded. 'I'll do it really well, promise. I'll let him kiss my hand and I'll say "Aksel Halldorsson, you are the winner" and I'll give him the cup very carefully. I won't drop it, promise I won't. Please, Papa?'

She wound a strand of his fair hair around her finger, something she was often wont to do, and he laughed and kissed her nose.

'It's your mama's cup to give, Maria.'

Maria looked at Lily, weighing up her chances, then back to Harald.

'But you're the king.'

Harald laughed louder.

'Queens count for more than kings, Maria, believe me.'

'Really? Is that, then, why you have two?'

The people around who had been indulgently watching their precocious princess sucked in their breath. Elizaveta glanced at Tora and to her astonishment the other woman came forward.

'No, Maria,' she said directly to the child in her soft voice, 'that is just because your papa is very, very lucky. Now look, the winners are coming – you'd better get the cup ready.'

Maria, thankfully, scrambled to do so, Harald ducking after her to 'help', and the two wives were left together.

'It's less lucky,' Elizaveta said under her breath, 'than greedy.'

'Probably,' came back the reply, 'but let's keep that one to ourselves.'

Elizaveta felt a ridiculous giggle building inside her. Her lips twitched and Tora, seeing it, smiled too.

'I'm meant to hate you,' Elizaveta said.

'You don't seem to me like a woman who does what she's meant to.'

'I try not to.'

Elizaveta looked on as Maria, clutched in Harald's arms, presented Aksel with his cup to cheers from the crowd. She noticed Halldor leaning against one prop of the grandstand trying to look nonchalant but beaming from ear to ear and was glad. He'd seemed out of sorts recently, grumpier than ever, and it was good to see him smile.

'I rode the rapids once,' she said, still watching the winners. 'You?'

Elizaveta smiled even wider at Tora's horror.

'I wasn't meant to. I sneaked out. Pretended I was a boy.'

'What happened?'

'I got into terrible trouble.'

'I'm sure, but did you win?'

Elizaveta whirled round to look at Tora, intrigued at the question.

'No,' she admitted. 'I was stopped halfway by my father, but thank you for believing that I could have done.'

Tora shook her head.

'I sometimes believe you could do anything, Elizaveta of Kiev.'

'Bar produce a son.'

Tora's jaw tightened and her hand went to her belly.

'We don't know that,' she said stiffly and turned away just as her uncle, Jarl Kalv, sidled between them.

Elizaveta shivered and looked for an escape. The jarl who'd returned from the Orkneys was exactly how she remembered him from her brief childhood encounter – as lithe and sly as a forest-weasel – and she distrusted his every move.

'A wonderful race,' he said, his voice as soft as cooking fat. 'A Kievan tradition?'

'It is.'

'It must bring back fond memories then, Princess.'

'Queen. I am queen now.'

'Of course. Foolish of me. You must miss Kiev.'

'As you must miss Orkney.'

'Ah, but it was never truly my home. I don't believe anyone can ever truly be at home away from their birth country.'

'You don't? Then you must be very unadaptable. I find myself every bit as settled here in Oslo as I ever was in Kiev.'

That silenced him, but only for a moment.

'There are traders here from the Rus, you know,' he said, his voice sly. 'I have been speaking with them. They were delighted to see the race. They said – what was it? – how pleased your father would be to see his influence spread so far.'

'My mother too, I'm sure,' Elizaveta agreed, looking desperately for a way past but the crowd around Aksel and his fellow riders was blocking her in.

'Your mother? Ah yes . . .'

Elizaveta saw a dark gleam in Kalv's eyes and her heart scudded.

'Excuse me, I must . . .'

'I have news of your mother actually. Sad news.'

Elizaveta would not look at him; would not give him the satisfaction.

'She is gone to God.' The world swam before Elizaveta's eyes, as if the great fjord had risen up in a wave and swamped her. Ingrid – dead? She could not be. The happy memories that this glorious race had released inside her just a short time ago seemed to loom up and threaten to tear her from within. 'There was a lump,' Kalv's voice went on. 'It grew until it suffocated her heart, or so they say. I am sorry, Princess.'

'Queen!' Elizaveta rounded on him, hating him and clutching at that hatred to keep her afloat on the waters of rising grief. 'I am the Queen of Norway – the only queen – and whatever nasty news you delight in bringing me, I ask you to remember that. All of you.'

She swung round to include Tora in her glare. For a moment

the hurt in the other woman's blue eyes – so very, very like Ingrid's – almost sent her staggering, but she set her legs against it.

'Dignity,' she reminded herself, hissing it through her teeth so that the crowd, unnerved, parted swiftly before her. Tears swam but she would not let Kalv or any of the damned Arnassons see them. She owed her mother that much.

'Aksel!' Elizaveta reached her squire and clasped his hands and, to his astonishment, brought them to her lips and kissed them flamboyantly. 'I'm so proud. You've honoured me with this win today, me and all my family. I shall ask my husband to make you a lord.'

And with that she grabbed her confused squire and led him away. She would save her grief until later. For now she would be the queen her mother had been proud of; the queen she had raised her to be; and the queen who would give Harald his King Olaf and silence the Arnassons once and for all.

CHAPTER TWENTY-SIX

Oslo, September 1050

*P*ain, that's all Elizaveta knew. She was swimming in pain, arms and legs flailing helplessly against it like a Danish prisoner in the mist, like a canoe beneath the rapids, like a dragon-ship folding in on itself and crashing through the ice to sink to oblivion.

'Oblivion,' she thought, forming the word like a liferaft, binding strakes of nothingness in her mind, yearning to sail. Her raft would have an eagle-prow and would take her out of this hell and into peace.

'Mother,' she rasped out. A shape formed before her eyes, moved away again. She put out a desperate hand. 'Mother?'

'No Lily, 'tis I, Harald. You . . . You are alive?'

'Not yet.'

Elizaveta fought to open her eyes. Was she alive? The eagle-prow receded a little and she was almost sad to see it go. Something cold was laid on her face – cold and slimy and clinging. She thrashed her head desperately against it and it was whipped away again.

'Sorry. I'm sorry. I thought it might help. Can you open your eyes, Lily?'

Could she? Slowly she forced her lids up and squinted out. A curtain of blonde hair shone in the dim lamplight.'

'Hari?'

'Lily, thank God.' Harald leaned forward but then checked himself. 'I'm not to touch you, they say.'

'Who say?' Even her throat hurt.

'The midwives.'

He glanced fearfully over his shoulder and memory slammed into Elizaveta – the endless pains, the blood, Greta's eyes clouding with fear even as her voice stayed calm, the midwife saying something about 'wrong way round' and everything, indeed, feeling turned and twisted and so, so painful.

'The baby?' she croaked.

'The baby is well. She is a fine child, Lily.'

'She?'

Disappointment thumped into her and she flinched at its impact on her bruised body.

'She,' Harald said firmly. 'I have named her Ingrid.'

'Ingrid?' The name jerked out of her on a rush of hot tears. 'Oh Hari, thank you. That's beautiful.'

'As is she, my sweet. As are *you*.'

The tears were soothing her eyes as the cloth had not and she let them flow gratefully.

'I am not, I think,' she managed, 'quite at my best at the moment,' and now Harald was crying too. Defying tuts behind him he put his arms around her and despite the pain searing through her body she clutched him close.

'I thought you had died, Lily,' he murmured into her hair.

'Me? No. Too much worth living for to die.'

He laughed, a strangled sound, half mirth, half agony.

'You have to be an empress, my sweet.'

'You've taken Denmark? How long have I been lying here?'

He flushed.

'Days, no more, and no, I've not taken it yet but I will. As soon as you are fully better I will sail on Svein again and this time I will bring you a throne.'

'I have a throne, Hari.' A new thought came to her. 'Tora?' Harald tensed.

'She is delivered too,' he said cautiously.

'Another boy?'

Of course it was; she had known really that it would be, just hoped that perhaps she would have one too.

'Another boy,' Harald confirmed.

'What have you named him?' He looked to the floor. 'Hari – what have you named him?'

Greta darted forward, alarmed at her harsh cry, but Harald waved her back. He tried to lay Elizaveta down on the mounds of pillows but she clutched at his arms.

'I have called him Olaf, Lily.' She closed her eyes. That was it then. It was over. Tora had, after all, won. The big, soft deer-queen had won and she – she might as well sail her eagle-raft into oblivion. 'Lily, listen – you must listen. I have called him Olaf so you do not have to go through this again. The midwives told me, my sweet – they told me they warned you that another child might kill you, especially had it been a boy. I cannot have that, Lily, for I do not want an Olaf if it costs me *you*. Do you see that?'

Elizaveta opened one eye. She felt tired now, so tired; fortune's wheel was riding over her. 'Hold fast,' her father's voice said inside her head, rich and tearfully sweet, like a fruit preserved in ice. 'Hold fast, Lily.' She gripped the damp sheets.

'Tora gives you kings,' she objected.

'Yes,' Harald agreed. 'It's what she does best but you, my Lilyveta, you give me the world. Let her raise Norway's next generation, but let you and I rule her now. Together.'

Elizaveta's mind spun again to her childhood in Kiev. 'Is

that all you want for yourself,' she'd demanded of Anastasia, 'to produce kings?' She'd been so scornful, so dismissive. 'I'd like to be a queen,' she'd gone on – she could almost hear herself now. 'A queen in my own right who can help my husband rule and shape a nation.' Had she set her own destiny then? Was this all her own wilful fault? Or her own wilful right?

'Stay with me, Lily,' Harald begged, her big warrior husband with his muscle-hard body and his Stikelstad scar and his beautiful hair.

She reached out a hand to him and he clasped it tight, so very tight that she felt the beautiful ring he had gifted her back in Kiev squeezing her tender flesh. She still hurt, she still hurt so very much, but she would heal.

'Ingrid,' she said softly, 'my Ingrid – is she blonde?'

'As an angel.'

Elizaveta smiled.

'I will stay with you, Hari,' she said softly, 'if you will stay with me.'

'Always,' he agreed and on that promise, she slept.

CHAPTER TWENTY-SEVEN

Jutland, Denmark, August 1051

Harald stood at the prow of his new warship and scanned the Danish beach before him. He was determined to take this country from Svein and to take it fast so he could get back to Elizaveta. She was much stronger now but he worried that she would sicken and that, despite his promise, he would not be there for her if she did.

He put up a hand to the neck of his grand dragon-head prow. He was having a new ship built out on the west coast, one that would bear his wife's precious eagle, but for now his brave dragon would have to do. At least his glorious landwaster flew high from the mast. Last winter Elizaveta had started to add a border in swirls of black and red but she had grown weary of stitching and it went only halfway around the flag. Harald smiled at the thought of his impetuous, impatient wife and vowed to take Denmark for her this time.

It was hard though. Wretched Svein never seemed to know when to admit defeat. Time and again Harald had launched attacks on him but always the usurper had splintered them by playing what Elizaveta had dismissed as 'silly games', ducking away from full battles and preferring to lead Harald round Denmark's endless islands, picking off single ships in ambush.

It made him a very frustrating quarry and left Harald with little choice but to raid his towns and villages like an old-style Viking in the hope that his people would turn on him. Yet never they did.

It was endless cat and mouse and today Harald felt too much like the mouse. He'd had no reports of Svein's fleet from his spies and the beach they were sailing towards looked suspiciously quiet. Usually the local militia would at least muster a defence but today the long stretch of sand sat still and bare.

'Where are they?' he said to Ulf, stood just behind him.

His marshal shrugged and pushed his curls from his face to look more closely.

'Maybe they have the fever?'

'Or maybe they are hiding.'

'Well, they can't do that for long and once they're out in the open we'll take them like we always do.'

Harald scanned the low horizon.

'Something feels wrong.'

'Maybe,' Halldor said darkly, 'that's not on land but in our own craft.'

Harald grimaced. Halldor, as usual, had put his wizened finger on the heart of the matter. In his own ship all was well. Most of his personal warband of fifty had been with him for years and he knew he could rely absolutely on their courage, their skill and, above all else, their loyalty. They had sailed into many battles together and sailed out again intact. Most of these men had grown rich enough in Harald's service to retire to farm and live out their lives in peace but every summer they came back to serve, not for the plunder, not even for the thrill, but because they belonged. Much the same was true of the other four ships at the centre of this fleet but the ones at either side . . .

Harald looked across to the lead ship. It was captained, at

the man's own request, by the reinstated Jarl Kalv and over these first weeks of raiding he had proved himself a wily and capable general. Harald trusted his abilities implicitly – but his loyalty? Kalv Arnasson's loyalty was to himself alone and that made him dangerous.

Kalv had taken Harald and Tora's sons under his fearsome wing in much the same way Einar had done with the last King Magnus. He had ordered them tutors, built them homes and commissioned them clothes befitting not just princes but kings. He paraded them at court whenever he could and Harald could scarcely object – Magnus and Olaf were his proclaimed heirs and fine boys besides. In a strange way, though, their very existence threatened his own. If Norway were to lose him now, they had kings to play with and powerful local lords to control them. It was a situation the county had oft been used to in its history. Even at the start of this century the jarls of the north had ruled for fifteen years without any king at all and Harald was increasingly convinced that Kalv was seeking a return to such blissful times. Plus, Elizaveta hated him.

Harald looked back to the beach, scanning the gentle rise of the grass-strewn dunes for any sign of an ambush. All was still.

'If Svein is setting a trap,' he said, 'he's doing it very well.'

'So we must turn it to our advantage,' Halldor said quietly. 'Send the lead ship in.'

Harald looked at him.

'To draw out the attack?'

'Exactly.'

'So we can then land strategically in the best place to back them up?'

'If that seems appropriate, yes.'

Harald eyed his hunched lieutenant curiously. Halldor had not spoken openly against Kalv but Harald had seen him watching the northern jarl very carefully and knew he distrusted him.

'What's your plan, Hal?'

Halldor kept his eyes firmly on the horizon.

'No plan. Simply that Jarl Kalv has a very high opinion of his generalship so it seems only fair to give him a chance to prove it.'

'It does,' Harald agreed, 'but Finn . . .'

He glanced back to his foster father's two ships, bringing up the rear. Finn was past his sixtieth year now and recently his proud frame had become hampered by a stiffening disease. He was slow to move in the mornings and his fingers, in particular, were twisting painfully, making it harder for him to accurately wield a sword. Harald had taken to putting him in the rearguard both for his calm head in a tricky situation and, increasingly, to protect him from the worst of the fighting.

'Finn is six boat-lengths back,' Ulf said, moving in at Halldor's side. 'He is not here to attack.'

Harald considered. His comrades spoke sound military sense. Their tactics were entirely justifiable – should they ever be called upon to justify them – and any other motivation would be lost in the fog of battle. If any such there was.

He looked across the water, ostensibly assessing his position, though in truth he was seeing Jarl Kalv's actions the day they had set sail from Norway. Much of the court had gathered on the beautiful new jetties at Oslo to see off the invasion force that had sworn, once again, to finally take Denmark. Harald had ordered pennies thrown into the crowd and two barrels of mead to be opened so all the fast-growing city could toast their king on his way, and the mood had been buoyant.

Harald's ship had been launched into the water to huge cheers and he had stepped confidently up to board her, turning first to bid his family farewell. Such events had become slightly awkward affairs with Tora and her two boys on one side and Elizaveta and her girls on the other but that day it had been made easy by Maria. His feisty little Maria, soon to turn five, was heart-breakingly similar to her wilful mother, with an all-too-large helping of his own daring and stubbornness thrown in, and he sometimes felt as if she could see into his own mind.

'Come on, Magnus,' she'd said loudly that day, grabbing his hand. 'Let's say Godspeed to Papa.'

Magnus, who, like much of the court, was dazzled by his confident half-sister, had gone eagerly enough and Harald had even, to his amazement, caught a look of almost complicit fondness between the two mothers. He'd held his arms wide to embrace both children, delighted that the world would see how obedient his unusual household was to his authority, but at that moment Magnus had been snatched back. The boy, startled, had cried and Maria, furious, had rounded on his captor, hands on her slim little hips.

'What are you doing?' she'd demanded of Jarl Kalv.

'What everyone else should,' he'd snarled back. 'You may kiss your precious papa if you must but Magnus will be the last to say farewell and alone.'

'Why?'

'Because he is the heir to Norway.'

'Why?'

Why was Maria's favourite word. Usually Harald found it endearing but that day with all of Norway looking on he had wished her, for once, a more passive child.

'Because he is a boy,' Kalv had told her, eyes narrow with patent hatred.

'And I,' Maria had fired back, 'am the eldest.'

Kalv had laughed nastily.

'That counts for nothing, Princess. Can you defend your country? Can you fight for it, as a ruler must?'

'I can fight better than him,' Maria had said, pointing disparagingly at Magnus, who'd obligingly shrunk back.

The crowd had started to laugh and, recognising the danger of that, Harald had quickly gathered Maria up, kissing her loudly. It had not mollified her and damned Elizaveta, whose sympathies were so clearly with her outspoken daughter, had done nothing to help.

'I will bring you fine jewels if you are a good girl and don't make a fuss,' Harald had whispered to Maria.

'Don't want jewels.'

'What then, sweetheart? What do you want?'

'A sword.'

He'd promised her – what else could he do? – and if Elizaveta didn't like it, it was her own fault. Except, he recalled now, that Elizaveta had liked it; had laughed and called Maria her little warrior. He shook his head as the thought of his beautiful wife made him ache with longing; why did he waste summers away from her?

'To win Denmark,' he reminded himself fiercely, 'and after Denmark, England.'

It was a far-off dream but were they not the best sort? Elizaveta often received news of England. Ever letters flowed in and out of her rooms, as if she and her sisters were weaving a web of words across the world and so far King Edward of England had no heir, though there was worrying talk of the bastard Duke William of Normandy paying court to the old king.

Now an adult, William had miraculously dodged all his would-be assassins to take full charge of his duchy and had recently wed Matilda, daughter of the powerful Baldwin of Flanders. But William was a brigand, a petty power-hunter whose only experience was with his own back-stabbing nobles;

he, Harald Hardrada, would make England a far more competent king. First, though, Denmark.

He looked to the beach. They had to attack now. If they had taken the locals by surprise they should capitalise on that and not bob out here like seals waiting to be hunted. And if it was an ambush they should draw it out or, rather, Kalv should.

'He's a nasty man, Papa,' Maria had said to him by way of parting.

'But a good fighter,' Harald had told her, putting her down to shake open, solemn hands with little Magnus. Well now they would find out *how* good.

He put up his arm to Kalv to signal an attack.

'You lead,' he called across the soft murmur of the light waves. 'We'll fan out to back you up when we see the lie of their troops – if there even are any.'

Kalv looked uncertain.

'To you the spoils,' Harald reminded him.

The lead ship always took the first choice of plunder and already the jarl's men were leaping eagerly to their oars so Kalv was left with no choice but to urge them on. Behind him, Harald commanded his central ships into a line parallel with the sloping shore, with Finn commanding the two rearguard vessels further out at sea. Harald watched from his dragon-prow as Kalv gave the order to up the rowing pace and his sleek warship shot through the gentle breakers and rammed onto the sand. Instantly his men were out, swords and shields to hand, scrambling through the shallows and onto the beach, coming together in a tight arrowhead formation with Kalv's patterned helmet clear just behind the tip.

For a moment it seemed as if nothing would happen, as if they would be able to march up the beach, shaking the sea from their boots as they went, and over the horizon into the first village to claim their spoils. But then suddenly a blood-curdling yell rang out from behind the dunes and the sea grasses came alive. Hundreds of soldiers – more than any local militia could ever command – flew out and poured down the beach, swords swinging.

'Massacre!'

The whisper went round Harald's boat like a death prayer and instinctively the rowers reversed their stroke, pushing the boats away from the carnage on the sand. The Danes reached Kalv's unit, coming at them from both sides, and crashed into their flanks. The Norwegians had closed into a tight shield wall but they were hopelessly outnumbered and could only last a short time without relief.

'Attack!' The cry came from the rearguard ship, hoarse and urgent. 'You must attack, Harald, or they will die.'

'But if we attack,' Harald said to Ulf and Halldor, 'we will surely *all* die? They have archers – see! They will be ready for us in the shallows and will have us down before we can even get over the gunwales.'

With a raven cry, the Danes split one side of Kalv's arrow-head and Harald caught the acrid tang of fresh blood on the seaward breeze. For a moment he recoiled from it then he dug his fingers into the whorls of his dragon's red neck and stood firm. Hardrada – ruthless.

'Retreat,' he called, putting up a hand to his trumpeter. 'Sound the retreat.'

The men in the ships did not need the horn's plaintive cry to respond. Already they were turning to the steer-board side, heaving the ship round for all they were worth. Within moments they were round, their fellow ships with them, and all five sails grabbed at the wind and took over, driving the boats towards the rearguard, which had not moved.

'Attack,' the cry came again, 'attack, you miserable cowards!'

Harald saw Finn pounding the gunwale as he roared the

command, his ageing face purple with rage, but no one paid any attention, not even his own crew, and quickly the main fleet drew level with his two craft.

'You are leaving them to die, Harald,' Finn screamed across the water.

'No,' Harald corrected him calmly, 'I am saving everyone else.'

'You sent him on purpose.'

'Who?'

'Kalv. You sent Kalv to his death on purpose.'

The men looked back. The Norwegians were flattened, carrion already, as the Danes scrambled over their savaged corpses to lay greedy hands on their deserted ship.

'Jarl Kalv asked to lead,' Harald said. 'He knew the risks and, as a noble Viking, he embraced them. He has died in glory.'

'He has died for your cowardice.'

Rage shot through Harald, as sharp as if a Danish archer had skewered him with it.

'I am many things, Jarl Finn,' he roared across the rising wind and the triumphant cries of the Danes on the beach, 'but I am *not* a coward.'

'Worse then – a murderer. Of your own men.'

'Have I murdered these men? Or will that, Finn, be your doing when the blood-drunk Danes come after us in our own ship? There was nothing I could do.'

'No,' Finn called back, 'you *chose* to do nothing. You have robbed me of a noble brother, Harald, and I no longer consider you my son, or my king.'

'Finn, no . . .'

But Finn was ordering his bewildered men towards the bloody shore, his gnarled fingers clutching at the gunwales in a sort of madness. Harald saw the soldiers looking at each other, torn between obeying their king or their captain, but in the end a good Viking always did as his immediate commander instructed and Harald wasn't surprised when they picked up their oars.

'You will die,' he called. 'Finn, please – I don't want you to die.' It sounded weak, pathetic almost. He could see the men exchanging sardonic glances but he didn't care. Finn Arnasson had raised him, had supported him as King of Norway. He could not lose him now. 'What about Tora's boys?' he demanded. 'Your future kings?'

Finn, however, was in a mist of his own making.

'Good luck to them,' he growled, turning back to his vessel. 'Row!'

He struck the first oarsman with the flat of his sword and the man began to row, the others following in a bedraggled, reluctant mess of white water.

'We will not die,' Finn was calling to them, 'but live to serve a true master who does not sacrifice his own. We will live to serve Svein Estrithson.'

And as Harald watched, horrified, his foster father – his ever-devious but ever-loyal foster father – ran a white flag up to the top of his mast and made for the heart of enemy territory as, on the dunes, a sparky young man in a shining crown appeared. Svein! Ulf nudged at Harald's arm.

'Hari, we must go – now. If Svein is there himself he will not be slow to use this. We could be trapped.'

'As an audience before a poet,' Harald said, his head swimming.

Kalv was gone, yes, but with him Finn and all Harald had to show for his fifth summer raiding Denmark was another 'bold escape' for the mead-hall's entertainment.

'Not so much "ruthless",' he told himself bitterly as the sails filled and they sped out into the sapphire-blue ocean, 'as useless.'

Maybe from now on he should concentrate on Norway and creating a solid, secure country for his children to grow up in – to inherit. It was a worthy aim, surely, but even as his ships limped away from Danish shores he was not sure it was one he could keep to. He was a Viking after all and his veins were only half blood. The other half – the itchy, fast-running, glorious half – was all sea.

CHAPTER TWENTY-EIGHT

Austratt, September 1051

The court stood sombre in the lashing rain as the choir, water streaming down their faces and into their mouths, drowning their notes, sang a requiem for Jarl Kalv and his men, lost in the service of the country to which he had so recently returned.

'I feel as if this is Finn's funeral too,' Harald whispered to Elizaveta, his fingers grinding into hers.

'More so,' she whispered back.

In truth no one would miss Kalv but even she would feel the lack of loud, lively Finn and she knew it stung Harald like a barb beneath his skin. She clasped his hand tight, trying to squeeze out the pain. Throughout the service he had stood dutifully at Tora's side, an arm around her shoulders, but now that the monument to mark Kalv's passing was being blessed, his hand-fast wife had stepped forward without him, taking just her two sons for company. Elizaveta watched Tora, her head high and her blonde hair bound up in a dark headdress, clutching Olaf to her hip and Magnus to her side, and knew that she, too, was mourning the loss of Finn, her beloved uncle, more than Kalv.

'Surely Finn will return,' she murmured to Harald. 'He would not leave Tora alone.'

'She is not alone.'

'No. She has you.'

'A bit of me, maybe.'

'Too little to be of real comfort,' Elizaveta said honestly.

She hadn't as much of her husband as she would choose but she had more than Tora and somewhere along the twisting path past her thirtieth year she had learned to be grateful for that. Was that dignity, or just compromise? Or did they, in the end, come to the same thing?

Tora, standing before everyone with water running off her headdress, was the picture of dignity. She always had been and Elizaveta felt something dangerously like admiration for her rival.

'I will send messages,' Harald was saying, still whispering as the choir struggled to the end of their requiem and the court looked longingly towards Kalv's great farmhouse, lit up in the mid-afternoon gloom and sending warm, meat-scented air out of the doors in steaming clouds. 'I will beg his forgiveness, even though I see nothing to forgive.'

'You acted as you had to.'

'Yes and yet . . .' He leaned in to Elizaveta, so close his wet hair tangled in hers. 'I wonder, if it had not been Kalv spearheading that first troop, would I have acted differently?'

'Harald, hush! Of course you would not.'

'No,' he agreed, kissing her cheek. 'No, you are right – of course not. But, Lily, the loss of Finn pulls at my heart. Perhaps I am growing old – old and soft.'

Elizaveta squeezed his arm, taut with muscle.

'You are not soft, Harald, or only occasionally.'

She looked pointedly at Maria, stood fiercely upright with her new sword strapped defiantly over her dark gown. It was made of blunted steel with a hilt set with amber and Maria wore it always, so that she would be ready to 'fight for Papa whenever he has need of me'.

'Maria is under my skin,' he admitted with a fond smile. 'But she makes me proud. And teaches me strength besides.'

Elizaveta smiled.

'This has just been a setback, Hari, like when Einar and Kalv came for Magnus. Kalv was plotting, I am sure, as Einar was plotting back then.'

'You told me I was stupid to kill Einar.'

'Maybe I was wrong. What's past is past. Come, the choir is finally done and you should lead Tora out of this hellish rain.'

Harald kissed her again.

'You are sending me to Tora, Lily? Perhaps it is *you* growing old and soft?'

'Perhaps it is.'

Elizaveta reflected on Harald's words as she took her place in the hall, accepting a soft linen cloth from Aksel to dry herself as best she could. This should have been a day of triumph for her with both senior Arnassons gone. Only Tora's brother Otto, now a man of thirty-two, was left to muster the northern jarls and he had been long in Harald's service and was devoted to him. Tora still had her precious princes but they were so very young and must be more a burden than a support.

Elizaveta found herself watching her rival throughout the feast, seeing how she picked at her food and only supped her wine when Kalv's health was drunk. Of Finn there was pointedly no mention – he was a traitor now. Elizaveta drank her own wine but it tasted somehow sickly. The rest of the courtiers were shedding their grief with their roast duck but Elizaveta had little appetite for revelry today. When, therefore, Tora made her excuses and fled to her chamber the moment the sun set,

Elizaveta took her own chance to withdraw too. It was a rough, damp night and she hastened towards shelter and Greta's ever-kindly care.

With this being Arnasson land she had brought her pavilion. It looked respectful not to demand a room in the farmhouse and, more importantly, it gave her space to avoid the tight-knit northern families. Whenever their petty sniping got too much for her she could retreat into the safety of her own walls, embroidered with patterns of her own choosing and sit on her own stool to play her own precious viol. Now she felt her fingers itch for the comfort of the strings, the way they would take her pent-up emotions and turn them into something sweet and purposeful.

Greta welcomed her in and fussed around her, settling a soft fur around her shoulders and plumping up the cushions at her back. Elizaveta was grateful but for once Greta's kindness irritated her; she just wanted to be alone.

'That's all, thank you, Greta,' she said, picking up her viol.

'You're sure, my lady?'

'Quite sure.'

Greta bobbed a curtsey but made no move to leave.

'You may go.'

'Yes, my lady, of course. Only . . .'

'What is it?' Elizaveta asked impatiently, lifting her bow from its case.

Greta gestured nervously to the door and to Elizaveta's great surprise she saw her steward standing there.

'Did you follow me here, Aksel?'

'Of course, to make sure you were safe, my lady.'

She smiled. These two, these gentle servants who had known her longer than most, were ever-watchful and she should be grateful.

'I am quite safe, Aksel, thank you. Why don't you escort

Greta to the hall for the dancing? I'm sure it will be no hardship for you.'

He blushed.

'Of course, my lady. But there is one more thing.'

Elizaveta bit back rising irritation.

'What is it, Aksel?'

'My father wishes to speak with you.'

'Halldor? Now?'

'If it suits you, my lady?'

It did not but Aksel so rarely asked anything of her that she did not feel she could refuse.

'Very well.' She tried for a smile. 'Best fetch wine then.'

Aksel bowed low and moved to the door and, to Elizaveta's surprise, ushered Halldor straight in.

'Were you waiting outside, Hal?' she asked, peering at the rain squalling in through the flap. 'What's the matter?'

'What isn't the matter on this dark day, my lady?'

Elizaveta frowned and ran a longing finger down the strings of her viol, making them cry plaintively.

'Spare me the dramatics, Hal, please. I am tired.'

'Sorry.'

She forced herself to put down her instrument and patted a seat at her side. Halldor edged forward to take it, fiddling with a frayed hem on his best tunic. Aksel and Greta stood behind him, close but not touching, both leaning slightly forward. Elizaveta waited, curious now.

'I am tired too, my lady,' Halldor said eventually. 'I want . . . Begging your pardon, truly, but I want to go home.'

'Home, Halldor?'

'To Iceland, my lady.'

Elizaveta felt as if her already-reeling body had been punched full on.

'To Iceland?' she repeated dumbly. 'For a visit?'

'For good, my lady.'

His head was down and he looked like a man confessing a crime, not begging leave for an honestly deserved retirement.

'Have you spoken to Harald of this?' Elizaveta asked him gently.

His fingers picked faster at the tunic edge and Aksel shuffled behind him. Elizaveta looked to her squire.

'You knew of this?'

Aksel's eyes were all misery.

'Father has been restless for some time, my lady. He is past his fortieth year now and ready for his farm.'

Elizaveta groaned.

'You Norsemen and your farms!'

Halldor half-smiled.

'I am hardly a city dweller, am I, my lady? A half troll like myself is best in the forests.'

'Oh Hal – you are no troll. That is but a jest.'

'And like the best jests it is half true. I am half of half a troll.'

'And as I told you once, my mother told me all manner of wonderful things about trolls.' She considered the grizzled warrior, sat so humbly before her whilst the rain lashed down on the linen roof above them. 'You wish then,' she said, touching his knee, 'to dig your hole beneath Iceland's trees?'

Halldor shook his head.

'But you said . . . ?'

'Iceland has no trees, my lady, or at least none with roots big enough for a fat old warrior like myself to dig beneath.'

'Really?' Elizaveta leaned forward, intrigued despite the uneasy conversation. 'No trees at all?'

'Very few.'

'Then Norway must be as strange for you as it is for me.'

'I have cherished my time here, my lady.'

'But that time is over?'

He bowed his head.

'I have been blessed in life, my lady, for I have loved serving Harald, but you remember how I could not bring myself to leave his service and retire to farming when Aksel here was born?' Elizaveta nodded. 'Well, now I find I am ready.'

'I see. And you want me to ask Harald?'

Halldor looked uncomfortably down and it was Aksel who replied.

'Persuade him perhaps, my lady?'

Elizaveta looked to her squire. He was a big man now, his young limbs long and strong, his jaw square, his beard full-grown. Greta looked neat and small at his side, though very comfortable. Cold dread flooded through her.

'And you, Aksel?' she asked, her voice squeaking. 'Do you wish to go with your father?'

His eyes filled and he looked at Greta, who almost imperceptibly nodded him on. So they had talked of this together? When? Elizaveta felt her heart flutter ridiculously in her chest. Aksel and Greta were the only ones bar Harald and Ulf who remembered her homeland, her family – was she to lose them too?

'You may speak,' she told Aksel.

'I wish to serve you, my lady.' Her heart leaped; thank God! 'But I fear for my father travelling alone, building his farm alone.'

'I see.' She would not cry; she would not. This wasn't over yet.

'And you, Greta?'

Her maid looked at Aksel then suddenly ran forward, clasping Elizaveta's hands in hers.

'I will stay, my lady, if you wish it.'

Of course she wished it. She could still remember Hedda suckling Greta on the very night Harald had first come to Kiev.

She had known her maid longer than she had known her husband, but this wasn't about her now. She saw Aksel straining forward, yearning to touch the girl, and remembered sharply how she had felt about Harald when they had first been courting.

'I wish you to be happy,' she said. Greta looked back to Aksel and the twist of her body spoke more than any words. 'Go,' Elizaveta urged her. 'Marry Aksel and go to Iceland and maybe I will persuade Harald – seeing as you seem to think that is so easy for me – to bring me to visit this strange, treeless country and to eat in Halldor's lovely farmhouse.'

'Truly? Oh my lady!'

To Elizaveta's great surprise, Aksel threw himself at her feet beside Greta, clasping his arms around her legs and holding on as if he might tumble off a cliff without her.

'Aksel. Aksel, please.'

He did not seem to hear and it was Greta who, with a gentle smile, prised him away. They rose and Halldor put an arm around them both, a firm, solemn threesome.

'We only leave, Elizaveta,' he said, 'because Harald is secure. No one can threaten his throne now and he has you to keep him safe.'

'Not just me.'

'Pah!' Halldor almost spat onto her Greek carpet but caught himself just in time. 'That Tora woman is not a taper to your oil lamp, my lady, not gruel to your venison, not a sparrow to your eagle, not . . .'

'Thank you, Hal.' She put up a hand; she just wanted them to go now; to release her to be sad. 'I think maybe I should sleep now.'

'What? Oh yes, of course. And you'll talk to Harald?'

'I will. Good night.'

'I'll stay,' Greta offered, her cheeks pink, but Elizaveta shook her head.

'Don't worry, Greta, I can manage alone.'

'But . . .'

'I can manage. I might play a little. Good night.'

Elizaveta pointedly picked up her viol and they went at last, bowing their way out. She lifted her bow to the strings but they sounded harsh, discordant. They needed tuning but she had not the heart for it now and thrust the instrument aside. Halldor leaving? Aksel and Greta too, and this on top of the loss of Finn? It felt as if the world was turning upside down and she was no longer sure who to hold onto to keep upright.

She moved to the door of the pavilion, taking in deep gulps of night air. The rain had stopped at last but it hung heavy in the dark sky and sat in rough puddles all across the grass. She could hear Halldor and Aksel's heavy treads sloshing back towards the farm and could just make out Greta's slim form pulled tight against the young man who had once followed Elizaveta around as if a string ran between them. Tears stung at her eyes.

She longed to hold her daughters but they would be tucked up safe and warm in the nursery and it was not fair to wake them. She could go to bed and await Harald's strong arms but the men had been settling to the ale barrel when she left the hall and she doubted he would be in for hours. She thought of her sisters but they were far away across foreign seas and a letter took weeks to reach even Anne, now happily in Paris with King Henry. She held all three of them dear in her heart but right now she needed someone to talk to.

Elizaveta looked across the meadow to the farmhouse. The glow of the fire in the main part of the building was strong and she was about to turn away when she noticed a dim light burning in the small window-opening of Tora's chamber. She stared at it, mesmerised by the tiny spark behind the lumpish shadows of the pavilions. Was the other woman as sad as she on this dark night? Could she go to find out? *Should* she? Elizaveta shook her head – who cared about *should*?

Picking up her skirts she trod determinedly out into the mud. When she reached the farmhouse porch, however, she avoided the riotous hall to the left, ducking instead into the slim corridor to the right and heading down towards the sleeping chambers at the far end.

'My lady?'

A maid, sat half-asleep in the doorway of Tora's chamber, leaped to her feet, all astonishment.

'Is your mistress asleep?' Elizaveta asked. The girl glanced nervously back and she took that as a no. 'Thank you,' she said firmly and, tapping gently on the door, slid it open.

It took a moment for her eyes to adjust to the low light and even then she heard rather than saw Harald's handfast wife. Tora was on the bed, a crumpled heap of clothing amid the covers, and she was shaking with grief.

'Tora?'

Elizaveta touched her shoulder and the other woman sprung up as if stabbed and scrabbled backwards.

'Why are you here?'

Elizaveta shrugged.

'Why indeed! You are sad, Tora.'

'How observant of you.'

'And I am sad too.'

'You? Why?'

'Halldor is leaving. Aksel and Greta with him.'

'Oh. Why?'

'You sound like Maria.' A glint of a smile ghosted across Tora's face and Elizaveta seized the chance to sit on the edge of her bed. 'We have little reason to like each other, Tora, I know, and far more to hate.'

Tora wiped at her eyes.

'I have never been good at hating.'

'And I, perhaps, have been *too* good at it. Though with you . . . You remind me too much of my mother to truly hate.'

'I do?' Surprise made Tora sit up straighter. 'In what way?'

'You look just like her. I know it's hard to believe but, aside from my littlest sister, Agatha, I am the odd one in my family. The rest are like you, like my mother – womanly, blonde, beautiful.'

'Nay, you are far more beautiful than me, Elizaveta.'

'Oh don't start that, Tora. Maybe we can't be friends but we do have a mutual interest.'

'Harald? I'm not sure he'd like it if we . . .'

'It's not up to him.' Tora looked startled and Elizaveta grabbed her hand. 'Look, Tora, you've lost Finn . . .' Tora's eyes welled up and Elizaveta cursed herself. 'For which I am very sorry, truly.'

'Me too. He was always very good to me in his own way.'

'And Aksel and Greta to me. They are only servants, I know, but we have been . . . close.'

'So you want me as your servant now instead?'

'No! I'm not doing this very well. Truth is, Tora, I don't know what I want or why I'm here, save that I looked out of my pavilion and I was alone and you were alone and it seemed . . . foolish.'

Tora picked up a cushion, pummelling it gently.

'It is foolish,' she agreed eventually, low-voiced.

Elizaveta rose and wandered across the room, surprised to see Olaf sleeping in a cot in the corner. She tiptoed over to look in at him sleeping peacefully, unaware of the swirls of alliances formed, broken, and reformed around him. She touched his tiny face.

'I have three sisters, you know,' she said quietly. 'Back in Kiev when we were young, we were always fighting.'

'I bet.'

'But I miss them every day. They have daughters themselves now – so many girls in our family – but I have never seen them.'

The other woman pummelled the cushion some more, then coughed awkwardly.

'You can have him, you know – Harald. At night, you can have him.'

'What?'

'If you want him. If you . . . can?'

Elizaveta found herself blushing; it was an odd sensation.

'I can.'

The midwives had shown her how to use moss to keep out his seed. Aksel had collected it for her but who would get it now? For a moment she felt dizzy then she looked at Tora, puffy-eyed with grief, and pulled herself together. She could take Maria and Ingrid moss-gathering. Maria would think it a great adventure to go into the forests, and quiet little Ingrid was already showing a remarkable understanding of plants and healing and would relish the chance to pick what she could. But if *she* did not bear Harald children . . .

'Surely you must have his heirs?' she said awkwardly, crossing back to Tora.

The other woman looked at her, her pretty head tipped on one side, and suddenly her eyes sparkled with more than just tears.

'I think he has enough heirs,' she said with a trace of laughter.

'Not if he wins Denmark and England – then he will need kings to put in both.'

'That is his plan? Really?'

'So he says – he needs another prince.'

Tora, however, shook her head, pushing her blonde hair back out of her drying eyes.

'Nonsense,' she said, 'Maria could rule any country. She even has the sword for it.'

Elizaveta laughed.

'Perhaps, though I pity the poor husband who'd have to go along for the ride.'

'She is very like you.'

'I suppose she is. Is that terrible?'

Tora tipped her head on one side.

'Not terrible, no, though a little . . . scary perhaps.'

Laughter burst from Elizaveta, surprising herself as much as Tora, and suddenly they were both laughing, clutching at each other and shaking with tears and merriment and relief and release. They laughed, unheard by the men huddled around the fire, unheard by Harald, or by their sleeping children, or by anyone under the cloud-clamped moon save each other, but that suited them. It was a strange new alliance but one that might just help them both.

PART THREE

CHAPTER TWENTY-NINE

Sognafjord, Western Norway, March 1057

'This is Norway!' Elizaveta watched as Harald, feet planted on the great law-rock, flung his arms out wide to the blue fjord behind him and the hills looming beyond. 'This is *our* Norway and she is thriving.'

The cheers of the crowd rang around the rocky valley and up into the bright skies above. It was the day of the Western Assembly out on Norway's evening-facing shores and spirits were high. People had trekked from far up and down the jagged shorelines to see the king and his court and to hear justice being dispensed. Some had brought grievances, some prisoners to be tried of crimes greater than the local lords could penalise, but most had just come to see government in action.

Their tents were all across the grasslands behind, rough versions of the elaborate royal pavilions clustered on a low ledge at the base of the hillside. There would be feasting tonight. The people would dance, marriages would be made and sealed in the welcoming crevices of the rocks, and when the moon was at its highest, the bravest – or most foolhardy – would dive from the law-rock into the ever-clear waters of the Sognafjord below.

Every year that Elizaveta had watched this tradition she had yearned to try it for herself but the custom was to dive naked and as queen – even her own, wild-edged version of queen – this was one step too far. Not dignified. She tore her eyes away from the crystal waters and back to the law-rock where Harald was addressing his nation, his great figure silhouetted against the dipping sun. His raven banner hung, as always, above him, though to Elizaveta it looked limp and almost purposeless in the still evening air.

'God blesses Norway,' he called out to his people. 'He sent a fine harvest last year – so fine that the byres bulge even now and despite the winter's snows we all bulge also.'

He patted his belly and his people laughed delightedly. Elizaveta, however, was not impressed.

'He does fatten,' she said.

'Lily!' Tora, at her side, put a finger to her lips.

'Well, he does. Too much sitting around on his throne looking at plans for churches. He used to have seawater in his veins, Tora, but now, it seems, he has limewash.'

'Lily, hush! You wanted a city.'

Elizaveta sighed.

'I know, I know.'

'And at least he is safe on his throne.'

'Bored.'

'He doesn't seem bored.'

'Not *him*.'

Tora chuckled.

'You need something to do, Lily.'

'I have my viol.'

It was true and she loved it still. It was a little battered now and Harald had offered to buy her a new one last Yuletide but she had declined. The instrument had come with her from Kiev and she could not bear to cast it aside. She still sometimes recalled that harsh winter when she and her siblings had danced in their own private, ice-bound world. She had felt bored then too but looking back it seemed idyllic.

Her family had danced on, though, weaving their influence across many countries – putting Yaroslav's stitches into the fabric of several royal houses to grow down the ages. Her brothers had married into the courts of Poland, and the Byzantine and Holy Roman Empires and her sisters, without exception, had now all produced sons for their royal husbands. Agatha had borne Edgar in 1051 and then, as if the Kievan blood had suddenly remembered how to do it, Anne had produced Phillipe and Anastasia, Solomon and, barely a year later, David. Anastasia's delighted relief had gushed across the vellum when the news had come to Oslo, though the other two had thankfully been more tactful.

The one sadness was that Yaroslav was no longer here to see his bloodline run through so many royal houses. He had followed their mother to heaven three years ago and now Elizaveta's eldest brothers ruled the lands of the Rus as a triumvirate. Yaroslav had died, what was more, before the greatest news of all had permeated the family's letters – that Agatha had travelled to England and his first lost prince, Edward, might finally be able to pay him back as he had always desired: with power. And what power!

Elizaveta had hardly been able to believe it when her littlest sister's letter had arrived in the hands of a hard-ridden emissary a month ago. Somehow, just as the Norwegian jarls had come to Kiev for Magnus and the Hungarian rebels for Andrew, Englishmen had arrived on the Danube to invite Edward home after forty years. The English King Edward, the prince's uncle, had no heir and with his wife, Aldyth Godwinson, now past childbearing, was unlikely to produce one. Aldyth's brother, Earl Harald, had therefore come himself to invite Edward to return to his heritage and be proclaimed aetheling – an ancient Saxon term marking him out as throneworthy.

Can you believe it, Lily? Agatha had written, her words tumbling onto the page, as wild as the dark curls Elizaveta recalled so fondly. *England. Remember how we used to talk of her? I made Edward learn her tongue for when he would be her king. He only agreed to please me but I was right; I was right, Lily, and now it might come true. Edward might be the next King of England and I – I might be her queen.*

It was an exciting prospect indeed and a potentially lucrative one. England was but two days' sail from Norway with a fine wind. She was a wealthy country with a powerful government and close links with her rulers could only help Norway. Harald had been delighted at the news.

'We will surely have what we want from England now, Lily,' he'd said, spinning her around, 'without any of the bother of conquest.'

She'd frozen, her own delight suddenly frosted.

'The *bother* of conquest, Hari?'

For her, it had said everything about her husband's new, relaxed, from-the-throne style of ruling and it made her nervous. Complacency didn't suit him; and it certainly didn't suit her.

'This year alone,' he was now saying to the crowd, 'we have opened three new mints and our coins are amongst the finest in the world.'

'Coins,' Elizaveta muttered crossly. 'What use are coins?'

'Well actually . . .' Tora started but Elizaveta waved her words away.

'Fine, fine. I understand. What *fun* are coins?'

'Life can't all be fun, Lily.'

'I know that but surely *some* of it could be?'

Tora touched her hand.

'What's wrong?'

'I told you, I'm bored. It's all so, so smug – all this sitting around congratulating ourselves on our churches and our mints and our law courts.'

'Is it not good to be secure, at peace, prosperous?'

Elizaveta waved an impatient hand.

'Of course it is but if we are so secure we should be looking for more.'

'More?' Tora looked out to the crowd gathered below them in a rich array of colours like butterflies crowded into the rocky hollow. 'What more is there?'

Elizaveta let out a strangled choke.

'Have you ever been out of Norway, Tora?' she demanded.

'You know I have not. Why should I?'

'Why should you not? Did you hear those men last night, the Icelanders?'

'Sssh!' Tora nodded to the people nearest who, drawn by Elizaveta's rising voice, were looking their way. 'Tell me later,' she whispered.

Cross, Elizaveta folded her hands into her lap and pursed her lips shut. She let Harald's talk of new administrative offices drift easily over her, recalling instead the tales of the travellers last night. Their gruff voices had sounded so like Halldor her heart had ached and even without his elaborate rhetoric she had been drawn into the world they had conjured up.

'An expedition has sailed west from Reyjavik,' they had told the court, sat on sturdy benches around a vast hearth beneath God's thankfully dry heavens. 'Their plan is to sail further even than Greenland, into the unchartered waters beyond as once our ancestors sailed west from Norway and found great riches.'

Now Elizaveta looked out down the Sognafjord. Here, towards its mouth, the sharp channel was opening out, its edges softening, its water swirling eagerly around the Solund islands – the last beautiful lumps of Norwegian land – excited to be free. No one could say where sea became fjord, or fjord sea, for it was a natural movement – one that had drawn men three hundred years ago to take those first voyages into the unknown.

Had they been scared, Elizaveta wondered, those pagan adventurers with their fickle gods and their strong hearts? Had they feared for their lives as they pointed their ships to the horizon? Had they dreaded falling off the edge or had they simply yearned to see over it? They had proved, those first men, that there was no edge. They had found the Orkneys, Shetland, England; England where even now Agatha could be arriving to join the great royal family in a place of honour. They had found Ireland and the Isle of Man – rich lands full of treasure. They had found Iceland and Greenland too – wilder places. Some said that the further west you went the harsher the land but no one knew that. Over the next edge might sit another Constantinople – a Miklegard of the west waiting to be discovered.

Elizaveta yearned to know more of this expedition, yearned to meet the men who would wager their lives on an unknown horizon. It had all started here, along this rugged evening-facing coastline on which they now sat in such splendour. Behind them, in Sweden and Denmark, men had sailed south, carving their way down the great rivers towards the golden waters of the Byzantine Empire, creating new worlds as they went – new worlds that included her own dear Kiev and its Rus lands. Here, though, in Norway, the true adventurers had set sail, not down rivers or over lands but across the open sea. Yes, it had all started here and now, it seemed, it had all stopped.

'I have a joyous announcement to make,' Harald was saying and Elizaveta felt Tora nudge her in her ribs.

'Stand up,' she hissed.

Obediently Elizaveta stood, though her eyes were still on

the sea which seemed almost to be winking at her as the low sun caught the ripples at the cusp of the open water.

'My daughter, my beautiful Maria, is to be betrothed.'

Elizaveta's attention snapped back to her husband. She looked around for Maria to pull her up but her daughter was already there at her side, standing tall and proud as all eyes turned their way. Elizaveta was pleased to see she had not brought her sword and stood like a lady, but her heart shook to see her so grown. Her daughter was not yet quite ten; so young to be betrothed.

'*You were young too,*' a voice whispered in her ear as if a troll had crept up and settled behind her. '*You were young when you first saw Harald and offered to become his treasure-keeper and already hoped for more. Yet you thought yourself more than ready for the world.*'

Maria was taller than she had been and her body was already curving towards womanhood. Elizaveta glanced at her daughter's hips, praying they would expand as her own had never done, for she would not wish her childbed experiences on her. Not that it need come to that yet. This betrothal was a formality, no more, and at the moment the only man Maria was devoted to was her father.

'I welcome Jarl Otto as my son,' Harald cried across the gathering. 'He is all I can ask for in a man – a strong warrior, a loyal servant and a true Norwegian.'

'A true Norwegian?' Elizaveta muttered sardonically and, like an unexpected scratch, she heard Kalv's sly voice – 'I don't believe anyone can ever truly be at home away from their birth country.' She had vehemently denied it at the time but was it true? She recalled her mother, every part of her the Grand Princess of Kiev, telling stories of trolls at bedtime, her eyes aglow in the candlelight. These northern lands had been a part of Elizaveta's mother in a way Elizaveta had never truly understood, as Maria and Ingrid would never understand the Rus in her, especially not if they married within their own shoreline, however beautiful.

'You do not approve?' Tora whispered over the raptures of the crowd as Otto, with great flamboyance, led his bride up to the law-rock to receive Harald's public blessing. 'I thought you were pleased?'

Elizaveta struggled to recall. She had been pleased when this had been proposed, had she not? Otto, Tora's brother, was a fine man, older than Maria by some years but honourable and handsome and true.

'A true Norwegian,' Elizaveta echoed.

'That is not, you know, a bad thing,' Tora said, her voice as near to angry as it ever could be, and Elizaveta put out a hand to her.

'I know and I'm sorry. I was just remembering my own father and how determined he was to marry us into new lands – to extend his borders and, beyond that, his influence. He was a very outward-looking man.'

'And Harald is not?'

'I thought he was; now I'm not so sure.'

Tora shifted her feet beneath her skirts.

'Otto is a worthy groom.'

'I know that, truly, Tora.'

'And when they wed we will be family.'

'Are we not already?'

Tora smiled awkwardly and turned to join in the clapping as Harald presented the couple to the crowd. Elizaveta clapped too, smiled, waved a little – she was good at this now.

'I'm truly sorry, Tora,' she said, nudging her. 'It *is* good. It is all good. I used to admire my parents' solid partnership when I was younger, you know. I used to believe the Rus could be strong just because they were, but it seems maybe three is an even more solid alliance. I just . . . Oh, you know me – I am restless. Sometimes I long for it to be as it was when Harald and I first sailed for Norway.'

'Tense and bitter and torn into factions and plots?'

Elizaveta smiled.

'You see everything so clearly, Tora, and so widely. You think more of Norway than of yourself.'

'Is that not what a queen should do?'

Elizaveta nodded and looked to the skies as Harald handed the newly betrotheds down from the law-rock and settled himself to the serious business of law-giving.

'You are a better queen than I,' she remarked but Tora shook her head.

'Harald,' she said quietly, 'would never agree,' but that did not settle the spiky feeling in Elizaveta's stomach.

'I think I shall ask him,' she persisted.

Tora simply sighed.

CHAPTER THIRTY

'Good business, was it?' Elizaveta demanded.

Harald, watching his wife of fourteen years pacing their bedchamber, answered her warily.

'Did you not think so?'

'Everyone seemed very satisfied.'

Her voice had an all-too-familiar edge to it and he tried not to let himself get too distracted by the way the light from the brazier was cutting through her shift, illuminating her still-lithe body.

'Save you?' he suggested.

'No.'

It was all she offered and, uncertain what to do with the curt word, he rose and went to her, waving away her new maid as he clasped his wife close.

'Come to bed, Lily.'

She was rigid in his arms.

'I have to say my prayers.'

Harald raised an eyebrow at that. They carried an elaborate prayer stool with them wherever they went but neither of them was often to be found upon it.

'You are unhappy, my sweet?'

'Not unhappy, Hari. Just . . .' She moved to the pavilion door and lifted the flap to look out. Young men were gathering on

310

the law-rock. She could see their naked forms silhouetted against the bruised sky as they gathered to jump and she pulled instinctively towards them, but at her side a guard stood instantly to attention and with a sigh she dropped the fabric back into place.

'Just . . . ?' Harald prompted.

Elizaveta waved him away.

'Do you think those men will find land?'

Harald blinked, confused.

'Which men, my sweet?'

'Which men?! The Icelanders – the ones who have sailed west.'

'Oh. I see. How would I know?'

'How indeed.'

Another cryptic remark. Harald sank onto the edge of the bed.

'Would you like, perhaps, to send for word of their journey?'

She whirled round.

'I would like, Harald, to go on it.'

'Oh.' God, she looked beautiful blazing towards him, eyes flashing. 'But Lily, it will be very dangerous.'

'Good.'

Harald swallowed. Lily, herself, was dangerous in this mood.

'You are bored, my sweet?'

'Are you not?'

'I'm very busy. The new law code is causing much debate and . . .?'

'New law code?' The words burst out of her mouth as if fired from a catapult. He did his best not to flinch.

'You object to the laws?'

'No. I'm sure they're lovely laws, with lovely lawyers to sort them out. I object, Harald, to them being the only thing you think about.'

So that was it!

'They are not all I think about, truly. Only just now I was thinking how much I would love to have that shift off you and . . .'

Her scream of fury made him jump. The flap shuddered and a guard called out: 'All well, my lord?'

'Quite well,' he called hastily back, grabbing his wife and whisking her onto the bed.

Elizaveta fought beneath him but he held her until she stilled and said petulantly, 'I hate that you're stronger than me.'

'Only in arm,' Harald said ruefully. 'Look, Lily, what would you like me to think about? Your father, you know, was famed for his law code.'

She huffed.

'My father is dead, Hari.'

'And his laws live on.'

'You used to want to be remembered for your deeds, not your laws.'

That stung. Letting go of her, Harald sat back.

'That is true. But Lily, I am doing much, truly I am. Norway is thriving.'

'So you said.' She pushed herself up the bed. 'Do you think I'm a good queen, Harald?'

'Of course, Lily, you're . . .'

'Only Tora seems to care much more about Norway than I.'

'Tora cares about her sons.'

'As she should. They are your sons too.'

Harald swallowed. Friendly as his wives seemed, thankfully, to be these days, there were still tricky moments, from Elizaveta at least. He felt carefully for an answer but before he could form one she was talking again:

'Agatha might be in England by now.'

Another change of direction; he fought to keep up.

'She might well be. I am sure Harold Godwinson will see them there safe. He is a great warrior, they say.'

'Like you?'

'Like me, Elizaveta, yes.'

'But not, I'll warrant, grown fat.'

She poked at his stomach and he looked down.

'I'm not fat,' he said indignantly.

It was true that there was a little more give in his skin than there had once been but was it any wonder? He was forty-two now and entitled to a little flesh. He seized Elizaveta's face in his hands to draw her eyes up from his midriff.

'I thought Agatha said King Edward promised the inheritance of England to Duke William of Normandy when he paid court to him back in 1051?'

She shifted.

'She did mention it, but why would he?'

'King Edward was harboured for many years by William's father and, indeed, by William himself in the early years of his rule.'

'He was a lost prince too?'

'There are a lot of them around, Lily, and not enough crowns to suit.'

She frowned.

'So Duke William and King Edward are friends?'

Harald laughed bitterly.

'From what *I* hear, Lily, no one is "friends" with Duke William. The Normans are a ruthless race. I saw them operating in Italy and Sicily and their passion for blood and for gain made my own men look like girls fighting over a posy. The English won't want a Norman duke as king.'

'Nor a Flanders princess – Matilda? – as their queen. But that won't happen, Hari, will it, once Agatha's Edward is there?

He is of the ancient royal line and he will be a good king – and Agatha a wonderful queen.'

Harald smiled, remembering his wife's madcap sister. It was hard to believe she was a woman now; they were all grown so old. He sat back, toying idly with the hem of Elizaveta's shift.

'I have a claim too, you know. Harthacnut named Magnus as his heir but Magnus was so busy fighting Svein for Denmark that he had no time to demand England. I inherited from Magnus, so I hold his claim still.'

Elizaveta shifted awkwardly.

'Do you wish to press it?'

'Do *you* wish me to?' he shot back, enjoying her unusual discomfiture. 'It would stop me growing stale – fat!'

'Yes, but Edward . . .'

He grinned.

'I will not press it if Edward inherits, my sweet, though Svein might invade. He is Cnut's nephew after all and was born and bred in England.'

She waved this away.

'You will have killed him by then, surely?'

'I will,' he agreed vowing, again, to somehow defeat the upstart Dane. 'He will not get England, Lily.'

'Good. And if Edward becomes her king we could visit, could we not?'

'I thought you hated sailing?'

A memory tipped over her, like a giant wave.

'Sailing cost us your son.'

Her pain spiked his flesh and he pulled her gently in against his chest.

'We have done much, you and I.'

He felt her gather herself, his brave Elizaveta. Her head came up again and she looked him straight in the eye.

'And can do more. I refuse to be afraid of the sea, Hari. And what about you – I thought Vikings' eyes were ever on the horizon?'

'Well, yes,' he conceded. 'But there is much to do at home.'

'Home will still be here when we come back. The boundaries of the world are changing. There are many countries out there and I would love to see more of them.'

'You would?'

'Is that so strange?'

'You're a woman, my sweet.'

Harald caressed her breast and felt her nipple harden but she was not ready to give in to him yet.

'I am a woman who rode the rapids, remember?'

'Not all the way.'

'Not yet.'

'Oh Lily.' He kissed her neck, dipped lower, felt her arch in response. 'If it is thrills you seek, we need go no further than here.'

He pushed her gently back and lifted her shift from her, running his hands across her skin and slowly down between her thighs. She moaned softly but then pushed him away.

'I will let you . . . thrill me, Hari.'

'Too kind.'

She smiled.

'But I want more too.'

'Always more,' he groaned but then she was pulling him down and wrapping her legs around him and he knew only the eternal rapids of his restless, difficult, delicious wife.

CHAPTER THIRTY-ONE

Oslo, April 1057

'Nice weather for the race.'

Tora indicated the sky where a brave sun was poking through the clouds, as if checking it was safe to come out over the rapids in time for what was now an annual event on the great river at Oslo.

'Isn't it?' Harald agreed, panting slightly as he plunged into another bout of sword play with Magnus in the spacious yard in front of Tora's house.

Her son, now ten, was proving himself, despite his small stature, to be athletic and quick. Harald, thank the Lord, was pleased with him and if, out of his father's sight, Magnus still chose studying bugs and furry creatures over battling, at least he was active. He was a fast and conscientious learner, Olaf too, and both were responding well to their tutors so that they stood up as skilled, if not crazed, fighters and that, for now, was enough to satisfy their father. As Magnus ducked Harald's thrust, sending him staggering, Tora took the chance to grab his arm.

'Time for a rest perhaps? You don't want to be all sweaty for the race.'

Harald grimaced.

'Got to keep up my public face, hey?'

'Well, haven't you? It's a big day for the city.'

'It is.'

Harald released Magnus and let Tora lead him to a bench in the corner of her yard. She dunked a cup into a bucket of fresh rainwater and passed it to him.

'She's fed up, you know, Hari.'

'Who is?' Harald wiped his brow. 'He's quick on his feet, isn't he, Magnus?'

'Very,' Tora agreed patiently, adding, 'Elizaveta.'

'Elizaveta is quick on her feet?'

'No! She's fed up.'

'I know that. I'm having to . . .'

He stopped and Tora looked politely away. She knew exactly how Harald would be keeping his other wife busy and found it curious that Elizaveta was still entertained by bedsport. When Harald spent an evening with her, as he sometimes did when he was in the north alone, they were more likely to play a game of tafel than with each other and for that she was grateful.

'I think,' Tora said carefully now, 'that however rigorous you are, Hari, it will not be enough.'

'She did say something of the sort but what can I do? I offered her a new viol but she didn't want it. Life is different now. We are older. I have new priorities. I was thinking, by the way, of taking Magnus journeying with me this summer.'

'Magnus?' Tora froze and looked across to her son, who had sheathed his sword and was peering into a bush, doubtless after some new species of spider for his records. 'He is so young, Harald.'

'Not really. He's ten, Tora. He will soon be a man in the eyes of the law.'

'Maybe but . . .' She fumbled desperately for convincing logic. 'He is so small.'

'In stature, yes, but not in temperament. Are you, my boy? Magnus?' Harald looked around and saw his son's blonde head sticking out from the foliage. 'Ah,' he said fondly, 'always in scrapes.'

It wasn't true. Magnus had never been a naughty child and now, on the cusp of manhood, he was more composed than ever. He would somehow emerge from that bush as immaculate as he had gone in, more concerned with his animal studies than with adventure, and the thought of him on a ship with only Harald's hardened warriors to look out for him chilled Tora's blood.

'What have you got there, lad?' Harald asked as Magnus backed cautiously out, hands clasped.

'I thought it might be a Thor's blue but it's just a normal skyberry.'

'Sorry?'

Harald peered at his son as if he were talking a foreign language and by way of explanation Magnus opened his fingers to let a bright blue butterfly spiral upwards to lose itself in the sky. Harald was silenced for a moment then roughly cleared his throat.

'How would you like to come on a journey with me, Magnus?'

Magnus glanced to Tora but she dared not interrupt and could only nod him helplessly on.

'I would like that very much, Father?' Magnus offered, more a question than a statement.

'Of course you would,' Harald confirmed. 'You are a big boy now and must learn how to become a king.'

'Must kings go on journeys, Father?'

'Of course – they cannot stay at home congratulating themselves on what they already have.' Tora heard the edge in Harald's voice and recognised the source of his words – Elizaveta had got to him then. 'The world is a large and exciting place, Magnus. Would you not like to see it?'

Magnus considered.

'I would,' he concluded. 'I would like to see all the different creatures in other lands.'

Harald looked both confused and, thankfully, intrigued by his son's view of the world.

'I hear they have many badgers in Ireland,' he offered.

'Iceland?'

'No, Magnus, Ireland – a country past England ruled by many kings, several of them our Viking allies. We could perhaps visit Iceland on the way though. Call in on Halldor. Would you like that?'

Magnus looked uncertain again. Halldor had frightened him as a child, but he knew his duty and stuck his little chin up.

'I would like to go wherever you think best, Father.'

'Good lad.'

'And wherever Mother would like too.'

'Mother? Ah!' Harald bent down before Magnus. 'Your mother will not be coming, son. This is a man's trip.'

Magnus's lip quivered and Tora felt her eyes start to fill. She looked away. She'd known this time would come; known her boys would become men, become warriors – it was the way – but she had not looked for it to happen so soon.

'Will Maria not, then, come either?'

Harald chuckled.

'She would, given half a chance, I'm sure, but no. You, Magnus, are my first son and my heir and your duties start now.'

'Yes, sir.'

'Good. Now, run along to your dinner. The race will be starting soon and we do not want to miss it, do we?'

Tora had rarely seen Magnus move so fast; he skittered across the yard and into the house as if there were a bear on the loose.

'See,' Harald said to her, 'he's delighted.'

Tora sighed. Harald saw what he wanted to see and she had not the guts to contradict him. A sudden thought occurred to her.

'Why not take Elizaveta journeying?'

'What? Oh honestly, Tora, not you too. Did you not hear me – this is a man's trip.'

Her fear for Magnus made her bold.

'Why?'

'Why?!'

'Will you be sailing to battle?'

'No.'

'Well then . . .'

'But you never know when a battle might arise.'

'And if Elizaveta is there she can keep Magnus safe.'

'Oh, I see.' He looked down at her. 'Why not you, Tora?'

She shivered.

'You have two wives, Harald,' she told him crisply, 'with two very different dispositions. Why take the wrong one for the task?'

Harald groaned.

'I think I preferred it when you two hated each other.' He took her hands. 'Look, Tora, I know you're concerned for Magnus. I understand that, but I'll take care of him. I'm no hot-headed young blood any more, just a fat old general.'

'Did Elizaveta tell you that?'

'She mentioned it and she's right. That's why I need to get into training again, why I need to sail, to see the islands that pay allegiance to me as a king. And it's why I need to be a man again, not some poultry-pecked stay-at-home king with more wives than anyone can easily cope with.'

Tora laughed, though her heart was still fearful.

'Elizaveta will not like this,' she warned.

'Elizaveta is busy organising the Rapids Race,' Harald countered. 'She will barely notice.'

'I'm not so sure,' Tora said but he had gone, striding after Magnus to dinner, and she could only pray she was proved wrong and that this afternoon's racing would be enough to keep Elizaveta at peace with herself.

Elizaveta shifted her boat, feeling its weight stinging her slender arms, and took the last few steps up the forest path to the start. She knew what to do. She'd practised, sneaking out of the palace at first light when the rest of the royal household were snoring in their feather beds and the guards on Oslo's new walls were too blurry-eyed to spot her slipping down the streets through the dawn mist to the chirpy waters of the river Lo, the banks of which she now trod with her fellow racers. She knew, because she'd been over and over it with Aksel before that first ever Norwegian race, how to spot the vicious downward suck of a whirlpool, the dark shadow of a rock too close to the surface, and the eerie light of a sandbank. She knew how to find the current that would carry her, swift and true, to the great rope, strung between the grandstands on the lower plains to mark the finish line. She knew it and she was determined to rise to it.

The others had looked at her a little strangely when they'd collected their boats but, eyeing up her slim figure in some of Aksel's old clothes, they had not, she was sure, considered her much of a threat and, indeed, she was not. She stood no chance of winning but she cared not. She wanted to finish, that was all. She wanted to feel again the thrill she'd known as a girl before she had been jolted from the water by the dark cloud of the preying net.

'How dare you stop me?' she'd shrieked at her captors back then

but they had been dancing to her father's tune and had simply said: 'How dare we let you continue?' Yet she remembered still the younger guard sneaking food to her bedchamber that night. 'Next time, Princess,' he'd told her, proffering stolen soup and ale, 'please adventure on someone else's watch,' and she'd smiled. She'd smiled as she smiled now because he'd said 'next time' and at last 'next time' was come.

Tora waved and smiled at the crowd, letting Magnus and Olaf walk before her so the people could see their future kings. Olaf, she knew, had not much hope at the crown unless anything were to befall his older brother, or Harald were to win more land, and as thoughts of the planned voyage crowded her brain, she prayed her younger son would never rule. Harald's blasted landwaster made her shiver. The raven's sharp wings made it look, to her, more like an angel of death than a conquering bird, and she hated the thought of her sons fighting beneath its cold heart. Olaf would be happy as Magnus's marshal, or maybe his Metropolitan, for the boy was enchanted by the rituals and music of the church. It would be a fine destiny for him, and a safe one.

Tora knew Elizaveta was frustrated by her lack of interest in the world beyond Norway, but what Elizaveta could not see was how her own refusal to settle frustrated Tora too. Why did she seek other countries, when this one was so rich in all they needed? Why did she always have to look for trouble?

She cast around for her fellow queen, her friend, but could see her nowhere. She would be with the racers, no doubt, giving them last-minute advice and seeing them off up the path to the start. She would soon join the royal party on the podium where Harald was already stood, courtiers crowding around him. They seemed twitchier than usual, Tora thought, but then she noticed that their feet were being jumped on by an over-excited Maria, welded to her father's side and already clutching the winner's cup. She smiled and waved, turning to gather six-year-old Ingrid, dawdling behind, and lead her up the steps into the grandstand with her and the boys.

'Where's Mama?' Ingrid asked anxiously.

'She'll be on her way,' Tora assured her. 'You know your mother – she never misses the Rapids Race.'

'Take your places,' the race-leader instructed and Elizaveta edged her canoe into the pool, slipping into it and wedging the skins around her body. The man – the only one in on the secret – looked nervous now.

'You are sure you know what you are doing?' he hissed at her, but she knew – oh, she knew exactly.

'I brought this race to Norway,' she reminded him and he retreated, dark-eyed, already perhaps seeing Harald's wrath.

'He will not blame you,' she assured him. 'He will know there was nothing you could do to stop me.'

'Save net you.'

She frowned furiously at him.

'No one nets me.'

'No, my la . . .' He looked nervously around. 'No. Not unless you are in trouble.'

'I will not get into trouble. Raise the flag.'

Nodding, he stepped back, checked all the canoes were in the pool, and gave the signal to the lad up in the trees, who lifted the great red and white flag. Elizaveta heard a cheer from the crowds below rise faintly up the river but it was muffled by the pines and the roar of the rapids and the sound of her own blood rushing around her head. She pointed her canoe to the edge, keeping a little back from the muscular young men jostling for the best line, and waited for the gong.

*

Harald looked around as the flag rose above the trees and the crowd cheered.

'Where's Elizaveta?'

'I'm not sure,' Tora admitted. 'I assumed she was with the racers but they're long gone up the hill.'

Maria tugged on her skirts.

'She's not well,' she said. 'She said she was exhausted and wanted to lie down before the race.'

Harald glared at his daughter.

'And no one woke her? She'll be furious.'

'*You* didn't wake her, Papa,' Maria pointed out.

Goodness, that girl had no fear, Tora thought, flinching back as Harald growled furiously.

'It is not *my* job, Maria. That's what she has maids for – and daughters.'

'Oh,' Maria said breezily, 'I was too busy placing my wager.'

'Maria! Princesses do not wager.'

'Of course they do. Everyone wagers.'

Harald shook his head in despair but he was smiling at his precocious eldest – the child, despite her sex, most like himself.

'What about Ingrid then?' he demanded now. 'Where is she?'

'She's here,' Tora put in quickly, 'with me. I brought her from the nursery with Olaf and . . .'

She stopped herself from adding 'Magnus'; he was not supposed to be in the nursery any more but he still liked to sneak inside when he got the chance. He and little Ingrid were happy together for hours, comparing their finds of plants and animals, and Tora loved to see them in such innocent amusements.

'Good God!' Harald, thankfully, was too distracted by his missing wife to think of Magnus. 'Someone had better go for her then. Ulf,' he turned back to his marshal, 'send someone for Lily, will you? She'll have my neck if she misses the race.'

Ulf sent a servant racing off the jetty and down the streets towards the palace then came back to Harald's side.

'It's not like Elizaveta to miss out on a big occasion, Hari – especially not this one. Is she well?'

Harald's eyes widened with sudden horror.

'Well? Of course she's well. Why would she not be well?' He looked to Tora. 'Why would she not be well, Tora?'

Tora spread her hands.

'She's been very busy with organising the race, Hari. I've hardly seen her these last few days. Perhaps it just got too much for her?'

Even as she said it, though, it sounded wrong. Nothing ever got too much for Elizaveta. She'd looked rather flushed these last few days, yes, but not in a feverish way, more with something like excitement.

No!

Tora pushed the dreadful thought away but it came leaping back at her.

'She wouldn't,' she whispered.

'Wouldn't what?' Harald demanded. 'She wouldn't what, Tora?'

'The flag!' the crowds called impatiently. 'They're on the start.'

They were looking expectantly to Harald, who had little choice but to lift the hammer, though Tora could see his hands shaking. She leaned close.

'I do not think she is ill, Hari. Mad maybe, but not ill.'

'Mad?' Harald swung the hammer into the gong and the low note echoed up the mountain to the boats at the start. 'Mad,' he repeated, his eyes following the sound upriver before he turned, horrified, to stare at Tora. 'No!'

'Let's hope not,' was all Tora said, for whatever was happening in the starting pool, it was too late to stop it now.

*

'Go!'

The first canoes leaped forward, over the lip of the pool and down through the cascading water, battling for position. Elizaveta let them go. She glanced at the race-leader and saw relief cross his face, poor man, before she launched herself after them, pushing her paddle into the water with all the force she could muster to shoot herself free of the first little waterfall.

She landed safely in the centre of the rushing current and forged after the rest, queen no more, woman no more, just a rider pitting herself against nature and against time. And now she could feel it again, as sharp as if she were ten years old – the surge of water through the thin skin of the tiny canoe, the sparkle of spray in her eyes, the rush of warm air against her face and, above all else, the roar of her heart as, again, she crested the rapids.

Elizaveta battled with the water, steering herself into the stream and willing herself to relax and let it carry her down, down towards the jetties of Oslo below. The great pines high up to her right were leaning in as if willing her on or, perhaps, waiting for her to fall but she would not fall, not this time. She followed the other riders – still less than a boat-length ahead – through the next little pool and over the waterfall, larger this time, so large that for a moment she felt she were cresting air not water. And now she could see the sun-blurred faces of the crowds hanging over the bank, all wide eyes and open mouths; their calls of encouragement scattered on the light breeze and were lost in the roar of the endless, treacherous, glorious run of blue water before her – hers to master. She dug in her paddle and, breathing tight, forced her way into the rapids.

'It's her,' Tora whispered to Harald as the boats came into view and the crowd surged forward. 'I swear that's her, at the back.'

'Can't be. She wouldn't do that, Tora. Surely she wouldn't?' They looked at each other. 'Why do you think that one's her?'

They looked back to the river where the canoes were battling down the lower reaches of the rapids.

'Have you ever seen anyone that slight ride the rapids before?' Tora asked and now others were noticing, pointing.

Harald pushed forward to the rail, elbowing courtiers aside. He leaned forward and Tora forced her way in beside him, straining her eyes to try and make out the face of the rider at the back. At that moment, however, his – or her – canoe hit a whirlpool and spun. Tora caught her breath as the boat swirled helplessly but somehow the rider dug in a paddle and pulled it out again. Water flew up over the canoe but it came safely out the other side, though the rider's cap had fallen off in the frenzy and now sleek, night-dark hair fell, glossy and wet, down her – definitely *her* – back.

'The queen!' The whisper ran around the crowd, rapidly gaining in volume. 'The queen. It's the queen – the queen is riding the rapids!'

The crowd were delighted but Harald did not seem to hear them. He was fixed on Elizaveta's tiny figure as she turned the canoe between two rocks and headed for the last stretch of rapids. She was gaining on the boat in front of her and as everyone watched, the lead riders forgotten in the unfolding drama, the other rider's canoe caught the jagged edge of a rock and flew into the air.

'No!' Harald cried, but Elizaveta shot beneath him, ducking her head down to skim past as the netters dragged him to safety.

'She's going to get hurt,' Magnus gasped. 'Mama – Elizaveta is going to get hurt.'

'No she isn't,' Tora said, more in hope than belief.

Her son was not fooled.

'You have to stop her, Father,' he insisted, tugging on Harald's gilt-edged tunic.

Harald looked to Tora, panic in his eyes.

'Do I?' he asked. 'Do I have to stop her?'

Tora thought of Elizaveta kicking against the complacency of the Western Assembly. She thought of her haunted look when she'd talked of journeying and her wild eyes these last few days.

'Don't stop her.'

'You're sure?'

'Sure. Don't stop her, Hari. It will break her heart.'

Harald nodded and clasped her hand for a second and then he was leaning out over the parapet, so far she thought he might tumble in after his Slav wife, and screaming like a peasant boy: 'Go on, Lily! Go on!'

The lead racer shot over the finish line to a mild cheer but all eyes were fixed further back as Elizaveta's little canoe tipped through the last of the rapids and she dug her paddle into the open waters of the fjord, pushing for the line. She would be last – save the poor man scrambling, red-faced, from the nets above – but there was a joy in her eyes that Tora swore she would never forget.

That, then, was why Elizaveta fought so hard at life – that elation, that consuming passion, that need for more. Tora looked at Harald and saw fierce, stupefied, dazzled pride written wide across his scarred face. She was the third in this strange triumvirate of theirs, she knew that today more than she ever had before, but if riding rapids was what it took to be first, she'd settle for being third.

Elizaveta shot over the finish line feeling as if her whole body might erupt. She'd done it. She'd ridden the rapids all the way to the end. She'd conquered them. She felt painfully, joyously alive as she circled in the finishing pool. The others riders were looking at her incredulously, belatedly terrified of hurting her but she just beamed at them.

'Well ridden,' one said and she clung to the words in delight. Well ridden!

Drawing in deep breaths, she turned her canoe and paddled for the shore and there was Harald, arms folded, legs wide, brow so low his scar seemed almost to dangle from it. She swallowed, attempted a wave. Still his arms were folded and she paddled slowly to the shore.

'I had to do it, Hari,' she called up to him, not caring who heard.

His words came back to her, loud and clear: 'I know you did, Lily, but could you not have won?' And then he was sweeping her up out of the canoe and lifting her high through the crowd as everyone went wild around them.

'Why, Lily?' he whispered into her hair. 'Was it a dare to shock me? Was I not paying you enough attention? Did . . .'

'None of that, Hari,' she assured him, squirming in his arms to bury her face in his neck. 'No dare, no whim, no cry for attention or accolades, just a desperate need, like an itch in my soul. Does that make sense?'

'An itch in your soul? Lily, my sweet – that's exactly what you are to me. And I love you for it.'

She looked up at him, his dear, scarred face filling her vision.

'Can I then,' she asked, 'come journeying with you?'

'I think,' Harald agreed ruefully, 'that for your own safety it would be best if you did. Now stop dripping on me and present your poor winner with his cup.'

CHAPTER THIRTY-TWO

Myvatyn, Iceland, July 1057

Elizaveta drew in a long, deep breath of tangy air and then let it slowly slip from her body as she looked around the wide bay of Reyjavik. This, she thought, was peace and she raised a prayer of thanks to God in his endless heavens that she had been privileged to come here to Iceland. Around her, Harald's men were rolling up the sail and shooting the long oars through the portals to guide them into the smart jetty on which Elizaveta could see Halldor, his squat frame square, his arms held wide in greeting. Behind them stood a couple who could only be Aksel and Greta, and Elizaveta suddenly felt as giddy as a child at Christ's mass. As soon as they pulled alongside, both she and Harald scrambled to disembark.

'Halldor, you old troll!' Harald cried, grabbing his friend in a wrestle of a clasp that, for all its outward show, was pure affection.

Ulf bounded up at his side and Elizaveta smiled to hear the three bluff warriors laughing like children. Leaving them to their raucous greetings, she turned to Aksel, drinking in the sight of him after seven long years away. Although now a man of twenty-three, he looked exactly as she remembered, save for a stronger shape to his shoulders and a line or two in his open face. Greta, too, had the same sweet face, though her hips were perhaps a little wider and she had four children around her knees. They scattered like chickens as their parents knelt before Elizaveta but she hastily raised them, beckoning their brood back in.

'Please, you are not my servants now.'

Aksel smiled.

'We will always be your servants, my lady.'

'Elizaveta.'

'Elizaveta, my lady.'

He and Greta both looked flushed and she turned to the children to spare their embarrassment.

'And who do we have here?'

'I'm Evert,' a bright-eyed boy told her, his voice gruff with the Icelandic inflection, 'and this is Mina. She's younger than me.'

'Only by a few minutes,' the pretty girl objected.

'Twins?' Elizaveta asked Greta, charmed. Greta grimaced.

''Fraid so, my lady. Two sets.'

'Two?!'

She looked to the younger pair and saw two miniature versions of their father as he'd once been when he'd sat at her feet in Yaroslav's grand hall in Kiev.

'That's Josef,' Evert told her, pointing to one, 'and that is Filip.'

'Filip?' Elizaveta choked, looking to Aksel. 'Like the toad?'

'What toad?' Evert demanded eagerly.

'No toad,' Aksel told him quickly, though to Elizaveta he said with a wink, 'I've liked the name ever since that day. Is Maria well?'

'Very well, though furious not to be journeying with us. Ingrid too, even after I'd told her Iceland has little in the way of herbs. We have had to promise to bring them when they are older but Magnus is here.'

Tora's son had clambered out of the boat behind them and now she drew him forward. He gazed up at Aksel, then back to Elizaveta, who nodded him forward to shake hands.

'He longs to see Iceland's wildlife,' she said to Evert.

'Well, here they are,' Aksel offered to squeals of protest from his children.

'I can take you up into the hills to see the reindeer if you like,' Evert offered.

Magnus looked again to Elizaveta.

'Can I?'

'Of course. Maybe tomorrow if Evert is free?'

'And me,' Mina said.

'No way,' Evert told her. 'It's too dangerous for girls.'

'Is not. Anyway, I'm braver than you. You're the one that cried when the whale jumped over the boat.'

'It was a very big whale.'

'A whale?' Magnus's eyes shone. 'When? Where?'

And they were off, chattering away, leaving Elizaveta to greet Halldor, who was talking like a man possessed as he, Harald and Ulf caught up on too many years apart. Together, they all moved towards the low buildings around the harbour that seemed to constitute Iceland's premier town.

'Magnus looks to you for guidance, Elizaveta?' Greta asked curiously as they fell in behind the men.

'He does and I promised Tora I would watch out for him.'

'Promised *Tora*?' Both she and Aksel spluttered at the notion and Elizaveta laughed.

'It's not just out here that things have moved on. We are friends now; it's easier that way.'

'As I recall, my lady,' Greta said lightly, 'you were never much inclined to make things easier.'

'Maybe not but now I am old and staid.'

'Never,' Aksel said gallantly. 'And besides, if you are feeling your age at all, Iceland will make you young again.'

He spoke true. Over the next few days as they journeyed gently across the island, stopping with smiling farmers along the way, Elizaveta felt herself unfolding. The place was magical. It moved and spoke as if it were alive – as if somewhere below the craggy surface lay a huge lung that, like her, drew in the rich air and then teasingly sent it out again through the bubbling pools and swirling springs and frothing waterfalls that poured through the whole landscape.

Halldor had been right that there were very few trees but the rocks seemed to grow instead, pushing up towards the clouds in strange twisting formations and Elizaveta could see why Harald's loyal warrior had yearned to return. Men sat easily in Iceland's busy geology, a natural part of the shifting seasons rather than a dominating force. Even their houses huddled into the hillsides, melding with them.

'Troll houses!' Ulf exclaimed delightedly as, on the third day, Halldor proudly led them up a gentle rise to his vast farm on the shores of Lake Myvatn.

Elizaveta looked where Ulf indicated and instantly saw what he meant. The buildings of Halldor's household were set deep into the hill, dug out of it who knew how far back, with only triangular porches jutting forth to mark the doors.

'There are no trolls in Iceland, fool,' Halldor told his old friend, swinging out of the saddle as they all drew up in the centre of the magical semicircle of doorways.

'Maybe one,' Ulf suggested and Halldor punched his arm.

'Not even one, my friend.' And in truth, in his homeland Halldor stood tall and straight, his brow clear and his shoulders square, as if he had become permanently his storyteller self. 'Out here on the edge of the world,' he went on as the rest of the party drew up, 'we have lighter creatures than trolls. We have fire pixies, so small you could mistake them for normal hearth sparks until they burrow into your tunic and bite at your heart.'

'At your heart?' Elizaveta gasped, encouraging him, for hearing his stories again was every bit as refreshing as seeing his world.

'At your heart,' he confirmed darkly, 'as fearsome as love.'

'Oh, Halldor . . .'

'You know it to be the truth, Elizaveta, and when that happens the only cure is to find the water sprites.'

'Water sprites?'

'Yes. For they slide across your heated skin like the breath of a maiden . . .'

'Still with the maidens, Hal?'

'Of course,' he agreed with a wink, 'everyone loves a maiden. And they smother the fire pixies and send them screaming back into the bowels of the earth from whence they came.'

'Fire beneath the ground? Really, Hal?'

At that, though, Halldor became solemn.

'Really,' he said, his voice dropping its storyteller's lilt for a moment and becoming more solidly Icelandic. 'There *is* fire beneath Iceland, Elizaveta. It keeps our waters warm and our land fertile even up here in these dark winter lands. It nurtures us but every so often it bursts out, to show us who is truly in charge.'

'Bursts out? Where?'

'In the hills. It blows the tops off and comes out in choking clouds and burning rivers.'

Elizaveta looked frantically around and Halldor laughed.

'We are safe here, my lady. The nearest one is a day's ride away. We feel it shake the ground a little sometimes but its tongues have never licked Myvatn. Fear not; the gods will not play with you in my home.'

'Gods, Halldor?'

'Forces if you prefer. I am no pagan, my lady. See our church.' He indicated a beautiful low structure, the only building not tucked into the hills. It was made of precious wood and carved and painted all over so it glowed. 'But I know why our ancestors were. Nature is a part of us here. Sometimes it makes mischief, sometimes it soothes, always it inspires. There are no gods, no creatures with a will of their own, but sometimes, even now, it feels as if there might be. I do not worship that, Elizaveta, but I embrace it.'

Elizaveta recalled Harald talking of the core truth of Valhalla and shivered.

'As you embrace the water sprites and the fire pixies?' she suggested lightly and a gleam came back into his eyes.

'Ah no, my lady,' he chuckled, wagging a finger at her, '*never* embrace a fire pixie. Now, let me welcome you to my home.'

And what a welcome it was. Halldor's farm, if farm it was, ran so far into the hillside that surely only his precious gods could have dug it out.

'Not gods,' Halldor said cheerfully as she suggested this, 'men; my men. They work hard – I feed them well. We're all happy.'

Over the next few hours Elizaveta was well able to believe that was true as dish after dish was served to their royal party in Halldor's mole-hall. The space was vast and lined with richly painted stone behind which, Halldor told them, moss and peat was stuffed to seal out the cold of the earth. The fire – also mainly peat, because wood, fished from the sea, was scarce – burned low but strong and the stone walls drew in the heat and held it so that you could lean back upon them and feel stroked by natural warmth. Light came from tunnels dug up to the surface and as night eventually fell, if you angled your-self carefully you could see the stars peeping in at you. Elizaveta loved it. Even more than the hall, though, she loved her bedchamber.

Entered through another porch, a little around the hillside from the hall, it was her and Harald's own private burrow. The whitewashed walls were painted with biblical scenes set not in the arid Holy Land but here in Iceland's own lush, rugged countryside, and hung with rich tapestries of such rough wool it seemed as if at any moment they might leap up and baa. The bed, to her great amusement and Harald's delight, was shaped as a longship with the feather mattress set beneath a mock mast which Harald stroked appreciatively and determined to 'put to good use'.

There was a copper looking-glass stood against one wall in a twisted gilt frame, and a coffer that sat on feet shaped like those of some mystical beast and – especially for Elizaveta – a music stool in the shape of a viol. It was a storyteller's room, full of quirks and humour, and Elizaveta vowed to attempt a replica at home. For now, though, she was content to enjoy the magic where it belonged especially when, a week later, Halldor promised to take them to the 'greatest miracle of the whole island'.

This 'miracle' was a whole morning's ride from the lake but their party was eager and excitable. There were some twenty local men and women on horseback and a dozen pack ponies behind carrying 'a little dinner' for when they arrived at their mystery destination. No one was telling Elizaveta what awaited her there, though she'd begged for information, and her antici-pation was growing. Even Aksel refused her entreaties and she could hardly wait to arrive.

'Is this not the most amazing country?' Harald said as they rode along together.

'Magical, Hari. I'm so glad I came with you.'

'So glad I permitted you to do so?'

'Exactly that, my lord and master.'

His eyes darkened.

'Don't cheek me, Elizaveta, or I shall have to tie you to the mast – again.'

Her loins shivered in remembrance. His time out here had already sculpted Harald's body as surely as if one of the fire pixies had licked his flesh away. They had feasted, yes, but he had been out every day with Halldor and Ulf, the three of them riding miles, or trekking along uphill paths and glaciers, or hunting boar and deer for the table.

Elizaveta had watched them ride in one day as she and Greta returned from moss-gathering – Greta being no keener on adding to her mischievous brood of children than Elizaveta – and had thought them all as young as they had been that first night they'd ridden into Kiev nearly thirty years past. And Harald's spirit had honed itself with his stomach. He spoke with new vigour, laughed louder than ever, and sparkled with the glow of adventure rediscovered. Magic indeed.

'In that case, *my lord*,' she said now, 'I fear you are grown unoriginal in your old age.'

'Unoriginal?! You wait, Elizaveta . . .'

She grinned up at him and he leaned over in his saddle to kiss her so hard she had to grip at the reins to steady herself. They rode on together in contented silence, watching Halldor's boisterous Icelandic companions racing each other across the open plain, before Harald said, 'Would you travel further, Lily?'

She thought carefully.

'I'm not sure, Hari. The idea of it captivated me, I admit, but there is only so much you can achieve in one lifetime and there is a great deal of the known world I would still like to see.'

'You are not tempted, then, by this new land they have found?'

'Vinland? I was drawn to the novelty of it,' Elizaveta admitted, 'but in truth it does not sound a very promising place.'

The explorers, to Elizaveta's delight, had sailed into Reyjavik from their journey west just two days after their own arrival and Halldor had invited them to his house to share their adventures with his royal guests. Both Elizaveta and Harald had quizzed them in detail on the new land they had found several days' sail west of Greenland but there had been disappointingly little to say.

'It seems a fertile place,' they had reported, 'with many trees and sprawling vines and huge salmon in the rivers.'

'We have trees aplenty in Norway,' Harald had said. 'Salmon too, and we can ship wine from over the Varangian Sea in just a day or two's sail. What else does this new country have that makes it worth battling the waves to reach?'

The men had looked at each other, a little lost.

'Space?' one had suggested.

'Space?!' Harald had laughed. 'God above, we have plenty of space. We need towns for trade, craftsmen with new goods, mines full of minerals. Have you found such things?'

'No, Sire. The natives are nomads, a quiet people who prefer to stay in the bushes than challenge new arrivals. A man could claim rights as their king without having to lift a sword.'

'And where would be the point in that? Who wants to be the king of a handful of tribesmen?'

'I might,' Elizaveta had heard their leader mumble and she'd risen.

'Then you are.'

'Beg pardon, my lady?'

'What is your name?'

He'd flushed and stammered: 'Erik, my lady, but I meant no insult, truly.'

'And I have taken none. Rest easy, Erik. Ambition is a worthy trait and yours should be rewarded. I pronounce you King of Vinland.'

'But . . .'

'Sail forth and enjoy your reign.'

'I . . . Thank you, my lady.'

Elizaveta smiled now at the remembrance of his confusion and his fellows' uncertain congratulations. She wished them well of the place, for it sounded too dull to tempt her.

'It seems to me,' she said to Harald as they reined their horses back to cross a rocky patch of land, 'that this Vinland is no match for the riches of Europe.'

'No indeed,' he agreed. 'It would be foolhardy to waste good men on such an empty place. England though . . .'

'Oh Hari,' Elizaveta begged, 'let's not think of politics. We are in Iceland. There are no kings, nor queens either, and it is very restful.'

'*Restful*, Lily? Has some troll stolen my wife away?'

'You know what I mean. Look – Halldor is reining in. Are we here?'

She looked around, confused. There was nothing to mark this place out as special, let alone as a 'miracle'.

'My lady, allow me!' Halldor was at her side, offering his arm with a flourish. Elizaveta took it and leaped from her saddle, peering curiously all around. 'Do you like it?'

'Like what, Halldor?'

'You do not see?'

Elizaveta looked harder but the only defining feature in the rugged plain was a rough crack in the rocky ground before them, as if someone had grabbed the edges and squeezed them together, forcing them to split upwards.

'See what, Hal?' The others were looking gleefully at each other and Elizaveta turned to Harald as he came to her side. 'Do *you* see anything, Hari?'

'Only a crack in the ground.'

'Only a crack!' the locals chuckled delightedly.

Elizaveta leaned in to Harald.

'I think maybe *they* are the cracked ones,' she whispered.

'Humour them.'

'Come, my lady,' Halldor was urging now, taking her arm and guiding her along the rough ridge to where it widened a little. 'In here.'

'In there?' Elizaveta squeaked, peering down the jagged crevice; was this a jest?

She looked desperately around and Aksel took pity on her.

'Allow me to escort you, my lady.'

'Underground?'

'It will be worth it, trust me.'

Greta was coming forward too so Elizaveta submitted, letting Aksel lift her into the mouth of the rocks. A slim corridor led downwards, twisting out of sight and Aksel, ducking low, made his way slowly along it. Elizaveta glanced back up at Halldor.

'Are there trolls here after all?'

'No trolls. Go!'

Elizaveta's heart was beating with fear. The rock seemed like a great jaw waiting to close in on her but Aksel, who had taken a lantern off one of the serving boys, was disappearing into it so, taking a shaky breath, she forced herself to follow him. A last glance up revealed myriad faces keenly waiting – for what? – but then her foot slipped and she had to turn hurriedly back and as she did so the tight walls suddenly stretched out and there before her, rippling softly between natural ledges and pillars, was a pool. She gasped in delight and heard Halldor's friends cheer above her.

'Oh Hari,' she called up, 'come and see this – it truly is a miracle.'

She took a few more cautious steps down to where the rock flattened out into a tiny natural jetty. It was warm down here, very warm, and the water, she noticed, was steaming like the shallow bowls in a sauna. Still moving very slowly, as if this might be some kind of dream, she crouched and dipped her fingers in the water.

'It's hot.'

'As a bath, my lady.'

Greta came in behind her, holding a lantern high, her eyes dancing with mischief.

'As a bath,' Elizaveta repeated. 'Can we . . . ?'

'We can.'

'But what will we wear?'

'Wear?'

Elizaveta's eyes widened and she turned to Harald as he scrambled in beside her and gazed around him, awed.

'We're going to swim,' she told her husband, 'naked?'

His eyes gleamed.

'All of us?'

Greta laughed.

'All of us, yes, but not together. This is the men's pool. Elizaveta, we ladies are through here.'

'Shame,' Harald objected but Greta was already tugging Elizaveta along the rocks and beneath a low archway through to a second pool.

Elizaveta looked around. The rocky roof was so low she could reach up and touch it and as she did so the soft mist gathered upon her fingers, coalescing into water that ran like a lover's stroke down her arm. Through the archway a splash, then another, told her the men were not hesitating and, with a nervous glance at Greta, she reached for her brooches. Three more ladies joined them and together they shed their gowns, laying them carefully over a rock.

'Shifts too?' Elizaveta asked.

'If you are happy to, my lady. I brought a spare in case you wished to preserve your dignity.'

'Dignity?' Elizaveta laughed and the sound carried around the little cavern. 'Dignity is not something I am known for.'

Elizaveta cast off her shift and plunged into the water. It was deliciously warm, warmer than even the most hastily filled bath could ever be, and it moved around her as the others jumped in. Ducking beneath the surface, she opened her eyes and, though it stung a little, she saw her own dark hair floating before her and the bodies of the others fragmented by the shifting water, and she felt like one of Halldor's mystical water sprites. She was hidden here in the breathing depths of this mystical island, miles away from anything as cumbersome as titles or responsibilities or ambitions, and as her breath caught at the thought, she broke the surface, sucking in air.

'A miracle, Elizaveta?' she heard Halldor's voice calling through.

She laughed again and called back: 'A miracle, Hal. It is the most stunning place I have ever seen.'

'I'm glad,' Halldor replied, his voice softer now. 'It is my gift to you and to Harald too for releasing me to return here.'

They bathed there, beneath the earth, for a time too hazed to count and then, as Elizaveta floated contentedly lost in the waters' embrace, she heard: 'Lily.' She jumped – the waters were whispering her name. 'Lily, in here.'

She cast around, confused, and suddenly Harald's face popped up through a crack in the back wall of the pool. With his hair slicked back by the water and his scar hidden in the low, flickering light of the lanterns he looked somehow boyish and she swam over to him, casting a quick, guilty glance towards the other ladies gossiping at the far edge.

'How did you get here?' she asked but Harald just dipped away.

She felt a gentle tug on her leg and, gazing down, saw a hole through the rock beneath the water. Taking a last look back at the others, she ducked through.

'Hari.' She kissed him. 'You're mad.'

'For you, yes.' He pulled her against him and she felt him hard beneath the water. 'I'm so glad we came here, Lily. Who cares for law courts and mints and churches?'

'Well, they are important, just . . .'

'Just not *that* important.' Harald pulled her onto him so the waters sloshed against the rocks. 'I feel alive again, Lily – alive and purposeful and adventurous.'

'So I see,' she giggled, sensations rising irresistibly inside her.

'I'm glad you're with me.'

'And I, or who knows which poor lady you would have set upon?'

'Lily – be serious.'

He stilled, holding her close and the world receded until there were no rocks, no cave, no water, just Harald, her Harald, and she knew that the fire pixies had bitten deep into her heart – too deep even for the water sprites to cure.

'I will always be with you,' she told him, as he had told her once before. 'Always.'

CHAPTER THIRTY-THREE

The Brough of Birsay, The Orkneys, May 1058

Elizaveta pressed herself against the rough stone wall, desperately seeking shelter from the sharp onshore wind. Where was Harald? She had not sailed west with him just to spend long days pacing a wild seashore alone. She drew her cloak closer around her body for, although it was fully springtime, the sun held little power and the winds seemed ever to cut through any slight warmth. She was weary of battling them out here on this lonely bunch of islands and longed for Norway.

Elizaveta had loved the Orkneys when they'd sailed into the elegant harbour of Birsay last autumn. Jarl Thorfinn, as big and hairy as a bear, had welcomed her, and his wife, Idonie, Finn's daughter, had showered her with hospitality and endless questions about the father she had not seen for years. Confessing he had shifted allegiance to Svein of Denmark had been hard but Idonie had taken it steadily.

'Kalv was ever a troublemaker. We were glad when he left us to return to Norway. A good soldier but a hard man.'

Elizaveta had nodded.

'That's true but I am sorry we lost your father.'

'Men are ever easy to anger,' Idonie had said simply and something about the kindly woman – the turn of her nose, the timbre of her voice, the soft blue of her eyes – had been so like her cousin Tora that Elizaveta had felt at least partway home in her care.

The islands, too, had felt like a miniature Norway. She'd loved how the knife-edge cliffs gave way to soft, rolling hills and how you could see the sea all around. She'd loved Thorfinn's courtyard of buildings, the curving timbers rising up out of the foundations of an ancient settlement built many, many years ago by Pictish natives. Most of all, she'd loved the way they were set on the Brough – a promontory that curved up out of the sea and was cut off from the mainland by the swirling tide for all bar two hours of every day.

Thorfinn and Idonie's palace was on the lower edge of the Brough, nudged up to the sheltered harbour where the jarl kept his small but very smart fleet of ships. Behind it the land rose steadily up to the high point where Elizaveta now stood, leaning in against the stone broch, or tower, that was the only remaining Pictish structure on this part of the isles. The broch was the width of three men laid head to toe at the base, but it narrowed as it rose so that if you stood inside and looked up it seemed as if it might drop in on your head at any time. It had stood, though, for a thousand years, maybe more, and despite the few crumbling stones around the top it seemed unlikely it would pick Elizaveta's lifetime to cave inwards.

Idonie had told her that no one knew exactly what the ancient peoples had used it for but it was believed to have been a watch-tower and certainly that was why Elizaveta was drawn more and more to its proud side – watching, always watching for Harald's ships to appear on the wide western ocean, his raven flying proudly before him. He had been gone nigh on three months and without him the days were stretching as far as the clouds above Orkney. His stated intention had been to sail with Thorfinn to Ireland to have talks with King Diarmid of Dublin, but Elizaveta had known his true purpose and the length of his trip should not surprise her – he had gone to England.

News had been waiting for them from Agatha when they'd sailed into the Brough – terrible news. She'd sent copies of the letter, so she'd said, to Iceland, the Shetlands and Norway in the hope of catching her sister somewhere on her travels but she must have crossed with the first for the news had already been months old and it had torn at Elizaveta's heart to think of little Agatha suffering whilst she had feasted obliviously on Iceland's delights.

Edward, Agatha's dear Edward, was dead. Elizaveta had seen the words shaking on the vellum and pictured poor Agatha trembling as she wrote them, unable to believe they were true. All had been well at first, her sister had written. They had sailed into London in triumph. The people of England had lined the banks of the Thames to cheer them in and King Edward himself had been at the docks to greet them. He had clasped her Edward in his arms, acknowledging him before the whole crowd as his chosen heir, and she had wanted to weep with joy. Three days later she had been weeping indeed, but over her husband's dead body.

Why? Agatha had raged, the words splodging with grief. *Why bring us all the way to England just to strike us down?* Elizaveta had felt her own anger rising but Agatha's next words had been confused. Edward had fallen ill, she'd said. A sudden fever. Several of the crew of their boat from Flanders had suffered too and Agatha admitted that it could have been a natural illness, though she clearly did not believe so. Edward had not felt very well on the journey, she'd said, but he'd gained colour and vitality the moment his feet had met the soil of England – his inheritance. Only no more.

Elizaveta had longed to see Agatha. Her little sister had never been alone. Always, even these last years as a married woman, she had been near Anastasia and of course ever since she could remember she'd had Edward. Stuck in a foreign country with just three small children for comfort, Elizaveta feared she might be crumbling. Young Edgar had been declared 'aetheling' – throne-worthy – in his father's stead, but he was just six years old. The court had made them welcome, Agatha had reported dully, but England was disappointed.

'Disppointed?' Elizaveta had raged, furious for her little sister. 'Has England lost a husband, a friend, a father – the life they've always known?'

Harald's eyes, though, had sharpened at the news and once Elizaveta's initial grief had played itself out he'd spoken.

'I have a claim.'

Elizaveta had rounded on him, shocked.

'You said you would not pursue it.'

'*If* Edward inherited. I said I would not pursue it if Edward inherited.'

It was true and Elizaveta's stomach had swirled with an uncomfortable mix of emotions. She could not condone stealing a throne from her own nephew and yet . . . If Harald were King of England she would be with Agatha.

'Queen in her place,' she'd reminded herself sternly and brushed the idea aside, though sometimes, especially in the dark of the lonely Orkney nights, it crept back, tormenting her with its promise. Agatha was staying in England for the sake of her son, but it was clear from her letters that her bruised heart was no longer alive to the country of her dreams. Was England, then, where Elizaveta had truly been journeying ever since she'd lapped up stories of the jewelled isle as a child? Had Norway just been a stopping-off point? Why not? She had easily trimmed her Rus Norse to its Norwegian version – English would be no more of a challenge.

'I will not invade if Edgar is pronounced king,' Harald had said before he'd sailed, but they'd both known that this was an unlikely prospect. King Edward grew old. He was unlikely to last the years it would take for Edgar to mature enough to take the throne of a country like England, especially with the threat of Svein of Denmark and William of Normandy, not to mention Harald himself. He had gone to England, she was sure of it. He had murmured to her that he might 'take a reckoning' of this much talked of land and she had closed her ears to what she knew that meant. Harald would be testing the strength of the opposition in the way he and his Viking warriors knew best – with the sword.

She cast her eyes across the mercilessly empty waves and ran her precious ring round and round on her finger, slimmer after the tough winter so that ever she worried the jewel might fall. She was beginning to fear he was not coming; to fear that these skin-freezing winds had not filled his sails but had tossed him into the depths. Someone in England had, surely, got rid of Agatha's poor Edward; why would they not do the same to Harald?

Elizaveta moved around the tower to look east. Somewhere out there was Norway and her children. It had been close to a year since she'd seen Maria or Ingrid and her heart ached for them. She had feared sometimes that she was an inattentive mother, always looking to the window for something more lively than children's games, but she felt right now as if she would happily sit in the bower all summer long if she could only have them at her side.

They had sent letters – long, careful ones from Ingrid, assuring her mother they were safe and well; and short, impatient ones from Maria, mainly protests at how little she was allowed to do. Elizaveta worried that her fiery elder girl would turn twelve without her and wondered how much time she spent with Otto, left behind to assist Tora as Harald's regent. Maria would always be close to her father but as she grew older she would understand the charms of other men and, although that was natural,

Elizaveta feared it for her daughter as she had never done for herself and was grateful Tora was there to keep an eye on her.

Tora had sent letters too but more points of government for Harald than anything of importance. Now Elizaveta looked across the choppy sea and wondered if they'd held the Rapids Race without her and who had won. Then she wondered – as always she wondered – when Harald would return to take her back to them.

'Elizaveta!'

She turned to see someone waving from the base of the hill – Greta, her saviour and her sanity in this empty spring. When they had left Iceland she and Aksel had shyly asked Elizaveta to let them serve her once more. They loved Iceland, Aksel had said, but they wanted to see more of the world. Did she understand that, he'd asked, and of course she had. Tears had formed dangerously in her eyes at the thought of having her Kievan friends back at her side and she had assured them she would dearly love them to sail with her if Halldor would permit it.

Halldor had been sad to let his precious family go but he had given his blessing and Aksel and Greta had boarded Harald's royal ship with their four children, beside themselves with excitement. Magnus and Evert had vied with each other for a place in the oar team and Elizaveta had delighted in seeing Harald's son growing stronger and braver with his challenging new companion. Harald had announced that both boys would accompany him and Aksel to Ireland and, despite her reservations about Magnus's safety, Elizaveta had acquiesced. She'd been sure Tora would forgive her when her son returned bronzed and muscled – a worthy heir for Norway – but now she cursed her stupidity. It would break Tora's heart if she had to sail home without Magnus.

She shook the dread away and waved to Greta as she battled up the slope, her three remaining children playing around her in the rough seaside grass, seemingly unaware of the chill of either the wind or the wait. Elizaveta abandoned the uncertain comfort of the Pictish tower and ran to meet them.

'No sign?' Greta asked.

She was as anxious as Elizaveta for the men's return, perhaps more so. Aksel, a skilled boatman, had lived his life in Iceland as a fisherman and she was not used, as Elizaveta sadly was, to having to wait more than the scope of a single day for his return to harbour.

'No sign,' Elizaveta admitted, 'but Harald has never failed to return to me yet. They will come, I know it.'

It wasn't true but speaking her fears out loud would only make them more solid and she could not bear that.

'What do you think they are doing?' Greta asked.

Elizaveta pulled a face.

'Harald did mention he might visit England on his way back from Dublin.'

'England? For how long?'

'Depends how rich the pickings are.'

Greta looked at her curiously.

'You don't mind?'

'Mind what?'

'That Harald is taking from people?'

'Taking?' Elizaveta considered this. 'I haven't thought about it much,' she admitted. 'Usually it's Denmark he's raiding, isn't it, and there's almost an understanding there – we take Svein's things and he takes ours.'

'I suppose so.' Greta wandered on up the hill, drawn by the view though the sea was, as ever, void of sails. Elizaveta followed and when they reached the top Greta spoke again: 'It is not Svein's land that he raids though, is it?'

'Well no, no the lands are rightfully Harald's but . . .'

'I mean, it is not the *king's* goods that he seizes, or the *king's* corn that he tramples or the *king's* cattle that he slaughters to feed his men.'

Elizaveta looked uncomfortably at her one-time servant. Greta had matured greatly from the Kievan maid she had taken with her across the Varangian Sea so long ago.

'What are you saying, Greta?'

Greta shrugged.

'I'm sorry. Maybe I've just forgotten how life is outside of Iceland's quiet borders, but it seems to me that the ones who really suffer are the simple farmers and fishermen – families who want only to harvest their crop, and milk their beasts, and bring up their children in peace. What have they done to deserve a Viking at their door?'

Elizaveta stared at her.

'I don't know,' she admitted, heading back to the rugged shelter of the looming broch, 'save that if their leader was strong enough they would not suffer so.'

'A leader cannot be everywhere.'

'No, but his influence can. No one has attacked Norway for years, for if they did Harald would hound them out – take back what they had stolen and their lives besides.'

'Hardrada,' Greta said, more to the sea than to Elizaveta but Elizaveta heard all the same.

'Ruthless,' she agreed. 'It is true, Greta, and maybe I am blind to what that means when he is off a-viking but I do see that it makes a strong and settled homeland.'

'And if Harald takes England?'

'He will do the same for her, far more so than young Edgar possibly could. With Harald as king no one else would dare attack so she would be secure.'

Greta sighed.

'I see that. Iceland has made me an innocent, Elizaveta.'

Elizaveta took her arm.

'Be thankful for it. Remember when the Pechenegs attacked Kiev?'

Greta nodded.

'I was only five but I saw it in my dreams for years after.'

'I was sixteen and, to my shame, I was more fascinated than horrified. We were celebrating victory before I could truly be shocked by the horror of death but I don't believe I am any the better for it. Tora is an innocent too and she is a far nicer person than I.'

'That's not true, my lady.'

'I've told you, Greta, call me Elizaveta – we are friends now, surely?'

'As you are with Tora?'

'Yes, though she may not remain so if I do not bring her son home. We think *we* have waited long but imagine how it must be for her. We set sail from Norway last June.'

'The winter kept us prisoner.'

That much was true. Harald was meant to have sailed for Ireland last November, as soon as he'd reprovisioned on Orkney, but winter had roared in like an arctic bear, trapping the ships in the storm-tossed harbour and sending early snow that drove them all into the great hall and made journeying either east or west impossible. It had been a lean winter with so many mouths to feed and it was only Aksel's brave team of fishermen spearing a whale in Scapa Flow that had kept them all alive. Elizaveta was grateful for it but she would be happy if she never tasted the soft wobbly flesh of the sea-beast ever again and swore nothing had ever tasted as good as when the snows had melted from the hare holes and the trappers had snared meat for the table at last.

Harald, Ulf, Aksel and their men had sailed the moment Harald had deemed the seas navigable but what if he'd been wrong? What if they'd never reached Ireland, let alone

England, and had all been dead for months? Surely she'd have sensed that? Surely her heart would have felt his absence? Maria's would have done, for her heart seemed to beat with her father's, but Maria was not here either.

'Look at me!' Elizaveta was distracted from her heavy thoughts by a piping call from little Filip. She glanced around but could not see him anywhere. 'Up here!'

She lifted her eyes and saw the boy halfway up the outer wall of the broch, his little hands and feet fitting nimbly into the cracks between the uneven stones.

'Filip – come down! It's dangerous.'

'I'm holding on tight,' he assured her, 'and I can see for miles. If I get to the top I might be able to spot Ireland.'

He moved up another course of stone, seemingly stuck to the rough surface of the broch. The walls thankfully leaned inwards a little as they narrowed but Filip was already more than halfway up – at least three times his own height. If he lost his grip the fall would be a terrible one. Elizaveta looked around for Greta but she had ducked inside the broch with Mina and Josef and was unaware of her adventurous son high above her head.

'Filip,' Elizaveta said, forcing herself to keep her voice calm though her heart was pumping like a hot spring. 'You're climbing very cleverly but the stones are loose further up.'

'They're not, honestly, they . . . oh!' Elizaveta's heart bubbled crazily as, with a sickening rattle, Filip dislodged some of the sandstone, sending it twisting down the side of the broch like deadly rain. 'I'll come down,' he said, his little voice strained.

'Good,' she agreed, moving below him and holding her hands out, praying she would not be needed to catch him for she was slighter than ever after the winter's privations and he was a stocky child. 'Slowly. Take care.'

'I am. Oh, but . . .'

'But what?' she demanded, putting up a warning hand as Greta ducked out of the curved doorway of the broch and gasped in horror.

'But,' Filip called down, his voice blithe again, 'I can see so well.'

'You can see down here too.'

'Not as well as up high.'

Something in his voice – a certain cocky knowing – caught at Elizaveta's ears.

'Why, Filip?' she demanded. 'What can you see?'

He looked down and grinned.

'Ships,' he said. 'I can see ships and they're heading this way.'

They were all at the docks as the ships sailed in and Elizaveta's heart swelled with joy as she spotted Harald's raven flapping vigorously from the foremost mast and Harald himself stood, arm around his dragon-headed prow and ice-blonde hair flowing behind him, as the now welcome wind blew him into land.

'Hari!' she called, unable to stop herself despite all the people gathered around. 'Hari – you're safe!'

'Of course I am safe, wife – would I dare leave you?'

The boat came alongside the jetty and as men grabbed the thrown ropes to haul it safely in Harald leaped onto the wood and caught Elizaveta up in his arms.

'I thought God had taken you,' she whispered against his lips as he kissed her.

'What would God want with a rough Varangian like myself? No, Lily, I am yours awhile yet.'

'I am glad of it. And Aksel? Magnus?'

Even as she asked, though, she saw Aksel running up the jetty to Greta with Evert and Magnus hot on his heels.

'All safe,' Harald confirmed. 'Safe and rich – in experience and in treasure.'

'More keys?'

'More keys, Lily – yes. And we will need them.'

'Why, Hari?'

He grinned so wide it creased his scar almost into hiding.

'I have been to England, my sweet. I raided with King Griffin and Lord Alfgar of Mercia.'

'King Griffin?'

'Of Wales, Lily – a fearsome warrior with hair the colour of burnished copper. They call him the "Red Devil" and with good reason. He is fierce.'

'As fierce as you?'

'*No one* is as fierce as me.' Elizaveta felt a tiny shiver down her spine, as if the Orkney wind had ducked beneath her collar, but she pushed it away for Harald was speaking still. 'He would be no threat were I to invade England.'

'Your mind is made up, Hari?'

She looked at him anxiously, unsure what she wanted the answer to be.

'They are talking of Harold Godwinson as the heir,' came the oblique reply.

'Harold Godwinson? The earl who went to fetch Edward and Agatha?'

'The very same. Edgar stands little chance, Lily. He is young and isolated, he barely even speaks English. We would be doing him a favour if we took power. We could protect him, protect Agatha.' Was it true? It was convenient, but was that enough? 'Harthacnut promised his inheritance to Magnus,' Harald was saying, his hands running up and down her back as if she were his sword hilt, ready for action. 'That claim lies with me and if Cnut can do it – Cnut whose forces killed my brother – then so can I.'

'You mean it?'

'I do, Lily, and it is all thanks to you. You showed me there was more to life than law courts and mints. You pointed me back to the horizon where a true Viking's eyes should always be and you were right to do so.'

He drew her to the seaward end of the jetty as men crowded round to unload the ship, cutting them off from the rest of the court. Elizaveta saw Thorfinn commanding his troops with Idonie hanging onto his arm as if afeard he might go aboard again and thought of all the wives still waiting for their menfolk back in Norway. Little did the poor women know that Harald already had his eyes on the next expedition. But now he was grabbing her hands to pull her back to him, forcing her to look deep into his flinty eyes.

'I'd lost myself, Lily,' he told her. 'I'd lost the man I wanted to be; lost the man I could see so clearly when I stood on the ridge above Stikelstad with Olaf, sword in my hand and fire in my heart. The night after that battle was the worst of my life. I was cold, I was wet, I was in pain – too much pain to even move – but above all other discomforts was the knowledge that I had lost. And, worse than that, that I had lived to lose. I had not given everything to the battle but had kept a bit back for myself. Had we all done that, I wondered as I lay beneath those thorns, curled in on myself like a baby? Was that why we'd lost?'

'Of course not, Hari. The odds were too great, that is all.'

'I know that here,' he dropped her hand to touch his head, 'but not here.' His fingers went to his heart. 'Here I fear my own cowardice.'

'Harald Hardrada,' Elizaveta told him stoutly, 'you are the bravest man I know.'

'Perhaps because of that fear. I do not think there truly is such a thing as bravery, Lily. You called me reckless once and

I think maybe that is closer to the mark. It is about reputation, about pride, about leaving behind stories that will honour your children and your country. Take you, my sweet, were you brave to go ahead and conceive a second child knowing it might – as it so nearly did – kill you?'

She considered this.

'I did not want to fail you.'

Harald clasped her to him.

'As if you could, but you have it exactly – you felt you had more to gain than to lose. You were wrong of course and should have deferred to me . . .'

'Deferred to you?!'

He kissed her.

'Maybe one day, but Lily, that is why we are so suited. You understand that life is about taking risks, about pushing for more, and that is what we must do now. You saw it first, my sweet. You saw us – me – sinking my feet too deep into Norway's comfortable soil. You saw my complacency, my ease . . .'

'You make me sound like some sort of tyrant. There is nothing wrong with taking your ease, especially once you are past your fortieth year.'

'But there is. There is if you are me – if you are you. Never, Lily, have I been more proud than when I watched you ride the rapids. You flew across that water, you battled it and you did not let it defeat you and your eyes, Lily, when you crossed the line – your eyes sparkled as if the gods were dancing in them.'

'The gods, Hari?'

He shrugged.

'I have a pagan heart. Perhaps that is my problem. I know that Valhalla does not exist. I know that a man cannot win his way into feasting with the gods through battle-glory. I know it as I know why we lost Stikelstad but I *feel* the core truth of

Valhalla all the same. I do not want to die cosy in my bed, Lily, not even with you in it. I want to die beneath my raven, fighting on. I want men in times yet to come to remember me as one who died striving for more.'

'I do not want you to die at all.'

He smiled.

'And I do not intend to. I am lucky in battle. Ulf says it's because I pick my conflicts carefully, prepare well beforehand and make fast decisions as they turn but Ulf is ever practical. I know not. In battle I do not think so much as move but it has got me this far and it will get me further yet, I swear it. Would you not like, my sweet Lilyveta, to be Queen of England?'

She looked out across the spray-whipped sea towards the south. She would like it. She would like it more than she dared say, even to herself.

'I have never seen England,' she whispered.

'You'd like it. It is Norway crossed with Kiev.'

'Nonsense, Hari.'

'It *is*. There are hills and lakes and fertile plains but the people live in towns and villages. Cities too, Lily, such cities. Not like Kiev – more wood – but large and well-defended with walls and palisades, and teeming with people. They have mints in every town and markets full of goods and they hold law courts . . .'

'Law courts, Hari? Mints, markets? Is this not what you are looking to escape?'

He laughed.

'And a system of officials, Lily, like you have never seen. A king need do nothing if he so chooses save order them around and count his treasure.'

'You have treasure, Hari – so much treasure.'

'Thanks to you, my treasure-keeper.'

Elizaveta pushed him away and looked over to his boat where

even now men were passing chests and barrels over the side, exclaiming with glee at the contents.

'That first time, Hari, when I offered to keep your caskets safe, how did you see me?'

'See you?'

'Yes. Did you see me as, you know, more than just a helping hand?'

His grey eyes twinkled like silver.

'I saw potential in you, my sweet.'

'Potential in my father's position, I'll wager.'

'That too. What?' he asked as she smacked at him. 'I was an ambitious young man. I'd have been a fool not to recognise the value of your title. I do remember you, though, when you rode into those funny little settlements on the Ros two years later, you took my breath away.'

'I did?'

'Oh yes. I lusted for you, Lily, as I have – to my peril – lusted for you ever since. I had uneasy dreams that night with you sleeping in that little wooden chapel just beyond my pavilion.'

Elizaveta smiled as he pulled her against him, and cast her mind back across years and lands to that far-off time. She remembered the flare of his hand on her ankle, his breath on her cheek, his hair entwined in hers. She separated out a lock now and looked at it.

'My hair is silvering, Hari.'

'Going blonde at last?'

She smiled and, reaching for a strand of his, still as sharply pale as ever, she twisted them together.

'You wish to ride on England?' she whispered.

'I do, Lily. For myself, for Norway, for your family honour, for the memory of Olaf and for *us*. And I *can* do it too, for I have the best warriors in the world – look.'

He gestured to the men greeting loved ones and showing

359

off treasure. She could hear chatter everywhere – England this, England that – and the enthusiasm was infectious, save that her heart was still aching from the lonely vigil of the last months. She looked up to the broch sitting high above them, dark and solid against the skyline, and shivered anew; she did not want it as her companion again.

'It would be very risky,' she suggested.

'Of course it would. As risky, perhaps, as a woman braving the rapids?'

He had her trapped there and he looked so handsome with his body as sculpted and lean as it had been when she'd first known him as a determined youth, and his hair blowing in the spring breeze, and his eyes aglow with the new challenge. She could not deny him this.

'Just make certain you get over the finishing line,' she told him.

'Of course.' He swept a big hand around her waist and pulled her tight against him as he led her through the crowds along the jetty and onto the land. 'I will invade. When the time is ripe I will invade and I will win the throne for you, my necklace goddess, all for you. Now come.'

His hand was so sure on her waist, his men so proud at her back, his ships so strong on the waves, that she had to believe him. She would write to Agatha – tell her they could be together again, pray her dear sister liked the idea. A new adventure was set, bigger perhaps than any she or Harald had yet attempted, and she could only pray they could paddle hard enough to rise to it.

CHAPTER THIRTY-FOUR

Nisa, The Danish Seas, August 1062

'Yes.' Harald spoke the word quietly into his own chest as he placed a hand to his heart. It was beating as firmly as ever; this was real. He lifted his head. 'Yes!' At his side, Ulf laughed.

'It seems, Hari, that we've finally got the bastard.'

'Yes!' This time Harald sent the cry out across the water, littered with torn vessels and men – *Svein's* vessels and men. The last of the dead king's ships were limping away, fit only to take news of this defeat to the womenfolk of Denmark and to warn them they had a new king. Harald's arm ached for he had taken a nasty slash across the wrist and blood was seeping through the hastily tied linen strip around it, but nothing could hurt him now. He glanced up to his landwaster and, seeing the raven flapping its glossy wings in triumph, he lifted his arms to it.

'I told you,' he said to Ulf, clapping him on the back. 'Didn't I always say that if we ever got the dodging rogue out in full battle we would defeat him?'

'You always said it, Hari, and now you have proved it.'

'*We* have proved it, my friend. You fought well today.'

'Not as well as young Aksel. Halldor would be proud.'

They both looked over to the lad's ship, a small but nimble vessel that he had used to deadly effect, nipping round the back of enemy vessels engaged with the core platform of Harald and Ulf's fleet of twelve, and picking them off with his little crew of lethal archers.

'He has an eye for an opportunity,' Harald agreed. 'And he's a determined young man.'

'As his father was – though can he tell a tale like Hal?'

'Full of maidens and popping eyeballs and heroes?'

'Exactly.' Ulf grinned at him. 'I was never half as much a hero in life as in Halldor's telling.'

Harald smiled. He had missed Halldor since leaving him in Iceland and had thought often of his friend's quirky mole-hall and his bubbling homeland. He had even wondered if, had he been born without royal blood, he could have lived in such a way himself, but he had the sea in his veins and today he had proved it.

'Imagine,' Ulf said now, 'what Halldor's rhetoric would have made of this battle – Svein drawn into the very centre of our formation like . . .'

'Like a man to a maiden?'

'Just like, though brought to a less enjoyable end.'

Harald laughed, then looked at Ulf, serious now as the import of the day sunk in.

'Is it true, old friend? Is Svein really defeated after all these years of petty battles?'

Ulf stroked his beard, still wild, though now as grey as steel.

'It seems so. His standard fell. I saw it myself and the men say he was tossed into the sea at sword-point and sank under the weight of his own armour. He can fight Neptune for a kingship now, Hari, for Denmark is yours.'

'As it should have been when Magnus died, had Einar not conspired against me.'

Ulf patted his back.

'Einar learned his lesson the hard way. Come, Hari, let us not dwell on the past but look to the future.'

'Let us,' Harald agreed, 'though the past, Ulf, is not easily avoided – look who stands prisoner.'

He kept his voice light though the sight of the man being bundled onto his ship, twisted hands tied before him, made his knees as shaky as one of Halldor's maidens on her wedding night. The unwanted metaphor reminded him, in a dagger-point flash, of Tora entering his pavilion before Stikelstad and he darted forward to untie Finn Arnasson. His one-time foster father now had hair as white as a gull's wing and his back was so bent that he stood nearly head and shoulders below Harald.

'You should not be fighting, Finn,' Harald said, more softly than he should have done to such a prize captive.

'I obey my king.'

'Good, for I am your king now.' Finn did not reply but looked to the shore and Harald glanced at Ulf who nodded him forward. 'I will forgive you, Finn.'

'Forgive me what?' The old man did not even look his way.

'Forgive you taking up arms against me – your king and your son-in-law.'

'Handfast only.'

'Finn! You desired the match.'

'I desired a *true* match, Harald, an honourable match, not a pagan second place to an upstart Rus princess.'

Harald bit back a fiery reply and drew in a deep breath, putting a hand to his aching wrist. Finn was old now and newly defeated; he could forgive him a little ill humour.

'Tora is not in second place, Finn; they are equal. She stood as regent of Norway for nigh on a year whilst I travelled to England and she will do so again. Her sons – your grandsons – grow strong and quick. You would be proud of them. You would surely like to see them, would you not?' Finn's white head stayed bowed, his eyes trained on the blood-washed deck of Harald's warship. 'I will forgive you, Finn,' Harald said again, 'for I know your intentions were true. I will forgive you and restore you to your lands in Austratt.'

'No.'

'No?'

Finn's head went up and he glared at Harald.

'Why would you do that, Harald?'

'Why? For Tora.'

'You do not care for her. You have never cared for her. You are enslaved by your Slav and have only used Tora for your own ends, as you used Kalv. As you used me.'

'That is not true.'

Harald looked around at his men, watching the scene curiously. He had to put an end to Finn's insidious talk and now. He took a firm step forward to grab the old man but Finn simply let him clasp the neck of his tunic, his clouded eyes looking straight into Harald's own as blood dripped from Harald's wrist through the links of his battered chain mail.

'Ambition is a disease, Harald Hardrada. That's what they call you now, isn't it? Proud of that, are you?'

'Accepting,' Harald said as quietly as he could. 'It is what I have had to be but I have cared for Norway well. The country thrives – will you not come back?'

'No. I prefer to serve a king who fights not to attack others but simply to defend his own.'

'Fought.'

'Sorry?'

'Svein is dead, Finn, and I am your king now, whether you choose to live in Norway or in Denmark.'

'You think so?'

'I know so. Svein is drowned.'

Finn just smiled and Harald felt an uneasy squirm of fear. He looked again to Ulf who strode to the other commanders, grouped around the steer-board. Alone for a moment, Harald let Finn's tunic drop.

'Finn, please. I'm sorry if you feel wronged but I seek to make amends. You were a good father to me; let me now be a good son to you.'

Something flickered in the old man's eyes – a stir of memory, a rekindled fondness? – but then he just put back his white head and laughed.

'Must you have *everyone* love you, Harald?'

Harald blinked at him again. He asked no man to love him, surely? He sought loyalty, yes – only a foolish leader would not – but *love*?

'I remember you, Harald,' Finn said, his voice so low Harald could hardly catch it over the fierce murmurs of the men further up the ship. 'I remember you with a wolf's head over your own, leaping to shore as if you owned all upon it though you were but twelve. You are greedy, Harald Hardrada, as greedy as your scavenging raven; you are greedy for treasure, for wives, for lands. Ambition is a disease, I tell you, and you have an infected soul. Now look – your men, I think, have news.'

Finn nodded gleefully to Ulf, sidling back towards them.

'What is it?' Harald snapped.

Finn's words had shaken him. It was stupid; they were the ramblings of a bitter old man, no more. Finn was probing for a weak spot, a chink in Harald's armour, but he would find none.

'It's Svein, Sire,' Ulf said, his voice low, and Harald froze; his old friend never called him by his formal title.

'What of him?'

'They say that he is not dead. They say he escaped in a skiff and is setting up camp even now.'

JOANNA COURTNEY

Ulf gestured to shore, to the spot Finn had been fixed upon, and Harald saw in the trees high up on the hillside Svein's banner flying crazily in the summer winds as if signalling the start of a Rapids Race.

'It could be a trick.'

'It could.'

They both knew it was not. Harald looked from Finn, smiling like a madman, to his huddled commanders, to his marshal. He brought his injured hand down so hard across the gunwale that the golden ring around the rowlock portal below sprung out and fell to the sea, spinning dizzily in the sun.

'Your men saw him die!' he roared.

'So they thought, but it seems, Sire . . .'

'Hari, Ulf – you call me Hari. You cannot get away from me that easily.'

'Sorry. It seems, Hari, that he dressed another man in his armour.'

'Another man? *Another* man? Svein let some poor stooge take his death for him?' He rounded on Finn. 'And this is the sort of coward king you wish to follow?' Finn looked to the floor and Harald spun away. 'Let him go then. Let him limp off to his treetop king to play make-believe if that's what he desires. I want only *real* men in my fleet.'

His 'real men' cheered loudly and Harald felt warmed by their approval. He spun away from Finn and marched up the centre of his ship towards them. He could not let Finn's sniping comments bring him down – he was a leader and he would lead, at home and abroad. If that was ambition, so be it. He would have Denmark yet and after Denmark, England.

CHAPTER THIRTY-FIVE

The Gault-Elf River, May 1064

*E*lizaveta looked around her companions and felt, despite the strange nature of their evening, a deep contentment.

She, Ulf, Johanna, Tora and Harald were sitting in the royal pavilion, set in meadowland outside Lilla Edet. This small boating station, halfway up the Gault-Elf River, the border between Norway and the Danish mainland province of Skaane to the south of Sweden, had been chosen to hammer out a truce. Just outside the door-flap Harald's ship and its four flanking vessels were moored on the bank, tied to land with great ropes and guarded by highly suspicious soldiers. For on the far bank, similar vessels were tied up, those of King Svein of Denmark.

Two more years of fighting had achieved nothing but a loss of ships and men on both sides and with news coming from Agatha that King Edward of England was ailing, Harald had reluctantly proposed this truce. Such negotiations did not, however, come naturally to him and though they were ostensibly here to broker a peace, there was every chance that, on a turn of a temper, the negotiations could descend into war.

'Peace,' Harald grumbled now, curling his lip disdainfully.

'You make it sound like a wart, Hari,' Elizaveta told him.

'It *is*. I have never made peace in my life, save with those I have conquered.'

He looked to Ulf for support and his marshal gave it with a raised goblet.

'Feels strange,' he agreed, 'negotiating without a victory to stand upon. Turns my stomach somehow.'

He glanced towards the door, though the sun had given way to the moon some time back and there was little to see of the old ship anchored in the centre of the river to host the peace talks.

'It feels good,' Johanna said gently, refilling his wine. 'Your stomach turns too often these days, Ulf – you eat too well. And did you and Harald not make peace with Magnus when first you came to Norway?'

'We agreed not to make war,' Ulf said carefully.

'Which is the same thing,' Johanna countered, 'is it not, Tora?'

Tora looked up from her embroidery and nodded.

'Truly,' she said, 'however strange it may feel, this peace is for the best. Denmark is surely of little interest to us anyway? Better to concentrate our energies on Norway.'

Harald looked at Elizaveta and they shared a smile.

'Or on England,' he said, taking her hand and squeezing it.

'When the time is ripe,' she reminded him, trying not to look at the Nisa scar across his wrist, a match for the Stikelstad one on his face.

This new wound troubled her far more than the earlier one for Maria had complained half last summer of an ache in her own arm, turning her hand endlessly round and round, seeking to ease it. Elizaveta had suggested it was overuse of her precious sword and still believed – hoped – that had been the reason.

Maria had begged Harald for years to bring her a bigger blade now she was full-grown but he had told her the original was perfect as a 'woman's weapon' and compromised by letting her have it sharpened. Her favourite trick was to slice the dinnertime bread with it, slashing it into strips in swift, precise movements. Last summer, though, she had used it little and her complaints about her wrist had ceased only as Harald had healed. Cease they had, though, and now Maria was as eager as any to talk of England.

'When the time is ripe,' Harald agreed easily now, but at his side Ulf shifted.

'Will it ever be so?'

Elizaveta and Harald looked to the big marshal in surprise.

'You do not like the idea, Ulf?' Harald asked.

'England is a long-established country.'

'Long established by *our* forefathers.'

'Three hundred years ago, Hari. I suspect they've changed a little.'

'Of course,' Harald allowed, 'but come, Ulf, we had little trouble breaking them down when we raided from Wales.'

Elizaveta shivered. 'Breaking them down' – what did that mean? She remembered Greta talking on Orkney about Harald targeting common farmers and fishermen, but her maid had said herself that she was innocent of the world. Even tonight she was safely in the pavilion with Aksel and their children, unencumbered by the wider decisions to be made here. Rulers could not get bogged down in such minute detail; it obscured the wider scope of the fresco.

'True,' Ulf was conceding now, 'but we had Earl Alfgar to direct us.'

'Alfgar was about as much use as a wooden cooking pot,' Harald scoffed.

'As a fighter, maybe, but he knew the land, Hari.' Harald leaped up at that and snatched the wine jug, sloshing more into his goblet before banging it back down on the side table.

'I am not opposed,' Ulf said quickly, though Elizaveta saw him clutch at his belly as if the words hurt him and wondered if he spoke the truth. 'I am simply saying that we need to plan carefully before committing good men to such a risky venture.'

'As we will, Ulf,' Harald snarled. 'As we always do.'

Elizaveta saw Johanna sidle closer to her husband and rose to join Harald, knowing his old friend had put his experienced warrior's finger on the same issue that, for perhaps the first time in their married life, was keeping Harald awake at night. She had rarely known him to pace the bedchamber as he had taken to doing recently and certainly never to refuse the distraction of any of her finest seductions. She did not think she had lost her charms for him. Indeed, just a few weeks back he had taken her aboard his new flagship, fronted by her very own eagle-prow, to 'christen' their joint creation as if they were youngsters, so the proposed invasion must be truly preying upon him.

'What bothers you so, Hari?' she'd begged him the other night when he'd pushed past her playing her viol naked, to get to the maps and sketches strewn across his desk.

He'd looked up, preparing, as always recently, to brush her concern aside, but something had changed his mind – perhaps the threatening way she'd pointed her bow at him, or perhaps the sight of her in his favourite outfit, or perhaps just the pressure of his worries finally growing too great, like the fire in an Icelandic hill.

'I do not know the land, Lily,' he'd admitted. 'I cannot take England in a sea-battle so I shall have to conquer her cities. I shall have to fight in her fields and they will know them so much better than I. They will know the slopes, the woods, the hiding places and the vantage points. That makes me vulnerable and I do not like being vulnerable.'

'No man does, Hari, nor woman neither.'

'Oh, I don't know about that.' He'd pulled her onto his desk, pushing the maps aside. 'You don't seem to mind.'

He'd grinned wickedly at her then as if, problem admitted, it already haunted him less, and she'd wrapped her legs around him, setting her viol aside to play with her husband instead.

'You did not know my body, Hari, when you first took it but you seemed to find the way.'

'I'd found my way around enough women, my Lilyveta, to work you out.'

'As you've found your way, my love, around enough battle-fields.'

'You compare yourself to a battlefield?'

That had stopped her for a moment.

'I fear I have, perhaps, put up something of a fight at times,' she'd admitted but he'd caught up her hand and kissed it.

'And I have loved you all the more for it. Now, though, I need you to fight *with* me.'

He had not meant in earnest, of course, weapon in hand like a shield-maiden of old, but he did need her support and she meant to give it wholeheartedly. The thought of him invading England made her every bit as fearful as Ulf, but Harald was alive with it and for that alone it meant the world to her. And they were making progress too. Already he had taken several keys from her neck chain and it was growing lighter as the mouth of the Sognafjord began to thicken with warships.

Boatbuilders all over Norway were delightedly receiving commissions and word was spreading through the mercenary community, bringing eager soldiers to Oslo in the hope of a share in this, the greatest mission west since King Cnut had set his own sails for England. Elizaveta embraced their spirit but as rulers they needed more; they needed plans, tactics. She drew Harald back to his seat beside Ulf and leaned between them.

'Svein, don't forget,' she said quietly, 'was born and raised in England.'

Both men looked up at her, eyes wide.

'Of course!' Harald cried. 'Svein knows England. You are suggesting, Elizaveta, that we share this invasion?'

She put up a hand.

'That would be for you to decide, Hari. I am simply saying that in all these negotiations Svein has something we want.'

'He also has a claim on the English throne himself,' Ulf warned. 'Stronger, perhaps, than our own, for he is Cnut's nephew whereas Harald's claim is based on Harthacnut's inheritance pact with Magnus. What if he joins our mission then steals it – as he stole Denmark from Magnus when the poor fool granted him the regency?'

'He seems,' Tora said mildly, 'to have been content with Denmark all these years. Mayhap he'd think invading England was foolish.'

Harald squinted at her.

'Mayhap *you* think invading England is foolish, Tora?' Tora looked hastily to her embroidery and Harald turned with a sigh to Elizaveta. 'And you, my sweet?'

Elizaveta looked down at him. She had written to Agatha, expressing sorrow for her loss and concern for her wellbeing. She had suggested, in veiled terms, how lovely it would be for them to see each other again and Agatha had written back all enthusiasm. If only Lily could be with her in England, she had said, everything would feel so much easier. Neither of them had dared speak openly for fear of seal-breaking spies but she could only hope that Agatha had understood and that she welcomed Harald's challenge.

'I think,' she said stoutly now, 'that England would be very lucky to have you on her throne.'

Harald smiled, a slow smile that gained in power, like the

sun rising, then suddenly pulled her onto his knee, spilling her wine down her gown.

'Hari!'

'Oh, don't mind that, Lily. You have to spill a little scarlet to win, but you are right – is she not, Ulf?'

Ulf inclined his greying head.

'In that, Hari, she is definitely right.'

'Good. So let's make peace with this rogue of a Danish king and set our sights west.'

CHAPTER THIRTY-SIX

Oslo, February 1066

'King Edward is dead!'

Elizaveta sat bolt upright in her bed as Harald burst into the chamber. He'd been up early again, conferring with his commander and boatbuilders, but she'd had no desire to leave the warmth of her fur covers – until now.

'King Edward?' she stuttered.

'Of England, yes. Dead. This month past and Harold Godwinson crowned king the very day of his funeral, with his new wife Edyth of Mercia as queen.'

'The Welshman's queen?'

'The Welshman's *widow*. Earl Harold took Griffin's life and now it seems he has his wife too. They have moved fast and we were right that Edgar stood no chance.'

Elizaveta jumped out of bed, grabbing her woollen robe for though the snows were melting early this year it was still icy cold.

'How do you know?' she demanded, grabbing Harald's hands to stop him twitching about the chamber like a grasshopper at mating season.

'Traders sailed into harbour late last night. They were

begging an audience before I even broke my fast, desperate to be first with the news. Lord help us, Lily – this is it.'

'The time is ripe,' she agreed slowly.

'It is.' Harald stilled. His hands squeezed hers. 'It truly is. I promised you England, my sweet, remember? When I leaped onto the fire-ship to beg your hand I promised your father I would take England for you. It was a madness then, a young man's ambition and for a time it looked as if her throne would turn to your sister instead but now . . .'

He stuttered to a halt and Elizaveta stared up at him.

'Now it is ours for the taking?'

'Now it is ours for the taking,' he agreed but his eyes had fixed on the rafters, or maybe somewhere beyond. She reached up and stroked his face, letting her fingers skim across his Stikelstad scar.

'You are afraid?'

'Afraid?' That pulled his eyes back to hers. 'No, Lily, I am not afraid. I was just thinking of something Finn said to me after Nisa. He said, Lily, that ambition is a disease.'

'A disease? Hari, that's fool's talk.'

'He said I had an infected soul.'

He looked tortured and she hated it.

'Oh Hari,' she said, 'of course you do. No man could be king otherwise and we should thank God for it.'

'You think so?'

'I know so. Who brought you up a warrior, Harald?'

'Finn.'

'Who taught you to fight? Who taught you courage and honour and *ambition*?'

'Finn?'

'It is why you loved him so. He is old, Hari, as his adopted king, Svein, is old.'

Svein had been a disappointment to her at the peace

negotiations. He had formally declared that he had no interest in invading England himself but had also, sadly, shown no inclination to aid Harald. He had at least, in return for Harald's full acceptance of his kingship of Denmark, sworn to leave Norway's borders unmolested during the proposed invasion but for intelligence about the land of his birth he had insisted they must look elsewhere. Harald had been downhearted but Elizaveta had been busy. She'd written again to Agatha and the reply had been most helpful.

'Those pseudo-Danes are men who have forgotten how to be ambitious,' she insisted now, 'but you, Hari, *you* have not.' He looked at her as if she had uncovered the secrets of the ancient world and, for once, she blushed. 'It is no great wisdom, just a simple truth.'

'A truth I had forgotten, but you are right – it was Finn who showed me how to embrace the desire to fight and how to *use* it. He is the one who has changed, not I.' He kissed her. 'What would I have done without you, Elizaveta?'

She smiled ruefully.

'Married Tora and ruled Norway in peace and prosperity?'

He shook his head.

'I think not. I have seawater in my veins, my sweet, and I would have itched to move on without you tumbling into boats to force me to it – but I would never have done it so well, nor so happily. You will come to England with me?'

'To fight?'

'No! Though I warrant you'd scare a few Saxons, my love. You can rest in the Orkneys until I have secured victory and then I will send for you to be queen.'

'In Westminster, where Agatha resides?'

'Eventually. To York first though, I think, as our ancestors did – if I can find it.'

Harald looked lost at the thought and Elizaveta shook at his hands.

'You *will* find it.'

'How do you know?'

She drew in a breath; it was time to confess.

'I have sent for someone. Or, rather, invited someone who will, I believe, be more amenable to working with you on this venture than Svein.'

'Who? Oh God, Lily, who have you sent for?'

''Tis my gift to you, as you have given so many to me.'

Elizaveta looked over to the neck chain, strung carefully on a wooden hook at her bedside. It was devoid of all but the very first keys but rich still with charms – a jingle of memories and promises.

'Who is it?' Harald asked, his voice hoarse. 'Who have you asked?'

She looked up at him, half-smiled.

'Lord Tostig Godwinson, once Earl of Northumbria and now, I am told, an exile and a seething mass of rage against his brother Harold – his brother who is now, it seems, king.'

Harald swept her into his arms, crushing her against his broad chest and pulling her up under his chin so that his moon-hair tangled with her night-time locks.

'I am not good at prayers, my sweet,' he said, 'but I thank God above every single day for giving you to me.'

Elizaveta reached her arms around his neck and kissed him.

'He may not be any use,' she warned, but Harald just grinned.

'Oh, he will be,' he said, kissing her back, 'I shall see to that.'

Lord Tostig arrived a few days later. Elizaveta and Harald, warned his ships were coming by riders posted at the mouth of the Oslofjord, were on the jetties to watch him sail in. He was a lean man, far slimmer than Harald and more than a head shorter, but he looked fighting fit and had hunger in his amber eyes and a fine sword at his belt and he leaped keenly from his boat to land almost directly at their feet.

'King Harald, Queen Elizaveta, I thank you for your welcome and hospitality.' His voice was smooth and, even in Old Norse, held hardly a trace of an English accent.

'Nay, do not thank us yet, Lord Tostig,' Harald countered.

'Torr, please – all my friends call me Torr.'

'Torr, I see – how do you know, though, Torr, that we are your friends? How do you know that we will not take you prisoner?'

'As my brother was taken prisoner by the Normans?'

Elizaveta felt Harald jump at this information and glanced at him, keen to know more, but Torr was watching them closely and Harald was never one to admit ignorance.

'Your brother Harold, now King of England?'

'The very same,' Torr growled.

'No longer prisoner then.'

'No, sadly, though by taking the throne he has foresworn Duke William.'

'Indeed,' Harald agreed, as if already apprised of the situation, though Elizaveta could see the clouds flitting across his pale grey eyes as he battled to work it out.

'Duke William has sworn vengeance,' Torr was saying, falling into step with Harald or, rather, trying to do so, for Harald's stride was long and he was forced to skip a little to keep pace.

'Duke William is a Norman,' Harald said sharply. 'I know his type well – brigands, scraping for a law to justify their aims whilst avoiding all its rules themselves. The Lombards invited the Normans into Italy and ended up losing it to them. If they get so much as a fingergrip on a country, they do not let go until they have it by the throat.'

Torr nodded keenly.

'Duke William says Harold swore to serve him as King of England. He means to invade.'

'So I hear,' Harald agreed again, though behind him Elizaveta noticed Ulf pulling men urgently aside – accidental spies would be sought in the taverns immediately for there was always a merchant as eager to sell information as wares.

'And you, Sire,' Torr demanded suddenly, stopping dead before the steps up to the grand royal buildings, 'do *you* mean to invade?'

Harald took his arm, guiding him on up, away from the eager ears of the bustling city.

'I could if I wanted to, but is it worth my while?'

'Oh yes,' the English lord said instantly.

'You think so? Worth *my* while, Lord Tostig – or worth yours?'

'Worth yours of course, Sire – you would be king.'

'If we won.'

'Yes, but I hear, Harald Hardrada, that you always win.'

'And I hear, Tostig Godwinson, that you were ousted by your own people. Why would they want you back?'

Torr's hands twitched at a loose thread on his fine tunic.

'Because,' he offered, 'I would bring them a king worthy to rule.'

Harald glanced back at Elizaveta.

'They talk well, these Englishmen,' he said lightly.

'They do,' she agreed, 'but do they *fight* well?'

Torr was onto that like a weasel on a mouse.

'Not as well as you, Sire, I am sure.'

Harald laughed.

'You manage our tongue smoothly, Lord Torr.'

'In Northumberland,' Torr agreed hastily, 'men speak a Norse akin to your own, Sire – they are, perhaps, more Norwegian than English.'

'You think?'

Harald waved his guest forward through the great doorway of the palace and leaned back to Elizaveta.

'He seems an empty sort of man,' he whispered.

'Good,' Elizaveta replied, 'we can fill him with our own goals.'

Harald nodded but now Ulf was coming up – clearly the spies had been busy already – and she went after Torr to give them time to talk. The English lord was strolling around the hall, ostensibly admiring the pillars, though Elizaveta noticed his long fingers picking again at the shining gold trim of his tunic.

'You like our carvings?' she asked, moving up at his side.

He snatched his fingers away from their fidgeting.

'I do. They are very fine and these frescoes at the top are astounding – we have nothing like this in England.'

'Nor much in Norway,' Elizaveta told him. 'The hall is Kievan in inspiration.'

'Of course.' Torr bowed. 'You are from the land of the Rus, my lady. Perhaps that is where I should turn my sail if everyone is as beautiful as you.'

Elizaveta laughed.

'Are you always this complimentary, Lord Torr?'

'Only where praise is warranted.'

'Or where you have need of something,' Harald suggested, striding up to rejoin them, Ulf at his back.

Torr turned to them and his amber eyes narrowed a little.

'Indeed,' he agreed, his voice harsher than before. 'I am not here to pretend, Sire, neither am I here out of the goodness of my heart. Harold has stolen the throne of England and I seek a partner to reclaim it.'

'For yourself?'

'I have no more royal blood than my brother.'

'What then, do you want?'

Harald's words echoed around the bright hall. He had set

guards on the door to give them privacy and their little group was alone in the vast building. Torr flinched but stood his ground.

'An earldom.'

'Northumbria?' Ulf suggested. 'That is what it is called, is it not, your earldom?'

'It is, my lord marshal, or rather it was, but I do not . . .'

'You lived in the north then?'

'I did and it's a godforsaken . . .'

'In York?'

'Further north even than that, in Durham, though I know York well and many of its lords too.'

'The lords who threw you out?' Harald asked.

'Those, yes,' Torr agreed, turning back to him, 'and the other, older, quieter majority who let the youngsters have their day believing, as I believed, that the king and my brother, who held the reins of power, would back me and I would be justly returned to office.'

'But you were not?'

'No. Harold pronounced me exile.'

'Harsh.'

'Very.' Torr's voice was almost a hiss now; it crept around the hall, low and venomous. 'He had his eye on the throne already, Sire, and knew he needed any opposition eliminated.'

'Eliminated? I see. But why, Lord Torr, would you oppose your own brother?'

'He is not a king, Sire, not as you are a king.'

'I would have thought, though,' Harald said casually to Ulf, 'that having a brother as king would be to a man's advantage?'

'Perhaps,' Torr said hastily, stepping between them, 'but a man must be honourable.'

'A man must, surely,' Ulf suggested, 'be loyal too?'

'I *am* loyal – to my country.'

'Why, then, would you wish a foreign king upon her?'

'Because I believe King Harald would rule well.'

'Do you?' Harald flashed, his voice rising as he took a step forward. 'Do you indeed, Lord Torr? In the same way as you believe Duke William would rule well, or Svein of Denmark would rule well?'

'No, Sire. No, I . . .'

'Because you have visited them before you came here, have you not?'

Torr paled. Elizaveta looked to Ulf – so this had been his news.

'I have,' Torr was forced to admit, 'and can bring you valuable intelligence of their plans.'

'Intelligence?' Harald looked down at Torr, then turned away to summon wine. 'How do I know,' he asked, his back to his guest, 'that you are not simply here collecting "intelligence" for *them*?'

Torr paled further and even Elizaveta, stood against a pillar, felt a little scared. This, then, was Harald Hardrada. He was an imposing man – an exciting one too. She moved to the side door to take the hastily fetched wine from the servant and offer it to Harald herself.

'Thank you, my sweet,' he said, apparently all ease now, 'and some for my guest if you will – he looks in need of refreshment.'

Sure enough, Torr took the goblet and drained it. She poured more, taking care not to meet his eye or offer him any reassurance, and after a couple more large sips he turned back to Harald.

'I will tell you true, Sire,' he said, 'and then you can judge me as you see fit.'

Harald inclined his head and moved to his great seat, offering Ulf the one at his side but Torr none of his own. The English lord shuffled before him.

'King Svein is my cousin on my mother's side so he was a

good choice for me, as you will surely recognise. He has no wish, however, to exert that claim in war, though I know not why.'

'He has lost a lot of ships recently,' Harald said, fingering the hilt of his sword.

'Of course. Yes, I see . . .'

'And Duke William?'

'Duke William is married to my wife's cousin, Sire, so for her sake I spoke with him. He plans to attack. I have seen his shipyards and they are already very busy. His stud farms too.'

'He will take cavalry to England?' Ulf asked, sitting forward.

'It is the only way he knows to fight.'

'Let's hope, then, that they are seasick!'

Torr managed a weak smile but did not dare laugh at the jest.

'He is gathering a formidable force, Sire,' he said to Harald. 'All his Norman nobles must contribute.'

'But he has no use for an exiled English one?'

'No, Sire.'

'Why not?'

'Maybe he lacks your wisdom.'

'Maybe he fears *your* treachery.'

Elizaveta could almost see Torr's slim legs shaking.

'Do I look like a traitor to you, Sire?' he asked Harald desperately.

'You look like a peacock, Torr,' Harald countered, his eyes on the now-loose thread at the base of his tunic. 'My friend here, Count Ulf, doubts the wisdom of invading this England of yours, though you are doing much to convince him there is little to fear from its men. So tell me, if you are so keen to prove your worth – how would a man best go about attacking her?'

'A man like yourself, Sire – a Northman? Why, he would sail his ships up the Ouse estuary to York and seize the city. He would establish a base there and take allegiance from the local lords, many of whom have Norse blood still, and he would especially do that, Sire, if he had with him a captain who knew the names and dwelling places of all those lords. Half of England would be secure within a week and from there such a man would march on Mercia where the ruling lord is young and nervous and once he had taken his allegiance also, he would attack Westminster.'

'You make it sound simple, Lord Torr, does he not, Ulf?'

Ulf merely grunted but Torr took an enthusiastic step forward.

'It *is* simple, Sire, with the right leader and the right men and the right knowledge.'

Elizaveta's heart turned. This man, despite his rich clothes and his blustering talk, was no fool and he knew his worth. But then, they knew it too.

'So, Sire?' Torr dared to ask.

Harald glanced at Ulf then back to his guest.

'We are happy, Lord Torr, for your ships to join ours if I should decide to invade England. How many do you have?'

'My captains are putting together a fleet in Flanders where Duke Baldwin, my wife's father, is happy to play host to my force.'

'But not so happy to invade with you?'

'Flanders is a small duchy, Sire.'

'As is Normandy.'

'But Duke Baldwin knows his limits.'

Harald chuckled, nudged Ulf.

'As Duke William does not,' he said and his marshal smiled for the first time in the sticky conversation.

'How many ships do your captains gather in Flanders?' Ulf asked Torr.

'Some thirty, my lord, and I plan to sail on the Isle of Wight, as my father did when he fought his glorious way back from exile in 1051. He gained much support on the south coast – as will I.'

'The south coast – your brother's lands, yes?'

'For now.'

'Ah!' Harald rose and strolled around Torr. 'I do not think, Ulf, that Lord Torr wants to return to Northumbria, do you, Lord Torr? You have your eyes on the south?'

'I would make it worth your while, Sire.'

'Perhaps.' Harald spun back to his seat, flinging himself carelessly into it. 'Go, Torr – pick up your fleet and harry the south. If you collect more vessels, sail them north and if we choose to sail too, we will join forces.'

'We will?' Torr looked as if he dared not quite believe it.

'Why not?' Harald said casually. 'You sail, I think, for vengeance.'

'I do.'

'I like that.'

'And you, Sire – what do you sail for?'

Harald glanced at Elizaveta and smiled.

'I sail – *if* I sail – for glory. Now come, you have travelled far, let us eat!'

He waved to his guards and they threw open the doors to admit the rest of the court, huddled outside, their gossiping breath a mist over their heads. Elizaveta stood back to watch Torr take a seat at Harald's side, looking dazed by his host's sudden benevolence. She almost pitied him but he was a man with little left to lose and much to gain and if he could be useful to Harald she was pleased.

'Will he do?' someone asked behind her and she turned to see Tora seating herself to her right.

'He'll do, I think, if Harald is careful.'

Tora sighed.

'There is a lot for Harald to be careful of in this venture. It feels, Lily, as if there are wolves at every turn.'

'Mayhap there are, but they all have their eyes on England, Tora, not on us.'

'Until we *are* England.'

Elizaveta had no time to reply before Harald leaped between them, making them squeal and pull apart.

'What are you two whispering about?' their husband asked, laughing at their surprise.

'Tora is worried for you,' Elizaveta said, recovering herself.

'Tora is good at that. Fret not, my dear – all will be well, I feel it. This Godwinson has a poor grasp on his stolen crown and I will not be beaten to it by some brigand Norman who has to build his fleet from scratch. They are not wolves, Tora – yes, I heard you – but barnyard kittens. *I* am the wolf, remember?'

Elizaveta saw Tora's eyes soften and felt a bitter stab of pain. Had he been Tora's wolf? When? And how? And why did it still matter after all these years?

'You are, Hari,' Tora agreed quietly and suddenly Elizaveta wanted to snatch the shortened name out of her lips. Tora never used to call him that; maybe he was her wolf still?

'Must I come, Hari?' she was asking now. 'Must I come to England?'

Elizaveta watched him smile at her.

'No, Tora. I need you to stay here in Norway, please – if we go.'

'You are not yet decided?'

'We must see how the winds blow. I will need my sails full to attack England.'

Tora nodded.

'You will take the boys?'

The boys – *their* boys, their fine young kings-to-be. Elizaveta dug her fingers into the arms of her chair and watched the

Norwegian court turn around her and suddenly felt almost as alone as Torr, sat nervously in the centre of them all.

'Just Olaf,' she heard Harald saying, as if from afar. 'He will learn to be my heir in England. Magnus will turn twenty this year – he will stay and rule Norway in my stead.'

'And me?'

'You, Tora, will rule Magnus. I trust you to hold Norway for me.'

It was too much. Elizaveta pushed back her chair and spun away. Tora was Harald's wife after all, his partner in rule, and she – she was merely his bedsport, his passion, his indulgence. Well, she would indulge him no more. Let him talk Norway with Tora and England with Torr, the man *she* had summoned though as like as not he had forgotten that already. Let him . . .

'Lily!' She heard Harald's voice but she would not stop; would not turn. She picked up her pace and gained the servant's door at the rear of the hall. 'Lily, stop!' She yanked the door open and two young servers, laden down with platters of goat-liver pâté, scuttled nervously back, clattering against each other. 'Lily, please stop.' Despite their best efforts to get out of her way, the servers had held her up enough for him to gain her side. Harald grabbed at her arm and pulled her round to face him. 'Why do you run, Lily? What's wrong?'

'Nothing. Why? Do you need me? Do you desire me, Hari? Do you fancy entering me here, against the kitchen wall to slake your lust after your manly sparring with Lord Torr?'

'What? No. I mean – is that what you want?'

'No!'

She jerked away and made for the street behind, wishing, for once, that she were out at one of Harald's precious farmhouses and could escape into Norway's endless pines.

'Elizaveta, stop now!'

'No,' she said over her shoulder. 'Go back to Tora, Harald.'

'Back to Tora?' She heard him chuckle, low and teasing. 'You are jealous, Lily?'

'No. I have just finally worked out my place.'

'Which is?'

Harald caught her up and pinned her to the wooden fencing of the nearest plot. She let herself go limp in his grasp.

'Just this,' she said.

'Oh my Lilyveta, you . . .'

'Don't call me that.'

'Why not? Lily, please – I don't understand.'

'Tora holds Norway for you, yes?'

Harald looked even more confused.

'Yes, as she did before. As . . .'

'And I, Harald – what do I hold for you? Nothing! I am a foreigner still in your beloved Norway. I have given you no noble connections and no sons and now even your treasure has almost run out. So tell me, Harald Hardrada, ruler – hero – what do I hold for you?'

'Can you really not see it?'

His voice was low and she looked up at him, at the scar his first battle had drawn across his gorgeous face, still raw even now that life had carved more lines into the corners of his eyes and round his mouth. It was a rougher face than it had been when first he'd asked for her hand but so, so dear to her, for whatever that was worth.

'Let me go, Hari,' she whispered.

'Never,' he said. 'Do you know what you hold for me, Elizaveta of Kiev? You hold my heart and if that were to stop beating – as without you it surely would – all else would be nought.'

'Your heart?' she echoed weakly, her own quavering in her chest.

''Tis a foolish thing, perhaps, for a king, but true. I told you once, Lily – Tora gives me sons but you give me the world. It is as true as ever. I cannot take England without you, my sweet – *will not* take England without you.'

Elizaveta felt herself swelling ridiculously, growing like a flower unfurling to the dawn. She held his heart and maybe that was a foolish thing, too, for a queen to draw strength from but draw it she did.

'You need not take England without me, Hari, because I will be your constant queen – there with you; there *for* you. '

He kissed her long and deep, pressing her against the fence, and she clung to him, kissing him back as if she were sixteen again and it was the first time their lips had met.

'And now . . . ?' he said, his voice light as he finally released her.

'Dinner?' Elizaveta suggested weakly.

'Dinner, yes, but first I think you said something about entering you against the kitchen wall?'

'Hari!'

He swept an arm around her waist, leading her back to the hall.

'Maybe later,' he said, kissing her again.

'Maybe,' she countered, 'they have fine kitchen walls in England?'

'Is that a dare?' he asked, his voice low as he opened the door and the noise of the court rushed out to them. 'My first act as their new king?'

'A dare,' she agreed, straightening her dress as he ushered her through and smiling back as she swept past, 'and a promise.'

CHAPTER THIRTY-SEVEN

Oslo, April 1066

'Ulf?' Harald approached the bed as softly as he could, though his big feet caught in the herb-strewn rushes on the chamber floor, making him stumble.

'It's all right, Hari,' came his old friend's gruff voice, 'I'm not dead yet.'

'And not like to be,' Harald told him firmly.

Ulf just smiled at him, a soft, wistful smile.

'Don't do that,' Harald said.

'Do what?'

'Smile like that, all serene. It doesn't suit you.'

'Neither does lying about in bed.'

'That's true.' Harald glanced around him. Ulf had been sickly for weeks, refusing to eat and griping like a wounded cub, but seeing him here, lost in his covers, was enough to turn Harald's stomach too. 'What are you lounging around for?' he asked, as lightly as he could. 'I need my marshal at my side.'

Ulf looked away.

'I think, my friend,' he said into his pillows, 'that you had best find a new marshal.'

'No!' Harald sank onto the stool at Ulf's bedside and laid a hand on his arm, still big and strong but incongruous against the linen sheets. 'You will be well soon.'

Ulf turned his face back round and up close Harald could see how thin and lined it had become.

'I have ever, Hari, have I not, been straight with you?'

'Too straight at times. I remember you asking me how much more of my hard-won treasure I intended to pour into a tankard and out of – what was it? – "my own foul bowels" before we could leave Novgorod for Norway.'

Ulf chuckled, then suddenly sucked in his breath.

'I was right,' he said when he'd drawn enough air to speak again. 'You were a mess.'

'A little,' Harald allowed, 'and without you and Hal I might never have gone back for Lily, so, yes, you were right.'

'As I am right now, Harald, when I say that you will need a new marshal to sail on England.'

'You have never been keen. Are you telling me now, Ulf, that you do not wish to come?'

'I am telling you, Hari, that I will be dead.'

Harald felt a sharp stab in his chest, as if an unseen enemy had sneaked up and plunged a knife between his ribs.

'Don't say that. You cannot die here, in bed. It is not a fitting end for a life lived so fiercely.'

That smile again. It made Harald want to punch it away but that would hardly be right. He ground the toes of his feet into the wooden floor.

'Don't hit a dying man, Hari.'

'I wouldn't.'

'Really? Come, I have followed you since I found you bedraggled and torn beneath a bush at Stikelstad; I can read you like a battlefield plan.'

'There will be no battlefield plans to read if you are not there, Ulf.'

'Rubbish. I was always more your scribe than your creator and you will have Lord Torr.'

'Lord Torr? Pah! He is not worth a hair on your big toe, my friend.'

'I'll have you know my toe . . .' Ulf's words descended into coughing and Harald watched, horrified, as Johanna rushed forward with a copper bowl and Ulf retched into it.

Blood hit the bottom, swirling iridescent in the sparkling container, and Harald felt caught in it, dizzied, drained.

'Ridiculous,' he admonished himself, turning away to give his friend the privacy to recover. 'You have lived a life of blood, Harald – you can face a tiny bowlful.' But right now he would take all the gore of the battlefield – all the hacked limbs and exposed sinews and spurting veins of open combat – rather than this. And so, he knew, would Ulf.

'Otto.'

Harald turned back at the word.

'Otto?'

'He should be your marshal. He is a good man, Hari, and your son-to-be. Let him take the office as my wedding gift.'

'I am in no mood for weddings.'

'You prefer a funeral?'

Harald threw up his hands.

'Ever, Ulf Ospakkson, you vex me!'

'Pleasure to serve.'

Ulf smiled, more his usual sardonic grin than before, but Harald could see the effort was costing him valuable strength. He glanced to Johanna, hovering anxiously to one side. She would not thank him for troubling her husband but he had to ask one more thing.

'Ulf?'

'Hari.'

'Should I invade England?'

'How should I know? Just because I can see my own death ahead of me does not make me a soothsayer.'

'I am not asking you to cast into the future, old friend, but into the past – *our* past. You know me better than anyone as a warrior so can I do it? Can I take the throne?'

Ulf reached out and took Harald's hand. It felt strange in his – big and masculine – but he clasped it tight.

'If any man can, Harald, it is you.'

'But you think it a fool's mission?'

'No, I . . .'

More coughing. Johanna pushed past Harald with the bowl and a glare and he put up his released hand.

'Just a moment more, please. I know he is your husband and I respect that, Johanna, truly, but he has been my friend all my adult life and I . . . I need . . .' Words failed him.

'You need my blessing?' Ulf suggested hoarsely.

'Maybe.'

Ulf took a sip of water and signalled Harald to pull him up on his pillows.

'I am sick, Hari,' he said. 'I have been sick longer, I think, than I have chosen to admit even to myself. I have had no stomach for anything for some time, least of all a voyage into the unknown. This canker has robbed me of my spirit, I fear, but I beg you not to let it rob you of yours. You will make England a fine king, Hari, so, yes – sail with my blessing.'

'But not your company?'

'Sadly God calls this Varangian too soon for that. It has been an honour to serve you, Harald.'

'Ulf, please . . .'

'An honour and a pleasure and I ask just one thing of you now – do not die in bed, like this. It is not, as you said, fitting.'

'No, Ulf, I was jesting. I . . .'

'I know and I thank you for it, but trust me – you were right.

393

Live well, Harald Hardrada. Die beneath your raven – though not for many years yet. I did not drag you out of that bush to get fat and lazy.'

Harald tried to smile but tears were in his eyes now and he dared not move a muscle for fear of releasing them.

'Now go,' Ulf said, offering him his arm. 'Leave me to the womenfolk, for you have an invasion to organise.'

'I cannot, I . . .'

'Please, Hari.' Ulf's voice broke. 'I do not wish you to see me this way. Please . . .'

Harald nodded. He rose and clutched his dear friend's arm tight, a warrior's clasp.

'God be with you, Ulf.'

'And with you, Hari. Though one thing more . . .'

'What is it?'

'I hear English beer is awful.'

He smiled, his full Ulf smile at last, and though the tears were falling now, Harald smiled back, then turned and left. He did not want to sail without his friend, his liegeman, but he would not fail him by refusing to do so. Let the winds blow – he would say his prayers for Ulf in York.

CHAPTER THIRTY-EIGHT

Sognafjord, July 1066

It was a sight to stir even a timid heart and though Tora knew hers was more timid than most, she could not help but feel strangely uplifted by the great mass of vessels at anchor in the mouth of the Sognafjord. Almost three hundred ships were ranged out across the sparkling water which lay as blue as Our Lady's robes. Forever after this Tora was sure she would see blue as the colour of hope. Hope and more – purpose, determination, ambition.

Elizaveta had told her what Finn had said to Harald of his ambition and she had hated her lost uncle for it. Her own heart would choose to keep Harald here, in Norway, living out his reign in peace but it was not what he wanted. Nor, it seemed, was it what anyone in the country wanted, for on those ships were the best part of ten thousand men, every single one of them eager to set their sails to the west and win those ever-glittering Viking prizes – land, riches and glory. They trusted Harald to lead them and to do that Harald needed to trust himself. It was not for Finn to rob him of his hard-won confidence.

For months now vessels had sailed into the mouth of the fjord, some great jarls' warships with full crews of sixty, some humbler fishing craft hastily adapted for braving the open seas.

They bobbed on the water like moons around the great sun that was Harald's magnificent new warship. Thirty-three benches long, with high sides and sleek ends curving gracefully up towards the sky, it was fronted by a huge eagle painted in gold, its wings spread wide over the waves. Elizaveta's eagle, Tora thought, brave and free and desperate to soar high. And perhaps she was right.

Even from up here on the hilltop, Tora could hear the excited cries of sailors preparing to journey. Between the warships hundreds of skiffs buzzed across the water like insects, carrying barrels of water and dried meat, of cheese and the precious cloudberry, gathered up on the heathlands to keep the sailor's disease at bay. On the sloping shores where the fjord gave way to the sea, men sat around fires mending ropes and sails, sanding steer-boards and oars, and weaving that most important of all journeyers' provisions – dreams.

'Is it not thrilling?'

Tora turned to see Elizaveta coming up the hillside, skirts clutched so high in her hands that she could see her ankles.

'Lily – dignity!'

'Dignity? Come, Tora, you know me better than that now. Sometimes I long for hose. When I wore them for the Rapids Race it was so easy to move.'

Tora pursed her lips over her instinctive response – Elizaveta was just looking to shock her as she always did and she would not rise.

'All is set?' she asked instead.

She longed for a negative, for a last reprieve, but Elizaveta just nodded.

'All is set. The men are taking to the boats now. Harald says the winds are with us and as soon as the tide turns he will set sail for the Orkneys.'

'And from there . . .'

'To England. Lord Torr has harried the south as he said he would. By all accounts he lost more ships than he gained but Harald does not need his men, just his maps. They look to meet at some river called the Forth where Torr takes shelter with King Malcolm of Scotland and from there to York where Harald says he will build Ulf a church.'

Tora smiled.

'Ulf would like that – though in truth he might prefer an alehouse.'

'As might Harald. He says he has a pagan heart, Tora.'

'He may be right. When news came that Duke William would be marching under a papal banner he said he did not see what use a jumped-up Roman priest in a white dress would be to an invader.'

'I hope he is right. He always said the Normans were fearsome fighters.'

Tora looked at Elizaveta and saw something new in her fiercely beautiful features.

'Lily – you are afraid for him?'

'Of course. I would be a fool not to be. He may have to defeat two armies: the English and the Normans. We can only hope they meet each other before he arrives then whichever is the victor will be weakened. If he must beat them both, though, he will – if any man can perform such a feat, it is Harald. He will follow his raven, Tora, and I will follow him.'

Tora jumped at the mention of the landwaster and felt in the leather bag she carried over her shoulder. The package was still there. She closed her fingers around it to pull it out but lost her nerve.

'If he wins, Lily,' she said, 'I may never see you again.'

Elizaveta frowned at her.

'Why not?'

'You will be Queen of England and you will have your sister Agatha at your side. You won't even think of me.'

'Now you are being foolish. Of course I will think of you. I will be Queen of England, yes, and you of Norway. We must write always.'

'We will be a whole sea apart.'

Elizaveta took hold of her face and planted a kiss, swift and sudden, on her nose.

'It is not a *big* sea, Tora.'

'It looks vast to me.'

Elizaveta peered closely at her.

'You have never sailed it?'

Tora shook her head.

'Only near to shore; never out in the ocean.'

'Then this, my sweet, will be the perfect chance to try it. 'Tis barely two days' sail to England and you will want, surely, to see Olaf in his new realm?'

Tora shuddered. Olaf was nearly sixteen. She could hardly bear to let him go and only his excitement at standing at his dizzying father's side had stopped her begging for him to remain behind. Waiting for Magnus to return from the west had been a year of purest agony and she wasn't sure she could face it again, especially with certain battle ahead. Olaf was tall enough, strong enough too but, like his brother, he was a peaceable soul. Her fault perhaps. She had cosseted them, kept them too close, and loved them perhaps too dearly.

'I will keep an eye on him, Tora,' Elizaveta said softly.

'As you did on Magnus?'

'Magnus came home,' Elizaveta said stiffly and Tora hated herself for being so mean. It was just that everything felt so spiky as if it were she, not the eager warriors below, held at sword-point.

'As did you,' she said softly, 'and you know, Lily, I was almost as pleased to see you as him.'

'You were?'

'I have a weak heart.'

'Nay, Tora, you have the strongest, biggest, dearest heart I know.'

'I do?'

'Of course. Why would you think otherwise?'

Tora shifted.

'I am not so . . . passionate as you.'

Elizaveta shook her head, smiled.

'I sometimes think passion is the weakness, Tora. I promised Harald once I would be his constant queen, but in truth you have been far more stable than I.'

Tora opened her mouth to deny it but for once she silenced her self-doubt. How many times had Harald come to her over the years? She had told Elizaveta the day they first met that Harald needed her and perhaps, despite all he had with his exotic Rus wife, it was just a little bit true.

'We have, it seems, worked well together,' she admitted.

'We have. It is hard to believe I hated you once.'

'Hated me?' As ever, Elizaveta's frankness caught Tora unawares.

'Of course – as you hated me.'

'Hate is a harsh word, Lily.'

'And they were harsh times but they are behind us. We have triumphed, have we not? Somehow we have been queens together and when I look back now I cannot imagine it any other way. You have given him sons to rule after him.'

'And you daughters to rule him now.'

Elizaveta smiled, stepped away.

'Maria seems sometimes almost to read his mind,' she

admitted, 'and certainly to twist it to her own ends. She unnerved me when her arm ached for Harald's injury at Nisa.'

'Coincidence?'

'Too much wistful sword play, or so I hope. And at least now she has Otto to preoccupy her. Harald says they will marry in England, when his new marshal is made earl.'

'Poor Maria.'

'The wife of an earl?'

'No, not that – she will like that. I mean the waiting. It is hard on her, I think.'

'You had to wait a long time for your marriage bed too, Tora. I am sorry for it.'

'Oh, not as long as you think.'

The words slipped out before she could catch them. Elizaveta stared at her and Tora feared a blast of her friend's stormy temper but instead she smiled.

'When?'

'No matter. I shouldn't . . .'

'When, Tora? Before he left Norway? Before Stikelstad? Oh!' Her hands went to her mouth. 'You were his first! You devil!'

'I'm sorry.' Tora knew she was blushing furiously. 'I was young, so was he. Did you think . . . ?'

'That it was me? Lord, no, but I always counted on some slippery Byzantine concubine. Oh Tora, I'm so glad it was you.'

'You are?'

Tora looked nervously into Elizaveta's dark eyes; even after all this time with her mercurial fellow queen she was never sure of the turn of her moods.

'Of course I am. It means he is all ours.'

'You think?' Tora waved sardonically to the myriad warships below. 'He is theirs, is he not? Their commander, their hero, their inspiration.'

Elizaveta slid an arm through hers.

'In a way, yes, for he is a king, Tora. It is how it has to be, but he is a man too and that bit, my sweet, is ours.'

'*That* bit?!'

'Tora, no! Honestly, I try to be serious for once and you . . .'

But now Harald was coming up the hillside, his chain mail glistening in the sun and his ice-blonde hair locked beneath an iron helmet and suddenly everything felt very, very serious. Tora looked to Elizaveta but for once her fellow queen was frozen, her eyes on the Norwegian grass around her dainty feet, and it was left to Tora to say the words she had long dreaded: 'You are ready to sail, Hari?'

'Almost. I need my banner.'

Tora's hand went again to her bag. Elizaveta stared at her.

'Tora? What do you have in there?'

Tora fumbled awkwardly with the package, half withdrew it.

'I asked Harald for it. I hope you don't mind. I knew you wouldn't have the time and you don't like sewing as I do and . . .'

'Oh Tora,' Elizaveta interrupted, 'stop gabbling and let me see.' She seized the package and unwrapped it. 'Oh!'

The raven flew free and now, all around the edges of the golden rectangle that contained it, the black and red border swirled, proud and glorious. Elizaveta stared at it and Tora thought she saw tears in her friend's eyes.

'You did this?'

'I wanted to help. To contribute.' Still Elizaveta stared and Tora felt herself curl up inside; she had not wanted to offend her, not now, with her sailing to the Lord knew what. 'I'm sorry. I thought . . .'

But suddenly Elizaveta was enveloping her in a hug so tight she thought a vice might have closed around her.

'It's beautiful, Tora. So, so much better than I could ever have done it. Now we will carry a little bit of you with us to England.'

Tora wiped away tears and clasped Elizaveta in return. She had never truly grasped her dear friend's moods and maybe now she never would. She looked to Harald.

'You will . . . you will take care.'

'Take care?' Harald lifted the banner high, admiring it. 'I will take care to ride into battle before they do.' Tora shivered and Elizaveta pushed at him. He relented. 'I will try, Tora, though it does not come naturally to me.'

'You will, at least then, win.'

He took her hand and bowed low.

'I will win.'

Tora saw him again, then, leaping from a skiff, a wolf in the magical dusk of midsummer. He had chased her down that night and she had been a willing prey. Through it all, she had been a willing prey but now he was sailing away again as if none of it had ever been.

'My wolf man,' she said fondly, and then she was in his arms, hugging him so tight his chain mail pressed into her skin and then tighter again in the hope that its ringed imprint would stay there, etched upon her, until she heard he had won and he was safe.

'You will come to the jetties, Tora?' he asked when finally they drew apart. 'You will come to see us off?'

She did not wish to. She wished to stay up here where the ships looked like toys and the men like speckles across her imagination. She wished to keep away from this mission that promised to gain them all so much and yet threatened to lose them everything. But she was Queen of Norway now, Harald's regent, and she knew her duty. Always she had known her duty.

'I will come,' she said.

*

And so Tora stood on Norway's western shore, Magnus at her side and a handful of guards at her back as the rest of her beloved country's men – or so it felt – drew up their anchors, turned their prows to the open sea and set sail. She stood with all her precious country's wives, mothers, and daughters, caught in the painful gap between pride and fear, and waved until the three hundred ships moved around the Solund Isles and tipped their red and white sails over the horizon.

A part of her wished she was like Harald and Elizaveta with their seawater veins and their adventurous spirits. She longed to know what it must feel like to have this itch inside you and yet it seemed such an uncomfortable, painful way to be ruled. Harald was a true Viking and everyone loved him for it, yet he worried about his pagan heart, as if it did not really belong in their modern world. Did Tora's yearning for peace fit the new, more stable way of governing better, or was her time yet to come? If so, she feared she would not live to see it, even safe on her own shores.

A huge cheer went up from the bay as Harald's eagle cut through the waters at the cusp of the open sea, the flag edged with her own embroidery flying proudly above it, and she shook her foolish musings away. What did it matter where anyone's spirit truly lay when their fate was in the here and now? They all had to fight. Harald and Elizaveta would sail forth into the attack and she – she would stand as bravely as she could here, at home.

Standing on her tiptoes to see as far over the treacherous horizon as she possibly could, Tora waved at Olaf and at Harald and at Elizaveta as they shrank and then tipped over the edge of her world. And when, finally, they were all gone, she took Magnus's arm and turned her steps back inland to wait.

CHAPTER THIRTY-NINE

The Orkneys, August 1066

'Lily, wake up!'

Elizaveta stirred, opened her eyes. Harald was stood over her, fully dressed, and she started awake.

'What is it Hari? You're not going already?'

'No. Hush.' He kissed her quiet. 'I just couldn't sleep. The day is dawning, Lily – *our* day is dawning. Will you come and see it rise with me?'

She looked up into his eyes, more gold than grey as they shone eagerly down at her in the half-light.

'Of course I will.'

She flung back the covers, drawing in a sharp breath as the autumn air bit at her bare skin, and gratefully pulled on the shift Harald held out for her. She covered it swiftly with the fine gown Greta had laid out last night. It was a rich purple, trimmed with gold, and was intended to make her look regal as she waved the troops off on their great mission but for now she was just grateful for its warmth.

Harald was already at the door of their bower and she pushed her feet into her calfskin shoes and went to join him. A single line of pink hovered along the horizon and she took his hand as they stepped out towards it.

'The girls . . . ?'

She glanced back; Maria and Ingrid were on the upper floor of the bower.

'They are well. I looked in on them.'

'You did?'

'Just to check. They're so funny, Lily, even now they are all but women. Ingrid is tucked up tight, even her hair neat on the pillow, and Maria is all limbs.'

'You like her best.'

'No. She just . . . lodges more sharply in my heart.'

'And you in hers. They are sleeping?'

'Like babies.'

Elizaveta smiled.

'As should we be.'

'Nay, wife – why sleep when there are adventures to be had? Come!'

He tugged her forward and together they crept across the central yard of Thorfinn's great compound, tiptoeing so as not to disturb the sleepers in the halls and outbuildings all round. They made it out into the meadow and began to climb the Brough just as, to their left, the topmost part of the sun broke free of the soft waves of the bay and reached out sparkling fingers across the land.

The light caught in the dew, so thick on the rough sea grass that it seemed for a moment as if the whole land were a pool of gold and their every step a ripple in the dawn. Elizaveta clutched tight at Harald's calloused fingers and he smiled down at her.

'All will be well, Lilyveta, I know it.'

She nodded but her body was too clogged with the effort of storing up the imprint of his hand to speak. She trod onwards but the calfskin shoes she'd foolishly chosen were sodden already and she could feel a chill damp penetrating to her toes.

Lifting her heavy skirts, she looked down at the delicate leather, dark with moisture.

'My feet are wet, Hari.'

He stopped.

'I'll carry you.'

'No!' She batted him away. 'I'm too heavy. You can hardly go into battle with a limp caused by lifting your wife.'

'Here then.'

He bent and untied his own sturdy soldier's boots then, before she could protest, lifted up one of her feet and, shoe and all, slid it into one of the boots.

'Hari . . .'

'And the other one. Perfect, Lily. Is that not perfect?'

'They sort of fit,' she admitted.

'Good.' He tied them around her ankles, his fingers like tiny spiders across her skin. 'Now hurry – I want to beat the sun to the top.'

She laughed and let him pull her forward again, though her feet were awkward with the new weight and she clumped after him like a fool.

'See, Lily,' he encouraged her, wriggling his own bare toes in the grass. 'Now you know what it's like to walk in my shoes.'

'I do. It is heavy, Hari.'

'I am trained to it.' He kissed her again. 'We're nearly there, my sweet. Look – there are the first of our ships.'

They'd crested the rise now and, sure enough, Elizaveta could see the tips of myriad masts poking up into the sky, swaying gently on the morning breeze.

'Like lances,' Harald said, 'ready to strike.'

He was right, she supposed, though she'd never have seen that for herself. She was standing in his shoes but she could not quite see with his eyes. Adventure she understood deep in her own soul, but war? War was his alone.

'You are sure about this invasion, Hari?' she said, pulling him to a halt in the shadow of the old broch.

'You ask me that *now*?'

She leaned in against him and felt his arms enfold her as they had done for so many years, even when she'd pushed him away.

'We have been on this journey a long time,' she whispered into his chest.

'And have plenty of years still to go – the best yet.'

'You will be careful?'

She heard his laugh, low and sweet against the sudden cry of a seabird rising over the cliff.

'You sound like Tora.'

Elizaveta tried to laugh with him but her mirth was fractured by a memory of her friend, stood on the jetty back in Norway. She had always before thought of Tora as a woman of presence with the big, voluptuous body of her own solid mother, but that day, on the arm of the son Elizaveta could so vividly remember being born, she had looked tiny.

Elizaveta had felt herself huge with excitement and anticipation in comparison and had pitied Tora's tight little frame as it had receded into a dot on the narrow stretch of the Sognafjord. This morning, though, with her own fears suddenly battering at her chest, she remembered Tora differently – her shoulders square against her fears and her back straight with her responsibilities.

'Perhaps Tora was right, Hari,' she said. 'Perhaps we should have contented ourselves with Norway.'

'And miss this?'

He reached down and gently took hold of her chin, tipping it up and out towards the sea. Elizaveta stared. The sun was a perfect disc atop the ocean, casting a path of white light all the way to their feet.

"Tis as bright as your hair,' she murmured, caught in its beauty.

'A sign,' he replied. 'I told you, Lily, all will be well. We were not content in Norway, not really.'

'*You* were.'

'Momentarily distracted, that's all. You freed me; took me back to my true self.'

'The man with seawater in his veins?'

He smiled and turned them both to the ocean below.

'When I limped away from Stikelstad aged fifteen, Lily, I became an adventurer – a Varangian. I was bitter at the time but I have seen so much because of it, done so much, and I have loved it all.'

Elizaveta looked across the water into the sun, embracing the intensity of its light.

'And me?' she asked. 'When did I become an adventurer, Hari? When I saw you?'

He kissed her, long and hard.

'Oh no. You, my Lilyveta, were *born* an adventurer and I love you for it. You will wait for me?'

'Always. You will come?'

'No.'

'No?'

'Because *you* will come to me. You will come to me in Westminster, to be crowned as Queen of England.'

'You promise?'

At that though he shifted, pulled away a little.

'I cannot promise, Lily, you know that, but have I ever failed to return from battle?'

She sighed. Calls were sounding from the ships below as men rose, stretched, checked for their swords. The sun's light was spreading, calling everyone to the day, and their stolen moment was leaking away. Hardly able to bear it, she pulled her husband's arms back around her and, locked together, they watched the Viking army unfurl before them.

'We are in God's hands now,' Harald murmured but Elizaveta shook her head fiercely.

'Not quite yet,' she insisted. 'For a few minutes more, Hari, we are still in each other's.'

Those precious minutes were soon swallowed up in the voracious jaws of a preparing army, and after that came two weeks of emptiness. Thorfinn, like Ulf, had gone to God last year and his two sons had sailed with Harald, taking Idonie along to visit the Scottish King Malcolm, to whom the family owed partial allegiance. The great compound on the Brough, therefore, was empty of all but a handful of servants, and Greta, Elizaveta, and their children rattled helplessly around in it. In the long days after the great fleet set forth from Scapa Flow, summer seemed to sigh itself out and autumn raced across the beautiful islands, turning the leaves golden and whipping them almost immediately from the trees as if refusing them their glory. Elizaveta had to fight herself hard not to see it as an omen, for that way madness lay.

Earlier in the year the night skies had been riven by a falling star, trailing fire like a backwards dragon. Many had hailed that as an omen, but of what? As Harald had calmly pointed out, the same star would blaze its trail across England, Normandy and Norway alike and who was to say which it favoured? The same was true now – the falling leaves could mark a loss for any of the contenders for the throne of England, or they could just be falling. And the winds, at least, would carry Harald's ships swiftly south, which was worth more than any imagined favour.

Exactly two weeks after Harald had left, Elizaveta pulled her cloak around her and took her viol up to the ancient broch. It was foolish, she knew – the very winds that had taken Harald to England would prevent his messengers reaching her, but at least up here on the cliffs at the edge of the Brough, where they had stood together that precious golden dawn, she felt as close to him as she could possibly be.

Was he there in Westminster yet? Were the messengers on their way to fetch her to him as he had promised? Was he, maybe, laughing with Agatha as he took the throne of the English from the upstart Earl Harold? Was he preparing to lead both his own men and the English against the Normans? Or had the Normans got to Harold first and it was Duke William he must now face to secure the throne? Surely, either way, the English would aid him in seeing off the upstart duke and his presumptuous Flanders wife?

Elizaveta tried to imagine Westminster but could only find images of Kiev, though there was no way the English first city could be like her childhood home, far away in the Rus. She had quizzed anyone she'd encountered who had ever been near London – though they were pitifully few – and she knew from Agatha's letters that Westminster was a low-lying island set within the embrace of a great river called the Thames, a wide, flat, rolling water without the cliffs and rapids of the Dnieper.

The rest of London, her sister had said, sprawled out from the palace and abbey at its heart, across what had once been meadowland and marshes, eating up new villages into its eager embrace with every passing year. It was built largely of wood, its streets were no more than trampled earth, and it was protected only by a palisade, and that bare in places. It was not, then, Kiev, with its paving and its cupolas and its rooved walls though there were apparently, at least, traders and merchants of all nations living there so it should be more at the centre of the advancing world than remote Norway. And so what if it lacked architecture? She could create that, as she had created it for Oslo. Yes, she tried hard to imagine Westminster for sometimes it felt like the only positive thing she could do.

Elizaveta fingered her viol bow, wondering how it must feel to wield instead an archer's bow, or a sword. She thought of Harald seeing lances in the ships' masts and remembered standing on Kiev's walls to watch her father's forces beat the Pechenegs – the only war, despite how many had raged around her, that she'd ever seen. That had been the summer weedy little Magnus had ridden to Norway in Harald's place. She had been so angry – too angry to even pay much attention to the battle.

From where they'd stood, some hundred paces from the fighting, it had been hard to see faces, to spot individual deaths, and Elizaveta's overwhelming impression had been of an ever-shifting sea of limbs, some flesh, some metal, moving like a changing tide on a piercing wind of pain. Her mother had tried to steer her into admiring her father's tactics – the precise movement of blocks of troops to enclose the crazed Pechenegs – and Elizaveta had heard enough of Harald and Ulf's talk since to now appreciate the skill of command. At the time, though, she had been too intrigued by the relentless smash of steel on bone to see the patterns.

'Where is Papa?' was all she'd wanted to know.

'A good commander stays in the rear,' her mother had assured her. 'He must view the whole field, not just the man in front of him.'

Elizaveta had seen that day how true that was, but only if the commander were winning. The Pecheneg leader had sunk with his lowliest soldiers, his battle-patterns, if he'd ever had any, carved to nought. She drew her bow determinedly across the strings. The winds whipped her notes away almost before they could form but that suited her for the poor instrument was old now and warped from its travels and she wanted it less for music than distraction from the discord of her own thoughts.

'Mama?'

She looked up to see Maria in the doorway of the broch, her dark hair whipping behind her as if one with her carelessly slung cloak.

'Maria! Come inside. There is precious little warmth but the walls keep the worst of the winds away.'

The young woman, newly turned twenty, stepped carefully over the rocky sill and joined her.

'You look for ships?'

'Foolish, I know.'

Maria did not contradict her.

'Josef is not well,' she said instead, 'so I have brought Filip out to give him and Greta some peace.'

Elizaveta leaned forward to see the twelve-year-old kicking a pig's bladder against the wall of the broch. The rough stones sent the ball flying in all directions and she envied Filip his concentration on its path. She was grateful Greta had chosen to come back to the Orkneys with her when Aksel had been made one of Harald's commanders in the mission to England. She was good company and the children were a blessed distraction and, besides, Greta had been with Elizaveta last time and last time Harald had returned – more omens!

'That's kind,' she said to Maria.

'It's not as if I had anything else to do, save drive myself insane with imaginings.'

'You too?'

'Yes. Ingrid is happy in Thorfinn's drying room, doing something strange with leaves. She's made a drink to bring Josef's fever down and is now concocting a potion to help soothe wounds but what's the point in that? I would rather be with the warriors, Mama, fighting alongside Papa with my sword, than stuck here like a cripple.'

'You love him very much, Maria.'

'As do you.'

Elizaveta looked at her.

'I do. I have been lucky. And you – you are looking forward to your wedding?'

Maria blushed.

'I am. It feels, Mama, as if everything between us has been on hold for this invasion.'

'Everything?'

'Yes – everything!' Maria said indignantly, adding, 'Though not for want of Otto's trying.'

'Clearly I have brought you up well.'

Maria smiled suddenly, releasing a cheeky dimple that made her look four years old all over again.

'I've been tempted. I used to think Papa was the only man in the world worth marrying but Otto has changed that. He's so handsome, Mama, and when he looks at me I, I . . .'

'Melt?'

'No! Goodness no, nothing so soft. I flame.'

Elizaveta kissed her cheek.

'There is nothing wrong with that, Maria. It is, indeed, a blessing – or it will be.'

Maria rose and paced the inside of the broch, running her hands along the wall as if feeling for its heartbeat.

'I was angry at him,' she said eventually.

'At Otto?'

'Yes. I was angry that he agreed to postpone our wedding for England. He was all caught up in being Papa's marshal and happy to do anything he said. I thought it was wrong to wait. I . . . I shouted at him.'

Elizaveta went to her daughter.

'Maria, sweetheart, I swear I have shouted at your father more times than I have broken my fast but he always comes back for more.'

'Maybe, but did he ride to battle in between?'

'You argued here?'

'The night before they sailed, yes. He wanted us to, to . . .'

'Know each other fully?'

'Yes. And I said that had he not let Papa postpone the wedding we could have known each other for weeks. I said . . . I said that if I had to wait, he had to wait too.'

'You said that?' Elizaveta gasped.

'Was I wrong?'

'No! Oh Maria, no, it's exactly what I said to your father in Kiev when he chose to sail back to Constantinople as a bachelor Varangian instead of with me to Norway.'

Maria stared at her.

'And what happened?'

Elizaveta smiled.

'Much, Maria, including more arguments, but in the end he rode back to me – rode down an icy river and leaped a burning ship to claim me as his bride.' Maria laughed, disbelievingly. 'It's true!'

'It sounds like one of Halldor's stories.'

'It does, doesn't it? Stories though, you know, can carry much truth.' As one they looked to the roughly arched window on the seaward side of the broch. 'And heroes,' Elizaveta added, 'do exist. We must trust to that. Trust and pray.'

CHAPTER FORTY

York, September 1066

*R*iding high on his horse Harald approached the walls of York and seeing the frightened huddle of women above the gates knew that news of his victory had reached the city. He smiled. Victory! It hadn't been easy but nothing worth winning ever was and besides it was good practice for the battles yet to come. If the men of northern England, their veins supposedly running with Norse blood, had put up such a fight, there would be battle aplenty in the south but he cared not. He was ready. He felt alive, on fire, like a bolt of smoothest silk shot through with gold. He would be king of this pretty country.

Not that the marshlands at Fulford were pretty now. It had been a bitter fight. The English earls had caught them halfway to York, their troops lined up between a wide, unfordable stretch of the Ouse to the west and marshlands to the east. It had been a brave stand, Harald had seen that from the moment he'd ridden over the hill. He'd admired the young commanders' guts in leaving themselves little room for retreat, but he'd also seen all too swiftly how that could be exploited.

Earls Edwin and Morcar had hit him fast, barely before he'd lined up his front troops and with half his army still strung out along the road from the ships at Riccall – though strung out, crucially, behind him so that as the front lines were engaged he was able to keep on filling his ranks from behind. He'd soon outnumbered the defenders – just the way he liked it.

'They will have to surrender, Sire.'

Harald was drawn from his thoughts by Torr, riding proudly at his side as if he had been instrumental in the battle, which in a way he had. The exiled earl had led them safely to the enemy and, once there, Harald had been able to station his rag-taggle troops to the right, in the marshiest of the marshy land the English had forced them to fight from. The enemy had been unable to resist the lure and had driven hard into them. Torr had not looked so cocky then, with men falling all around him, but he had, at least, held out long enough for Harald to send his own powerful force driving round the side to push the English, giddy on their initial success, deep into the marshland. The fighting had been long and hard but with more troops still arriving from up the road Harald had slowly but surely decimated the English and once their earls had turned tail it had all been over.

'Surrender?' he queried Torr now, for the English had already surrendered. He had personally driven his horse over a putrid pathway of 'surrendered' English soldiers to lead a rout of the fleeing remnant of their lines.

'The city,' Torr said, gesturing to the great walls before them. 'The city of York. She is still held, though only by the queen now. That is, the, er . . .'

Harald put up a hand, still gloved in chain mail.

'She is the queen, Lord Torr, though not I trust for long. And yes, she will surrender. Edyth, I believe she is called. I met her once in Wales, a resourceful woman and no fool. Wait here.'

Torr obediently drew rein, the rest of the core troops with him, and Harald rode forward alone, assessing the ancient stone walls of the old Roman city before him – they were weak, he decided, crumbling. They'd need replacing, but not until Ulf's church was built.

'You are defeated, my lady,' he called up to the cluster of women on the parapet above the gate.

One stepped forward and he recognised her immediately. She had been Queen of Wales when he'd seen her last and now it seemed she was Queen of England, though not, as he had told Torr, for long. That honour would be Elizaveta's – he had promised it to her and he would deliver.

'So it seems,' Edyth called down, her voice steady, 'for this day at least.'

Harald laughed.

'Your noble brothers are fled,' he told her and saw, to his surprise, a flicker not of dismay but of hope. Did she think they would come again? She would not be so foolish when she saw the weight of men sunk in Fulford's marshes.

'What do you want of us?' she demanded.

'We seek entry into York which we claim as our own.'

'I cannot oppose you, Sire,' Edyth said and he felt Torr twitch delightedly behind him, 'but I can ask that you honour me and all of my people.'

She glanced to her women and he felt a flash of anger as he understood her implication; he might be a Viking but he was no barbarian.

'We come not to pillage, my queen,' he told her stiffly, 'but to conquer. Today is but a step on our path.'

'A victory on the way to defeat.'

Damn her, she was insolent. It fired his anger but also his admiration. She reminded him a little of Elizaveta and he smiled to himself. His wife would be half-mad with waiting but now he could send good news. He would order a messenger to the Orkneys with report of this, his first triumph, as soon as he was inside York's *walls. He would tell her that she would soon be dining with her sister in the new palace at Westminster.*

'*If it suits you to see it that way,*' *he called up to the English queen. '*It makes no odds to me. I seek food, I seek wine and I seek terms – hostages.*'

The women whimpered pathetically and he knew, whatever his own feelings, that he would have to keep a tight rein on his men this night. This was no Viking raid, no smash-and-grab looting. He was here in England to be their king and he would behave as their king all the way to Westminster.

'Maria, Maria, come and see!'

At the sound of Filip's voice, Maria leaped up and ducked out of the broch doorway. She looked around, puzzled, and Elizaveta, knowing already what she would find, ran after her. Sure enough, Filip was halfway up the outer wall and making steady progress towards the top.

'Filip,' she called, 'come down.'

It was growing late. The sun was diving towards the darkening ocean and already it was hard to make out Filip's fingers as they darted across the stones seeking solid holds. Elizaveta thought of Greta, back at the hall with ailing Josef, and tried not to panic.

'This tower is York,' the boy called down, 'and this time I will master it, as Harald will master that city.'

'How do you know?' Elizaveta asked him, for at least when he was talking he was still.

'How? Why, because he is the biggest, strongest man in the whole Viking world.'

'England is not in the Viking world,' Elizaveta objected.

'I'll wager it is by now.'

Maria clapped her hands together.

'I'll wager it is too.'

'Maria . . .' Elizaveta warned.

'What, Mama? Filip is right. Papa will win; mayhap he already has.' She peered out to sea. 'How long would a messenger take to reach us?'

Elizaveta sighed. She had discussed this with Harald before he left but neither of them had known.

'It could be as much as a week's hard ride if a man came overland through Scotland, though possibly more as I hear it is mountainous terrain and the local tribes are fierce.'

Maria sighed but now Filip called out triumphantly from above them and Elizaveta looked up to see him right at the top of the broch, a dark silhouette against the purpling sky.

'I can see England!' he called. '*Our* England.'

'Can you? Can you really?'

Maria made a dive for the broch and Elizaveta grabbed her arm.

'Of course he cannot, Maria. There are all the mountains of Scotland in between.'

'I can,' Filip called down defiantly. 'Oh!'

His foot wobbled and a stone crashed into the centre of the broch, smashing to pieces on the earthen floor. Maria dived for the wall and this time Elizaveta did not stop her but before she could so much as hitch up her skirts Filip was sitting safely down, holding the edge to steady himself.

'I'm fine,' he called, though Elizaveta heard the tremor in his voice.

'Please come down, Filip,' she implored. 'Your poor mother would be very vexed if she saw you up there and it grows dark. We must get back to her. And carefully,' she added as he began slowly to turn himself for the descent.

Maria's hands were clasping the wall and her right foot had already found a toe-hold two courses up but Elizaveta tugged at her arm.

'Stand back, Maria – give him space.'

Her daughter nodded and together they stood and held their breath as Filip slowly, painstakingly crawled down the curved wall towards them. When he was just a little above their heads he looked down, his sudden smile broad in the rising moonlight.

'I'm quite safe,' he said and then, without warning, leaped to the ground, landing before them and steadying himself with just a slight bend of his young knees.

'Home!' Elizaveta said darkly and set off down the curve of the Brough towards the hall, glowing in the dusk as the servants lit the rush lights.

She set a brisk pace, more to walk off her own unease than because there was any real rush. She wanted to deliver Filip safely back to Greta and to see Ingrid, whose calm, however much it might frustrate Maria, always soothed her. The youngsters, though, lagged behind.

'Could you really see England?' she heard Maria ask Filip.

'I believe so.'

'And what did you see?'

'Victory.'

'Victory?' Maria was scornful. 'What does victory look like?'

Filip chuckled.

'You'll have to see for yourself,' was his cheeky reply and then he was running past Elizaveta, Maria hot on his tail, and Elizaveta was so glad to see her unusually sombre daughter losing herself in a child's chase that she did not think to warn her against doing so.

CHAPTER FORTY-ONE

Stamford Bridge, 25 September 1066

*T*he life of a conqueror, Harald had decided, was a good one. The sun was shining on him and his men as they sat in the sloping grasslands above the babbling River Derwent, coaxing a fire into life to roast the meat the younger soldiers were even now rounding up on the pastures over the wooden bridge at Stamford.

'Catch him, Tomas,' Aksel called. 'Surely you can outrun a cow, man?'

Harald smiled to hear Halldor's rough humour running through his son's voice. Here in the strange fields of England he had missed his old friend's vibrant enthusiasm nearly as much as he had missed Ulf's quiet pragmatism. Aksel's bright presence in his army was a balm to the wound of their absence on this, his greatest campaign, and he was unendingly grateful that Hal's boy had sailed with him from Iceland back when this invasion was little more than a dream.

It was a dream no longer though. He was here and he must make the most of it. Shaking off the ghosts of the past, he laughed with the rest of his men as the cow, a sprightly young heifer, ducked Tomas's clumsy attempt to rope her and danced off, hooves kicking high in the autumn air.

'Jump on his back,' someone suggested and they all laughed again.

'Can we not stick an arrow in the beast?' another grumbled. 'Tomas will be all day playing tag with it and I'm hungry.'

'It might be best,' Harald agreed.

The men had broken their fast heartily on board the ships, still moored at Riccall, but it had been a twelve-mile march here, to the assigned point for the English to hand over their hostages and treasure, and a man soon worked up an appetite on such a trip, especially in this warm weather. Even in the lightest armour Harald had allowed them they had all been sweating within minutes and many had chosen to throw off their heavy chain mail on arrival in the sweeping fields above the bridge to duck themselves in the blissfully cool waters of the Derwent. Now they sat steaming gently, taking their ease around the landwaster banner, struck into the ground on a long stave, but they did need food.

'Aksel,' Harald said over his shoulder, 'set your archers on the cattle, lad.'

Aksel rose and, taking two of his best men down the bank, waved to poor Tomas and his fellows to stand aside. The heifer was felled with a single strike, offering no more than a strangled moo before it fell to earth with a loud thud and a call of delight from over the bank.

'Good work,' Harald called to the archer. 'Save those arrows for the English.'

The men jeered obligingly then turned their attention to the entertaining spectacle of the younger men trying to drag the dead cow across to the bridge. The fire, as if sensing meat, leaped to life and they called out to them to hurry.

Harald rose and moved aside, his eyes scanning the horizon. He had not been jesting about the arrows. The English in York had seemed docile enough, the women terrified and those men

who'd escaped Fulford in no mood to do battle again, but he still
had to be careful. He had set guards on all the roads and outside
York's big south gates to watch for treachery but so far all was
quiet. It would soon be midday and the hostages should come. He
flexed his wrists, his right one a little sore still from the action at
Fulford. It had ached ever since Nisa but he welcomed the reminder.
He had made peace with Denmark so he could put all his energies
into gaining England and he must stay alert.

'The time draws close,' Harald said, turning. 'We should arm
ourselves.'

His men, though, had crowded down to the river. The youngsters on the far side looked hopefully at them, awaiting help, but
if Harald knew his warriors they would get none, not to tug the
beast over the bridge, nor to gut it on the other side. That was a
novice's task and they would enjoy the show. As should he. Picking
up his own helmet, he gave a last glance to the horizon – still
empty – and wandered down to join them. It was a fine cow; it
would be a good feast indeed, especially with English hostages
to serve it.

'An outdoor dinner?' Elizaveta asked, frowning at her eldest
daughter.

'An outdoor dinner,' Maria agreed, adding as she saw Elizaveta's face, 'it was Ingrid's idea.'

'And it's a good one,' Ingrid said unusually firmly. 'Josef is
healing and he needs fresh air, as does Greta. She is too pale.'

That much at least was true. But . . .

'An outdoor dinner?' Elizaveta repeated and Ingrid leaped
forward to take her hands.

'Why not, Mama? We cannot just sit around staring at walls.
It could be weeks until we hear news.'

'Of the victory?'

'Of the victory, yes, so why should we not enjoy ourselves in the meantime? Please, Mama, it is a glorious day.'

That was true too. The winds had lessened and the sun, though low, shone with real warmth.

'Where?' Elizaveta asked.

'Up at the broch,' Maria told her instantly, tugging her towards the door, Ingrid in tow. 'The children love to play there and it will offer some shelter if the winds rise.'

'As,' Elizaveta pointed out, resisting, 'would staying in the hall.'

'Oh, Mama – don't be so dull.'

That arrow hit home. Dull? Is that what she had become?

'I'll have you know,' she said, 'that I am not dull. I rode the rapids.'

'I remember,' Maria said, glancing to her sister. 'Do you, Ingrid?'

'Mother kayaking dressed as a boy?' Ingrid wrinkled up her nose. 'Of course I remember.'

'I was so proud,' Maria said defiantly.

'You were?' Elizaveta smiled and stepped towards the door, suddenly twitching to look out to the south, for all the use it would be. 'The broch it is, then. We must get food.'

'All arranged.'

Elizaveta looked at her daughters, women now but looking as guilty as little girls at the admission. She drank in the sight of pretty, blonde Ingrid, so like her grandmother and namesake in both looks and temperament, then dark-haired Maria, too like her mother and father for her own good. She sighed.

'You knew I would agree?'

'You're always up there, Mama. At least this way you can enjoy your dinner instead of scratching away on that old viol.'

'Scratching . . . ?' Elizaveta protested but the girls were already spinning away and Greta was calling to the children

424

that it was time to go. 'Scratching?' she repeated indignantly to herself but in the doorway Maria spun back.

'I really *was* proud of you,' she said and then she was truly gone, leaving Elizaveta to pick up her skirts and follow with a reluctant smile.

'Goodness, Tomas, we'll all starve at this rate and then we'll never defeat Harold's damned southerners. Pull it by the horns!'

'I'll pull you by the horns,' came the ferocious reply and the men roared with laughter.

The group of youngsters had dragged the cow almost to the riverbank now but were in confusion about how best to get it across. The bridge was sturdy but narrow, barely wide enough for two men side by side, and the cow would fill it. Across the pasture behind them another group had somehow succeeded in lassoing a second beast and were leading it, still very much alive, towards them. Harald saw Tomas look round in something close to panic and took pity on him.

'Get the ropes,' he called to the men on his side, 'or we'll never have it cooked before dusk. And besides, we don't want the English to think us fools, do we?'

That set them moving. Aksel led a group up the hill where two lengths of rope sat coiled amongst the discarded mail like adders in a nest. He bent to pick up the first one and then froze.

'Hurry, Aksel,' Harald prompted but in reply Aksel pointed a hand towards the York road and now Harald saw it too – dust rising. 'They're coming,' he roared to his men. 'The hostages are coming. Get that bloody cow over here now!'

Aksel picked the ropes up, slinging them over his shoulder, but then paused again.

'Aksel!' Harald shouted, irritated. 'Move!'

Aksel looked down the slope at him and Harald saw raw dread in his eyes – Halldor's eyes. For a moment he was in Miklegard again, a young man fighting with his friends against pirates, and then the lad's shout ripped through his warped mind: 'Soldiers!'

He blinked. Soldiers? It couldn't be. There were no soldiers left in the north, or none ready for fighting at least. They were all face down in Fulford's marshes.

'Soldiers!' came Aksel's cry again, then, 'A banner. 'Tis, 'tis . . .'

''Tis what?' Harald snapped, though he could see it for himself now – a white banner with a black warrior picked out upon it, sword raised: the fighting man, the standard of Harold Godwinson, once Earl of Wessex and now King of England. 'It cannot be,' he muttered.

'Sire, 'tis the king.'

'It cannot be,' he said, louder. 'He is in the south waiting for Duke William.'

But there was no doubting the banner, nor the gilded armour, nor the huge host at the man's back. Was he a magician to have brought so many so far? And how had he evaded the guard outside York? Were those poor men dead already? There was no time to think of them now and Harald's mind raced into action, seeking advantage. If this was truly Harold Godwinson, his men would be tired. They would be no match for his own troops, rested and ready and . . . He glanced back to the armour, strewn carelessly across the hillside. Never had Harald been caught so unprepared and he felt panic surge through his big body before, swift on its tail, the hotter rush of battle-anger.

'To arms!' he cried, snatching up the landwaster and leading the way himself. 'Man the bridge. We must keep them back long enough to form a wall.'

He ran up the hill, flinging mail at men as he went so that it clashed and tangled in their legs. Harold Godwinson had caught him out with barely half his warriors and they were unarmed and sluggish with sun and ale. Ulf would never have allowed this, he realised with a bitter pang. He had been a fool and now he had to move fast.

'Did you know about this?' he hissed at Torr, grabbing the man's collar as he tried to dart past.

'No, Sire, truly. I have no idea how he has done it.'

'Well he has,' Harald said grimly, 'and now we will have to fight as we have never fought before.'

Already the English were streaming out across the pasture, some fighting on horseback like Pechenegs, cutting down the Viking cattle rustlers in swift, easy strokes.

'Send to the ships,' Harald commanded one of his best riders. 'Take horses and ride hard. Tell Otto he must bring troops now.'

The man nodded, looking fearfully back at the English as they drove through the Norwegians still caught on the far bank.

'Sire, 'tis twelve miles.'

'I know, you fool. Ride hard.'

The man ran for his horse, leaped in the saddle and was gone, up through the trees towards Riccall. Otto would come, Harald knew, but not for some hours. They would have to defend as they had never defended before.

'Men!' he roared into the autumn air, planting the landwaster into the ground. 'To me! We knew we would have to fight Harold of Wessex to win England and it seems the time has come to do so. He has spared us a march, bless him – so let us welcome him in true Viking style!'

His men let out a huge roar and Harald thought he saw the English line falter across the pretty river between them. Good. He had not picked this time nor this place but he was ready. He had always been ready – let them come.

Elizaveta felt she had not laughed so much in weeks, certainly not since Harald had sailed for England and perhaps for a long time before that. Everything had been so bound up in the invasion, as if normal life had ceased and all Norway had been hunkered in a dragon boat pointed west. She had breathed battle plans, drawing them in from Harald with every snatched kiss, and all else had seemed somehow frivolous. Today though, perched up on the Brough of Birsay, avoiding the shadow of the ancient broch, she felt as if she had been gifted life again.

She sat back on the woollen rug laid out on battered leather hides to keep the September damp from seeping through, and watched as Filip, hands clutched around his ankles, leaped across the grass before them. She had finally told them of the toad, his namesake, and how Maria had smuggled him into the great hall at Oslo, and now he was acting out the scene, eyes forced wide and cheeks blown out as he croaked his way across the cliff top.

'Ah!' Greta screeched, throwing her hands up to her cheeks in mock horror. 'It's so ugly!'

'And so slimy,' Mina cried at her side.

'And so warty,' Ingrid added.

'Oh no,' Maria objected, hands on her heart, 'I think he is beautiful and I shall make him a lord.'

She jumped up and ran over to Filip, seizing her precious sword from the food basket and holding it before him. Elizaveta watched the amber hilt glowing golden in the dipping sun and prayed Harald's sword, too, was glowing gold, not red.

'Swear fealty, Lord Toad,' Maria commanded.

'Never,' Filip cried in a croaking voice, trying to leap back and tangling himself in his own fool's grip. 'I will only swear,' he went on from his position on his back in the grass, 'to the King of England, King Harald.'

'King Harald Hardrada,' Elizaveta said quickly.

'Of course,' Maria agreed, just as swiftly, 'what other Harald is there?'

'None,' Filip called, 'save he be a toad like myself.'

It was a brave jest but the laughter had gone out of the scene and all eyes turned to the sea. It lay a benign blue before them – the colour of hope, Tora had called it, and Elizaveta seized at that now.

'Who would like an apple tart?' she called brightly, reaching to the servant for the basket.

The children tumbled towards her but Maria did not move, save to step towards the cliffs. Elizaveta handed the basket to Greta and went to her eldest girl.

'Maria? You are cold?'

Her daughter's skin, exposed where she had pushed back her sleeves in the game, was as dimpled as gooseflesh. Maria snatched the fabric back into place.

'A little. It is late in the year after all, Mama, for eating outdoors.'

Elizaveta refrained from pointing out that the whole jaunt had been Maria's idea.

'It is time, perhaps, to head for home,' she suggested instead but at that Maria shook her head.

She was turning her little sword over and over in her hands, staring at it as if she might gaze right into the heart of the steel and suddenly she said: 'I want to see.'

'See what, Maria?' Her daughter did not reply, just moved to the broch and put a hand on its rough walls. 'No!' Elizaveta darted after her. 'No, Maria, please. You cannot see England even from the top. You know you cannot.'

'I might.'

'And even if you could, what then? Papa is at least three days' sail away – you will hardly pick him out from here.'

'I might,' Maria said again, her face set. 'I feel him, Mama – in here.'

She pressed her hand to her heart and tipped her head back to fix her eyes on the topmost stones of the broch.

'Maria,' Elizaveta begged, 'you cannot climb. Your skirts . . .' But now Maria was setting her sword against the base of the broch and unclipping her shoulder brooches. Elizaveta hastened to stop her but as the skirts fell to the floor she froze. 'You are wearing hose.'

'I am not a fool, Mama.'

'Not a fool,' Elizaveta allowed, 'but foolish all the same. Maria, it is dangerous.'

'So is sailing to England but if Otto can do that, if Papa can do that, then I can climb this.'

'It does not work that way,' Elizaveta insisted. The others were gathering around now and Maria was grasping the first stones. Elizaveta grabbed at her waist. 'There are no omens, Maria, no deals to be made with God. This is but a tower, a collection of stones; you cannot reach Harald this way.'

Maria looked down at her.

'Mayhap not, but I need to try.'

Elizaveta stilled. She knew that feeling. It was a feeling that had sent her, canoe above her head, up the steep riverside path in Kiev and then again in Oslo. It was an itch in the soul and it seemed her daughter had caught it from her. She took first one hand and then the other from Maria's waist.

'Take care,' she told her softly and then, standing back and taking Ingrid's arm, watched her elder daughter start to climb.

Harald felt as if he were on an endless upwards struggle. His limbs screamed, his head pulsed. He slashed and parried, blocking blows with his shield and casting them with his sword. Deep within the shield wall he was sheltered from the ferocity of the full attack but his men were falling away like moths in a candle flame, and the English were driving fervently on towards them.

Stuck on open hillside he'd had little choice but to form a shield-wall in full turtle formation around his banner with his men in an arrow shape, the best fighters on the two longer sides protecting the softer rear. He and his personal warband were a little back from the tip, supposedly commanding the movement of the battle but in truth there was no command to issue save: 'Hold!'

Already the field was littered with bodies, most of them Norwegian. On the bridge poor Tomas had abandoned his cow and, fighting alone with a sword flung his way by a comrade, had held off the entire English host for wave after wave, buying Harald the priceless time needed to arm and group the core of his warriors. Finally he had fallen but with unending courage and Harald vowed he would see him honoured. Once the reserves made it from the ships and sprung the English from behind to secure the victory, he would see him honoured. He just needed to last out a little more. He was not a natural defender – already he felt cramped, tied in by his own battling men – but he could do it. He would do it.

Harald set his feet more firmly in the soft ground but then a sharp cry told him that the left side of his wall had split. Looking over he saw the English driving into the central section, soldiers pouring in like ants onto honey, only with murder in their eyes. For a moment all seemed helpless but then he glanced back up the hill and saw a flash of steel in the dipping sun. Otto was come! Otto was come and not a moment too late. He need stand here, penned in, no more.

He looked out across the battlefield and his heart soared. This was him. He was Harald Hardrada – Viking, Varangian, King. He wiped sweat from his brow and swept his eyes around, taking in the ferocious shield-push of his men, the chaos of the English, and the sparkle of his own reserves roaring down the hill, swords high. There was no battlefield plan now, no calm command, no space for manoeuvre. There was just one thing left – spirit.

Glancing to his landwaster he saw his raven, wings triumphantly wide, sewn with the loving, believing stitches of his wives. Planting his feet, he drew in a deep breath. He would fight as he had fought all his life and he would not end this day beneath a bush. He threw back his head, raised his sword and roared a single word – 'Charge!'

The world had concentrated, focused down into one tiny figure, dark against the soft sandstone of the broch as the sun dropped behind. It seemed as if there was no time any more: Elizaveta was listening to her mother's stories and feeling trolls clutching at her ankles; she was riding up the banks of the Ros, resettled foreigners cheering her in; she was on her childbed, wreathed in agony; then cresting the rapids, spirits as high as the tumbling waters. And there was no place either: she was on the walls of Kiev, ice in her face; riding up to a royal farmhouse, fighting disappointment; ordering architects to spin a city from half-remembered plans; then plunging into a steaming pool beneath a fire-riven land.

She was watching Maria and seeing Harald, his blonde hair entwined in their daughter's dark locks as it had for so long been entwined in her own. She felt Ingrid at her side and Greta behind, and sensed little Filip, so like Aksel as her young squire, fighting to go after Maria.

'No,' she heard Greta say, 'not this time.'

The words were picked up on the rising wind and thrown around the broch – *not this time, not this time*. Elizaveta threaded her hands together, driving her nails into her palms, and willed Maria on. The girl was feeling her way so, so carefully, picking the widest stones and the deepest gaps to plant her feet and grip with her dainty fingers. They were leading her round the broch, towards the cliff side, spiralling upwards, and all their eyes followed. A cloud crossed the dying sun and was gone again as if God had winked. A gull dived in, screeching its protest at a human striving so high, then whirled away, plummeting towards the sea in search of easier prey. And still Maria climbed.

The point of the wall split before Harald as if his soldiers, like him, were eager to throw up their shields and fight like men. Harald felt as if his body were filled with blood. It surged through his veins and sang at his temples and pushed at his limbs, forcing them forwards. He was not simply in the battle; he was the battle.

The reserves were entering the fray. In the fading light he could see them beyond the English, cutting into the rear, and he thrust forward, slashing men from his path to meet them. Let these Englishmen, like the last, pave his way to victory. Somewhere out there was Harold Godwinson. If Harald could find him, he could kill him and this would all be over. He cut again and again but these Englishmen were stubborn. Their limbs were tough and their eyes fierce and now they were fighting on two fronts, turning back Otto's men who seemed to be crumbling like soft cheese or, perhaps, like men who had run twelve miles in full armour.

'You might lose.'

Harald heard the thought but cut it away with a slash of his sword. He would not lose. He could not lose. Elizaveta was waiting. Elizaveta was waiting to join him on his throne. He stepped forward, cutting a man to the floor with a single swipe of his sword, then felt pain rear, like an out-of-control stallion, across his arm. He stared at the ripped flesh, then at the man who had attacked from his side and who looked almost as astonished as he.

'No!'

Harald swung again, slashing the man to the ground, though pain rode high on every sinew of his flesh and his eyes saw red, nothing but red. He blinked furiously as the silk of the land-waster clapped in the sharp wind above him and there was Tora, stood in the doorway of his pavilion, throwing back her cloak with a heavenly mix of shyness and audacity to reveal her nakedness beneath. Then Lily, his Lily, dragging him onto her boatbuilder's bed and ripping his clothes from him as her eagle-prow looked on – the eagle-prow that had crested the waves to England.

'Do not die in bed,' Ulf had told him and he had been right to do so. Valhalla might not live in the skies but it lived in Harald's heart. He cast around again for Harold Godwinson, but the battle-field was a mass of swords and spears, and however hard he strained, even at his great height, he could not find him. He stretched out, his sword still swinging and his shield still pushing men aside. The battle consumed him and he knew that whether he won or he died, either way would be glory.

He did not, in the end, feel the arrow as it pierced his throat. He just felt a searing stab, like the arousing anger of a beautiful wife, and he fell gratefully before her.

Maria did not call. She did not, as Filip had done, crow when she reached the top of the broch and threw her hose-clad leg over the sill. She said nothing at all. Neither did she stand but sat, demure as the maiden she had professed herself to be, hands tight on the stone either side of her as she looked out to sea.

'Can you see it?' Ingrid called when no one could bear the silence any longer. 'Can you see England?'

Still Maria did not speak but Elizaveta saw her lean forward a little, as if catching a cry on the wind. She saw her dark hair lift and watched, caught on the edge with her first-born, as she raised a hand to the skies.

'Maria,' she wanted to call, 'hold on,' but she dared not break the spell holding her daughter to the top of the ancient tower.

'I see nothing.' Suddenly Maria's voice came down to them, clear and sad. 'I see nothing, Mama. 'Tis a fool's errand.'

'As I said,' Elizaveta thought but she shored up the words, a painful ball inside her throat as, praise God, Maria turned and dropped one foot down to find a hold.

'Go back,' she threw at a servant, 'go back and heat water. She will be chilled.'

She saw again Maria's purpled flesh beneath her thin sleeves and prayed her daughter's cold fingers did not lose their grip. She saw one foot find its step and the second move across the broch, slowly, carefully.

The stone snapped as if whipped from the wall. It tumbled down and ricocheted off another where the wall turned outwards, spinning into the air and tumbling over the cliff. Maria's foot dangled a moment, suspended on the clouds, but somehow she found a hold beneath.

She paused against the wall and glanced down, safe, and Elizaveta breathed again. Their eyes met and Maria half-smiled before something, some sound in the sky Elizaveta did not catch, drew her to look upwards and she seemed to jerk. She put a hand to her throat, her eyes twisted in their sockets, then her knee turned and her leg crumpled. Her hands scrabbled helplessly at the broch but its ancient stone gave way in her frantic grasp and, in a shower of darkness, she fell – a stark, wingless angel.

She hit the earth with a thud and a crack of bone, her foot catching her sword and sending it flying into the air. It spun once, the amber hilt flashing red in the setting sun, and then dropped over the cliff and was gone. Maria lay as still as the rocks around her.

For a moment Elizaveta was frozen too, but then she was

running, clasping her daughter into her arms and shaking her limp, cracked body in a desperate attempt to free the life that had beat so vitally within it just a moment before. How could she be gone? Surely a gull had just snatched her spirit, taken it for a mischievous dive into the waves. It would be back. Maria would breathe again.

'Come back,' she begged. 'Come back, Maria. We need you. I need you. *Papa* needs you.'

The word caught in her windpipe, tangling with her earlier protests at Maria's desperate climb. She looked down at her daughter, into her dark, unseeing eyes, and pictured the sudden jerk of her white throat at the top of the broch – Maria had felt something.

'No!'

Elizaveta threw back her head and hollered. She sensed the others at Maria's feet, heard their cries, their tears, their prayers to a God high above the careless Brough, but she knew now that her dear Maria was not the entirety of their grief, just its beginning.

'Hari,' she whispered. 'Hari, my love.'

She pulled Maria's limp body as tight against her as she had pulled Harald that golden dawn before he sailed for England. She'd begged him to promise to return, but he had not promised and he would not return. It had all been for nought.

Slowly she stroked the dark tangles of Maria's hair away from her beautiful face and kissed her young eyes closed. For a moment she thought she saw a line across her cheek, the shadow of a scar, and she traced it desperately with her finger, longing to find Harald in his daughter's flesh, longing for this to be Stikelstad again – the start, not the end. But the lines across her own old hand told her that could not be.

'No!' she cried again, tossing her defiance over the cliff as if it might somehow pull Harald back to mourn their daughter with her. But he was gone and the word was whipped uselessly south – chasing her love, chasing her dreams, chasing her soul across an empty ocean.

Twenty Norwegian ships sailed back into Scapa Flow; twenty of the three hundred that had sailed so hopefully out of the mouth of the Sognafjord. They brought Harald's body, Otto's beside him, and Elizaveta laid them both by Maria's in the little stone church at the base of the Brough of Birsay. Even before they'd returned, she'd ordered the broch torn down and its treacherous stones hurled over the cliff to bury any glint from the sword Harald had gifted Maria, and only the healing company of Ingrid, her quiet, golden little Ingrid, stopped Elizaveta hurling herself after them. But when the ships came, she was glad she had not. For on board the first vessel was Aksel, scarred but whole, and with him Tora's Olaf.

Elizaveta ran, as Greta ran to Aksel, and Olaf clasped her in his arms as if she were his own mother, as, in part, she was.

'He fought so well,' was all he could say. 'They trapped him, Lily, trapped him with only half his men and they barely armed, but still he fought so well. Right to the end.'

'Did you see him die?' Elizaveta asked.

Olaf nodded and his face clouded.

'From afar. I was with the ships and barely made it to the battlefield in time for the final stand but I saw Father die and Lord Tostig too. With them gone, we had little choice but to surrender. Harold Godwinson pardoned me, released me. He was a noble opponent, truly.'

'A worthy king after all?'

But at that the boy shook his head.

'He is dead too, slaughtered by Duke William.'

'The brigand Norman?' Elizaveta choked out, Harald's words echoing down to her, still rich with his dear tones.

'Now King of England.'

It was a harsh end to all their hopes. Elizaveta thought of Agatha. She would be in danger. King William would not want Edgar around as a threat to his stolen throne. If they stayed in England the boy might die, as his father had died ten years before, and she prayed that someone, somewhere, was helping them to escape this island of death.

Her thoughts strayed mercilessly on to the other Harold's queen – Edyth. Was she in flight too? She must have been wed to him to hold England together, but instead England had torn her life apart, as it had torn Elizaveta's. Queens, it seemed, were made to be broken.

'Ambition is a disease,' she mumbled bitterly but at that Olaf caught her hands.

'No. No, do not believe so. I saw Father die and it will scar my soul forever, but before that I saw him fight. I do not think, Elizaveta, that I have ever seen a man more alive than in those last few minutes of the battle. He fought so well.'

'You said.'

'And he died in glory.'

'As he wanted.' She drew in a long breath. 'Come,' she said to Olaf, taking his arm and looking over to Aksel, lost in Greta's embrace, 'you must rest and then we must sail. We must take those we have lost home and we must return you to your mother. She will be waiting for us. Tora will be waiting and we must go to her.'

She pictured her friend, stood on the jetties still, waiting to draw them into the safety of Norway's rugged harbour, and for the first time since that terrible day a smile tugged at Elizaveta's lips. Turning her head into the wind, she felt memories whisper across them like a kiss from her lost husband – battles and fights of their own, but passion too, and love and a life lived fully. Lived together.

EPILOGUE

Today, when she closes her eyes against the mourners lining the streets to honour Harald's great coffin, Elizaveta can feel it still – the headlong, giddy challenge of pitting herself against the world – and she is, once more, lost in the rush of that far-off race. She can feel the surge of water through the thin skin of the tiny canoe, the sparkle of spray in her eyes, the rush of warm air against her face. And, above all else, she can feel the roar of her heart as, at last, she crests the tumbling river.

The walls of the city, high on the cliff, mingle with dark pines and sparkle in the sharp light as they lean in willing her on or, perhaps, waiting for her to up-end. The sun-blurred faces of the crowds hang over the bank, all wide eyes and open mouths, their calls of encouragement scattering on the light breeze. And then there is the blue of the water; the endless, treacherous, glorious blue of the water – hers to master.

She shudders, as years and sense fall away beneath the crash of life's current, and she loses her grip on the paddle. It catches a rock and is pulled from her, splintering against the jagged surface and flying into the air. She ducks but it is gone already and the boat rushes on, spinning wildly. She sees the dark cloud of the saving net but she is moving too fast now, shooting too swiftly down the frothing current with no way of controlling her path.

She puts her hands to her eyes, watching her own fate between them as the canoe, giddy with freedom, dives into a sharp edge, smashing the craft apart and sending it whirling into the sky in a splintering of strakes and bones. For a moment she is mid-air, flying freer than ever before, then she thuds into the water and is sucked down, down into its clawing grasp until there is no breath and no beat and no sound.

The swirling current stills. Her scudding heart slows. The water catches her arms and legs and for a moment she is lost, but then, slowly, it warms as if a volcanic heat is surging through it. Then, in a liquid haze, she sees the ripple of a warrior before her, his strong body sinuous in the flow, his coffin cast aside, his scar washed away, and his hair, caught in the last spin of the bubbles, shining golden in the sunshine.

HISTORICAL NOTES

As with *The Chosen Queen*, the first book in *The Queens of the Conquest* series, I have loved doing the research for this novel. The battle has been more about what to force myself to leave out than what to include. I have done my very best to keep the plot within the bounds of the known facts but in the end I did not seek to write a summary of the period, but Elizaveta's story. As a result, some of the amazing characters and places that I discovered during my research could not be allowed much space within the final novel.

I am aware that there will be misinterpretations within my work but here at least are some explanations of areas where I chose to bend the facts a little for the sake of the narrative, as well as some added details that may help curious readers to explore this fascinating period of history further.

Elizaveta's Neck Chain

This is a product of my imagination, but based on a key piece of information from a known love poem by Harald himself, written during his service in the Byzantine Empire and reported by Snorri Sturluson (an Icelandic saga-writer, author of *King*

Harald's Saga, written in the twelfth century) as referring to Elizaveta. It includes the verse: *Yet the goddess in Russia / will not accept my gold rings*, which can also be translated to describe Elizaveta as Harald's bracelet goddess or necklace goddess. The *Morkinskinna* (an early thirteenth-century Norse saga telling the history of the Norwegian kings) suggests that Harald had spoken with Yaroslav during his first time in Rus, requesting to marry Elizaveta, only to be rejected because he was not yet wealthy enough. During his mercenary work in the Byzantine Empire he seems to have regularly sent his gains to Yaroslav's vaults for safekeeping and from these shadowy facts I derived the idea of Elizaveta becoming his 'treasure-keeper' and their romance progressed from there.

Harald's Raven Banner

It was traditional for war leaders in this period to have a personal flag or banner carried before them into battle. Harold of Wessex was known by his 'fighting man' and King Olaf fought beneath a dragon, as described in the novel. The traditional Viking flag, however, was known as the 'landwaster', for obvious reasons, and usually bore a raven – the bird of the battlefield. This classic symbol is the one Harald chose to use for himself.

There is a tantalising possibility that a part of Harald's banner still exists, in the form of the legendary 'fairy flag' of the chiefs of Clan MacLeod. This tattered and fragile 46cm² piece of yellow-brown silk is kept in Dunvegan Castle in Scotland. The silk is believed to have come from the Far East and when it was examined in the early twentieth century, it was suggested that it may have come to England with Harald, believed to be an ancestor of Leod, the first leader of the MacLeod clan.

Later this flag was associated with a whole range of myths about its magical properties, including the belief that it extinguished a fire at Dunvegan Castle in the mid-twentieth century, and that it brought luck to servicemen flying bombing missions in the Second World War. We will probably never know the truth of its origin (or its magical properties!) but it is very pleasing to imagine that it might be possible to stand before the very banner that Harald carried into the terrible Battle of Stamford Bridge and I could not resist weaving its creation into Elizaveta and Tora's stories.

Harald's Return to Norway

Harald married Elizaveta in early 1043. The marriage probably took place at the time of the Winter Festival (see below for more on this midwinter celebration) as suggested rather dramatically in the novel. The pair moved from Kiev to Novgorod and then at some point on to Ladoga to make the sea crossing to Scandinavia but they do not seem to have actually set sail until 1045. This gap of two whole years remains unexplained.

It is certainly possible that, as I suggest in Chapter Seventeen, they were detained helping Vladimir fight rebels in the north as this was a perennial problem. It is also true that in this period Magnus was locked in bitter battles with Svein, who had seized Denmark, and Harald may have been hoping that they would kill each other, leaving the way clear – or, at least, clearer – for him to take the throne.

When they finally did sail, their return to Norway was not as simple as I have – for the sake of not labouring or clogging the narrative – suggested here. Harald's acceptance as joint King of Norway with his nephew was peacefully made in 1046, but only after some classic medieval raiding and looting to impose his terms on Magnus.

In fact, when Harald and Elizaveta arrived in Sigtuna, Svein was also there, in exile from his wars with Magnus. He and Harald allied (at least superficially) and raided Denmark all summer before Magnus's men secretly approached Harald to offer him a share in Norway in return for his help against Svein and a share of his vast treasure. At this, Harald unceremoniously ditched his tentative ally and left for Norway, where negotiations were almost certainly held, as I have described, in the borderlands and the uneasy joint tenure began.

The Solstice Festivals of Midsummer and Midwinter

The Viking (and Anglo-Saxon) year was still, in this period, ruled by divisions into seasonal quarters, with the summer and winter solstices on the longest and shortest days and the equinoxes in between. These 'quarter days' were often when servants were hired and rents paid so they had a vital influence on daily life and were marked with celebrations.

Much of this also tapped into pagan practices as the early church was careful to adopt ancient ceremonies and adapt them into Christian ones to ensure continuity and therefore encourage people to move easily to the new religion. Thus, Easter grew out of Mithras and Christmas out of Yule, and the other divisions of the calendar were also cunningly tied into key feast days on the quarterly divisions of the calendar.

Much of this assimilation was cleverly managed but the two solstice celebrations could, for the Christian church, be considered as 'the ones that got away' and they remain (bar maybe Halloween) as the most pagan of all celebrations.

Midsummer

It is at this festival, celebrated on the beach at Giske in Chapter Six, where we first meet Tora. I hope this scene captures the very natural feel of this ancient day. Although 24 June was proclaimed as the feast day of St John the Baptist and the observance of St John's – or Sankt Hans in Norse – was accepted, it remained as much a celebration of nature as of religion.

In England Mayday became the predominant summer festival, as shown in Chapter Twenty-nine of *The Chosen Queen*, but in Scandinavia, where the solstice in most places means a twenty-four-hour daytime, this was the key celebration. It remains so important even now that in Sweden the government are still considering changing their national day from 6 June to Midsummer's Eve.

Midwinter

It is at this mirror festival, celebrated on the Dnieper, where Harald finally secures Elizaveta's hand with his dramatic proposal from the burning dragon-ship in Chapter Fifteen. This celebration has its roots very firmly in pagan tradition, echoing the classic cremation of great chieftains in their ships, accompanied by all their belongings to see them comfortable in Valhalla – the great feasting hall in the sky. It also draws on the ancient practice of sacrificing a ship to welcome the sun back as the days begin to lengthen and to ensure the gods' favour on travels for the coming year.

Readers who wish to know more of this would do best to visit the Shetlands in January as the festival of Up Helly Aa, held in Lerwick on the last Tuesday of that month, still upholds many ancient Viking traditions, including Viking dress, torchlit processions and a burning ship.

Norwegian Assemblies

At the start of Part Three, Harald addresses a great assembly of his people and these governmental meetings, much like those of the 'Witan' or royal council in England, were central to Norwegian rule in this period. In Norse they were called 'Things' but for ease of comprehension (as 'thing' is clearly a common word in English with a very different meaning), I have referred to them simply as assemblies.

Smaller Things operated at a local level, but there were three supra-Things led by the king for higher-level law cases and crucial issues of law and government. The Eidsivathing was for central Uppland about Lake Mjosa (in the east). The Eyrathing was near the mouth of the River Nid for Trondelag (in the north). The Gulathing (as seen in the novel) was for Sogndal, Hardaland and the fjords just south of the mouth of Sognafjord (in the west). It seems to have been the model for the great Icelandic Thing around which the world's earliest-known democracy was established and I was delighted to be able to take Elizaveta to this amazing country in Chapter Thirty-two. I very much hope that including this scene shows the reader that the Vikings, at least by this late period, were not just bloodthirsty raiders but also settled men of intelligence, rational organisation and culture.

The Rapids Races

These great races, both in Kiev and subsequently in Oslo, are, I must confess, a product of my own imagination, though based on geographical possibility. The rapids of the Dnieper were legendary. The river was only navigable in a short window during the early summer, after the winter thaws had dropped enough to calm the raging currents, but before they dropped so far as to expose the great rocks on the river bed.

Viking traders always gathered in Kiev in spring to collate the goods collected from all over the lands of the Rus during the winter tribute gathering and to load them onto boats at the docking station at Vitichev (a few miles south of the city) ready for the great trip down to Constantinople once the water level was deemed navigable. It is therefore, I hope, more than likely that some form of race could have marked the readiness of the waters for this vital trading run.

Winter Tribute Gathering

Prince Edward of England, Prince Andrew of Hungary and Harald are all mentioned in the novel as taking part in Grand Prince Yaroslav's winter tribute gathering. This was a punishing task that involved riding all over the vast lands of the Rus to collect tax from the various remote tribes in the form of goods – often furs. This collection was made during the winter because the simplest way to travel was up the frozen rivers. The tribute-gatherers and their considerable armed guard would ride on horses wearing specially spiked shoes to grip the ice and would draw sleds to transport the goods. No doubt the collected furs were more than welcome in Russia's freezing winters!

*H*alldor's *T*ales

All of Halldor's extravagant tales are based on known facts, as discussed below:

Darkness at Stikelstad

In Chapter Two, Halldor tells how, in the Battle of Stikelstad, darkness fell at the crucial point in the fighting. His interpretation of it as King Cnut sending 'a devil with a black cloak across the sun' is clearly imaginative, but there was a recorded solar eclipse in that year. It took place on 31 August 1030, rather than the traditional date of the battle, 29 July. Dates at this period do not seem to have been as vital as they are to us now and are often confused and there is a clear oral tradition that the battle was fought in darkness. The eclipse started at 13.40, becoming total by 14.53 and over by 16.00, so it may well have overshadowed the battlefield at a crucial point.

Jumping the Chain at Miklegard

Halldor's grand tale of Harald's men jumping the great chain across the harbour at Miklegard in Chapter Thirteen is also based on a known story, recorded by the famous Icelandic saga-writer Snorri Sturluson (see above). He was not a man known to be a slave to facts, but the dramatic trick of tipping the boat over the chain by running from one end to the other is recorded in detail so I considered it worthy of inclusion here.

Greek Fire

Halldor also delights, in Chapter Seven, in telling of 'Greek fire'. This mysterious weapon of the Byzantines, first recorded in the 600s, was a huge fascination for storytellers and audiences throughout this period and, intriguingly, remains an unexplained weapon. 'Greek fire' was the name given – along with others like 'sea fire', 'liquid fire' and 'sticky fire' – to flames projected at speed from some sort of pressurised nozzle. It was held in awe and fear by other nations as it burned on water so was a huge advantage in naval warfare, although clearly it had its limitations, including the need for calm seas and close-range deployment.

Its composition was a closely guarded secret and remains a mystery to this day. Even when the Arabs succeeded in capturing some of the substance and the siphons used to dispense it in the 800s, they still failed to copy it successfully for their own manufacture. This was perhaps because the different elements of this weapon system – the formula, the specialised ships that carried it, the device used to heat and pressurise it, and the nozzle projecting it – were kept separate, with the engineers aware of the secrets of only one component, so no enemy could gain knowledge of it in its entirety. This may also explain why it eventually fell out of use in the twelfth century.

The closest we have to any form of recipe is from Anna Komnene, a twelfth-century imperial princess who wrote *The Alexiad*, an extant historical and biographical text about her father, Alexius I. She suggests that 'Greek fire' was made by collecting inflammable resin from pines, rubbing it with sulphur and propelling it with hot air through tubes of reed so it caught light. There seems, however, to have been more to it than this and over the years historians and scientists have explored the possibility of its base ingredient being saltpetre (which would make it the earliest known use of gunpowder) or quicklime. General opinion now seems to be that it was some form of crude petroleum, a little like modern napalm – clearly a terrifying weapon indeed.

Geographical Considerations

Sigtuna

Sigtuna, the capital of Sweden in this period, was situated on the banks of Lake Malaren which was a deep bay of the Varangian, or Baltic, Sea. Post-glacial rebound (the rising of land no longer pushed down by the weight of ice) subsequently caused many islands and promontories to rise out of the water, eventually cutting Malaren off into an inland lake around 1200. This was about the point when Stockholm, at the outer 'choking point' of the channel, rose as a city and it replaced Sigtuna as capital around 1300. These days you would have to follow tight channels to reach Sigtuna by boat but when Harald and Elizaveta sailed in, as shown in Chapter Seventeen, the way would have been much more open.

The Gault-Elf River

The Gault-Elf River no longer exists by that name, but seems to correspond most closely to the Gota Alv, running from Lake Vanern to the Kattegat sea between modern-day Sweden and the Danish mainland. In Viking times Skaane – the area now forming the southernmost province of Sweden – belonged to Denmark. The Gault-Elf River, therefore, marked the boundary between the Danish mainland and Norwegian soil which also ran into what is now Sweden below the Oslofjord. It was, therefore, the perfect place to make a peace between the two countries, as shown in Chapter Thirty-five.

*C*haracters

Below is a little more detail both about characters included in this book and some that I was forced, in the interests of a tight narrative, to leave out.

Andrew of Hungary and Anastasia

Although evidence is uncertain, it is probable that Andrew was not actually in Kiev until 1031 or even possibly some years later. He and his two brothers, Béla and Levente, may well have at first sought safety in Poland where Béla, the youngest of the three, married the daughter of King Miesko II, before the other two moved on to Kiev. I chose, however, to place Andrew there from the start of the novel so he was involved in the narrative all the way through.

Andrew was invited to return to Hungary, though clearly he had to fight his way to the throne. Some sources suggest that Levente was actually the elder brother but did not take the throne because he was still a pagan, unlike Andrew who had converted to Christianity in Kiev. Andrew was crowned in either late 1046 or early 1047 but the story doesn't actually end there, especially for Anastasia. For Andrew's younger brother Béla rose up in rebellion in 1060 and defeated Andrew, who died shortly afterwards. Anastasia and her son, Solomon, escaped to Austria where Anastasia, not one to give up easily, sought the help of King Henry IV of Germany, whose sister Judith was engaged to Solomon. In 1063 German troops invaded Hungary on their behalf, but luckily Béla died (seemingly of natural causes) and his sons fled, leaving Solomon to be crowned King of Hungary under Anastasia's regency. I would love to explore Elizaveta's spiky sister's story further at a later date but, as with so much, there was no room for it in *The Constant Queen*.

Henry I of France and Anne

After the death of his first wife, Matilda of Frisia, Henry seems, in a rather fairytale manner, to have hunted far and wide to find a new bride. Sadly the hunt seems to have been protracted not by romance but by the need to find a woman noble enough to be a queen but not so closely related to Henry for their match to be prohibited by the church – apparently a tough ask. The desperate king sent agents to all the courts of Europe and eventually they found their way to Kiev in time to secure Anne as Henry's bride in 1051.

It was not, perhaps, the most flattering way to be chosen but it was a good match for Anne. She does not, mind you, seem to have been very impressed with her new home at first, writing to Yaroslav that France was 'a barbarous country where the houses are gloomy, the churches ugly and the customs revolting.' She seems to have been particularly appalled that many of the French were illiterate and spoke few languages, that they did not wash often enough, and, perhaps most amusingly, that their cuisine was very poor compared to what she'd been used to in Kiev.

She must, however, have settled and soon gained a strong

reputation for her intelligence and political understanding. In her husband's lifetime she often co-signed charters with him, showing his respect for her, and when he died in 1060 and their eldest son, Phillipe, succeeded aged only eight, Anne was made regent – the first Queen of France ever to have been afforded this privilege. She shared the role with Baldwin of Flanders, the father of Matilda, wife of William the Conqueror, and so I will be able to return a little to her story in *The Conqueror's Queen*, the third book in this series.

King Svein of Denmark

I have also had to cut back Svein's role in this novel. Throughout his reign in Norway, Harald was perpetually engaged in summer skirmishing with Svein over the hugely disputed possession of Denmark. It seems almost to have been a form of noble game with the two men respecting each other even whilst they fought and I would have liked to include more of their rivalry, but in the end this is Elizaveta's story and the intriguing scrapping of the rulers had to take a back seat.

Svein seems to have been a lively and exciting character. He was reported as a large, charming man with three successive wives and any number of mistresses, who provided him with at least twenty children between them.

An audacious, impressive and seemingly much-loved King of Denmark, he could so easily have imprinted himself on our own history as, born in England to Cnut's sister Estrith, he was a stronger contender for the English throne than either Harald or William. It seems almost certain that his battles with Harald had made him too weak to take advantage of the chaos in 1066, but he did make determined, though failed, bids for England in both 1069 and 1074.

He also seems to have married Harald's widow, though sources are unclear as to whether this was Tora or Elizaveta (see below).

Empress Zoe

This novel only just touches on the life of the Empress Zoe of Byzantium. She was 'Porphyrogenita', meaning 'born into the purple' – i.e. to a reigning emperor, though apparently the imperial bedchamber actually had purple walls so this is a literal as well as a figurative expression. She was born in about 978 to Constantine VIII, and her father was apparently so reluctant to let another man anywhere near power that, despite numerous proposals, she didn't marry until the age of fifty when, with her father dying in 1028, she wed Romanus Argyros, who swiftly became Emperor Romanus III.

Making up for lost time, Zoe tried desperately to fall pregnant using magic charms, amulets and potions, all (not surprisingly) without effect. This was an obsession which she seems to have pursued all her remaining life and her rooms in the palace were filled with apparatus for the manufacture of ointments and perfumes with which she was apparently able to hold onto her beauty and even keep her face free of wrinkles until she was sixty – though not to conceive the longed-for heir.

I have portrayed her as something of a man eater, both for narrative entertainment and as it seems to run close to the truth. Romanus, who quickly lost interest in impregnating his wife, was found dead in his bath in 1034 and later the same day Zoe married Michael, a courtier and her open lover. Michael IV, however, soon proved of weak health and not really up to the task (if anyone was) of giving the ageing Zoe babies, and when he died in 1041, the imperial crown passed to his nephew Michael V. He had to rule jointly with Zoe – still the Porphyrogenita – but he swiftly banished her to a monastery, causing the popular uprising in Constantinople described in Chapter Twelve.

Michael was blinded, almost certainly by a force led by Harald, to prevent him challenging for power again and Harald does appear to have had to flee under cover of darkness from the predatory Zoe. She went on to marry a third husband, a former lover Constantine Monomachos, who was then formally proclaimed emperor alongside Zoe and her sister Theodora. To add to the excitement Constantine brought along his mistress, Maria Skleraina, whom Zoe seems to have, to some extent, welcomed into the strange imperial fold. A striking woman, indeed, and one I would love to learn more about when time allows.

Grand Prince Yaroslav

Elizaveta's father seems to have been a genuinely inspirational and forward-thinking ruler but he was not actually Grand Prince of all Russia until 1036 when his brother Mstislav, with whom he had co-ruled at the end of a series of fraternal disputes, died. Mstislav's base had been in Chernigov and he seems to have kept largely to the east of Russia so I felt his presence in this story would overcomplicate events. It is also possible that Yaroslav only fully moved his royal power base from Novgorod to Kiev in this year but in the absence of any true proof either way, I chose to house his family there from the start of the story to avoid unnecessary complications.

Earl Hakon

Chapter Thirty-four shows us the Battle of Nisa and Harald's victory over Svein, including Aksel as the brave commander of the loose ships which helped turn the battle the Norwegians' way. In reality, however, it was not Aksel (an invented character) who managed this but Jarl Hakon, a nephew of Einar Tambarskelve who led the northern jarls after Einar's death.

Hakon's story is very interesting in its own right, as he, like Finn, defected to the Danes after a disagreement with Harald but was later forgiven and returned to his service, marrying Ragnhild, King Magnus's illegitimate daughter (see below). He argued with Harald again a little time later when it emerged that it may well have been he who, perhaps swayed by the Danish king's kindness to him in times past, let Svein escape the same Battle of Nisa alive, robbing Harald of his chance at the Danish throne. Harald subsequently killed Hakon at the Battle of Vanern in autumn 1064. I hoped to include him in this story but he proved too cumbersome to fit. I could not, however, resist borrowing his brave exploits for Aksel.

Ragnhild

King Magnus had a daughter called Ragnhild by an unknown mistress, probably conceived when he was relatively young. She seems to have been a strong-willed type who, in a reported tantrum more typical of skaldic tradition than reality, refused a young northern lord because he was not an earl. That lord was Hakon, he of prowess at Nisa (see above) but as there was, in the end, no room for his story in this novel, Ragnhild had to be lost too.

What Happened After 1066

King Harold was merciful to the defeated Norwegians in the wake of the battle of Stamford Bridge, allowing those not killed on the field – including Tora's son Olaf – to retreat to their ships in safety. This was not, sadly for Norway, a large number and reports have it that although three hundred ships sailed forth on the quest to conquer England in 1066, only twenty-four limped home.

They returned, first, to Elizaveta in the Orkneys where they over-wintered with Jarls Paul and Erlend, Thorfinn's sons, who had both survived the carnage in England. In the spring of 1067 they retrieved Harald's body (where from, we do not know, but he must have been kept safe by someone, again showing mercy by the English, especially in comparison to Duke William's contemptuous treatment of Harold after Hastings), and took both his and Maria's corpses home for honourable burial. Maria's death, which was really recorded as occurring on the very day of the Battle of Stamford Bridge, was thought at the time to have a rather mystical significance which I have made the most of in this novel.

The rule of Norway was at first shared by Tora's two sons, Magnus and Olaf, but in only 1069 Magnus died (of what, we do not know) leaving Olaf to be sole king. He is known to posterity as Olaf the Quiet, and I like to think that this reflects Tora's careful upbringing as well as, perhaps, a surfeit of war under Harald's ambitious reign.

As discussed above, Adam of Bremen (a scholarly man who lived through the events of this period and wrote about them in his *Gesta Hammaburgensis Ecclesiae Pontificum*, or *Deeds of the Bishops of Hamburg*) reports that Svein took as his third wife 'the mother of King Olav Kyrre' though we do not know if this refers to his actual mother, Tora, or his stepmother Elizaveta. The marriage seems to have been part of a batch arranged shortly after 1066 to cement a peace treaty with Denmark. Ingrid, Elizaveta's daughter, married Prince Olaf, Svein's third son by an unknown concubine and King Olaf, Tora's son, married Princess Ingrid, another of Svein's children.

King Svein himself could easily have married either of Harald's widows but within the scope of this story I like to believe that it was Tora who allied herself to this very Scandinavian ruler. After this brief mention, however, no more is said of either of my heroines and we do not even know when or where either queen died. I very much hope that this novel, although as much the product of my own imagination as of historical record, goes some way to reviving their sadly lost stories.

CHANGED NAMES

Yaroslav's children:

Iziaslav Ivan

Sviatoslav Stefan

Vsevolod Viktor

Vyacheslav Yuri

Ingigerd (Elizaveta's mother and daughter) Ingrid

Ingigerd (Finn's daughter) Idonie

Bergljot (Einar's wife) Brigid

Jorunn (Tora's sister) Johanna

Oystein (Tora's brother) Otto

Sveyn (Cnut's son) Steven

ACKNOWLEDGEMENTS

I filled the first book in this trilogy with thank-yous so wondered, at first, who to thank in this second one, but the fact remains that all the same people, and a few more besides, have been every bit as important in the creation of this novel, so I think they deserve another mention:

My husband for his unending patience and indulgence – I promise not to have the bright idea of inviting everyone we know for a party this time round . . .

My children – to whom this book is dedicated – for putting up with endless talk of Vikings and not groaning too loud whenever I say 'Do you know, it was the Vikings who . . . ' Similarly for trailing round various battle sites/castles/exhibitions with me and even, at times, showing an interest. I know Vikings didn't have iPhones but they were still pretty cool.

My parents for being so excited for me and for not, thank heavens, passing their chemists' genes on! And all the rest of my family for their input, though I'm afraid the orders for Ferraris, holiday homes, motorbikes and the like will have to wait a while yet . . .

My friends everywhere, who have been so incredibly supportive with *The Chosen Queen*. I sometimes feel ashamed of myself for making such a fuss about just doing my job and consider myself blessed that everyone else is so happy for me. Thank you.

Kate, my agent, who has been behind me for longer than anyone outside my own immediate friends and family and whose continued enthusiasm and advice is so much appreciated.

Natasha, my editor, without whose wisdom, eye for detail, and endless patience this book would not be anywhere near as sharp. And for her lovely, supportive margin comments – 'I'm sobbing now,' being perhaps my favourite so far.

And finally the whole dedicated, friendly, enthusiastic team at Pan Macmillan – in particular Susan for fantastic copy-editing, Katie for incredible publicity, and Jo for her gorgeous cover designs. It's been a pleasure to take this publishing journey with such a strong team and I'm so grateful you chose to back me.

Thank you all,
Joanna

extracts reading groups events
competitions books new
discounts extracts extracts
competitions
books new extracts events
events books
extracts new reading groups
new titles reading groups
interviews
events extracts
discounts
new books events
events new events
discounts extracts discounts
www.panmacmillan.com
extracts events reading groups
competitions books extracts new